RIDE ON

For
Kieran and Margaret ...

RIDE ON

STEPHEN J. MARTIN

MERCIER PRESS

WHAT YOU NEED TO READ

MERCIER PRESS
Douglas Village, Cork
www.mercierpress.ie

Trade enquiries to Columba Mercier Distribution,
55a Spruce Avenue, Stillorgan Industrial Park, Blackrock, Dublin

 Mercier Press receives financial assistance from
the Arts Council / An Chomhairle Ealaíon

Printed and bound by J.H. Haynes & Co. Ltd, Sparkford.

PRAISE FOR STEPHEN J. MARTIN

'If you put Bono and Brendan O'Carroll into a DNA blending device, then you would end up with Stephen J. Martin – a wordsmith with one ear for rock music and another for Dublin's vernacular ... the dialogue drips with authenticity.'

– Irish Examiner

'Martin brilliantly evokes the cruelty, the fun, the allure of the impossible dream. I laughed, thought back - and then laughed again!'

– Tom Dunne, TodayFM

'One hilarious incident after another ... irreverent and amusing ...'

– Irish Emigrant

'... rollicks along in a jolly fashion ...'

– Ireland on Sunday

'Whether you're a musician yourself or simply a music lover, Superchick will rock your world!'

- Stephen Lawson, Total Guitar

'Brilliant! A laugh a minute ... rich, humorous and incredibly vivid...'

- Irish Echo

Chapter One

'PROBLEM SOLVED,' said Aesop, bouncing into the studio and taking off his coat. 'I have our song. Came to me in my sleep last night.'

'Good stuff. I suppose it's subtle and evocative, is it?' said Dónal Steele, The Grove's manager, without looking up from the mixing desk where he was going over some notes with Sparky, the engineer.

'Evocative … I betcha that means girly, doesn't it?' said Aesop.

Aesop went through phases. This week, his girly cut-off point was somewhere around the live version of 'War Pigs'.

Dónal thought about it for a second.

'Kind of.'

'Thought so. No then. It's not girly. Not like you mean anyway.'

'I see. And what's it about?'

'Where's Jimmy? He'll want to hear this.'

'He's out there,' said Dónal, pointing through the soundproofed window of the control room with his coffee cup.

Aesop pressed the intercom button.

'Jimmy?'

Jimmy's head popped up. He'd been adjusting one of the settings on his stompbox.

'Howya,' he said, standing to speak into his mike. 'What's up?'

'I have a song.'

'Do you? Brilliant. So do I.'

'Yeah? What's yours about?' said Aesop.

'Actually, it's for Jen's wedding. I've been at it for a while. I never thought of putting it on the album, and then last night I just said, fuck it, why not? I came in early this morning to put some tracks down for it.'

Jimmy didn't give a shite about what was girly and what wasn't, once he was sure it was coming from the right place. In his drunker moments, he just felt like he was freeing it from his soul. But he'd only ever said that to Aesop once and then suffered an unmerciful slagging. These days, he kept his more poetic musings to himself until it was time to put them to music.

'Oh Christ no,' said Aesop, rubbing his eyes with one hand. 'Here we fuckin' go again.' He looked up. 'A wedding song?'

'Yeah. Well, kind of. Listen …'

Jimmy started a guitar intro and then began to sing. It was beautiful. Simple. A voice and a guitar and sibilant lyrics that whispered to the heart of promises and devotion as a summer breeze might tease an aspen to shimmer. Aesop looked around at Sparky and Dónal. They were both grinning and nodding and tapping their fingers in time to the song. It faded out in softly beating echoes and Jimmy looked back through to the control room, his eyebrows raised.

'What do you think? It's called "More Than Me".'

'It's brilliant,' said Dónal. He'd heard it three times already this morning. 'Jesus. I think that's the one.'

'It's good stuff Jimmy,' said Sparky. 'Lovely.'

'It's the foulest fucking thing I've ever heard in my life,' said Aesop. 'And it's way too early in the morning to be subjecting me to it too, you fucker.'

Jimmy stepped away from the mike and came in through the big heavy double doors.

'But it's a wedding present, Aesop. For your bleedin' sister. It's s'posed to be romantic and sweet.'

'And evocative?'

'Yeah, exactly.'

'Well, you fucking nailed it then,' said Aesop. 'Cos my breakfast is on its way up. Where do you keep getting lyrics like that, for fuck sake? I swear, it's like you have a girl's knicker-drawer for a brain sometimes Jimmy, the shite you pull out of it.'

'We've already got some rockers on the album Aesop,' said Dónal. 'We thought we'd close it out with a simple ballad.'

'And anyway,' said Jimmy, 'it still needs a bit of work. And I've another verse to write.'

'Oh brilliant. One about snowdrops and daffodils?'

'No, Aesop. The song is about …'

'Cream-coloured ponies? Fairies and fucking lollipops?'

'Aesop?' said Sparky at last, putting down his tea and looking up. He always had a short fuse around Aesop.

'What?'

'Shut your bollocks.'

Aesop blinked at him and then sat down and picked up a bikkie from the plate in front of Dónal.

'Well I wrote a song too, yiz bastards.'

'Let's hear it then,' said Jimmy, handing him the guitar. 'Come on. What's it about? We're all listening.'

'You'll think it's crap.'

'We won't.'

'Yeah you fucking will. After the pole-smoker song you just sang? Jesus, all it needs is a recorder solo in the middle. If it went on any longer I was afraid Sparky and Dónal were going to start fingering each other in here, the heads on them.'

'What's your song Aesop?'

Aesop grinned at him.

'It's called "Brokeback Fountain".'

Jimmy frowned.

'And what's it about?'

'It's about this pair of lesbians.'

'Right. How many songs about lesbians is that now you're after writing, Aesop?'

'Only two.'

Jimmy nodded.

'So what about them anyway?'

'Well, one of them is after spilling ice-cream all over her tits.'

'Jesus,' Jimmy sighed, shaking his head. 'What was she doing with it, for fuck sake?'

'I don't know. It doesn't matter. So anyway the other one gets to work, but sure one lesbian can only eat so much ice-cream, right? And …'

'Okay Aesop. Right, I get it. But the thing is …'

'So, into the shower with them. That's kind of it. Well, there's lots of bubbles and all. And they keep dropping the sponge and stuff ...'

'Right. But Aesop, we're not really ...'

'You think it's stupid, don't you?'

'It is fucking stupid, Aesop. But that's not the point. We're not writing that kind of album. It's not really our genre, is it? Y'see, we do this thing called rock music. What you're after writing there is called lesbian porn. See how they're not the same thing?'

'They could be.'

'No they couldn't, Aesop.'

'I have one about eating porridge as well,' said Aesop. 'I thought of it this morning.'

'Did you? Well, there you go. That's fucking stupid as well.'

'You haven't even heard what it's about yet!'

'Is it about porridge?'

'Yeah.'

'Right then.'

'Do you want to hear it?'

Jimmy looked up at the clock over the desk. It was time to stop fucking around and get a bit of work done.

'Later Aesop,' he said, grabbing his guitar and heading back out the doors into the recording room. 'Come on. Let's see if we can get some clicks down for "More Than Me" to get us started. I've got a bass line down on track one there, Sparky. There's an arpeggiated loop on track two that'll get us to the chorus, so just kill it then and bring it back when I give you the nod. You'll get the idea. I'll play the melody here. Aesop, it's four-four, no tricks. I need you to play off the high hat until the chorus but I want it to build up to the first verse, so open it up gradually until I start singing. Sparky, that's when you bring in track one. The bass will hold us up there until the change. Track two is from the top. Four bar intro. Plus one to count us in. Are we right? Dónal, will you keep an ear out for an acoustic part. We'll need one to fill it out for us, but I didn't get a chance to put one down this morning. If anyone has any better ideas on any of this, let me know when we're done.'

They all got themselves ready. Aesop just got in behind the drums, took off his jumper and settled his headphones over his ears. By the end of the day he'd have forgotten all about his lesbian and porridge songs, so Jimmy wasn't worried about him getting sulky. Slagging and shite-talking aside, when it came to this type of thing Jimmy was the boss and everyone was cool with that. Aesop was his best mate, but The Grove was his baby.

Dónal smiled. He'd been hoping that Jimmy would come up with something good to finish the album, and here he was now after pulling this total fucking cracker out of nowhere. It was single material. It'd be all over late-night radio. The tune was already in his head and would be for the rest of the day.

Jimmy counted them in when they were all ready to go, his eyes closed and his head nodding as everyone came in where they were supposed to. The song sounded even better now with all the work he'd done putting backing tracks down before everyone else had gotten in. Then he started singing, leaving them behind in the studio and going with the song until it finished in a clutch of ringing notes on his guitar. He opened his eyes and held his bottom lip in his teeth for a second, just staring at the wall opposite him. The others waited. Then he looked at Aesop and grinned.

'Jaysis, Aesop, I think you were right,' he said. 'It does need a recorder solo.'

Aesop just raised his eyes to heaven and shook his head. Then he turned to Dónal and Sparky in the other room and leaned into his mike.

'Into the jacks with the pair of you, now, and wash your hands.'

IT WAS a good morning in Sin Bin. They got a lot of work done on 'More Than Me' and then found time to tidy up the chorus on one of the other songs before lunch. Another week or two and the whole thing would be in the bag. Jimmy and Aesop decided to go for a sandwich, and maybe a pint, for lunch. Just one, because Jimmy had to go back to the studio afterwards. He'd be there all afternoon and most of the evening. As well as being in The Grove and contracted to Sin Bin Productions in that capacity, Jimmy was also a business partner of Dónal's and Sparky's. He'd bought in a few months ago with a payout he'd gotten from his previous job in IT. Dónal had been short of dosh and Jimmy had been flush. They got on and respected each other. Right time, right place, right circumstances. Jimmy was the kind of bloke who wouldn't be happy just singing in a band anyway, so when he suggested to Dónal and Sparky that he get on board properly with Sin Bin, it all just fell into place. So now he was helping produce other bands too and learning the ropes when he wasn't doing his own stuff with Aesop and The Grove.

Aesop wasn't doing any of that. He was just the drummer in the band and that's the way he liked it. He'd be spending the afternoon looking at furniture for the place he'd bought with Jimmy from their album advance. He was living there on his own and paying rent for the moment to Jimmy. Jimmy already had a house so it was all working out fine so far. Aesop had a bit of money coming in for the first time ever in his thirty-three years, and his old man had been fairly keen that he get out of his house, take his fucking drumkit with him, and learn what it was like to have a bit of responsibility for a change. Everyone was up on the deal, as long as the band kept up some momentum and the arse didn't completely fall out of the property market. If they got the projected royalty cheques over the next few months, then Aesop would give Jimmy back twice the money that he'd put into the apartment, pay the balance of the mortgage off completely and own the thing outright. He still grinned to himself every time he walked in the front door. His front door. His gaff. From playing the drums with Jimmy. Who'd have fucking thought it?

'What are they like, this crowd you're seeing later?' said Aesop as they headed down the stairs just after one o'clock.

'Young fellas. Not bad. I've only heard a couple of bits from them. Be interesting to meet them. They're s'posed to have one song that Dónal reckons could be a starter. They call themselves Leet.'

'Leet? What's that mean?'

Jimmy shrugged.

'No idea.'

They got out onto the street and stepped around two young lads who were standing against the wall outside.

'What's their sound?'

'That's the thing. It's a bit mad. Imagine The Specials mixed with Coldplay …'

'So … brilliant mixed with shite, like? Very novel.'

'Yeah. But it works, apparently. They've a bit of a following around the city.'

'Jesus, who'd have guessed there'd be that many gay ska-heads in Dublin?'

'Well anyway, they're catchy enough. The arrangements are a bit obvious, but we can fix that. The singer has a good set of lungs on him. The drummer writes all the songs, Dónal says.'

'Drummers are always the best songwriters, aren't they?'

'Yeah. "Brokeback Fountain", "Octopus's Garden" … it's a fucking quality list that just goes on and on, isn't it?'

Jimmy heard something behind him and looked around. The two kids that had been outside the studio were walking behind them. A bit young for fans, although it wasn't at all uncommon these days for people to stare or point or even follow them. Sometimes they didn't even say anything, which Jimmy found a bit unsettling. He turned back to Aesop.

'So what are you up to tonight, after you go shopping for rugs and coffee tables?'

'I'm heading over to Donnycarney first to see me Nan. She's been giving Jen shit that I haven't been over. Then they're showing a Cure gig on the telly and …'

'The Cure? But you hate The Cure!'

'I know. Isn't it funny? But they were playing "A Forest" on the radio this morning when I was getting up and I can't get it out of me head now. They weren't that bad, were they?'

'They were fucking brilliant! Jesus, the shite you used to give me in school for liking them. Cheeky fucker now. And the … wait … hang on a minute, Aesop …'

Jimmy turned around. They were after going around a couple of corners now and the two boys were still behind them.

'Are yiz all right lads?' said Jimmy, stopping. They were only about eleven, but Jimmy just wasn't used to this kind of attention yet and it gave him the willies a bit.

The smaller one looked at the very slightly bigger one.

'Are youse The Grove?' said the bigger one.

'Yeah.'

'We weren't sure. Where's the Chinese fella?'

'Shiggy? He's in Japan. What's the story?'

'Me sister likes you.'

'Your …'

'She wants to meet you.'

Aesop snorted and stopped to light up a smoke. Wherever this went, it'd be good for a slagging in the pub afterwards.

'Eh … that's nice,' said Jimmy. He looked around the street to see if anyone else was listening to this.

'Will you meet her?'

'Ah listen, I'm kind of busy, y'know? But … how did you know where we'd be?'

'Your website said you were making a CD in that Sin Bin place. I got the bus in with Conor. He's me brother.'

'Oh. Right. Eh, howya Conor. And what's your name?'

'Liam Flanigan.'

'Liam. Okay. Em … but … and how old is your sister?'

'Fourteen.'

Aesop gave another little giggle.

'When will she be fifteen?' he said, grinning over at Jimmy. 'Fifteen all right for you, Collins?'

'Shut up will ye?' said Jimmy over his shoulder. He turned back to the kids. 'Where is she? I'll say hello. Did she not come out with you?'

'He called you Collins,' said the kid, pointing at Aesop. 'Are you not Aesop?'

'What?' said Jimmy. 'No. No, he's Aesop. I'm …'

'Right. It's not you then. She wants to meet him. Aesop.'

Aesop was chuckling now.

'She likes me, does she?'

'Yeah.'

'That'd make more sense all right. And what did she say about Jimmy?'

'Who's Jimmy?'

Aesop threw his head back and roared laughing.

'Ah that's so cool, that is. The lads will love this. Nothing's changed in twenty years, has it Jimmy? It's Cathleen McGovern all over again. Jaysis, remember when …'

'Shut up, you clown,' said Jimmy, straightening up. He couldn't help being embarrassed even though it was a stupid situation and not even his fault. 'Here, you sort this out. Gimme that smoke.'

'Your sister didn't come out with you?' said Aesop, taking over. He was great with kids. He had two nephews not much younger than this pair and he was mad about them. 'Is she shy?'

'No, she's sick,' said Liam. 'She's not allowed out. But she has a picture of The Grove on her wall and she's always talking about you, so she is. It's her birthday next week. I said I'd come in and ask you to go to her party. Conor wanted to come as well.'

'I see. Aren't you great brothers, aren't you? I have two brothers as well, but they wouldn't do that for me. And your sister's sick? Well, that's no good, is it? But c'mere, should you not be in school?'

'We're mitching.'

'Ah Jaysis lads, yiz shouldn't come into town when you're mitching. They have inspectors out on the streets. You'll be snared. How long were you standing outside the studio? You should have come up and …'

'For Christ sake Aesop …' said Jimmy, looking over. 'Stop encouraging them, will you? They shouldn't be on the mitch at all.'

'Ah stop it Jimmy, ye big granny. Leave them alone. Did you never go on the mitch?'

'No, I bloody didn't!'

'Don't mind him lads. He was always a big swot when he was in school.'

'Will you come to her birthday?' said Liam.

'The thing is lads, we're very busy making this record, y'see? Maybe when we … what's her name?'

'Philomena … Mena.'

'Well, you tell Mena when she gets better that if she wants to say hello, she can call Sin Bin and … hey Jimmy, is the Sin Bin number on the web site?'

Jimmy nodded.

'Right,' said Aesop. 'Call Sin Bin and they'll tell her when I'm in there and then she can come in with your folks and I'll show her how to play the drums. Will you do that?'

Liam was grinning.

'That'd be great, mister!'

'I'm Aesop, Liam. Just Aesop.' He winked at Conor. 'Who am I?'

'Aesop,' said Conor, blushing.

'That's right,' said Aesop with a big smile. 'And c'mere. Maybe I'll teach the two of you to play the drums as well. Would you be into that?'

Conor and Liam looked at each other like it was Santy they were after meeting. They nodded like they were trying to dislodge their heads.

'Good stuff. Right, well me and Jimmy here are off now to have a bit of lunch, okay? So you tell Mena I said hello and Happy Birthday and to give the studio a call when she's feeling better. Tell her I'll teach her how to play her favourite song. Will you do that?'

'Yeah,' said Conor.

'Right. Off yiz go then. Go back to school and, Liam, you tell your teacher that you had to bring Conor to the dentist this morning all right? And you forgot the note. And go easy on the jelly and ice-cream at Mena's birthday party next week, ye here me?'

The kids laughed and then turned and headed off back down towards the river. Aesop watched them for a while, grinning, and then turned around to Jimmy, who was leaning against the wall and putting the cigarette out.

'Y'right?' said Aesop.

'Yeah. Fuck sake, aren't you fucking great, aren't you? It's a wonder you didn't start doing magic for them.'

'Ah, kids are brilliant Jimmy. Jaysis, you were bending over poor Liam like you were his headmaster about to give him a box. Hands behind your back and everything.'

'Yeah, whatever. Can we go for a pint now ... fucking ... Ronald McDonald? I've to be back in an hour.'

'You're just grumpy because Mena likes me instead of you.'

'Am I? And what are you going to do when Mena comes knocking at the door of Sin Bin next week?'

'I'm going to teach her how to play the drums, amn't I?'

'And what if she wants you to be her new boyfriend?'

'Ah don't be fucking stupid Jimmy. I'll sign a CD and a t-shirt for her and she'll be all chuffed and run off to show her mates. Y'know something, for someone who spent twenty years dreaming about being a rockstar, you haven't given much thought to the fans, have you?'

'What fans?'

'All the kids who bought the singles for starters, you muppet. There's more to it than just playing music Jimmy. And would you ever try not to look like you're going to call the cops every time a fan comes up to you in the street.'

Jimmy shook his head as he pushed the door of the pub open.

'Will you fucking give over. We've got two singles out. Anyway, she's your bleedin' fan, not mine, remember?'

Aesop roared laughing.

'You think I'm going to forget that, Jimmy?'

Jimmy looked across the road, where two teenage girls were staring at them.

'Jesus, come on for fuck sake, look.'

Aesop looked over and gave them a wave and a big grin.

'Howzit goin' girls?' he called.

They giggled and one of them waved back.

'Aesop, will you come on?' said Jimmy.

'You go on in Jimmy. Get me a pint. I'll just say hello …'

'Christ, they're only young ones, Aesop.'

'I'm not trying to score. For fuck sake, if it wasn't for them and their mates, I'd still be on the dole. It's only manners. Go on. I'll be in in a minute.'

Jimmy watched him cross the road and thought for a second about going over too. But then he went into the pub and up to the bar to order the sandwiches and drinks. He just couldn't get used to all this. On the stage was one thing. That was his job. But when he was just trying to get a bit of lunch?

The barman came over to him and stopped, frowning. He was new, this barman.

'Are you Jimmy Collins?'

Jimmy sighed inwardly.

Fuck sake.

Chapter Two

'CUP OF tea?'

Norman looked up from where he was lying on the ground on a black plastic bag. The sun was up above the wall now and shining in his face. He raised his hand over his eyes to see if the voice was talking to him, but before he could see properly or even say anything, it spoke again.

'I've the kettle on. Will you have a cup of tea? It's a cold morning to be out working.'

Norman put down the secateurs and smiled at the silhouette on the other side of the rosebed.

'I've love a cup. I didn't realise what time it was.'

'Come on so. I'm Trish.'

'I'm Norman. Or, Robert I mean. Robert.'

He stood up and grimaced slightly at the creak in his knee and the twinge that shot down to his ankle.

'Are you sure now?' she said smiling. She had a coat on and her arms folded tightly against the wind that was coming in off the sea. A few bits of hair were after coming loose from under her cap and she pulled them from her lips. Lovely lips they were too. He'd been admiring them from afar for about a week and now here they were, pointing at him and moving and nice words coming out of them.

'Yeah. Robert. Well, my mates call me Norman. Long story.'

'Come on in then. You'll have to take those boots off, though, or the charge nurse will have you scrubbing the place with a bucket and mop. I saw her doing it once to the poor lad who delivers the vegetables.'

'I'll leave them in the porch here.'

He sat on the step and pulled his wellies off as she hung up her coat and waited just inside the door. Then he followed her into the dark corridor and past the huge statues of Our Lady on one side and St Francis of Assisi on the other. It was under the cold marble stares of that holy brace that Norman's eyes adjusted to the murkiness and he found himself gazing, with frankly confused surprise given the time of the morning, at the perfect shape of the snow-white form that was leading him towards the warm lights of the kitchen up ahead. Not that it was a uniform designed to arouse a man. God no. The last thing the nursing home needed was for the male residents to be getting the horn and annoying everyone with their delusions of virility. Christ knows, some of them were bad enough as it was. The nurses wore a plain white uniform that was crisp, no-nonsense and subdued. Herself didn't like any silliness under her roof and none of the girls felt inclined to test a ninety-kilo, sixty-year-old woman with the makings of a fairly respectable beard when the light caught her from the right angle.

But such qualities as no-nonsense and subdued are often in the eye of the beholder and Norman's eyes were following the figure-of-eight sway of Nurse Trish's hips as though tied to them by string. He'd never actually been this close to her before and none of the furtive glances of the past few days did her justice. The back of her dress was pinched very slightly half-way down to allow the merest sugges- tion of a tapering waist and then, below those hypnotic hips that dipped and rose in time with the tapping echoes of her shoes, there was nothing but falling fabric to the backs of her knees. But then, suddenly, like a bet you thought you'd lost, appeared her legs. Strong, firm almond-shaped calves that dived into neat white nylon ankles. By Christ, she was a fine woman. Norman picked up his pace.

There was no one else in the small kitchen.

'They're all coming down for their breakfast now,' said Trish. 'Everyone's in the main canteen. I'm just coming off.'

'You work nights? That's tough.'

'Well, we take turns. I've a few days off now and then I'll be on the morning shift. Sugar?'

'No. No thanks. I'm grand. This is lovely. Thanks very much.'

'That's all right. I could see you through the window when you went chasing that bag.'

Norman laughed.

'The feckin' wind took it before I could find a stone.'

'Bikkie?'

'Oh lovely. Hob Nobs. Mam doesn't usually get the chocolate ones.'

Christ, will you shut your hole about Mam? Jesus …

'Ah, sure one or two won't kill you. So how are our roses doing? Will they survive the blizzard everyone's talking about?'

'They'll be grand. I guarantee it now, come the summer they'll be exploding into every gorgeous red and pink you've ever seen, so they will. People will be stopping on the street outside, watch.'

Trish laughed.

'Herself upstairs will love that. They better not make a racket.'

Norman grinned back. Fuck sake, this was easy! Chatting away like old mates. He was on fire!

'Eh … so … em …'

Fuck. Now his head was completely empty. That's what he got for being cocky.

She looked at him for a minute.

'Would you be able to help me with something, Norman?' she said. 'I don't s'pose you know anything at all about cars?'

His heart took a little jump for itself. She was after calling him Norman and it felt brilliant.

'I … I do a bit. What's the problem?'

'Well, I've a lend of my Dad's and it was acting up last night. It might be just the cold weather, but if it won't start you wouldn't be able to have a look at it or give me a little push, would you?'

'Of course I will. Come on and we'll have a look at it.'

'No, no. Finish your tea.'

'I'm done sure, look. Thanks, that was lovely.'

'Are you sure now? I don't want to keep you from your work.'

'Two minutes, sure. Come on. No problem at all.'

She led him out to the car park and up to the car. It was a big old Sierra. A bit of a banger of a yoke. She got in and tried to start it. It lurched forward suddenly and then stopped dead.

'Jesus,' said Norman. He'd had to jump back out of the way. 'That didn't look good. Was it doing that this morning when you came in?'

She nodded back at him through the windscreen.

'Lift up the bonnet there,' he said.

She released the catch and Norman bent over and stuck his head in over the engine, biting his lip.

'See anything?' she said.

'Hang on a sec,' said Norman, rubbing the stubble on his chin. He knew fuck all about cars, but that was okay because he wasn't planning on fixing it anyway. He just needed to give himself time to think. He might never get another chance at her. 'Hang on. I'll just try and give the … eh … spark plugs a quick wipe. Sometimes they can get dirty. Wait now. So anyway … you're not working tonight …'

'No. I'm off now till Monday. I was going to drive home this afternoon.'

'Where's home? That's a Kerry accent.'

She laughed.

'God, my friends say I'm getting a Dublin one.'

'You are not, don't mind them.'

'I'm from Sneem. You know Sneem?'

'I do of course. God, Sneem's a beautiful part of the world.'

'It's a bloody freezing part of the world too, at the moment. I'll be in front of the fire all weekend.'

'Sure won't we all. Try it now.'

He stepped back as the car lurched again and died.

'Yeah. The spark plugs are manky. I'm going to have to clean them all.'

He hoped she stayed in the car because all he was doing was taking some dirt from the underside of the bonnet and rubbing a bit on his face. He wouldn't know a spark plug if he sat on the pointy end of one.

'So you won't be around tonight?' he said. 'Ah well …'

'What?'

'Well, I was going to say … ah, sure, if you're not here …'

'Yeah?'

'I was going to say … like … would you like to go out for a drink later?'

He was glad she couldn't see him. He knew he looked petrified. He heard her laugh and felt like a total dickhead. Fuck. He was going down again. 'Kamikaze' was what Aesop used to call him at school discos. But then …

'I'd love to Norman. But I usually like to be able to see a fella when he's asking me out, and not be talking to the bonnet of me car, like.'

He grimaced and stood up to go around to the open door on the driver's side.

'Sorry.' He was purple now and smiling like a dope. 'Would you be on for a drink tonight? Maybe you could drive home to Kerry tomorrow morning? Only if it suited you, like. If you have something on at home, of course …'

'I'd love a drink.' She was smiling at him. Something a bit cheeky in her eyes. 'That'd be great.'

He smiled back, a big huge one. He felt sixteen feet tall and about six and a half stone in weight, instead of the other way around.

'Yeah? Brilliant!'

Then he looked around at the open bonnet of the car and decided he better get back under it while the going was good and before he said something that would fuck everything up.

'How is it now?' he called.

Back in the car, she pulled it out of gear and into neutral, laughing to herself. That had been a doddle. The engine roared into life.

'Norman, you're a genius!'

'Ah stop. It probably just needed a few goes with the cold this morning.'

He was chuffed with himself. He hadn't done anything and now she thought he was the dog's bollocks. He came back to her and leaned down on the window.

'I'll give you a call later this afternoon?'

'Yeah. Wait till about two, will you? I'll be asleep.'

'Course.'

She scribbled her number on a piece of paper from the glove compartment and handed it to him with a grin.

'Thanks for fixing the car.'

He shook his head.

'Thanks for the tea.'

She grinned and reached out through the window to wipe at his cheek. She showed him her fingers.

'From the spark plugs …'

'Oh right, thanks.'

He took out his hanky and wiped his face.

'Talk to you later so.'

'Grand.'

The car took off down the driveway and Norman watched it for a bit. Then he trudged back to the rosebed, a big happy head on him. He didn't even notice the four nurses in the main front window laughing and pushing each other. It was the first time he'd asked a girl out in six months.

'AH … well, fuck it anyway!' shouted Jimmy at himself in the kitchen that night. He put the tin down on the counter and hung his head in disgust.

He had a deadly recipe for smoked salmon fillets with a cream pasta sauce and he was just after making a balls of it. He got the wrong salmon. It wasn't the smoked stuff at all, it was just regular tinned fucking salmon chunks that would taste of nothing by the time he'd fried up the onions and garlic and added the few chopped chives he had in the fridge.

He cooked it all up anyway rather than waste the food and sat watching the telly as he ate, still pissed off with himself. The cordless handset of his phone was sitting on the arm of the couch across the room from him and every few minutes he found himself looking away from the news to make sure it was still there. When he was finished eating, he went over to pick it up and click it on and off to make sure it wasn't out of battery or something. It hadn't rung in ages. But it was fine.

He put the plate into the sink and checked the clock in the kitchen. He put the kettle on and sat looking at it for a minute as it started to hiss.

They hadn't spoken in about three weeks. Not even an email. Jimmy remembered meeting her in Thailand the previous summer. That week often played itself out like a movie in his mind afterwards. He'd been through a fairly dry patch before that and she was just so fucking beautiful and so cool. But then when he got back to Dublin he'd had all this crap in his old IT job, and then he'd quit that as The Grove had started to take off in a big way and he suddenly found his face on the front of magazines and his voice coming out of the radio in his car. He just didn't have the time for an long distance girlfriend. Any girlfriend in fact. Certainly not one that deserved all the attention that he couldn't give Susan. She was cool and relaxed but she wasn't a sap. Someone else would edge his way sooner or later into the gap Jimmy had left and then she really would be gone. Maybe it had already happened. Maybe that's why she hadn't called him

But it wasn't right. If it was going to be over, if he was going to let Susan go and get on with her life, he should do it properly. But he didn't want to. He didn't want it to be over and he didn't want to let her get on with her life. He wanted to come off the stage and see her there waiting for him, to have her share the insanity with him and then to grab his hand so that they could run off and hide from it all together when it got too mental. Six months. If he just had six months to wrap everything up, the album, the tour, and get the whole thing moving. Twelve months tops. In a year he'd be able to give her so much more than he could now. But, Jesus, was she going to wait around for a year for him to get his shit together? What if … if …

Bollocks to this. He had to call her.

'Hello?'

'Susan?'

'Jimmy?!'

'Yeah. How's it …'

'Hang on a second, Jimmy. Just … hang on, give me a second.'

He could hear her hushing someone in the background, her hand on the mouthpiece making everything muffled. Who was there?

Some bloke probably. A bottle of wine in one hand and a tin of smoked fucking salmon chunks in the other, the bastard.

'Jimmy?'

'Yeah. Still here.'

'Sorry, it's a bit loud here.'

'Entertaining?'

'Kind of. Amanda is heading off tomorrow. There's a few people over.'

Amanda had been out in Thailand with Susan on holidays when they'd met. Aesop had ... well, he'd made sure that Jimmy had plenty of time alone with Susan.

'Where's she going?'

'She's just going off travelling she says. Doesn't even know where. Said she'll head to Paris first and see what happens. She hasn't really had a great time of it recently, poor thing. They let her go in work, well she kind of quit, and she ... she hasn't really been herself for a while now. But I told you all that, didn't I?'

Jimmy didn't remember.

'Yeah, yeah,' he said. 'That's tough.'

'But anyway, how are things with you? It's been a while.'

Her voice was bringing it all back now. Thailand, Dublin, her laugh, the feel of her skin.

'Three weeks and three days,' said Jimmy.

'Wow. You're counting. I didn't think ...'

'Susan, why didn't you call?'

Fuck it, this was hard enough without dancing around.

'Jimmy, it's ... I'm ... God, I wasn't expecting you to call tonight. Jimmy, I'm ... I ...' Big sigh. 'I'm not enjoying this. Us. It's too hard. We're not even really a couple, are we? It's not one thing, it's not the other thing. I don't want to get ... to be the one who ... it's just hard Jimmy. And you never call. I know, I know, you're busy. You've got so much you need to do. I know that. I mean, it's great. It really is.'

Jimmy was sitting right on the edge of one of the hard kitchen chairs; elbows on knees, hand on forehead and the phone jammed up against his face. He was rocking back and forth a little.

'Susan, I'm … sorry.'

'The last time I called you, you were in such a hurry to get off the phone. I felt like I was just in the way.'

'It wasn't like that Susan. I had a film crew costing a thousand quid an hour waiting to roll. There was a cranky make-up lady tapping her watch at me, and Aesop running around the TV studio in a towel and a Cradle of Filth t-shirt trying to find his lucky under-pants. It was just bad timing.'

'I know, Jimmy. You told me. But you never called me back.'

'Well, you sounded pissed off. I thought I'd give you a bit of time to, y'know …'

'How much time did you think I needed?'

'I …'

'Jimmy, I'm not sixteen any more, y'know? Going out with the lead singer in the band was all well and good when he was just on the posters on your bedroom wall and it wasn't real. But this is different. Even when I was in Dublin, the way people kept coming up to you in the street, I felt like I was getting in the way. Like I was taking up time you should have been spending with them. I'd just kind of stand to one side and try not to look too much like some groupie you'd just picked up.'

'Ah Jesus, Susan, it's not like that. And it's all new to me too, believe me. I still get surprised when it happens and then I don't know what to say to them. I mean, this is Dublin, right? Half the time they just come up and go, "hey you, singer bloke, you think you're fuckin' great, don't ye?" and then walk off.'

She laughed. It was the sweetest sound he'd heard in weeks.

'Susan …'

'Jimmy listen to me. I told you before that not a lot of people can do what you can do. You have so much talent, God. I don't want to be the one who stops you showing it off. You deserve everything you have now. You should enjoy it.'

'But I'm not. It's not like it was meant to be. There's something … fucked up about it all. Something's missing or something.'

'What could be missing?'

'I … I'm not sure.'

Don't fucking say it, Jimmy. It's not fair. Don't mess with her head like that. You're either in or you're fucking out. Where's your balls? There was another pause. Then …

'I saw the Strut video yesterday.'

'Oh, did you? So, what did you think?'

'It's so weird to see you on the TV like that! You wouldn't believe it. But, no, it's really great! It's a good change after "Caillte". Shows that you're versatile. Aesop smiles a lot when he's playing the drums, doesn't he?'

'Depends on the song. You should have seen the head on him this morning when we played my latest masterpiece in the studio.'

'You both looked great. Very sexy. I didn't see the Japanese guy you were talking about though. Is he not coming back to play with you?'

'Probably not. Maybe. He doesn't know yet. It'd be great though, he's a great bloke.'

'Who were the girls?'

'Who?'

'The girls in the video.'

'Oh, just some dancers. We hired them for the shoot. Probably another reason Aesop was smiling like that.'

'And you?'

'Nah. Not my scene.'

'Jimmy?'

'Yeah?'

'It's … I guess it's kind of hard to sit all the way over here and wonder. I mean, I know what Aesop's like. Amanda sent him a few emails, but I don't think he replied. I can only imagine what you guys are getting up to, the things that are happening around you now.'

'Susan, it's not like that. I swear to God.'

'Isn't it?'

'No! Well, maybe a little bit. I mean it's there all right. Aesop is certainly enjoying himself. But I've known him since school and,

28

believe me, he's been living this life since he was about thirteen. The only difference is that he doesn't have to borrow money off me all the time now. He's the rockstar. I'm just a musician, same as I always was. And I don't get caught up in all that shite. It's a bit distracting to be honest. I'm too busy. And anyway it's embarrassing.'

'Jimmy, be a rockstar.'

'What?'

'Go and be a rockstar. Please. It'd make me happy to know that everything you've worked for all these years is paying off. Live the life and see what you think. You'll only get one chance to do it, right?'

'Susan, I don't want that.'

'Well … what do you want?'

Fuck it, he was walking straight into these.

'I … just want it to really get going so I can … y'know …'

He heard her sigh.

'Jimmy, Amanda's heading off tomorrow. I don't know when she'll be back and I need to spend a bit of time with her before she goes. She really hasn't been herself. I should go.'

'Susan … can I call you?'

'Of course. Hey, you owe me a song, remember?'

'I do remember.'

'Any progress?'

'Well …'

'Too busy I guess, right?'

'Ah Susan, it's not like that … I just have all this …'

'I'm only joking Jimmy. Look, I need to go.'

'I'll call you. Soon.'

'Do if you like.'

'I will.'

'I mean it Jimmy. Call me because you want to. Not because you think you should. Okay?'

'Yeah. Sure. But of course I want to. I want to talk to you properly. Not like this. I need … I mean I want to …'

Susan laughed again.

'Jimmy, I don't think you know what you want right now.'

'Susan …'

'Seeya Jimmy. Take care of yourself. And, hey, give me a wave from your next video. That'd be cool.'

She hung up.

He sat up straight and felt the sweat trickle down his back. His hands and the phone were slimey and hot. Susan was nobody's fucking idiot. She was afraid of the very same thing that Jimmy was. That he'd drift away from her, that he'd let the circus he was part of now pack up and leave her behind. He wanted so much to promise her that it wouldn't happen. But how the fuck could he do that? It was getting so big now that he felt like he was just one of the clowns.

NORMAN MET Trish out in The Yacht in Clontarf. A few pints, a bit of dinner and a couple of pints, and then a few quick pints before they walked back along the coast as far as Fairview, where he stopped a taxi for her and held her hand as she sat into it. His heart was going nineteen to the dozen as she sat there looking up at him. He had no clue what she wanted to happen next, but he wasn't about to risk making a balls of the whole thing by opening his gob and so he just smiled at her and then cleared his throat.

'So … would it be okay if I called you again, Trish? I had a great night tonight.'

'Will you not be out in Baldoyle?'

'Ah, I'm pretty much done out there. I will be anyway by the time you get back next week.'

'Ah, that's a shame. What about our poor roses?'

'Sure, it was only a small job. They'll be grand for another while. So …'

'Give me a call next week. I'll be working but I should be able to get off again on Friday night. They're usually cool with the country girls getting home for the weekend if they can.'

'So you'll be going back to Kerry?'

She grinned up at him from the back of the taxi.

'Well … that might be up to you.'

His belly did a flip and then they heard another voice muttering.

'Fuck sake …'

It was the taxi man.

'Maybe you want to turn on your radio there?' said Norman, leaning down.

'It's broke. Go on. Pretend I'm not here. I've heard worse in annyway. I'll start whistling if it gets too painful.'

Norman turned back to Trish.

'So, maybe we can go for a meal next Friday? A proper one.'

'I'd love to.'

Norman suddenly put his hands on his face.

'Oh no! Fuck!'

'Jesus. What? What is it?'

'Oh God, sorry Trish. I just remembered I'm going to a gig next Friday. Feck it anyway. Unless … do you like music? Would that be okay instead?'

'Is that all? Christ, I didn't know what was wrong with you.'

'I just remembered. But what do you think? Would you be on for a bit of live music?'

'Of course I would. Who is it?'

'The Grove. You know them?'

'Of course, yeah. But are they not over in England or something? Didn't I read that?'

'Not for a while yet. They're playing in Vicar Street next week. Will you go with me?'

'Do you have a spare ticket?'

'I … eh … I know a fella can get me one.'

The taxi man stopped whistling.

'Can he get me one?'

'What?'

'Can he get me one? My mot is mad into that shower. That Irish song they do, y'know? She's always singing along to it on the radio. She was trying to get tickets to that gig but they were all gone. You should've seen the puss on her. It used to be Robbie this and Robbie

31

that, but now she never shuts up about yer man Aesop. Some shaper, that bloke.'

'Eh …'

'I'll bring you and your bird home for no fare. Where are yiz going?'

'I … what? She's not my …'

'Can you get two tickets?'

'I don't know if I …'

'Look, sit in there in annyway. I'll give you me phone number and if you can do anything you give me a call. If you can't, then no sweat. Right? Now where am I going?'

Norman didn't know what to say, but Trish moved along the seat, laughing. He sighed and got in.

'That's it, you do what your bird says,' said the taxi man.

'She's not my … bird,' said Norman.

The taxi man looked in his rearview mirror at Trish and then turned around to Norman again.

'Well you better get your fuckin' skates on pal, before she's some-one else's bird.'

Trish looked up at Norman with a big grin and put one hand on his leg. Norman caught a wink in the mirror from his new ally and just closed his eyes, his face burning in the dark.

Chapter Three

AESOP AND Jimmy met up for breakfast two days later. They didn't usually bother hooking up outside the studio so early in the day, but today was going to be, hopefully, a landmark day for The Grove. There was still some mixing and tidying up to do, but they were going in to cut the last song. The album was pretty much done.

Jimmy sat opposite Aesop, half a fried tomato en route to his mouth.

'Who?' said Aesop, frowning into the distance.

'Jesus Christ,' said Jimmy, putting down his fork and shaking his head. He looked up. 'Do I have to go through this every fucking time? Amanda! The girl you rode in Thailand, Aesop. English. Green eyes. Freckles. Friend of Susan, the girl I've been going mad over for the last six months, who came to visit me from London and got Peggy all excited because she brought a scarf from Harrods …'

'Amanda … Amanda …' said Aesop, tapping the table in front of him. 'Was she the one whose husband pissed off and took the car? A nice one too, wasn't it? A GT-R or something. Jimmy, that's got a steel turbine, ball bearing core, eighteen-inch …'

'She wasn't married. They were engaged. But yeah, he took some dosh and did a runner. I don't know anything about a GT-R.'

'I think she said it was blue. Did she not say it was blue?'

'Fuck the car Aesop. Do you remember her? It's not even a year ago.'

'I do yeah. I think so. So what about her?'

'She's gone … she … ah, it doesn't matter.'

'No, tell me.'

'What's the point if you don't remember her?'

'You were going to tell me, so just tell me.'

'She's gone off travelling. I was talking to Susan the other day and Amanda is gone off travelling because she was let go out of work and I think she's still upset about yer man legging it. So Susan

33

said she's gone off on a trip to get her head together or something. That's it.'

'She's gone travelling.'

'Yeah.'

'Ah that's nice. Great. So … eh … so, where's she off to then?'

'You have no fucking idea who I'm talking about, do you?'

'I'm trying me best Jimmy for fuck sake. I remember the car.'

'You never even saw the car! If there was one. Christ. Forget about it. It doesn't matter.'

Aesop relaxed and took up his coffee. Thank fuck that was over. Jimmy got all excited sometimes and Aesop would have to weather the storm till he got it out of his system and calmed down. Anyway, how are you meant to remember every single girl in the world you ever met or talked to or rode?

'So what were Dónal's new band like,' he said. 'What are they called? Feet?'

'Leet. Yeah, they're pretty good actually. Y'know who they reminded me of? The Stranglers. Take something like The Killers, right? Add a big keyboard sound like The Doors and a bit of ska. They sound like that. Y'know what I mean?'

Aesop had his face scrunched up.

'The Killers, Stranglers and the Doors. And ska.'

'Yeah.'

'I'll have to take your word for it Jimmy, at this hour of the morning. The Stranglers were fucking deadly, but.'

'Add more Killers.'

'Not Coldplay though?'

'No. I don't know where Dónal got that from. They're not whingy like that.'

'Thank fuck.'

'Anyway, they're good. Catchy. Man, they've got some tunes.'

'Do they know a bass player?'

'Ah shite. Forgot to ask them. I'll ask them the next time. So c'mere, did you find anything when you were out shopping for your new den of iniquity yesterday?'

'Nah. Actually, I went to the zoo instead.'

'Dublin Zoo?'

'No, Jimmy. One of our many other zoos.'

'But what was in the zoo?'

'Monkeys. Well, buff-cheeked gibbons.'

Jimmy just looked at him and said nothing.

'Y'see, I read in the paper last week that one of them had a baby about two months ago and that this week would be the first week it'd be on display.'

'So … what, you brought Phil's kids?'

'No. They have football on Saturdays, sure. I just went on me own.'

'What? Why for fuck sake?'

'Man, monkeys are brilliant. Them fuckers make me laugh. The buff-cheeked gibbons don't use their legs. They just swing out of trees, the cages, ropes. Like Tarzan, y'know? It's amazing. They lash around the place, just swinging from arm to arm, and they never fall. The speed of them. And the baby, his name's Jai, was hanging onto his mammy for dear life and her pissing around the cage being chased by the daddy. I think he was after some sweet monkey love, but she was probably still sore from Jai and she wasn't having any of it. He ended up giving Jai a smack on the head and then went off into a corner to sulk. It was brilliant. You should see them.'

Jimmy shook his head.

'I don't believe you.'

'Which part?'

'All of it. You reading the newspaper for starters.'

'Sure, I go to the zoo every few weeks to look at the monkeys and chill.'

'On your own?'

'Yeah!'

'Since when?'

'I've been doing it for months now!'

Jimmy just sighed. He probably shouldn't have been surprised. Aesop had a thing for funny animals. He went to see 'March of the Penguins' about five times when it came out and was probably the first person in Dublin to buy it on DVD. He'd come home from the pub, roll a big spliff and then stick on the movie and break his bollocks laughing at the telly for two hours before he went to bed. He did it at least three times a week. He had one about dolphins too.

'You're a bleedin' looper Aesop.'

Aesop shrugged and picked up his coffee.

'Isn't it better to go to the zoo for the afternoon than go out robbing shops?'

'I s'pose it is. Who robs shops?'

'Some people rob shops. Those fuckers were funny today, but. You should've seen them.'

Jimmy nodded.

'You know you can't have pets in that place?'

'Yeah, I know.'

'So you're not allowed buy a monkey.'

'Actually they're apes, Jimmy. If you want to be technical about it. Yeah, I know. I wasn't planning on getting one.'

'Yeah, well I was just making sure. Look, we better go and get our arses to the studio. We told Sparky we'd be in at eight and you know the way he gets when people are late.'

'I know. Hey, let's give him another fifteen minutes, will we? He'll be pacing around the place and kicking things and talking to himself. It's so bleedin' funny. He's like a caged animal when he's angry, isn't he?'

'Well you'd fuckin' know, by the sounds of things.'

JIMMY AND Aesop finished playing and looked up through the window at Sparky. He gave them the thumbs-up to say it was a wrap, and then they took off their headphones and started to yawn and stretch. Jesus, that had been a long session, but at least they were done. The rest of the work would be done by Sparky at the console, Jimmy lending a hand. Their debut album, which Senturian Records were going to release in the UK, would be winging its way to London and all the lads would have to do then would be wave and smile for the cameras. Everything was cool. Well, they had to find a fucking bass player of course. Jimmy had done all of the bass on the album except for the two versions of 'Caillte', which Shiggy had already recorded in Dublin and in Japan when the lads were out there with Johnnie Fingers the previous year.

'Aesop, there's a call on hold for you here,' said Sparky into his mike.

'Is it the president of me fan club again? Will you tell her I have her pencilled in for Tuesday and Thurday evenings and not to be such an itchy trollop. And would she ever try and have a bit of respect for herself.'

'I told you not to be giving this number out like that, didn't I? Anyway, it doesn't sound like one of your little floozies. It might be one of their Daddys, though, looking to kick the hole off you, please God.'

'A bloke? Jaysis. Tell him to hang on, will you? I'm going for a piss.'

'Hang on? I'll hang your bollocks off the monitors you cheeky prick. You can take it now or I'm cutting the fucker off. He's tying up the line for ten minutes, the cunt.'

Aesop nodded.

'Where was that finishing school you went to again, Sparky? Switzerland, was it?'

'You've five seconds.'

Aesop went in to take the call as Jimmy and Sparky started to tidy up. Leet were coming in a bit later to start putting down a demo that Dónal hoped would get Senturian interested in them. Jimmy was finding it hard to multitask like this – his debut album one minute, getting a deal for a bunch of kids the next. Dónal was out now at a meeting with some music lawyers.

'Wotcha reckon Sparky?' said Jimmy.

'Hopefully it is some girl's Da looking to kick the hole off him.'

'I meant about the album.'

'Tops, Jimmy. Here you go …'

Sparky took a CD out of his breast pocket and handed it across to Jimmy.

'Unit number one.'

Jimmy took it in his hands. It was just a blank-looking CD, no artwork or anything. No indication that it contained a large part of his spirit, his soul, the musical ideas that had been with him since he was a teenager, most of his aspirations for the future. It was going to be called "Brazen Songs and Stories".

'So how long will you need to spend on it, Sparky?' said Jimmy.

'By the end of next week it'll be in London. No problem.'

'I'd say you'll be glad to see the back of it then, yeah?'

'I'll tell you Jimmy, you've some good stuff on there. I'd say you'll do well out of it. But it's all down to the money and Senturian look like they're behind it. That's what's important in the end. If it's not being pushed along like a bastard, nothing will happen. That's the business these days. Good songs mean nothing.'

'That's a jolly bleedin' thought.'

'Sorry man. It's business. You see that fucking eejit that won Big Brother? Number one for the last six weeks and all he does is talk over a song that was shite when it came out the first time in 1966. More talent in my snot so there is. He'll have an album out now too, watch. Make a million quid. In six months time, no one will remember the cunt and we'll never hear from him again and that's the only good thing about it. Hand us those cans will you?'

Jimmy picked up his headphones and gave them to him.

'You don't think much of the music industry, do you Sparky?'

'Full of pricks, Jimmy. Always was, actually. These days more than ever. And I don't mean the likes of that gurrier in there on the phone. I'm talking about fuckers would sell their own mammies. Greedy bastards. It's got nothing to do with music.'

'So why do you do it?'

'Why?'

Sparky looked at Jimmy like it was the strangest thing he'd ever been asked.

'Yeah,' said Jimmy. 'I mean, if you think they're all bastards, why not do something else?'

Sparky laughed.

'Like what?' he said. 'Kindergarten teacher? Nah Jimmy, this is my job. The only one I can do. But I don't do it for the money.'

'Why then?'

'See that gobshite in there?'

'Aesop?'

'Yeah. Aesop. You know what I caught him doing last week?'

'Oh Christ, don't tell me …'

'Nah, it's not bad. He was loosening up before you got here. Playing that old Van Halen song he likes. You know it?'

'"Hot for Teacher"? He plays that to warm up when he can get his hands on two bass drums.'

'Yeah, well he was playing it the other day. I happened to be recording at the same time, just to get some levels for later.'

'What happened?'

'He played it perfectly.'

'Yeah, he's good at it all right.'

'No, Jimmy. Perfectly. I have that album on the computer. I brought it up and put the Van Halen intro next to his to check the waves. Identical. He didn't miss one single beat.'

'Right. Eh … is that good?'

'If you'd told me I'd have called you a lying cunt.'

'Really?'

Jimmy looked back in at Aesop who was still on the phone.

'It's that hard to do?'

'It's not fuckin' easy. So anyway, that's why I do it Jimmy. Cos every now and then, when you work with artists, you come across something that you can't explain. That's God shining through, Jimmy. It's a little glimpse of God. I need that in my life. We all do. God is brilliant, so he is.'

Oh fuck, thought Jimmy. Sparky was going mad again. Steady … steady …

'Of course,' continued Sparky, 'then you look at the people that God chooses to use as his instrument. And, taking that fucker in there as an example, the holiness of it all kind of falls on its tits, doesn't it?'

Jimmy laughed.

'I s'pose, yeah.'

'But it doesn't matter, Jimmy. I heard it. He hadn't even taken off his jacket. He just pulls out the sticks and goes straight into it. He didn't even know I was in here. Thirty seconds of the intro. Then he stands up, sees me and goes, "Hey Sparky, is the kettle boiled? I'd a skinful of pints and two French slappers last night. Hairy yokes they were too, but I'd be lying if I said I didn't enjoy meself. Is there bikkies?".'

Jimmy laughed.

'Sounds like the Holy Spirit working through him all right.'

'I know. But you can't question God, Jimmy.'

'I don't, Sparky. I don't. But ... I wouldn't have figured you for ...'

'Ah, I'm not going to stick a bible in your face Jimmy, but when I hit the bottom of the shitter twenty years ago and I couldn't climb out, it was God who reached down for me.'

'Fuck. I never knew that.'

'Yeah. Well that's between me and him. The point is, most people don't give a fuck about anything they can't show off to their greedy bastard mates, and you can't show off your soul. This isn't about heaven and hell or any of that manmade shite, Jimmy. It's not even about music. My job isn't really about music. It's about getting into someone's head and showing them the way out. Fuck knows, I've had a lot of practice flying in and out of me own head. For a while there I used to be gone for days. Sometimes me head wouldn't let me back in and we'd have a big row. Confusing as fuck that was.'

'Jesus. What were you on? LSD, coke ...?'

'LSD and coke? Christ, you don't want to take LSD and coke together Jimmy. The fuckin' last thing you need when you're hallucinating is a confidence booster, I'm telling you. Anyway, I don't do that shit any more, but when an artist – like you for instance – wants something, I can usually get a feel for it and help them bring it out. And I thank God for giving me that gift. You've got your gifts too, as does that little delinquent in there. But the music industry doesn't give a fuck about any of that. No more than any other industry. It's about money, Jimmy.'

'You're fucking bumming me out here Sparky. Jesus …'

'Ah, I don't mean to Jimmy. The important thing is how *you* feel about the album. Where it came from, what it means … are you cool with it? Your name is on it. Can you stand next to it?'

'Yeah. Yeah I can.'

'Then fuck them all.'

Aesop came back into them. He had the knuckle of one index finger in his mouth and was frowning.

'What's up?' said Jimmy. 'You in the shit over some bird?'

'What? Oh. No. No, it's not that.'

'Who was it then?'

'Remember Mena?'

'Probably not, Aesop. Around when was she having the pleasure?'

'No Jimmy. Mena. Remember them two little young fellas were outside here a while back? Wanted me to go to their sister's birthday party. She was sick, right?'

'Oh yeah. Eh … Liam, wasn't it? And the little fella.'

'Yeah. Well, that was their Da on the phone. Turns out that the poor young one is out in Crumlin in the hospital out there. She's not fucking doing well either.'

'Jesus. That's fucking terrible. Is it bad?'

'Yeah. They're only letting her home for her birthday cos they aren't sure she'll be having another one.'

Sparky blessed himself and shook his head.

'Poor child.'

'Her birthday is Friday night. I said we'd drop in.'

'Okay. But … eh … we're playing Vicar Street on Friday, Aesop.'

'We'll just say hello on the way to the gig. I know it'll be tight but, listen man, apparently I'm all she talks about, right? She thinks I'm fuckin brilliant or whatever. And now Liam is after copping that something's going on with her. He's starting to go off the rails at school, his Da says, and he keeps fuckin running away and all, y'know? And the Da sounds like he's only barely holding it together himself. C'mon. We'll drop in, Jimmy. Half an hour, right?'

Jimmy just nodded.

'Okay. Yeah, no problem.'

The three of them stood there for a minute.

'Cup of tea Aesop?' said Sparky, eventually.

'Thanks man.'

Chapter Four

NORMAN LOOKED at himself in the mirror. He was just out of the shower, standing in his jocks and cursing at the spot of blood on his neck. His Mam kept buying him cheap disposable razors and they were making shite of his face. He smiled at that. He couldn't even use a crappy blade now without cutting himself and yet he could still remember being crouched over a small stream in the mountains of Afghanistan, shaving with a Bowie knife so that the locals wouldn't notice the big red head on him if he had to unwrap the thick scarf that covered his face. Freezing cold water and a nine-inch blade. The lads would only laugh at him if he told them about it. They were always taking the piss about when he was a soldier. He didn't mind that much. And anyway, there was nothing cool about shaving with a knife. No more than there being anything cool about having to carry your gick around in plastic bags when you were on a mission so that animals wouldn't sniff it out and give your position away. They tended to leave stuff like that out of the Rambo movies.

He was all excited tonight. The lads had finished their album, and they were celebrating with the gig in Vicar Street. They'd blown everyone away the last time they played there and this time was going to be even better. The press would be in, the new songs would be on show, the venue was sold out. After this one they'd be taking a couple of weeks off and then the CD would be in the shops and the whole thing would start up again. Dónal was already finalising the details of the tour. Yeah, it was going great for the lads. But that's not why Norman was excited. The reason he was clipping his toenails and scanning frantically through the shirts in his wardrobe was that he had another date with Trish.

Earlier that day, he'd talked to Jimmy and Aesop on the phone. He wanted everything to go perfectly tonight.

'JIMMY?'

'Norman. What's the story?'

'Listen Jimmy, I'm on a date tonight.'

'Yeah? Brilliant. Who is she?'

'A nurse from out in Baldoyle, at work.'

'Great stuff.'

'Yeah. I'm picking her up at eight. What time are you on?'

'We'll be on around nine-thirty I'd say. Leet are supporting us. Remember that band I said I was doing a bit of work with? They'll be on at eight.'

'We'll probably grab a quick bite, but we'll be there for when you come on. Listen, can I buy a ticket for Trish?'

'Jesus Norman, didn't I say to you …'

'Ah no, Jimmy. That's not fair. I don't want to impose. You said I could just show up and I appreciate that, but I only met this one recently and then she wasn't sure if she was free tonight so I didn't want to …'

'Ah Christ, Norman. You're already on the guest list. Guests can bring guests. Bring whoever you like, really. Get her to bring her mates, sure, if you want. There's a few dozen spare spots. Half of the press won't turn up anyway, the pricks. It's no problem. Just tell the guy on the door your name and you're in, done deal.'

'Ah Jimmy, I feel like a terrible …'

'Norman, for fuck sake it's nothing. We've been over all this before! Please, you and Trish come backstage afterwards. I want you to. And don't queue up either when you get there, right? Just come in.'

They'd actually nearly had a row over it before. The last time The Grove played Vicar Street, Norman had actually paid for his ticket and then was too embarrassed to ask to go backstage afterwards to see the lads. Jimmy went spare when he found out. Him and Aesop had been mates with Norman for twenty years. Norman had come to see the band play when there was more people on the stage than in the audience. He wasn't fucking having him pay in to see them now.

'Jimmy, it's awkward, y'know? The fella won't know me and he'll be giving me that look, like I'm only …'

'He'll fucking know you tonight, don't worry about it.'

'How will he?'

'I'll tell him a fucking huge Corkman will be in tonight with his bird and if he's not nice to you, he'll be cleaning the jacks next week. Okay?'

'Ah, Jimmy, see what I mean? Going to the trouble …'

'I'm joking Norman. Look, it'll be grand. Seeya there, okay?'

'Okay Jimmy. Okay. I'll seeya later. If I don't see you before you're on, good luck.'

'Thanks man.'

'AESOP?'

'Norman. Howya. What's up?'

'Listen, Aesop, I'm bringing a girl tonight to the gig.'

'Sorry, I'm confused. Which Norman is this?'

'I'm serious Aesop. I'm bringing a girl.'

'A real one?'

'Yes, a real one. From Kerry.'

'Okay. Well it's starting to make sense now. Fair enough. Good man. Why are you telling me, but? Did I ride her or something?'

'No. But I'm just telling you that I really like this girl and there's a good chance we'll both be backstage afterwards. Okay?'

'Right. Eh, Norman?'

'Yeah?'

'I'm only out of bed. What are you fucking talking about?'

'I'm just telling you. I like this girl a lot, and it's our second date.'

'Okay … right. And it's my turn to say something now, is it?'

'Did you hear what I just said?'

'Yes, I fucking heard you Norman! You've got a bird. Brilliant. Porky Pig is hang gliding past the window here. Are you going to tell me why you fucking rang me?'

'Okay, I'll spell it out. I know you're playing a big gig and all tonight, and I don't want to distract you, but I'm just telling you now not to fucking annoy me this evening or I swear to God I'll kick your bollocks into your throat.'

'What? You rang me to tell me that?'

'Yes.'

'You went to the trouble of ringing me to tell me you're going to kick me in the bollocks if I annoy you tonight in front of some bird I haven't even met.'

'Yes.'

'Norman, I was sitting here quite happily having a cup of tea and a bit of toast. Do you think I need this fucking abuse when I pick up the phone? I don't know who I'll be annoying today. I haven't given it any thought yet.'

'Well, I'm just saying to you that it better not be me. And you're to be a gentleman around Trish too, or that'll be another kick in the bollocks.'

'Fuck sake. Okay. Fine. I'll be nice to your bird. Can I go now?'

'Yeah. Seeya later.'

'Fuck sake …'

'WAS THE limo really necessary?' said Jimmy. He was looking around the inside of the car, feeling the leather of the seats and pulling at all the drawers and gadgets.

'Of course!' said Aesop. 'And listen, you're to be on your best rockstar behaviour when we get there, right? The big swagger up to the front door in your leather jacket, the shades, and then I want to see some shapes when we get inside.'

'What shapes for fuck sake?'

'Just pretend you're on the stage.'

'But I'm not on a stage, Aesop. I'm at a fifteen-year-old girl's birthday party.'

'It's a stage tonight, man. No offence, but Daytime Jimmy is a bit of a boring fucker sometimes. We need Rockstar Jimmy to put in an appearance this evening.'

'I'm not boring.'

'Are you not?'

Aesop did a Jimmy impersonation.

'Ooh, look at me, I'm Jimmy the artist … I'm so confused … life is heavy and sad … I can't say two words to a woman without falling arse-about-tit in love with her … hang on till I find a dark corner so I can write a nice song about rabbits … sad ones … and candy floss … and being so into some tart, that I don't know who I fucking am any more … oh, what does it all mean …'

'Aesop …'

' … I wish I was in Radiohead …'

'Get fucked. I'm not like that.'

'Ah, you are a bit, but, aren't you?'

'No. Jesus, just because your life revolves around your cock, it doesn't mean other people don't have things going on in their head.'

'Whatever, Jimmy. I'm just saying that when we go in there tonight you're to be all cool and chilled, right?'

'You keep fucking telling me! Will you fuck off?'

'Okay, okay. Look, this is Sandymount now. We're nearly there. Where's your shades?'

'Jesus fu … they're in me pocket.'

'Grand, grand. Just checking.'

Five minutes later they pulled up outside Mena's place. Aesop had called her Dad and he was already standing outside the front door waving at them as the car stopped.

'Right Jimmy, now …'

'I know, I know. Come on. We've only got half an hour and then we've to get to the gig.'

'Help me with this, will you?'

'What's in it?'

'Ah, t-shirts, posters, a few bits and pieces. For the young ones at the party.'

'Here, give me one of the bags.'

Mr Flanigan was all smiles for them at the porch. He shook their hands and welcomed them inside. Jimmy looked back at the car from the hall. There was already a bunch of neighbours starting to gawk.

'Tommy Flanigan,' said Mena's Dad. 'You're very good for coming.'

'Not at all Tommy. I'm Aesop, and this is Jimmy. We're chuffed we could make it. Is she inside?'

'She's on the couch in the living room. All her mates are in there with her. She can't get about, so the party is kind of arranged around her.'

'Does she know we're coming?'

'No. And I didn't tell Liam or Conor either or they'd tell her.'

'Grand so. How's Liam?'

Tommy sighed and ran a hand through his hair.

'He's not great Aesop, to be honest. He was always a bit of a handful, God knows, but himself and Mena are … y'know, when they were growing up and all, they were very close. Listen, he thinks the world of you too, same as herself. You wouldn't … you don't think you might just have a little word with him? Just, the two of you. A bit of attention. He'd love that from you, so he would. He's nearly a bigger fan that she is, sure.'

'No problem, Tommy,' said Aesop. 'I'll have a laugh with him.'

'Thanks. Look they're just in here.'

Tommy nodded at a door just off the hall.

'I'll go in first and say we have a surprise for her. Wait here a sec.'

'Okay.'

Tommy went inside and the lads could hear him hushing everyone.

'All right?' said Aesop to Jimmy.

'I'm grand. And listen man … this is a good thing you're after doing. Fair play to you. I know you've been bloody annoying me all day about it but, y'know, at the same time …'

'Shades Jimmy. Where's the shades?'

'Oh for fuck sake … you'd have a saint wanting to kick the arse off you, you know that?' said Jimmy, fishing them out of his pocket and putting them on. 'Okay? Is that all right?'

'Lovely. You're a ride.

'Did Sparky want to come? I mean, he's kind of in the band at the moment.'

'Nah. Children give him heartburn in the arse he says. But he wants the limo on the way back from the gig. I think he's bringing his old dear for a spin around Dublin on the way home. Is that all right? We'll have to get taxis home like real people.'

'I am a real person, Aesop.'

'Are you?' said Aesop, grinning. 'Do real people wear shades indoors? Look at the state of you.'

'This was your fucking …'

'Lads?' said Tommy, pulling the door open again.

Aesop winked at Jimmy and strolled in first. Jimmy took a breath and followed.

There was about one second of total, stunned silence in the Flanigan living room and then the eardrums in Jimmy's head nearly exploded with the screams of two dozen teenage girls.

'OKAY MAM, I'm off now,' said Norman.

'Have a good night love.'

'I'll be late. Or I might even stay in Aesop's in town if it's very late.'

'Okay. Well, I'll see you in the morning then.'

'Goodnight.'

Norman got the bus into town and stood next to Molly on Grafton Street, pulling his collar tight around him and sticking his hands in his pockets. There was a guy in a tracksuit standing just next to him with a huge basket of individually-wrapped red roses. He was shifting from foot to foot in the cold and looking around hopefully. Norman was thinking about it. After all, himself and Trish had pretty much met because of roses. It'd be cool. Or would it be fucking corny and crap? Norman wasn't brilliant at this type of thing. Still, he hadn't fucked anything up yet. He turned around.

'Are you selling the roses?'

The guy looked down at his basket and shook his head.

'Nah. I just thought I'd come out tonight and stand around in the cold like a cunt.'

Norman blinked at him.

'Christ. I'd say you don't sell many, do you, charming fucker that you are?'

'Not in this weather. Everyone's meeting their women in pubs, the bastards.'

'I'll have one. How much?'

'Fiver.'

'A fiver? Are you mad?'

'You're going to start haggling, are ye? And the fingers fuckin' frozen off me?'

'Jesus, okay. Well just give me one so, please.'

'Here you go.'

'Thanks.'

'No problem.'

Norman took the rose and looked at it. It was a bit shite-looking. Still, it wasn't exactly the season. He wondered where they got them. He folded his arms against the cold, tucking the flower into the crook of his elbow, and waited. It was five past eight. No sign of her yet. Another two minutes. Then he turned around again, frowning. The roses guy looked up.

'What?' he said.

'Are you going to just stand there?' said Norman.

'What?'

'Are you going to just stand there? Right next to me with a big basket of roses? She'll know where I got this one.'

'What are you talking about?'

'She'll be along in a minute. What kind of a prick will I look like? Can you not go and stand somewhere else?'

'Where would you like me to go for fuck sake?'

'I don't know. Around the other side of the statue or something?'

'A fiver.'

'What?'

'Gimme a fiver and I'll go away.'

'You can fuck off with yourself!'

'Then I'm staying put. You make a good windbreaker, big fucker like you.'

'I'm asking you now as a favour.'

'Sorry pal. This is where the business is.'

'There's no business you said a minute ago.'

'Things have picked up a bit.'

'Jesus, you're some bollocks. Here's your bloody fiver. Give me another rose.'

'What? What are you going to do with two of them?'

'I'll think of something. Now give me the rose and go off away around the other side of the statue. Oh Jesus. Here she is. Quick …'

'Yer one in the boots? Jaysis, that's a bit of all right, that is. What's her name?'

'You're looking for a basket up the hole now, is it?'

Norman was finally standing alone next to Molly as Trish walked up.

'Hi. Sorry I'm late. Bloody buses.'

'That's okay. Here.'

'Oh, God, thanks! They're lovely. You shouldn't have. Two?'

'Eh, yeah. In case you lose one.'

Nice one. Fuckin' eejit.

'Are you hungry?' he said. 'We've a good while before the gig. Or maybe a pint? Up to you …'

'Actually, a pint would be good. I'm not that hungry. I never am when I work nights.'

'McDaids?'

'Yeah, great.'

There was a good Friday night crowd in the pub. Norman found one stool at the window just inside the door and helped Trish off with her coat. He just about managed not to bless himself when he saw what was hidden under it. This outfit she had on her now was a different story altogether from the nurse's uniform or the last time they were out. The coat slipped off her shoulders and into his faintly quivering hands to properly reveal the kind of woman that Norman had been fantasising about since he was twelve. Tall, strong, curvy. Not like the little tarts on the telly with nothing to them.

'You look very … eh … you look very pretty tonight,' he said, folding her coat. He was all red.

'Thanks,' she smiled. 'Without the coat, like?'

'Oh Jesus, no. That's not what I meant. You looked lovely outside too. I just meant …'

She laughed.

'Only joking Norman. Hey, you look lovely too.' She looked into his face. 'You're pretty cute when you're flustered, do you know that?'

He shook his head, looking at the floor, and muttered something.

'What's that?' she said, leaning in.

'I said I must look like fucking Bambi so, at the moment.'

She kissed him on the cheek with a grin, one hand on his side as she stretched up to him. She wasn't at all shy about personal space, Trish. Probably came from being a nurse. The things they saw and did all day, there was hardly much room for being sensitive about shite like that.

'That's for the roses,' she said. 'And hey, let me get you a pint too.'

'No, no. I'll get the drinks. What are you having?'

She got up on her toes again to try and see the taps at the bar. Her big breasts bounced slightly under her blouse with the sudden movement and he gawked at her without meaning to, a funny noise coming out of his throat on its own.

'Do they have Murphys here?' she said, turning back to him.

Murphys? His bad leg nearly gave way on him.

NORMAN RELAXED over the next hour. She was so natural and easy that he forgot his usual worries about fucking everything up every time he opened his gob. By the time he was holding out her coat for again, he was feeling the glow from three pints and getting a bit excited about seeing the lads on the stage. It turned out that she'd seen The Grove before, years ago, in the Baggot, when she'd just moved to Dublin.

'I remember the drummer. He was chatting up all the girls at the bar afterwards. Mind you, that's a long time ago. It mightn't even be the same guy they have now.'

Norman said nothing.

They headed around to Thomas Street and saw the queue tail around the corner.

'Hope it's moving,' said Trish. 'It's a bit cold to be standing around.'

Norman took a deep breath and her hand in his, closing his eyes for a second and praying that Jimmy had remembered to say something to the doorman.

'Come on,' he said. 'We'll be grand.'

They walked up the top of the queue, Norman trying to be nonchalant but convinced that he had a head on him like a tomato.

'Yes sir?'

Posh accent. Not like they used to be, bouncers.

'Norman Kelly,' said Norman, swallowing. 'I think … eh …'

'Ah yes, Mr. Kelly. Please, would you like to follow me?'

'Eh … okay … thanks.'

The guy led them into the venue and through a couple of doors until they found themselves in what Norman took to be some kind of member's lounge. Well-dressed people were mingling, the tinkle of ice and hum of poser bullshit hanging in the air. He could feel Trish staring at him, but he didn't want to say anything until he knew what was going on.

'The VIP room, Mr. Kelly. Please help yourself to refreshments. Will I tell the band that you've arrived?'

'Ah … eh … no. No. Leave them be. I'll talk to them later, sure.'

'Very good, sir.' He shook Norman's hand. 'On behalf of the management here at Vicar Street, I hope you have a great evening.' Then he turned to Trish and gave a small bow. 'Miss.'

And then he was gone.

Norman finally looked down at Trish, with a small embarrassed smile. She was looking at him like someone had just groped her arse.

'What the fuck was that?' she said, her Kerry accent on full now and her eyes huge. '"Will I tell the band you've arrived?" Who are you? Jesus, is the gardening just a part-time thing with you or what's the story? Should I be ringing the girls?'

'Sorry,' said Norman. 'I forgot to tell you. I'm just mates with the band.'

'Jesus, yer man looked like he'd been waiting all night for you to show up.'

'Well … eh … I've known the lads for a good while, like …'

'Look at this place! Oh, is that … look, Norman, there's our taxi man from last week.'

He was standing with a girl at the bar, waving over and giving Norman the thumbs up.

'Yeah. Jimmy said it was okay if I brought a few people and then I remembered that I'd made that fella a promise, so I called him earlier. Told him to mention my name at the door.'

'Lucky him. He probably wasn't expecting the VIP treatment.'

'Yeah. Well Jesus, neither was I, to be honest.'

The taxi man was making his way over. Norman had never seen a grin that big before.

'The mot thinks I'm bleedin' ice cream,' said the guy, shaking Norman's hand. 'You could sprinkle nuts on me. If you're ever stuck for a taxi, Norman, you give me a bell, right? Day or night. No problem.'

'Thanks.'

'Howarya again,' he said to Trish.

'Hi.'

He nodded back to Norman.

'Has this fella got the clamps on you yet?'

'Maybe I'm the one with the clamps,' said Trish, smiling.

'Jaysis, I don't think you need them. But he's a good bloke. Fair play to him for giving me a bell today. A lot of blokes wouldn't bother their arse. You could do a lot worse for yourself.'

'I think you might be right.'

She looked up at Norman and grinned. Norman just fidgeted and looked away.

NORMAN AND Trish stayed in Aesop's that night. If Aesop came home at all later they didn't hear him. Norman turned the key and they went straight up the stairs to the spare bedroom. It was nearly as big as the main one and had just been fitted with a king-sized bed. Aesop's sister had spent the previous Wednesday buying all the trimmings and it looked brilliant.

Trish turned on the light and then looked around at Norman.

'Aren't you full of surprises?'

He gave a small shrug.

'Sure, it was me that painted it for the bollocks.'

'Ah, Aesop's great. They both are. God, I can't believe you've all been mates since you were kids.'

Norman nodded and tried to smile. He was a little bit down. After the gig, backstage, Trish and Aesop had gotten on like a house on fire. Norman was trying to be sociable and talking to whoever was around, but he kept hearing her laugh and he'd look over to see Aesop telling her something, all arms and mad expressions the way he was when he was on the pull. The two of them had found a small sofa and she'd probably spent an hour at least being charmed by the fucker and howling her head off with him. Norman knew it was pointless being jealous over someone like Aesop. When it came to women, he couldn't compete with that. It fucking hurt him a bit though. He really liked Trish and the idea that she'd fall for Aesop … and to think that he'd been the one that actually told him to be fucking nice to her!

'Yeah. I noticed you were talking to Aesop a lot all right. The girls seem to go for him.'

'I can see why!'

'Yeah …'

'What?'

'Hmm? Nothing.'

'Is something wrong?'

'No. No.'

'Oh God. It's not Aesop, is it?'

'What? No. Don't be silly. What are you talking about?'

'Norman, look at me.'

'What?'

'Where's Aesop?'

'Christ only knows.'

'Right. And where are you?'

'I'm here.'

'Yeah. And where am I?'

'You're here.'

She nodded and put her hand on his face, going up on her toes to kiss him.

'And what does that tell you? Don't be going and getting all peculiar now on me. I've had a brilliant night.'

'Ah, I'm sorry Trish. I've just known him for a long time and … he's a great bloke, but …'

She shook her head at him, her eyes closed, and he stopped talking. Then she started to unbutton her top, letting it and her bra fall to the floor. Norman looked down at her, his breath catching.

'Holy fuck,' he said, unable to help himself.

She started to unbutton his shirt then, and reached up to pull it from his shoulders. She ran her hands down his chest and around by his sides to pull him closer. Something under her fingers caught her attention. She lifted up his arm to look and found the beginning of the twenty-inch scar that ran in jagged angles from his ribs down and then around to the middle of his back. She frowned at him, but he just shrugged at her and sighed.

'Collapsed lung. When I was younger. They had to operate.'

She ran her finger along the raised flesh again and looked up at him, but his eyes were closed. Okay. If that's the way he wanted it. But she wasn't stupid. Plus, she knew a thing or two about scars. And collapsed lungs for that matter. No surgeon had done that to him.

But that was fine; he didn't want her to know.

'You should have sued,' she said.

Chapter Five

A FEW weeks later, Jimmy was heading into the studio with a guitar riff going through his head. It wasn't really a Grove thing, but he knew that it would suit Leet for one of their songs. He wasn't interested in getting a writing credit, or even one for performance on the Leet album, but he'd teach it to Eamonn the guitar player the next day. In the meantime he wanted to get the thing recorded with their click tracks before he bloody forgot it. He'd been fucking useless for months and didn't trust himself to hang onto an actual decent piece of music in his head for more than one day at a time any more. He'd only been able to finish out their own album with 'More Than Me' because he'd started the song months before, when Marco had asked him to be his best man.

He rounded the corner and started making his way up the street to the front door of Sin Bin, not even noticing the cop car that was parked on the kerb right outside.

He opened up the door and stepped into the warmth of the studio with a big sigh of relief, taking off his coat and slapping his hands together to get some blood back into them. Another fucking cracking Irish winter so it was, the stinging wind outside whipping your nipples into points you could use to cut glass.

'Jesus,' he said, opening the control room door. 'Poxy cold out there again ...'

He stopped. No one was there. He looked through the window into the main room and gasped, feeling something like a smack in his chest. Dónal, Sparky and Aesop were out there with two cops. Aesop. Jimmy hadn't seen him all week. Oh ... fuck, no. What was the gobshite after doing? Was he after getting snared with gange? The dopey bastard. I'll fucking kill him. Hang on, Jimmy. Hang on. He's never been caught before. They'll only give him a bollocking. Right? They only gave you a bollocking the first time, didn't they? But ... why would they send two cops around to the studio just for that? Didn't sound right. Something was up. Fuck, please let it only have been gange. Please, please, please. Jimmy was pretty sure that Aesop didn't mess around with other stuff, but there were a lot of new people hanging around them these days after gigs and all. Sparky had already given them a pointed and carefully rehearsed speech about it. 'Keep an eye out for cunts', he'd said.

Jimmy watched his hand go out to the handle of the door and push it open. He heart was hammering like it was about to give out on him.

'Wh … wha …' he stammered, stepping inside and looking at everyone.

Garda Number One turned around to him. He was a big bloke. Big as Norman and made even bigger by the huge yellow shiny anoraks they have to wear.

'Who are you?' he said. Culchie.

'I'm Jimmy. What did he do?' He looked at Aesop. 'What are you after doing?'

'Jaysis, Jimmy,' said Aesop, laughing. 'You're some best friend, you know that? The boys in blue call around … "The man we're holding says that you can attest to his whereabouts yesterday afternoon. Is this true?" "Yes Garda, he was out robbing the post office."'

'Jimmy,' said Dónal. 'I tried calling you earlier but you weren't picking up.'

'I was at Ma's all morning. I left me phone at home and haven't been back. What's going on?'

'I'm afraid we have a bit of a problem. The two Gardaí here are helping us out with it.'

'What did he do?'

'He didn't do anything. It's okay Jimmy. He's not in trouble. Well, not like that …'

'What? What's happening then?'

'Well, we're just trying to find out.'

'Garda Egan,' said the big one, from behind a moustache he could have used to grow cabbage.

'I'm Garda Ní Mhurchú,' said his mate, who was a girl copper. Fairly short for a copper, and a bit pudgy. Very short hair and a not a whole lot of soft feminine vibes. A bit of a bulldog head on her. 'We're just asking Mr. Murray a few questions to help us in connection with an incident that's been reported. You're Jimmy Collins, right? I've seen you guys play. Last October it was, in the Town Hall in Galway. It was a great night.'

'Oh. Eh … okay. Thanks. And … so … and … what's wrong now?'

Garda Ní Mhurchú turned to the others and raised her eyebrows.

'Oh, it's grand, you can tell him,' said Aesop, waving a hand at her. 'He probably won't even be surprised.'

'It seems that Mr. Murray has offended someone to the point where they've been threatening him.'

Jimmy just nodded at her slowly.

'Told you,' said Aesop, opening a Twix.

'What kind of threats?'

'Well … we don't need to go into that just now. Do you mind if I take off this coat? It's very warm in here.'

'Not at all,' said Dónal. 'Go mad. Do you want a cup of tea?'

They both nodded.

'Lovely.'

'Sparky, would you mind doing the honours?'

When they were all settled around a low coffee table in the lounge area, Garda Ní Mhurchú took out her notebook and started writing in it. Jimmy was just sitting on the edge of his chair, his tea getting cold in front of him.

'So, first of all, you don't know who's been doing this?' said Garda Ní Mhurchú.

'No clue,' said Aesop.

'But it would seem to be a woman, based on what we know?'

'Yeah.'

'Okay. And is there one particular woman in your life right now? A girlfriend or partner, or … ?'

'No. Well, just Jennifer I s'pose.'

'Jennifer?'

'Me sister.'

'And would you say your sister is … estranged at all?'

'Ah she can be, yeah. Well, she's always talking to her goldfish, y'know? Stuff like that. You'd swear they were … but, nah, not anything this bad. And anyway, I know her. When she's annoyed with me she usually just tells me I'm a fu … fool.'

Jimmy closed his eyes and sighed. He was used to jumping in when Aesop met new people, but he didn't know if he was supposed to do it when he was being interviewed by the police.

'Okay. And what about other women in your life, Mr. Murray? I mean in a social context. Do you … date for instance? Or are you seeing anyone regularly?'

'This should be fucking good,' muttered Jimmy under his breath, as he picked up his cup and sat back in his chair for the first time. Sparky suddenly cleared his throat and left to put the kettle on again. Dónal started to fidget on the sofa.

Aesop was finishing the Twix and fingering the wrapper as he thought.

'Mr. Murray?'

'Well, Garda Ní Mhurchú … y'see … eh … sorry, would you mind calling me Aesop? I feel like me Da's standing right behind me or something. It's making me nervous.'

'Of course. Aesop. So … do you see anyone regularly, Aesop?'

'Well … no. Not any one girl in particular.'

'But you've been with a number of women recently?'

'What's recently?'

'Well, let's say since Christmas.'

'Yes. A number.'

'A big number?'

'Well … medium-sized. I had a bit of a cold there a few weeks ago.'

'I see. Aesop, maybe if we started with the last woman you … em … wooed.'

'Okay.'

'When was that?'

60

'Yesterday. No, no … the day before. Tuesday.'

'You're not sure?'

'Well I was with a girl yesterday all right, but I wouldn't say I wooed her exactly. But that's grand as well sometimes, y'know?'

'I'm sorry?'

'Well, some young ones are just quiet, like. But I definitely wooed the one on Tuesday. We had an hour to kill before "Desperate Housewives" so I thought I might as well take her the scenic route. She wooed a fair bit. I remember it because I don't have much furniture yet, so there's a bit of an echo around the gaff and I was afraid that …'

Everyone was looking at him.

'What?'

Jimmy looked around at Garda Ní Mhurchú. She had a nice big frosty head on her now. She glared at Aesop for a minute and then tapped her notepad.

'You said you were with someone last night?'

'Eh … yeah. Out in Drimnagh somewhere. Had to get a taxi back.'

'Okay. But these threats started last week. Did you know this girl before last night? Had you met her before?'

'Eh … not sure. But it's fairly unlikely. I'm not really one for swapping numbers afterwards and being mates and all, y'know?'

'Mr Murray … Aesop … if we were just to take the last few weeks, since the New Year, how many girls' names would I be able to put in this notebook?'

'Their names?' Aesop scratched his head. 'Jaysis … well, you won't have to go looking for your pencil parer.'

'So … a few, just?'

'No. More than that.'

'So then … what's … is it that you can't remember their names?'

Aesop sighed.

'I don't really like to get attached, Garda. I tend to forget names. You know the way hoors don't like kissing you on the lips? That's me with names. Otherwise it gets all personal and you end up with a

61

head full of women and you're trying to match names with faces and what you said to who and what happened … ah, it makes things very complicated, y'know? If it'll help I'd say there was probably about a dozen of them. God, that makes them all sound like slappers, doesn't it? They weren't though. They were lovely. And one of them was definitely Russian. Or she had that accent anyway. Russian … German … Norwegian … y'know that kind of way? Nice girl. She was wearing this blue yoke.'

Garda Ní Mhurchú had stopped taking notes now. She was just staring at Aesop.

'And, just out of interest, the last six months?'

Aesop frowned off into the distance and started to try and count in his head, his lips and fingers moving for a couple of minutes.

'Jimmy, when were we in Japan?' he said eventually.

'About six months ago Aesop.'

Jimmy was mortified, his head hanging down. Dónal had already gone to help Sparky in the kitchen.

'Will I include that?' said Aesop to Garda Ní Mhurchú. 'I was a teacher out there for a bit. It's a deadly way to meet girls, y'know yourself …'

'No I don't,' she said. She'd put down the pad again and was sitting back against the chair just looking at him.

'Okay, well, sure I'll add them in too. Right. Now where … ah shite. I'm after losing where I was. Will I use your pad?'

'Just an estimate is fine. No need to be exact at this point. I'm just trying to get a feel for what we're up against.' She looked at her colleague. 'I think I'm starting to get an idea.'

'Okay. Eh … and it's only riding now we're talking about, right? Not birds I just got talking to down the shops or whatever …'

Jimmy couldn't take it any more. He stood up and started walking into the kitchen.

'I'll … just see if that kettle is boiled yet.'

JIMMY SHOWED the Gardaí out. At the door, Garda Ní Mhurchú turned to him.

'Mr. Collins, I take it you're the … brains of the operation?'

Jimmy shrugged and gave a little nod.

'There's no reason to panic or anything, but Mr. Murray needs to be vigilant until this is sorted out. I'm not sure he's … on the same page as everyone else.'

'He's not even in the same library.'

'Right. Well, here's my number in case he does manage to piece together any of his … encounters. Maybe he'll be able to give us a bit more information.'

'Thanks Garda.'

'He mentioned that he used to give your name out to girls? I'm afraid I had to stop listening when he was explaining why.'

'Yeah. Well he doesn't do it any more. I told him to stop. Anyway, we're both kind of well-known now, so there wouldn't be much point.'

'Right. Well, just in case, you be a little careful yourself. It's possible that the …' She paused to get the right words. ' … utterly demented … girl that has a fixation on him might find her way to you by accident.'

'Jesus, I never thought of that. I still don't even know what happened.'

'They can tell you upstairs. But, again, no need to panic. I'm sure we'll be able to deal with this quickly and quietly.'

'I really appreciate this Garda. Thanks for coming out today.'

'No problem at all. And best of luck with the new album. I hear it's coming out soon?'

'Oh yeah. Thanks. Couple of weeks.'

'I'll be sure to pick up a copy.'

'Great.'

Jimmy came back up the stairs to find the others all sitting around the coffee table looking at him.

'So, will someone tell me what the fuck is going on?' said Jimmy.

Dónal picked up the empty cups and started bringing them into the kitchen.

'It seems that one of the girls this dirty little bastard has been sniffing around didn't appreciate the way she was treated either during or after the liason,' he said.

'A tenner says it was after,' said Aesop.

'Aesop, there were two Gardaí in here a minute ago,' said Jimmy. 'This is not the best time for you to be fucking about.'

'Yeah. I don't think Garda Ní Mhurchú liked me. The head on him.'

Jimmy frowned at him.

'What?'

'What?'

'Aesop, you do know that Garda Ní Mhurchú was a woman, don't you?'

'What? Get fucked.'

'Aesop, she was a girl!'

'She was not. Why do you think that?'

'Well, her fucking name for starters.'

'What are you on about? It's just Mhurchú. Murphy, right?'

'It's Ní Mhurchú! Ní is what women use in Irish.'

'Me bollocks! And anyway, why didn't she call herself Ban Garda Ní Mhurchú then, if she's a woman?'

'Because they don't do that any more. They're all just Garda.'

'But … Jimmy, did you not see the fucking awful-looking mess of a face on it … it couldn't have been …'

'Okay. It doesn't matter. Whatever. Will you tell me …'

'She was a bit short for a bloke copper all right, but I thought that was just because she was standing next to that big long lanky streak of piss she came in with. But she'd no make-up on or anything.'

'She's a fuckin' copper, Aesop, not a bleedin' Avon lady. And anyway, I think she might have been … eh …'

'Been what?'

'Y'know …'

'A short fat bloke?'

'No. A lesbian.'

Aesop roared laughing.

'No fucking way, Jimmy. I've seen hundreds of lesbians, and they don't look like that.'

'What? That's exactly the way they look. For fuck sake, sorry for ruining your favourite fantasy, Aesop, but lesbians aren't all six foot tall with long blonde hair, big tits and red lipstick.'

'Of course they are! Jimmy, come around to the flat afterwards and I'll stick on some ...'

'Aesop. First of all, fuck off. I just want to know why two cops were here today and no fucker's told me yet. What the fuck is going on? And second of all, I promise you the girls in your videos are doing it for money, not for love. Real lesbians probably laugh their bollocks off at that stuff. So to speak.'

'But Jimmy, I can prove that you're wrong.'

'Aesop, I don't care.'

'You like girls, right? So would you prefer a six-foot blonde with big tits and red lipstick, or would you prefer Garda Ní Mhurchú with that train-wreck of a boxer's face she lugs around with her?'

'Aesop ...'

'You'd go for the peach, wouldn't you?'

'Listen to me ...'

'And the only difference between lesbians and other women is that lesbians like women. So if they like women, why would they all go for women that look like blokes?'

'They don't look like ...'

'Y'see? If they wanted to go for people that looked like blokes, they'd just go for blokes, wouldn't they? And then they wouldn't be lesbians. Plus, they'd get the bonus of having someone with a lad. Something they can actually use, like.'

'Maybe they don't want a lad. Maybe they like ...'

'But do you see my point, Jimmy?'

'You don't have a point Aesop. You're a fucking eejit who thinks porn is real life. Now will you please ...'

'Admit it Jimmy. I'm right.'

Jimmy sighed.

'Aesop, I don't know everything about lesbians, but ...'

'Ah-ha! Backing down now! Captain fuckin' Lesbian you were a minute ago, weren't you?'

'Whatever! I don't care, Aesop. I'm just saying that lesbians tend to go for a certain look and it's not a very flouncy one. Now shut your bollocks about them. Right. Tell me.'

'Tell you what?'

'Why were the fuckin' police here?'

'Ah right. Well it started last week. Wednesday. Someone kept ringing the door and then legging it. They were at it for about an hour. Eventually I just stood at the door having a smoke for a bit and when I went back inside it stopped.'

'Maybe it was just kids doing nick-nacks.'

'Yeah, that's what I thought. But a couple of days later when I got up, the fuckers were after stuffing all these dead flowers in through the letterbox.'

'They what? For fuck sake!'

'Yeah. I never did that when I was doing nick-nacks. What the fuck, y'know? It was a bit freaky. Anyway, I still thought it was just some youngfellas messing, so I kind of forgot about it. Then on Saturday night I came in from the pub and the geebags were after drawing a loveheart on the door with a bleedin' felt-tip marker. And it had an "A" on one side and a "P" on the other. Oh, and more bleedin' flowers in the hall.'

'That's not young fellas Aesop. That's a bird.'

'Do you think so, Sherlock?'

Jimmy turned his head a bit, frowning.

'Paula ... Penny ... Peggy ... Ma? No, fuck, she likes him ...'

'A bit pointless trying to narrow it down by name Jimmy, y'know? Remember poor Garda Ní Mhurchú's dilemma?'

'What? Oh, yeah. See what happens now? See what happens when you're a trollop? And you ... but why didn't you tell me this was going on, you spa?'

'What? Sure you'd only bleedin' laugh at me for scoring with a psycho.'

'I wouldn't Aesop. Jesus, this is serious, this is. Some mad one is

66

stalking you!'

'It gets better.'

'Christ. What happened then?'

'The gaff was broken into last night.'

'Fuck! What did she take?'

'Nothing. Well, there wasn't much to take was there? She didn't even like me new curtains. But a few bits and pieces were knocked over and she left a letter. Well, it was kind of like the page of a diary.'

'What did it say?'

'I gave it to the cops before you got here. But basically it was saying that she loved me and she's looking forward to us being together. Eh … permanently. More lovehearts on the letter, y'know? Like the door.'

'Fuckin' hell! I'm getting the heebie-jeebies here, Aesop. What did she mean by that? Permanently. Is that … does she mean … y'know …'

'Don't know. Sounds a bit like it though, doesn't it? So I called Dónal this morning and he called the cops and told them to come in here.'

Jimmy stood up and walked around the room.

'That's fucking terrible! Jesus, what are we going to do?'

'It's okay Jimmy,' said Dónal, standing up too. 'We're working on it. I've had a little bit of experience with this type of thing. I know it looks bad but, really, it's not all that uncommon. Sometimes people see their heroes on the telly and if they're a bit fucked in the head they can get … obsessive.'

'But for fuck sake, Dónal … she threatened to kill him!'

'I know, I know. Well … she didn't technically say that, right? It's … it's probably not that bad. The cops will find her and she'll just turn out to be some girl with a bit of a problem. Depression or something. Last time I remember it happening, they just got her some therapy and she was grand. She was having problems herself and didn't realise the harm she was doing.'

'Ah Jesus … I don't know, man …'

'Jimmy, it'll be fine,' said Aesop.

'How come you're so fucking calm?'

'I'm sure it's just like Dónal said. It'll be grand. C'mon man, what's the chances of me getting bumped off by some mad bird?'

'Aesop, these things do happen! Look at Lennon.'

'Lennon was a god, Jimmy. Who the fuck am I?'

'Yeah, but it doesn't matter that *we* all know you're a total fucking eejit who isn't worth a wank Aesop, does it?'

'Well Jesus, thanks for the boost there Jimmy. Fuck sake …'

'The point is Aesop, you don't know what goes on in these mad fuckers' heads. It could be a religious thing or anything. There's loads of that shite about. Maybe she thinks you're the second coming of Christ for fuck sake.'

'Well then she wouldn't want to kill me, would she? She'd be coming around with buns and stuff. Bringing me children to kiss and all, y'know?'

'That's … it's … I don't know. I'm just saying you need to be careful. Really. I know you like to go through life like it's all a big fucking laugh, but … Dónal, tell him will you?'

'Well, he's right about being careful Aesop. The Guards said that too.'

'I'm always careful.'

'You fucking are not, Aesop! You stop and chat to everyone on the street that comes up to you. You shag your way around the city without even knowing who these girls are.'

'If they come from good families, like?'

'I'm serious Aesop. You need to keep a low profile for a bit. What did the cops say?'

'They said they'll get back to me when they have any news. And they're coming out to the gaff this afternoon to have a look.'

'Is that all?'

'Well, they said they didn't have much to go on. Apparently, she said, they'll have to cast a wider net than they were hoping. Look, it's grand. Will you stop worrying? That's why I called Dónal, sure. I knew you'd only get your knickers in a twist like a big girl. And listen, don't say anything to Jennifer about this, right? She's as bad as you.'

'Well … but … I mean, Jennifer's been in your gaff Aesop. For the curtains and all that. What happens if the nutter comes back when she's there and thinks Jennifer is your bird or something? Y'know? Aesop, this is not a small thing. You're the one who's always watching telly, aren't you?'

For the first time, Aesop didn't say anything.

'Maybe you should move in with Jimmy for a bit?' said Dónal.

'Yeah. Come on. Tonight. Pack a bag and you can come over tonight.'

'Ah, will you stop. It's not that bad!'

'It fucking is!'

'I'm not moving in with you, Jimmy. That's just stupid. And I like living in town. I'll just tell Jennifer the place was broken into and I had to change the locks. She won't be able to call over unless I'm there. And I'll tell her to come with Marco. He's got a black belt and all, right? Actually, I'm not sure I even locked the gaff last night. Maybe that's how she got in?'

They all looked at each other for a bit. Then Jimmy rubbed his face and turned to Aesop again.

'Look, just be careful okay? Keep your head down till the cops find her. This is serious.'

'Ah I know. It'll be okay. All right? Can we all just unclench a little bit here? Garda Ní Mhurchú is probably down the cop shop right now, reading her tea leaves. They'll find her.'

'But you're not to …'

'I won't try and score for a few nights, okay? Keep me head down. And I'll keep an eye out for anything weird. What else am I meant to do? Lock meself in the jacks for the next two weeks, for fuck sake? It'll be okay, right? Look, fuck this, I'm going to head into the zoo. Does anyone want to come?'

They all looked at him but didn't say anything.

'Right. I'll give yiz a call later.'

He stood up and went to get his coat.

Jimmy turned to Dónal.

'He has to be careful.'

'I know. He will.'

'I don't know if he's taking this seriously, man. Y'know … Lennon, Dimebag …'

'I know Jimmy. He knows too. He is taking it seriously. Listen, if anything else happens, I'll look into getting some kind of security. I think I have a few numbers.'

'Will you? That'd be good Dónal. Because he is always getting into trouble. He doesn't give a fuck what he says. To big fuckers and everything. It's all a giggle, I swear. Sometimes I wonder how he ever made it to adulthood at all.'

'I'm telling you, Jimmy. He knows it's serious. He won't mess about.'

Aesop passed them by again with a wave and opened the door to go out. He looked down into the hall and stopped.

'Hey, did anyone leave a dead fish out here?'

Then he broke his bollocks laughing and went out, slamming the door behind him.

Jimmy put his head in his hands before looking up.

'I'd start looking up those numbers Dónal.'

LATER IN the pub, Aesop was a bit quiet.

'Thinking about your mad little friend?' said Jimmy.

'Nah. Actually Jimmy, I was just thinking about some of the things I said to Garda Ní Mhurchú when I thought she was a bloke. They weren't really … proper. Were they?'

'No, Aesop, they weren't.'

'I feel a bit bad.'

'Good.'

'I feel like I should give her a bell to apologise or something. You don't talk like that to women. She looked a bit upset when she was leaving.'

'But probably thankful that she's a lesbian. How are you going to apologise?'

'I'll just tell her what happened.'

'Well, that'll make her feel better, won't it? What are you going to say? "I'm very sorry Garda Ní Mhurchú but I thought you were a bloke, the head on you.""

'Or I could make something up?'

'Ah, just leave her alone. I'm sure she doesn't give a fuck what you think. She was probably only upset because now she has to interview every bird in Dublin.'

'And a few in Tokyo as well. Remember that little thing I was riding?'

'Yuki-chan.'

'Is that her? She looked like she might go off the deep end a bit, didn't she? Remember we got ambushed in your gaff that time?'

'She's in Japan. I can't see her coming all the way over here just to start stalking you.'

'I don't know. I can have a strange effect on women Jimmy.'

'I know Aesop. Garda Ní Mhurchú probably spent the afternoon scrubbing herself in the shower.'

'You still think she's a lesbian?'

'I don't know what she's into Aesop. I'm just saying, lesbians sometimes look a bit like that. Short hair, a bit stocky, no nonsense …'

'Man, you really need to get yourself some new porn …'

Chapter Six

AESOP CAME home from the zoo a few days later with a shopping bag of milk, bread and eight tins of beans. Now that he was at home he was a bit uneasy. The door was definitely locked this time because he'd checked it twice before heading out. He put down the bag and gave it a push. Still locked. He opened it and went inside, walking slowly to the kitchen. There wasn't a sound. He did a quick tour of the whole gaff, opening doors and sticking his head around them before walking into the rooms. Everything was fine. Well, the bedroom needed a bit of airing, but that was nothing new. He'd been eating a lot of beans since he moved in on his own. Still though. Fuck it, this was a load of bollocks. Creeping around your own pad because you're worried that some mad slapper is going to jump out from under the bed and start screaming and slashing away at your mickey with a big knife or something, just because she doesn't approve of your lifestyle choices.

He made himself some beans on toast and turned on the telly to watch Eastenders. When it was over and Aesop had finished picking beans off his t-shirt and putting them in his mouth, he sat and pushed the buttons on his remote for about ten minutes. Nothing but shite. He'd normally be calling Norman or Jimmy or Marco to go for a scoop around about now, but he'd promised Jimmy that he'd keep his head down for a while. Probably a good thing anyway. If he went for a pint, there was a good chance he'd score and the quality of the riding had really gone way down since he'd become famous. It was a bit of a bummer. One girl even tried to pretend that she didn't know who he was, but Aesop wasn't stupid. The big delighted head on her. He hated that. Aesop's philosophies on the equality of the sexes weren't particularly well developed in his mind but, when he was with a girl, he knew what felt right and what didn't; and this kind of awe felt wrong. Well, it was fine afterwards, obviously. Expected and appreciated, even. He dropped his plate into the sink and flicked on the kettle for a cup of tea. Yeah, a little bit of awe was all right. But you had to earn it for fuck sake or you were only codding yourself.

The doorbell rang and Aesop froze.

What the fuck? After last week, he hadn't had a single unannounced caller. Come to think of it, who came up to your door these days without ringing first to make sure you were at home? No one did. It just wasn't the done thing any more. Everyone called. He looked around the kitchen for a weapon. There was nothing. He didn't even have a decent knife because he didn't cook. All he had was a plate, a knife and fork for eating, two cups – one spare in case he was entertaining – and a teaspoon. The doorbell rang again and he swallowed. He picked up the fork, still covered in tomato sauce but probably sharper than the knife, and started down the hall with it gripped tightly in his hand. At the door he peaked through the peephole quickly and then pulled his head back because of something he remembered from an old Jean Reno movie involving a bullet and an eyeball. It was a bird out there. Oh fuck.

He couldn't tell who she was though. She was all wrapped up in a scarf and hat. Too tall for Jennifer. Aesop took another quick goosey through the peephole. She'd turned around now and was facing out into the courtyard. There was no chain on the door. He'd meant to get one, but kept forgetting. First thing tomorrow, assuming this one didn't murder him first.

'Who is it?' he said, one hand on the doorknob and the other brandishing the fork. He was standing up against the wall now, in case she tried to shoot him through the door.

'Hi Aesop,' said a voice. 'Sorry for bothering you. It's Trish. I left something behind when I was here before.'

Aesop's mind raced, filtering through all the names of girls he knew … Jennifer … Jennifer's friends … Jimmy's Mam … no Trish's there. He was out of names. He must have rode this bird.

'Trish?'

'Yeah. I was with Norman. We met at Vicar Street?'

Ah right. Thank fuck. Norman's bird. Yeah, he'd talked to her after the gig. This was the one Norman threatened to kick his bollocks over if he wasn't nice to her, so he'd laid on the good stuff and then backed off to leave her wandering through whatever dreamy fantasies he'd conjured up, so that by the time she got hold of Norman later she'd ride the lad off him. Okay. Grand. So what the fuck was she doing here? Did she get the wrong idea that night? Did the mad cow think he'd ever, in a million years, shag Norman's girlfriend? Besides the fact that he wouldn't do something like that anyway, had she not seen the size of the fucker? There wasn't a deathwish-driven nutcase in Dublin would go near her now. Someone should tell her.

He opened the door and looked around and past her before looking at her.

'Howya.'

'Hi. I'm very sorry for not calling. I didn't have your number.'

'Oh right. Yeah. Norman has it.'

'Yeah. I know. But he said he was having an early night tonight and I didn't want to wake him. He's working early this week.'

'Eh. Okay. So …'

She looked behind her and then turned around again to Aesop.

'I'm sorry, do you mind if I come in?'

'No. Not at all,' said Aesop. 'Come on in.'

He did mind as it happened. He'd enough on his plate these days without Norman hunting him down too and fucking skinning him like a rabbit.

She saw the fork.

'Oh God, I'm sorry. I'm interrupting your dinner.'

'It's grand. I was just finished.'

'Have something nice?'

'Yeah. Well, beans on toast.'

She laughed.

'You're such a boy.'

'Yeah. Thanks. So … you forgot something?'

'Yeah. I left a chain upstairs. I kept meaning to get it.'

'Ah. Right. Well, go on up and get it so.'

'Do you mind? I'm on my way to work, so I just thought I'd drop by to see if you were in. I was here last week too, but there was no answer.'

'Sorry about that. You should have gotten Norman to get it off me.'

'Yeah, I know. I kept forgetting. I'll just pop up and get it?'

'No problem.'

He shut the door to stop letting the heat out as she ran up the stairs. He watched her go up and then started down to the kitchen again to lose the bloody fork. He was pouring water onto his teabag when he heard her coming back up the hall.

'Found it! It was on the floor next to the bed. Lucky. It could easily have disappeared up the hoover.'

'That'd be fairly unlikely,' said Aesop, without looking around. He glanced up and saw her looking at his teacup.

'Do you want a cup of tea?'

He wanted her to fuck off, but he didn't want to be rude either. What was she after? The only reason women forgot jewellery was to come back and get it later. This bird was odds-on looking for a portion. But on the off-chance that she wasn't, he had to be nice too. Bollocks to this. The Simpsons would be on soon.

She looked at her watch.

'Yeah. Why not. I have a bit of time.'

'Great.'

He got another teabag.

'Inside? I don't have a kitchen table out here yet.'

'I noticed that. You don't have much furniture at all, do you?'

'Still moving in. Grab the Jaffa Cakes there.'

They went into the living room and she laughed again.

'You got a big telly though.'

'Well, you get the important stuff first, y'know?'

'And curtains?'

'Yeah. I had some help there. Anyway, they keep the paparazzi from annoying me.'

They sat down on two big beanbags. He still hadn't mustered up the resolve to get a couch yet either.

'Does it happen much?'

'Which?'

'Paparazzi.'

'Ah not really. There was a picture in one of the papers of me having a pint in McDaids a few weeks ago. They had a little story under it about me meeting Colin Farrell in there.'

'Wow! What's he like?'

'I've never met the fucker. I don't know where they got that from. I was just having a pint.'

'Oh. Shame. I think he's absolutely lovely. He's just so sexy. Isn't he?'

'He's a ride, yeah. So what time are you working?'

'Eleven.'

'Right. That must be tough.'

'Ah it's not too bad. I like it at night. I like it when it's all dark and quiet. Don't you?'

She turned to face him, bending one knee so that her weight shifted and the stuffing in the beanbag rolled until she was suddenly six inches closer to him. Her foot was practically touching him. His eyes flicked down and then up again.

'Eh … well …'

'You actually look a bit like him. Colin Farrell. Did anyone ever tell you that? Cute, but in a kind of … dirty way.'

Dirty? You fucking slapper! Right. This was getting fucked up. She wanted him to ride her. Fuck it anyway. There was no way this wouldn't get messy. Even if he politely declined with all the sensitivity in the world and told her to fuck off, Norman would still be left with a girlfriend who was up for it with other men. And Norman was funny about that stuff. Plus, he'd blame Aesop.

'So … Norman's working early, is he? Will you … eh … will you be seeing him tomorrow so?'

'Aesop?'

'Yeah?'

'You don't remember me, do you?'

'Sorry?'

76

'You don't remember me.'

'What? Of course I do. You're Trish. Weren't we talking for ages after the gig?'

'I don't mean that. We met before. A long time ago. And you don't remember? I'm hurt.'

She turned towards him more fully and pouted. There was suddenly something very strange about this girl. Even stranger than her wanting a poke off him.

Oh fuck. No! What had he done? He realised the situation he was after getting himself into and it started to make a kind of horror-movie sense. His hands were all sweaty all of a sudden. Then she was smiling at him again. Big grin. He started to push himself very gradually further back in his beanbag. His dinner was sitting heavily in his belly and felt like it was being churned about in there. She ... she ... was she the one who ... oh Jesus, oh fuck. Jimmy says be careful and then he goes and lets her into the gaff and makes her a cup of tea. All this time it was Norman's ...

'Eh ...'

Now she was laughing, leaning even more towards him.

'You look very nervous all of a sudden. I wonder why that is. Maybe you do remember? Is that it?'

Aesop picked up his cup. He probably had one chance to talk his way out of being gutted by a psycho and he wanted an extra second to think about how to do it.

'Trish, listen ...'

'Yes?'

'Eh ... Trish ... I don't know where we met before.' He had his free hand up in supplication. 'But I'm very sorry if things didn't work out.'

'What?'

'I'm just saying, like ... I'm sorry if I ... y'know ...'

'Aesop, I have something for you.'

She slowly reached into the bag at her feet and suddenly pulled out something shiny.

Chapter Seven

JIMMY SAT bolt upright in the bed. Someone was trying to bang down his front door. Jesus, the cops were right. She was coming after him now. That stupid fucker Aesop and his uncontainable dick were finally going to get him killed. There'd been close calls before – angry boyfriends, outraged brothers and mates, the girls themselves fuming and upset – but this was the big one. He'd finally managed to stoke up a nutter and now she was coming after Jimmy because she hadn't managed to catch Aesop yet. The bastard. It wasn't fair! Jimmy was always nice to women. He sat in terror for a second. The thumping downstairs wasn't letting up. He had to get out of bed and try and protect himself before she broke down the door and cornered him. The doorbell started ringing now too. Christ. He was fucked. And he only had his jocks on.

He started down the stairs with his pillow clutched to his chest and the blood roaring through his head. Then he heard the voice outside, whispering in hoarse, guttural panic.

'Jimmy? Jimmy? Open the fucking door quick!'

'Aesop?'

'Yeah Aesop. Open the fucking door!'

Jimmy was standing right at the door.

'Who's out there?'

'I'm fucking out here. Will you open the door?'

'Is there anyone else?'

'What? No. I hope not anyway. Will you hurry up for fuck sake before she finds me?'

'Jesus …'

Jimmy pulled the door open and Aesop barrelled through it, knocking Jimmy onto the floor and standing on his arm as he slammed the door closed again and ran into the kitchen. Jimmy was still picking himself up when Aesop appeared back in the hall with a big bread knife.

'Ye fuckin' bastard,' grunted Jimmy, crouched over and rubbing his shoulder.

'Shush Jimmy,' said Aesop, looking through the peephole. He was sweating like a racehorse, his breath coming hard and heavy.

'What the fuck happened?'

'It was Trish.'

'Who?'

'Fucking Trish! Norman's bird. The culchie.'

'What about her?'

'She's the one who's been after me. I must have rode her.'

'What? Are you sure?'

'Yeah! She came around tonight and tried to stab me, the mad bitch. I let her in and everything. Jesus, see what happens when Norman scores? He shouldn't be let near women. He can't get a bird for years and then when he does pick one up, she's the Angel of fucking Death.'

'You're mad. Trish was lovely. How did she try and stab you?'

'How? She had a knife in her bag! Oh Jesus, man, what are we going to do?'

'Calm down, will you? Jesus. Okay. We're going to call the police. Fuck, we better call Norman too. Now tell me what happened will you?'

'Yeah … yeah. I was just … I was … what's with the pillow?'

'What? Oh … I was in bed when you started going at the door with a bleedin' sledgehammer.'

'And you brought your pillow down with you? What were you going to do with it?'

'I wasn't fucking thinking, was I? I thought there was a madwoman out there.'

'And you were going to subdue her with a pillow?'

'Will you fuck off? I got a fright. Now tell me what happened. Jesus …'

'Yeah. Right. Okay. Okay, well I was at home making the tea …'

JIMMY HAD put the phone down and was looking at Aesop on the couch.

'So you didn't actually see a knife?'

'I saw enough. She had it in her bag and she was going for it.'

'Aesop …'

'Jimmy, you should have heard her. She was going on about how much she likes the night and being in the bleedin' dark and that she was into blokes that are cute and dirty like me and Colin Farrell. At first I thought she wanted me to fu …'

'You and Colin …'

'I'm telling you man. She's off her fucking trolley. Call the cops, will you?'

'Aesop, she didn't actually do anything.'

'What?!'

'She didn't stab you. You didn't see a knife. All she did was sit down for a chat and a cup of tea.'

Aesop stared at Jimmy for a minute. Then another minute as he played the whole thing over again in his head. Then he looked at the floor.

'Two cups,' he said eventually.

'What?'

'When I saw her going for the knife, I fired me cup of tea at her and legged it.'

'You threw your tea at her?'

'Right in the chops man.'

'Jesus Aesop …'

'But I didn't hang about. I was down the hall and out the door before she had a chance to come after me. I caught a taxi on the quays – what are the fucking chances, right? – and came straight here.'

Jimmy looked at the phone again and back at Aesop.

'Aesop, is there any chance – any chance at all – that you over-reacted?'

'Over-reacted? Smacked her with a pillow, like? For fuck sake, what was I s'posed to do? I was sure I was about to get a Bowie knife up the hole!'

'But all she said was that she liked the night time. I like the night-time. I'm always up late writing. It's nice and quiet. So what? And

80

she likes Colin Farrell? Every bird on the planet likes Colin Farrell. They're not all serial killers.'

'But she said I was dirty.'

'You are dirty. You're a filthy bastard. Everyone knows that.'

'But girls aren't s'posed to talk like that.'

'It's not the first time you've been called names by a bird, Aesop.'

'And she said she met me before.'

'Yeah. In the Baggot.'

'What?'

'She told me in Vicar Street. She saw us play in the Baggot years ago. She was out with her buddies and saw us. You were chatting up her and her mates at the bar afterwards, acting the slut.'

'But ...'

'Aesop ...'

'But ...'

'Aesop ... did you throw scalding hot tea on Norman's bird for no reason?'

'No ... I ... I ... No! What about the knife?'

'What knife?'

'The one in ... the one ...'

Aesop turned to face the empty fireplace. If he looked frightened before, the dawning realisation of what he may have just done was starting to sink in.

'Jimmy ...'

'We need to call Norman.'

'What? Are you fucking insane? He'll kill me!'

'Aesop, we have to. You just assaulted his bird with a cup of tea.'

'Oh fuck. Jimmy. What am I going to do? What if he ...'

'Listen, you fucking lemon, she might be hurt. We have to call him.'

Aesop stood up. He looked like a man on his way to the gallows. He turned back to Jimmy.

'She's grand.'

'What?'

'She's grand. It wasn't hot.'

'The tea?'

'Yeah. It was half milk. Ah, it's a thing I do. If I'm trying to get rid of a bird but I can't get out of making her a cup of tea, I make sure it's only lukewarm. They either don't finish it or else it's gone in five minutes. A decent cup of tea can take twenty minutes of sipping.'

'But it was your tea you threw.'

'Yeah, I make them both like that so I can down mine in a hurry too. No excuses then. If we're done riding and both staring at empty cups, she pretty much has to fuck off, doesn't she?'

'For fuck … okay. Well, I s'pose that's something. Are you sure?'

'It was piss. Definitely. Before I thought she was trying to kill me, I thought she was trying to get me to ride her. Man, I wanted her the fuck out of there before she started dropping the cacks. The tea was grand.'

'Well … thank fuck for that anyway. But we still have to call Norman, man.'

'Christ. What's he going to do?'

'I don't know. But I'm going to guess that he won't be happy with you.'

'He'll kill me.'

'He won't kill you.'

'He will! Jimmy, he never gets his hole. He's finally getting some now and then I go and drown his bird in Barrys and then run out of the house screaming like a little girl. She'll think we're all fucking mad.'

'Probably. Fuck sake, I would. Can you imagine the fright she got?'

Aesop nodded.

'She wouldn't have been expecting it all right. Fuck. But I was just so freaked out. The stuff she was saying and then when she went for the bag … Christ. And anyway, it was you that told me to keep an eye out and be careful.'

'So it's my fault now, is it?'

'Well, you can't blame me for all of it.'

'I bloody can. And another thing, …'

Jimmy's phone rang and they both looked at it.

'I'm dead,' said Aesop.

Jimmy picked up the phone to look at it and nodded.

'Norman,' he said. He switched it on. 'Norman? Yeah … yeah, I know … he's here. Yeah … Sorry man, I'm not sure exactly. It was a misunderstanding … I don't know. Is she okay? Right … right. Well that's good … where is she now? … Okay. Okay, hang on a minute … here he is.'

Jimmy held out the phone but Aesop just shook his head and backed away.

'Aesop, he wants to talk to you.'

'Tell him I ran away.'

'He knows you're here.'

'Tell him I'm gone to Australia.'

'Aesop …'

But Aesop just sat down with his arms folded and his eyes shut tight. Jimmy sighed and put the phone to his head again.

'Sorry man … he's afraid you're going to kill him. Yeah … I know … I know. Aesop, he says Australia isn't far enough … and he is going to kill you … Okay Norman. Yeah … Right … I'll tell him.'

Jimmy hung up and looked over at Aesop.

'He's coming over.'

Aesop swallowed and went green.

'A PHOTOGRAPH?' said Aesop.

'Yes,' said Norman. 'You total fucking langer. She was showing you a photograph.'

'Of what?'

'She was out with her mates in the Baggot years ago for a birthday. They got talking to you and Jimmy after the gig and one of them took a picture. Trish found it in a box last week and stuck it in a frame. She was going to give it to you. She was being nice. A photo of you surrounded by girls. She thought you'd like it.'

'Well it looked like a knife. It was shiny.'

'The frame was shiny. Are you going to come out of there?'

When Norman had arrived earlier, Aesop locked himself in the toilet upstairs and said he wouldn't come out until Jimmy had explained that there was a stalker after him and that's why he freaked out with Trish.

'Are you calm?'

'Yes.'

'Jimmy, does he look calm?'

'He's grand. Will you come out of there, you eejit? He won't do anything.'

'Make him promise.'

'For fuck sake Aesop,' said Norman. 'Come out of the toilet. I'm meant to be in work in six hours and I want to sort this out.'

'Go down to the living room. I'll be down in a minute.'

'Aesop …'

'Go on. I don't want there to be any accidents on the stairs.'

'For fuck sake …'

Aesop eventually crept downstairs and peeped around the living room door.

'Will you come in and sit down?' said Norman. 'If I wanted to kill you, you'd have been a corpse ten minutes ago.'

'I'm sorry Norman.'

'It's not me you need to be apologising to.'

'I know. Where's Trish?'

'She's at work. She had to go home and change first though. Tea, Aesop? You threw your tea at her?'

'It's all I had.'

'Fuck sake. Isn't it just as well you weren't chopping vegetables? Why did you think she was the one stalking you?'

'I … I … was a bit nervous. I s'pose I picked up a few things she said the wrong way. And then when she went for the knife …'

'Photo.'

'Yeah. Well, when she went for it, I panicked. She wasn't hurt was she?'

'No. Well, she was fucking freaked out. You scared the hell out of her, you tool. But apparently you make a shite cup of tea, she says.

84

She gets worse spilled on her at work.'

'Well that's good.'

'So what did she say?'

'What?'

'What did she say that you picked up on the wrong way?'

'Oh. Eh … ah, we were just talking about stuff and she said she likes Colin Farrell.'

'So what?'

'Well, she said I look a bit like him.'

'And?'

'I thought she was looking for a … for me to … y'know … eh … nothing.'

'Aesop, are you telling me you thought my girlfriend came over to your place for sex?'

'No! Well … maybe. A little bit.'

'What kind of delusional fucker are you?!'

'It's just … well, it's the kind of thing that happens Norman.'

'Is it? Jesus, that must be grand. Is this the latest thing now for you, is it? Other people's girlfriends calling around to you for a servicing? Christ, aren't you the lucky man with the horse's mickey?'

'No, it's not like that. It's just that … well, women are always … when they leave something behind, it usually means …'

'She's with me!'

'I know! And she's great. I'm happy for you. But with everything that's going on and all, I wasn't really thinking properly. And when she said I was dirty …'

'Dirty?'

'Yeah. Like Colin Farrell, y'know?'

'What are you on about?'

'Nothing. Nothing. I fucked up Norman. I'm sorry. Are you sure she's okay?'

'She's fine. Now. She was in a right state when she called me though, you muppet.'

'I know. Christ. What must she think of me …'

'You don't want to know.'

They all looked at the floor.

'Fuck sake,' said Norman, shaking his head.

The others nodded.

'And all this stalker shite started last week?'

'Wednesday,' said Jimmy.

'Over this clown?'

'Yeah.'

'Fuck sake.'

'Yeah.'

'Do the police know?'

'Yeah.'

'What did they say?'

'They're looking into it. We've to be careful in the meantime.'

Norman nodded.

'Keep yourselves armed and ready, is it? With cold tea. Christ, that'll do the job all right.'

'Well I didn't have a pillow handy,' muttered Aesop.

'So what now?' said Norman.

'What?' said Jimmy.

'You need to call someone. If there is someone out there looking to slice up this bollocks, you'll need to get some close protection.'

'Close protection?'

'Security. A bodyguard.'

'Dónal said he might know someone. We were going to wait to see if she stopped though. Now that the coppers are involved, like.'

'No,' said Norman. 'That's no good. You need to hire someone now. Tomorrow. The police could take weeks finding this one, or they might never find her. You need someone keeping an eye on you. Obviously. Look what happens when you try to do it yourself. Jesus …'

'I'll talk to Dónal tomorrow,' said Jimmy.

'I'll talk to him. I know a few people. Specialists. What's his number there?'

Norman took it down and stood up.

'Right. I'm going home to bed. Are you staying here tonight Aesop?'

'Yeah.'

'Okay. And you're sure you'll be able to make it till the morning on your own?'

'I'm grand.'

'You're not going to attack Jimmy here if he has to go to the jacks during the night?'

'No.'

'Right then.' He started towards the door. 'Well, thanks for all that anyway. I only know the girl a few weeks and I've already had her hysterical on the phone. That must be a record.'

'Sorry man.'

'Didn't I tell you that I liked her? Didn't I? Be nice to her, I said. And then you have to go and give her a fucking heart attack like that and destroy her dress.'

Aesop nodded.

'Will you tell her I said sorry?'

'I will. And you'll be telling her too when you see her and explain yourself. You can leave out the part about thinking she wanted to have sex with you.'

'Right. I won't mention it so.'

'I'll talk to yiz tomorrow.'

'Right,' said Jimmy. 'And thanks for coming over. Sorting it out, y'know?'

Norman nodded and walked out.

Jimmy went back in to Aesop and found him staring at his hands on his lap. He sighed and sat down next to him. He checked the clock on the DVD player.

'Will I put the kettle on?'

'Jesus, no. I can't be trusted. A dog outside will bark or something and then that'll be you and your couch fucked.'

NORMAN GOT into his van and put on his seatbelt. He didn't start the engine yet. He was pissed off. About everything. But the thing he was most pissed off about was Trish. Aesop was a gobs-hite, but then Norman knew that already. Tonight's episode wasn't exactly one that anyone could have seen coming, but it was only one of a long list of fucking stupid situations that Aesop had gotten himself into over the years. Trish was a different story though. What was she doing, calling over to Aesop like that at night? She could easily have gotten the necklace off Norman if she'd asked, but she hadn't even mentioned it, let alone mentioning the fact that she was going to actually call around for it. And she did it when she knew that Norman wouldn't be around. She hadn't even said a word about the photo until she'd called from her gaff after Aesop had thrown the tea at her. He gunned the engine and took off. He only lived five minutes away from Jimmy and was in bed five minutes after that. He lay there, staring at the ceiling, wide-awake with his thoughts racing. He knew what was wrong and it was annoying the fuck out of him. He was jealous. Pure and simple.

He turned onto his side and stuck his arm under the pillow. He'd fuck it up eventually. Brood and sulk until she left him. He'd try and be his usual self around his Mam and the lads, but inside he'd be sick to his stomach for weeks every time he thought of her until maybe – maybe – he'd bring himself to try again with someone else months later. Someone that could light up some of the shadows inside him with a smile that was just for him. That's all it would take. But Trish wasn't the one. She'd dump him. She'd ultimately dump him because of his insecurities and leave him with a whole set of new ones. That's the way it would go.

Bollocks anyway. Three weeks and it was like watching a train wreck already.

Chapter Eight

AESOP BOUNDED up the stairs and into the reception. He stopped. There they were; Jimmy, Dónal … and Norman.

'Howyiz lads,' he said quietly.

'Aesop.'

'Eh … howya Norman. How's things?'

'Grand.'

'How was … work?'

'Grand.'

'Eh … why are you here?'

Dónal leaned back in his chair and threw his pen onto the pages on the coffee table in front of him.

'Norman is helping us out with our … security issue.'

'Oh. So you know someone then Norman?'

'Yeah. Me.'

'What?'

'We went over some of the names that I know, people that I've worked with before who are in this game now, and I realised that any bloke we got to keep an eye on you would eventually only wind up getting annoyed and kicking the shite of you himself. So I'm going to do it.'

'Kick the shite out of me?'

'I haven't ruled it out.'

'Right. Eh, Dónal, can we keep looking? I'm not feeling the love here.'

'Sorry man,' said Jimmy, smiling. 'It's a done deal. Actually, it's perfect. He knows you, knows your habits, knows your mates and your family. He'll be able to spot anything that doesn't look right. Isn't that right, Norman?'

'Yep. A large initial part of this work is research on the principal. That's you. I've had a lifetime doing that, God help me. This way I won't have to waste any time briefing someone else and trying to explain that you're like that all the time.'

'So … and what happens now?'

'Me and you go back to your place and I check it out. Then I'll go home and get some things and bring them over.'

'What things?'

'Clothes, toothbrush, rubber ducky …'

'You're moving in?!'

'Yep.'

'But … but …'

'I can't keep an eye on you if I'm not there, can I?'

'But I only just moved in. I was starting to get the hang of the place, y'know? And anyway, who said I needed someone to live in the gaff? Can I not just give you a bell if I'm going out or something?'

'As far as we understand it, Aesop, all the problems you've had so far have been at home, right?'

'Well … yeah.'

'So that's where you need looking after.'

'But the … will you stop saying it like that? I'm not a fucking baby.'

The others all looked at each other.

'I'm not!'

Jimmy stood up and handed Aesop a sheet of paper.

'We know you're not. But this is the way these things work. Look …'

Aesop started to read.

'Discreet?'

'Yeah,' said Norman, smiling. 'One of my attributes as a close protection professional. I printed some stuff off the Web earlier so you'd have an idea of what to expect.'

'Look at the size of you and the big red head! How is that discreet? You don't exactly blend in around normal people, do you?'

'Yeah, well she's not trying to cut my bollocks off.'

'Don't say that! She just … she probably just needs a hug.'

'Yeah, you just keep telling yourself she's only after a hug.'

'I am.'

'Good luck with that.'

'Fuck sake. You're s'posed to be on my side Norman. Some bleedin' bodyguard you are, saying shite like that. Am I not s'posed to feel relaxed when you're around?'

'Actually, you should just think of me as a chaperone.'

'I don't need a chaperone.'

'That's kind of what it is though,' said Dónal. 'A lot of time, the management of a … wayward … talent makes sure someone responsible is around so he doesn't get himself into trouble.'

'What are you on about? I thought we were worried about trouble I'm already in, not trouble I'm planning to get into in the future.'

'Two birds,' said Jimmy. 'Till this thing blows over.'

'So … so that's it then? Kevin fuckin' Costner here is going to move in with me, is he?'

'That's right Whitney. Me and you. Except I'm not planning on getting shot.'

'But you're not even a bodyguard, Norman. You're a bleedin' gardener.'

'Not much work in the oul' gardening this weather.'

'But still. I mean … have you ever even done this before?'

'Is it an interview now you're giving me?'

'No. Well, yeah. A bit. Are you qualified?'

Norman laughed.

'How many times have I saved your bollocks over the years when your big gob ran away from your brain?'

'But this is different.'

'I know. I'm getting paid this time.'

'How much?'

'That's between me and your manager.'

'Well, who was the last person you bleedin' … chaperoned, then?'

'You wouldn't have heard of him.'

'Try me.'

'Well, I can't tell you about the last one. But, just to set your mind at ease, back in the nineties I was deployed in Sierra Leone as part of an international covert Special Forces team to support and train

ECOMOG troops trying to restore stability to the region after one of the more brutal RUF incursions towards Freetown. I had to train and supervise the troops that were assigned as close protection to one of the government envoys trying to broker a ceasefire. You probably remember from the telly that ECOMOG eventually managed to overthrow the Koromah junta and then later on UNAMSIL got involved and the Brits helped them catch Sankoh?'

'Eh … was that on a Wednesday? Cos I was probably watching Coronation Street. Was it the time you fell and cut your leg?'

'Yeah. I fell. It wasn't a sniper round at all. Langer. Anyway, I think the point is that I'm qualified to keep an eye on a little shitebag like you. I'm assuming that this young one who's after you doesn't have access to automatic weapons or keep a stash of frag grenades under her bed, so I think I should be able to manage.'

Aesop sighed and looked down at his page again. He saw something and pointed to it.

'Yeah? Well it says here you're not s'posed to be making assumptions.'

'Oh right. I must be rusty so.'

'Actually, speaking of beds …' Aesop sighed. 'Looks like I had a visitor last night.'

'What?'

They all looked at him.

'I went home this morning from Jimmy's and the door was bloody open.'

'Jesus. Not again,' said Jimmy.

'Yeah. Well, obviously I didn't lock it myself when I … left. And I don't know if Trish closed it properly after her either when she was going out.'

'Trish who?' said Dónal.

'Eh …'

'It doesn't matter,' said Norman. 'So, what happened?'

'Well, I went in and looked around. No problem. I went upstairs to change and when I came out of the shower, the fresh jocks I was after putting out ready on the bed were all damp.'

'What do you mean damp?' said Norman.

'I mean the bed was wet.'

'She put water on the bed.'

'Not water. Piss.'

'What?!'

'She pissed on the bed.'

'Are you serious?' said Jimmy.

'Why would I fucking make that up?'

'Fuck sake!'

'But why did you put clothes on the bed if it was after being pissed on?'

'I didn't realise.'

'Someone pisses on your bed and you don't notice?'

'Well the room is only after being painted, isn't it? There's a funny smell in it anyway.'

'Paint doesn't smell like piss Aesop.'

'I know that. Can we stop with the fucking clever observations? She was there last night after I left and she pissed on the bed. That's all I'm saying.'

'Was there anything else?'

'Well … I'm not sure. But I can't find me Cradle of Filth t-shirt.'

'Jesus, Aesop, that could be anywhere. The state of your bedroom, you messy bastard.'

'Well, I thought it was on the shelf. Although, to be fair, it might have been this young one I rode a couple of weeks ago that took it. She was doing some ironing for me …'

'You have them doing your fucking ironing now?! For fu …'

'No Jimmy, Jesus. What do you take me for? Just this one. And she offered. Y'see, she was trying to get the nozzle of the hoover under the tumble dryer and saw that it was full of clothes, so the next thing …'

'You're actually going to make me listen to this shite, are you?'

'I'm just saying, maybe that might be what happened to the t-shirt. Cos I'm after losing a few bits of clothes over the last while. It's not enough that I'm giving them half a kilo of pud, now they want a souvenir as well to take home with them afterwards, greedy bastards. Man, I loved that t-shirt. It's one of me favourites, Jimmy. Remember when I got it? Remember that time when we were all down in …'

'Aesop …'

'But I could've nearly sworn it was on the shelf next to the …'

'Aesop, can we talk about it later? Stupid fucking t-shirts aside, was anything else taken?'

'Don't think so. Just that and the pissy bed. Oh, and more bleedin' flowers. Except in the kitchen sink this time, with water and everything. So I, got dressed and came here.'

'I'll call Garda Ní Mhurchú,' said Jimmy, standing up.

Norman nodded and bit at his lip, saying nothing.

'What now?' said Aesop.

'I'm thinking that maybe you staying there isn't such a good idea,' said Norman.

'Ah Jaysis. Why?'

'Why? Because it's too dangerous.'

'But you'll be there. If she turns up, you can just grab her and beat the fuck out of her.'

'That's not how it works Aesop.'

'Of course it is. She comes along when she's dying for a shite, or whatever she has planned next for me, and you drop out of a tree and grab her head – twist, crunch, the job is done. She falls to the ground twitching.'

'This isn't "Enter the Ninja", Aesop. The whole point of what I'm there for is to avoid any confrontation at all and let the police do their job.'

'You fuckin' chicken.'

'I'm serious Aesop, if you or I ever have to get involved with this girl then something has already gone arseways.'

'I'm already involved with her Norman. I have a mattress full of her wee for fuck sake.'

'Ah, you know what I mean. But, seriously … pissing on your bed … Christ, what did you do to this girl?'

'Who's the bleedin' victim here Norman? It's not my fault she's a spacer.'

Norman nodded. He was thinking about Aesop's townhouse, the courtyard outside, the door and windows. He thought about Trish being there on her own last night, however briefly, and about Jennifer, Jimmy and everyone else who went there. Including other girls that Aesop had been picking up. No. It was no good. He'd check it out, get the place locked up properly and then get Aesop out of there and fixed up somewhere else. His own place was no good. He wasn't bringing Aesop into the same house as his Mam. Jimmy's was no good either. They had to go somewhere completely different. Dónal would have to pay for a hotel in town or something. But … no. That wouldn't work either. If Aesop was still living in town, he'd be walking around and going out to all his usual haunts. Norman would have to handcuff him to the bathroom sink or he'd never stay still. They had to get out of town completely for a week or two.

'Is he needed?' he said to Dónal and Jimmy, pointing at Aesop.

'Needed?'

'Are you lot working on a record or something?'

'Well, no. We've got a tour coming up though. Rehearsals. Why?'

'I'm thinking maybe it's a better idea if he wasn't in Dublin.'

'Where are you thinking?'

'Don't know. Down the country somewhere. Just some place out of the way.'

'There's no point in asking for trouble with him hanging around the city, is all.'

'Where were you thinking of bringing him?' said Dónal.

'Not sure yet. Away though. He doesn't exactly keep a low profile, does he?'

'No he doesn't.'

'Who the fuck is "he"?' said Aesop, looking around at everyone. 'The cat's mother?'

'Can he be gone for a couple of weeks just?'

Jimmy and Dónal looked at each other, weighing it up.

'Well it's not ideal,' said Jimmy. 'But I s'pose he could come back for a few sessions with me and then head off again.'

'Come back from fucking where?' said Aesop, but no one was listening.

'Yeah, yeah …' said Norman. 'That might work.'

Norman was starting to have an idea. His Granny's old house in Cork. He knew everyone in the village and Aesop wouldn't be able to do anything or go anywhere without Norman knowing about it.

'Okay, I have it,' he said. 'We'll go to Cork.'

'We'll what?' said Aesop. 'Cork?'

'I have a place there we can use.'

'Your Granny's?' said Jimmy. 'Are you sure that's all right?'

'It'll be grand.'

'Cork?' said Aesop again.

'And it's exactly what we want. Away from everything that's going on here. Two weeks, say, and the guards should have an idea of the score with the other one.'

Dónal looked at Jimmy.

'Well … if you're sure,' he said. 'We really appreciate this Norman.'

'It's fine. No problem.'

'Cork?'

'We'll get going this afternoon. I just need to make a few calls around the family to make sure nothing's going on, but I'm sure we'll be grand.'

Aesop eventually put his hands up in the air and stood up.

'Excuse me a fucking minute please,' he said.

They all looked up at him.

'What?'

'Why is no one talking to me about any of this?'

'We are.'

'You're not. You're telling me I'm going to go down the bog and live with Sergeant Slaughter here, but I don't hear anyone asking me what I think about it.'

'Well, what do you think about it?'

'I'm not going! Cork? Will you get fucked, will you? You can eat my black shite if you think I'm spending a fortnight in the arsehole of nowhere in Norman's Granny's farmhouse.'

'Aesop, it's to make sure no one knows where you are.'

'Fuck off! What am I meant to do in Cork?'

'Not get your throat slit for starters.'

'Not get my throat slit? Jimmy, you know what I'm like around culchies. They're always trying to beat me up.'

'That's because you're always annoying them.'

'It's just a bit of slagging.'

Norman stood up and clapped Aesop on the back.

'Well Aesop, you're about to learn to have some respect for your country brethren. You might even learn more than manners.'

'This is bollocks!' said Aesop. 'You're not s'posed to give in to mad people! It's only when we … when … the terrorists make everyone afraid of … the … when you stop being … and it's because terrorism is after making you not do the things that … that's … that's when they win!'

'Well done Aesop,' said Jimmy. 'You should write a newsletter.'

'Piss off you. You know what I mean. She's fucking up me life here.'

'I know, man. Sorry. But Norman knows what he's talking about. It really is better if you get out of Dublin for a little while. The cops will catch up with her and it'll be all over. Look, I'm going to call Garda Ní Mhurchú now and tell her about the piss. I'll tell her you'll be heading off to Cork this afternoon as well.'

'Dónal. Help me out here.'

'Sorry Aesop. Norman's the boss and he knows what's best. It won't be for long. No one will know you're there.'

'But you lot know, don't you?'

'Well we won't say anything.'

'And what if she grabs one of you and tortures you to find out where I am?'

'I can't see her doing that,' said Norman.

'There we go again with the fucking assumptions, Norman!' said Aesop, waving his page in the air.

'Well, they don't know where the house is anyway, do they? She can torture them to death and they still wouldn't be able to give anything away.'

'Fuck sake Norman,' said Jimmy, scratching his head and looking at Dónal.

'Fuck sake is right,' said Aesop. 'Two weeks in the crotch of Cork? What is there to do? I betcha they don't even have a zoo down there, do they?'

'What do you want a zoo for?' said Norman. 'You'll be out in the countryside. There's animals all over the place.'

'What animals?'

'Cows and sheep and …'

'Oh fucking marvellous. Cows. The great natural entertainers of the animal kingdom. For fuck sake Norman, I want monkeys.'

'Well there's rabbits. Rabbits are a laugh.'

'Rabbits. Jesus.'

'And foxes and squirrels and stoats and badgers …'

'Me hole.'

'And the birdlife down there is …'

'Birds are shite.'

'Well, Christ Aesop, I'm sorry the granny didn't leave us a house in Borneo.'

'Borneo? They've good zoos there, do they?'

Chapter Nine

AESOP HEARD the knocking on the door, but it was like it was happening somewhere else. In the next townhouse or something. Then it thudded again, a bit closer this time.

'Aesop. Get up.'

Aesop didn't move. It was one of those mad dreams he had sometimes, when he hadn't scored, hadn't been riding late into the night and hadn't been drinking or smoking a spliff. His head was always racing those nights. He stuck the quilt under his chin and up around his ears and began to sink back into quiet blackness. The door burst open.

'Get up you sleepy fucker.'

That wasn't a dream. It had a Cork accent.

'Hmm?'

'Come on. Time to get moving.'

Who he was, where he was, who was trying to get him to wake up … all these things chugged into Aesop's head and finally managed to eject him from blessed, sweet sleep into a panicked alertness. One eye unstuck and popped open, facing the window. It was pitch dark.

'Fuck. Is she here?'

His head was two inches off his pillow, waiting for the answer.

'No one's here. It's time for us to get going. Up you get and into the shower. I'm finished already. The kettle's on.'

'What time is it?'

'Ten to six.'

Aesop's head sank back into the pillow and he conked out immediately to sleep again.

'Aesop.'

Nothing.

'Aesop!'

'What?!'

'Get up!'

'Is it still ten to six?'

'Yes.'

'Then fuck off.'

'We have to get going.'

'We don't.'

'We do. The traffic will start getting bad in another hour and we'll be stuck again.'

'I'll follow you down later. I'll get a train.'

'You won't. Come on, the traffic …'

'I don't care!'

'I care. Get up.'

Aesop sat up in the bed and looked at the big figure standing in the door.

'Norman, listen to me okay? You're just having a bad dream. We both are. Now go back to bed and I'll see ya later. There's no such thing as ten to six in the morning.'

'Of course there is.'

'Why have I never seen it then?'

'Because you're a lazy shite. Are you getting up or am I getting you up?'

'What are you going to do? Carry me out of the bed?'

Three seconds later the light in the bedroom was on and Aesop was curled up on his bed and squinting through his fingers as his quilt disappeared out the door.

'Ye fuckin' bastard!' he yelled after it.

'Downstairs in ten minutes,' called Norman from the stairs. 'I'll have the tea made.'

Norman carried the quilt into the kitchen and threw it into a corner. He stuck some toast on, and heated up the kettle again to scald the pot. Then he walked down the hall and cocked his head up the stairs. He could hear the shower running, so he went back to the kitchen to rinse the cups from last night. When Aesop didn't appear after twenty minutes, he started up the stairs to find out what he was doing now. He knocked on the bathroom door.

'Aesop, are you right?'

Nothing.

'Jesus, did you fall asleep in the shower now?'

He flicked the lightswitch on and off a couple of times.

'Aesop?'

Still nothing. He grabbed the door and pushed it open. Another unlocked door, the gobshite. The bathroom was full of steam but Norman could see well enough to know that Aesop wasn't in the shower cubicle. Oh fuck. What was going on? This wasn't good. He ran back into Aesop's room. The light was still on, but there was no sign of Aesop. Good and worried now, Norman ran down the stairs and checked all the rooms. The front and back door were still locked. The radio was on in the kitchen, but Norman was sure that he'd have been able to hear anything going on in the house while he was getting breakfast together. He ran back up the stairs and checked the bathroom and Aesop's room again. It was only when he practically sprinted into the spare room he'd slept in himself that he found his quarry, curled up in the bed and fast asleep.

THEY WERE just coming through Abbeyleix before Norman would talk to him except to bark orders.

'Will you be careful?' said Norman, looking around. 'You're getting milk everywhere.'

Aesop was eating a casserole dish full of Rice Krispies next to him in the van.

'Well stop driving like a fucking madman then.'

'I s'pose you thought it was funny back there in the house.'

'Honestly Norman, I wasn't thinking at all. I was just trying to get some kip and this big fucker switching lights on and robbing me quilt.'

'You turned on the shower, sure! Why didn't you just get into it?'

'Hard to get some kip in the shower. I knew it'd give me ten minutes of peace and quiet.'

'Well, aren't you the resourceful prick when you want to be. That's something anyway I s'pose.'

'Would I have made a good Ranger?'

Norman grunted and shook his head.

'Christ, they'd eat you.'

'Speaking of which, why did you fuck my toast out the window?'

'I don't want crumbs in the van.'

'Yeah, well can we stop? I need to get a sausage or something. I'm still hungry.'

'We'll stop in Johnstown. Half an hour.'

'You're just fucking getting me back now.'

'I want to get into Kilkenny before we stop.'

'Kilkenny? You mean that's a real place?'

'As opposed to what?'

'I thought it was just a word, y'know? Like Carlow or one of them makey-up places.'

'No, Aesop, it's a real place. Sure where do you think Kilkenny beer comes from?'

'Oh right, yeah. They named it after the beer?'

'Christ,' said Norman, checking the odometer to see how long more he'd have to put up with this shite. 'We should have flown.'

'And another thing …' said Aesop.

'Jesus, what now?'

'Can we change the fucking music?'

'What's wrong with it?'

'What's wrong with Joe Dolan at this hour of the morning? Will I make a list for you?'

'Well put on whatever you want. The CDs are under the dash there.'

Aesop pulled out a CD case and flicked through it. Then he looked over at Norman.

'Are you fucking winding me up?'

'What?'

'Is this it?'

'What's wrong with it?'

'The Fureys, Planxty, Stocktons Wing …'

'That's fine music for you now, boy.'

'It's fucking not. It's bogger music.'

'Have a look out the window, Aesop, and tell me what you see.'

Aesop rubbed the window and peered out.

'Desolation,' he said.

'Well, it's New York City compared to where we're going. You might as well stick on some Planxty there and get yourself in the mood.'

Aesop stared out the window for a minute and then his mouth dropped open.

'Look at the size of them shites! How big are the cows in Kilkenny for fuck sake?'

Norman looked out at the stacks of turf drying in the bog they were driving past. He shook his head and sighed.

'Christ save us from dopey jackeen fuckwits.'

Aesop folded his arms and said nothing for a minute. Then he looked up.

'I miss Dublin,' he said.

WHEN THEY finally pulled up outside Norman's Granny's cottage, Aesop was asleep. Norman cut the engine and gave him an elbow.

'Come on Sleeping Beauty. We're here.'

Aesop opened his eyes and looked around in confusion.

'What's up?' he said, rubbing his face and sitting up straight.

'We're here. Come on. I need to get a cup of tea into me.'

They both got out of the van and stood there, stretching and bending to get the kinks out. Then Aesop looked around.

'This is it?'

'Yep. What do you think?'

Aesop did a full three-sixty, taking in the fields, the other houses dotted around miles away and finally the cottage itself. Then he looked at Norman.

'It's quiet,' he said. 'Too quiet.'

'Grab your stuff there.'

'Where is everyone?'

'We're both here. Are you right?'

'No welcoming party? And what are you bleedin' grinning at?'

'I'm home Aesop. I love it here. Christ, can you smell that air?'

Aesop took a whiff.

'I smell something all right. I thought you were after letting one go.'

'Fresh country air Aesop. Fill up your lungs with that and it'll put hairs on your chest.'

'And your back too probably. And where's the noise. What's going on?'

'What's out here to make noise? Look at the view, sure.'

'All I can see are mountains and rivers and sheep.'

'Yeah, that's what a view is Aesop. And nice job spotting the sheep by the way. I thought I'd have to explain to you what they are.'

'What's that over there?'

'Where?'

'Over there next to the cow looking at us.'

'That's the holy well.'

'What does it do?'

'It's just a holy well. People come to pray for healing or luck or to find something they lost.'

'That's a bit fucked, isn't it? You're not allowed pray for luck. That's like asking God to let you win at poker. He'll just tell you to fuck off.'

'There's wells like that all over Ireland. They were here before Christianity came along, so a lot of the older traditions are still attached to them. The church took them over, but didn't change too much. That one is for Saint Ita. They say she lives in it still as a trout.'

Aesop looked away from the well over to Norman, frowning.

'Saint Ita the trout? I would've thought I'd remember something like that from religion.'

'Serious. You go over there and make an offering and circle the well three times clockwise as you're praying and Saint Ita will see what she can do for you in terms of bringing it up with Himself.'

'Can you see the trout?'

'I never have. Granny did, she said.'

'And the mucksavages around here believe that shite?'

'They do. Are you planning on making any friends in Cork, Aesop?'

'Hadn't thought about it.'

'Because you go around calling people mucksavages and they're going to get annoyed with you and take it out on your bollocks.'

'Ah, come on Norman. A magic fucking trout …'

'It's just a tradition. We have them in some parts of the country, y'know? That well goes back fifteen hundred years at least.'

'Is that your Granny's land it's on?'

'Yeah.'

'And did she not get a pain in her hole with people traipsing through it the whole time and leaving footprints and butts all over the place while they're waiting for their turn to have a word with the trout.'

'It's a holy well, Aesop, not a street corner for people to hang around on. Will you get your bag and come on? It's cold out here.'

'That cow is still looking at us. What does he want?'

'It's a bullock. And he's probably wondering what the fuck you are.'

'Who owns him?'

'Mikey Pat.'

'Mikey Pat?' Aesop laughed. 'Jesus, I can just picture the fucking head of Mikey Pat now and the smell of cabbage off him.'

'Mikey Pat is about six foot six Aesop. County hurler in his day. A lovely man, my cousin and a legend in the parish. I'm telling you boy, you'll have to try and keep that big gob of yours from swinging between your ears like a skipping rope or someone will let fly at you.'

'And yet this is where you bring me for me own protection? I haven't even gotten me bags out of the van and I'm being threatened by my so-called fucking bodyguard. And by the way, do you realise that the further we got from Dublin, the more you started talking like a mullah? And what's a bullock anyway? Is it the same as a bull?'

'It's a bull that's been squeezed, Aesop. Will you get your bags and come on?'

'You squeeze them? When you get lonely, is it? For fuck sake, what would you squeeze a bull for? Would he not get annoyed?'

'He gets a bit of a shock all right.'

'So why don't you just leave him alone? Do yiz not have women down here to squeeze when you get the horn?'

'I'll explain it to you later Aesop. Come on.'

'Do you squeeze the sheep as well?'

'We do.'

'Yiz filthy fuckers. And I thought Jimmy's porn was sad. So what do you call a squeezed sheep?'

'A wether.'

'Whether what?'

'Fuck sake. I'm going inside to get the fire going. You can do what you fucking like.'

Aesop stood on his own for a minute looking at the bullock through the slight drizzle and then shouted in the door.

'I think he needs another squeeze, the head on him.'

'BUT WHY?' said Aesop. He was staring into the fire, his hands wrapped around a mug of tea and his face a picture of disbelief and pain.

'You have to.'

'But why?'

'They're no good to you otherwise. They'll be worrying the heifers.'

'But … you castrate them!'

'Yeah. It's what you have to do. Otherwise they'll be no end of trouble.'

'Jesus, what do you do to your kids when they get out of hand?'

'Aesop …'

'Would you not be better off letting them ride all the girl cows and then you'd have more baby cows? It's simple maths, Norman.'

'The calves would be shite at giving milk later.'

'But you didn't even give the poor bloke a chance. Maybe his kids would be brilliant at being milked.'

'They wouldn't. It's a business they're running, Aesop. They can't afford to take any chances. You only let prize bulls near your cows. And anyway, that doesn't even happen all that much any more. You get the AI man in.'

'Who?'

'You buy the semen of prize bulls and this bloke comes around and impregnates your cows for you.'

'Ugh! What? How, for fuck sake? Or, hang on a minute, do I even want to know? Tell me he doesn't …'

'Fuck sake Aesop, he injects the stuff up the cow and she gets pregnant and then you've a good idea what to expect from her calves. That's all there is to it.'

'You sick bastards. Wait till I tell Jimmy about this.'

'You've never heard of the AI man?'

'Well we wouldn't have had much use for the fucker in Drumcondra, Norman, would we? And c'mere to me, how in the name of fuck do you collect a bull's baby batter anyway?'

'There's a couple of ways. You can use an artifical vagina. He starts to mount the heifer, but then you whip his cock into that instead and let him pump away.'

Aesop put his mug down by the fire and stood up, pointing at Norman.

'You're fucking taking the piss out of me now.'

'It's true.'

'Does he not fucking notice?'

'He's distracted.'

'By what? You have Barry White on in the background, is it? And what about the poor girl cow? She's getting herself all ready for the bull's mickey, delighted with herself, and then you leave her hanging.'

'It's not a match-making service we're providing Aesop. She'll get over it.'

'And have you ever done this?'

'No. Sure we never had a prize bull. I've been there at the other end though. Helped out the AI man when he came to sort out the heifers. When I was a young fella. For a treat, like. If I've been doing a good job helping Mikey Pat out around the farm, he'd let me help the AI man.'

'For a *treat*?' Aesop sat down again and shook his head at the fire. 'Fuck sake, we used to get Jaffa Cakes.'

AESOP WAS lying in bed that night. It was only about eleven o'clock and here he was; sober and alone in the bed with a quilt that must once have been about seven flocks of ducks. It was fucking huge and weighed a ton and it was pulled up to his nose. His eyes flicked around the room. It was freezing outside the bed but in here he felt like he was still on top of the fire out in the living room. But man, it was quiet. The wind had dropped off and only came now in bursts, flinging big drops on the windows when it did. Besides that there was nothing. Maybe the odd crack from the dying embers outside, but that was it. No piss-heads stumbling home, no cars beeping or sirens going. No girl in the bed with him, soft and purring and trying to get into his head. Now it was just blackness and total quiet.

How the fuck was he meant to get any sleep?

Chapter Ten

NORMAN HAD to get some kind of physical exercise every day or else he'd be all cranky. Now that he wouldn't be out gardening for the next couple of weeks, he went for a run first thing the next morning instead. He walked out to the road and started jogging up the hill slowly to get himself warm. It was freezing but the sky was clear, the sun low over the mountains to the south. Every kilometre or so he'd get down and do thirty quick press-ups before setting off again, leaving a black circle in the frost where his breath had huffed out of him in short blowing bursts. He ran the roads with a big smile despite his exertions. He'd spent his childhood summers around these fields and he knew every twist in the route and every tree he sped past. Every now and again a car would come towards him and he'd get a salute from the driver and give one back, the grin on him getting bigger for a minute. Sometimes he wondered what he was doing living in Dublin at all.

Back at the house, he let himself in and looked around. There still wasn't a peep out of Aesop, although Norman wasn't really expecting much activity. It wasn't even eight o'clock yet. He cleaned out the grate and set the fire going again, then he had a shower to get the sweat and soot off him. He ate a couple of apples and put the kettle on. There wasn't much in the fridge, so he decided to go to the shops to stock up.

He knocked on Aesop's door. Nothing.

'Aesop?'

Nada.

He opened the door and went in.

'Aesop?'

The big mound hidden under the quilt moved slightly.

'Aesop?'

'Ugh.'

'Come on. The early bird catches the worm and all that.'

'Me hole.'

'Aesop …'

'No one ever talks about the worm.'

'What?'

'The fuckin' worm is up early, isn't he? And look what happens to him.'

'Will you ever get up, will you?'

Aesop sat up.

'Norman, is this the way it's going to be, is it, ye bollocks? You coming in to torment me at the crack of dawn every day. Will you fuck off out of me room and come back when it's around the time that normal people get up. This isn't boot camp we're in and you can kiss my arse if you think I'm keeping the same insane hours that you do. Go back to bed and I'll see you later, okay?'

'So you don't want breakfast then?'

There was a pause.

'I didn't say that.'

'I'm going to the shops. What do you want?'

'Sausages.'

'Just sausages?'

'And coffee. And will you get me smokes as well?'

'Are you going to apologise for being rude to me?'

'I am.'

'Go on so.'

'I want to see the sausages first.'

'You'll be getting no sausages until I hear you say sorry for being a rude fucker when I was only seeing what you wanted for breakfast.'

'I'm sorry.'

'For what?'

'Being a rude fucker.'

'And what'll happen the next time you do it?'

'You'll kick the shite out of me.'

'Right. I'll be back in fifteen minutes.'

'Will you get rashers too? Do they have rashers in the country?'

'Do they have rashers? Where do you think rashers come from?'

'Ah. I know that one. Pigs. But I haven't seen any pigs in the fields yet. I thought maybe the ones in Dublin come in from England or something.'

'Pigs don't live in fields, Aesop.'

'Do they not?'

'No.'

'Jaysis. I'm going to be an expert on the country soon, amn't I?'

'No.'

'You'll have to start calling me … eh … what's that word?'

'Langer.'

THERE WAS a red Fiesta parked outside the house when Norman got back. He grabbed the bags of groceries and went in, pushing the open door with his foot. He could hear girls laughing inside.

'Hello?'

'Norman!' said Aesop.

He was next to the fire, dressed just in a t-shirt and his boxers. On the other armchair was a girl in her mid-twenties. It was Helen, Norman's cousin. Sitting on the couch was her mate Jessica. They were all drinking tea.

'Hiya Robert,' said Helen. Everyone down here called him by his real name. She got up to give him a hug. 'Great to see you.'

'Heya Helen. How's things?'

'Grand. Mam sent me up on the way to work with some milk and eggs for you. Noreen was on to her last night. I didn't know you were entertaining.'

'Yeah. I see you've met Aesop.'

'We have yeah. God, I was expecting you to open the door and then the next thing we get this famous rockstar instead. I nearly fell over when I saw who it was. Jessica screamed, didn't you Jessie?'

'The shock I got!' said Jessica.

'I got a bit of jolt meself,' said Aesop, picking up his cup.

'How are you Jessie?' said Norman.

'I'm grand. Now I am, anyway.'

'So Aesop was telling me that you're down for a couple of weeks,' said Helen.

'Yeah. Just taking a break.'

'How come you two know each other?'

'Ah, we were in school, like.'

'Will you have a cup of tea Norman?' said Aesop. 'I'll put the kettle on again.'

'That'd be grand Aesop,' said Norman, looking at the scene in front of him. 'Do you want to put a pair of trousers on you too while you're at it?'

'No problem. I was in bed when the girls knocked.'

'Well you're up now. I'm sure they'd be just as happy for you to be decent.'

'He's grand,' said Helen. 'Sure won't they all be jealous in school. And c'mere to me, tell us all about this Trish one. Aesop was saying you've got a thing going on.'

'Ah Jesus, Aesop. Can you not keep your gob shut for five minutes?'

'Leave him alone Robert and tell us all about her. Noreen didn't mention it to Mam or I'd know already.'

'Do you see this Aesop?' said Norman. 'Do you see what you're after starting? Listen Helen, don't be telling Bridie anything or else my Mam will get wind of it and then I won't get a minute's peace.'

'I won't say a word,' said Helen, winking at Jessie. 'Come on, tell me.'

'Ah, I've only been seeing her for a few weeks. It's nothing.'

'He's madly in love with this chick, girls, I'm telling you,' said Aesop. 'He spends half his time walking around the park at home, talking to the trees and laughing to himself.'

'Aesop! Will you shut up? Jesus, what are you trying to do to me?'

'Are you all right there Norman?' said Aesop. 'Are you standing too close to the fire or something? Your face is gone a bit red.'

'Fucking hell, I don't believe this,' said Norman, rubbing his face. 'You're not even in the place a day and you're hanging me in front of the family.'

'She's a cracking girl, Helen. A nurse. Big and tall and legs up to her ears. She's from Kerry or somewhere like that. And I'll tell you something, she's mad about this fella. Never shuts up about him. Norman this and Norman that and listen till I tell you about Norman.'

'Aesop, shut up!' said Norman. He was blushing furiously now. 'Don't mind him. He's talking shite. We're only …'

'I'd be surprised if you didn't meet her while we're down here to be honest.'

'Really?' said Helen, laughing.

'Ah yeah. Sure they can't keep their hands off each other! They're like a couple of chimps, sitting there grooming and touching each other.'

'Fuck sake, that's enough!' said Norman. He checked his watch. 'What time is school?'

Jessie looked at her phone.

'Oh God. We'd better get moving, Helen, look at the time.'

'Right, yeah. We better go. So are you going for a pint tonight lads?'

'Well …' said Norman.

'Definitely,' said Aesop. 'See you there?'

'We'll be in Kavanaghs I'd say. Rob?'

'What? Oh, eh … yeah, maybe. Kavanaghs? I s'pose so.'

He was still all flustered and hot.

'Don't mind him girls. He's only thinking of Trish now. He'll have to go in for a cold shower or he'll be chewing on the kitchen table for the rest of the day.'

'Fuck sake, Aesop. What does it take for you to shut your hole? Go in there and put some pants on you for God sake and give your mouth a rest.'

Aesop laughed and got up.

'I'll see you later, ladies. Thanks for the eggs and the milk.'

'You're very welcome,' said Helen. 'Hey, is Jimmy Collins coming down at all?'

'Jimmy? He might show his face all right. He's doing a bit of work up in Dublin, but he said he'll try and get down for a few nights. Why's that? Soft spot for Jimmy, is it?'

Helen looked at Jessie. Now it was Jessie's turn to go red.

'Ah,' said Aesop, with a wink. 'I see. I'll say nothing so. But I'll make sure and let you know if he's on his way, so you can say hello.'

Helen laughed again.

'We'll have our prettiest frocks out and ready to go, so.'

'God, I'm telling you, girls, you don't have to go to any trouble. You're a feast for the eyes on a cold dark morning like this, honestly. A lovely way to start the day so it is, chatting with the pair of you.'

'Bloody hell Aesop,' said Norman. 'Sorry Helen, he's always like this.'

They both laughed and stood up to grab their coats.

'Flattery will get you everywhere Aesop. Lovely meeting you.'

'And you. Seeya in the pub later.'

'Bye now.'

They went off, leaving the two lads standing at the door.

'Well, you're some bollocks anyway,' said Norman.

'What did I do?'

'Going on about Trish like that. Christ, everyone will know now.'

'So what? And anyway, have they nothing else to be talking about?'

'Everyone knows everyone's business down here. Mam will know about it by lunchtime. And what are you shiteing on about, with your feast for the eyes.'

'I was being serious. Two gorgeous young things like that. I haven't seen a woman in two days, and then they arrive on the doorstep and invite me out for a drink. Lovely girls.'

'Were they? Well, Helen is my cousin so don't even think about it.'

'Why not? Sure Marco is marrying my sister and you don't hear me getting arsey with him.'

'Yeah, well Helen isn't Jennifer and I'm not you. Keep away from them, I'm telling you. We're not down here so you can scandalise the place. Now get dressed, will you? I want to show you some things after breakfast.'

'What things?'

'A couple of moves that might help you if you're stuck.'

'Martial arts?!'

'Just a couple of defensive moves.'

'Deadly! Oh, can we do the Five Point Palm Exploding Heart Technique? That'd be brilliant.'

'Aesop, it's just a couple of ways to get out of a corner. You already know the most important move, and I've seen you do it a couple of times.'

'Run like a fucker?'

'That's the one. That's Plan A.'

AFTER BREAKFAST Norman pushed the table and chairs out of the way and made some space in the kitchen.

'Are you right?'

Aesop was starting to look a bit nervous.

'Eh, Norman ... what are you going to do? Are you going to hurt me?'

'Not if you get out of the way in time.'

'Well, last time I looked, you were a trained killer and I was just a sexy rockstar.'

'You're a drummer, aren't you? You should have good hand-eye co-ordination. Let's see.'

'Yeah. But the thing about the drums Norman, is that they don't actually hit you back. They stay fairly still most of the time.'

'Come on. Stand up here next to me.'

'What's with the rolling pin?'

'Pretend it's a knife. I'm going to come at you with it.'

'You are in your fuck.'

'I won't hit you. Will you come on? This is to show you how to protect your head.'

'From a rolling pin?'

'Just pretend I'm holding a knife.'

'How about you pretend you're holding a rolling pin?'

'For fuck … okay. There. It's gone, right? Now will you stand up?'

'I'm trusting you here Norman! Go easy.'

'Right. Now. Most people will come at you like this and then … where are you going?'

'I'm practising Plan A,' said Aesop, one hand on the front door.

'Come back you big girl. You already know how to run.'

'Why don't we pretend that I'm the attacker?'

'Will you keep still if we do it that way? Come on so.'

'Will I use the rolling pin?'

'Doesn't matter. I'd have your arm broken before you got near me with it.'

'You'd have … I don't want to play any more.'

'Aesop, I won't hurt you. Jesus, you think you're going to get a chance to converse with this girl before she slices you?'

'No! I'm expecting you to drop out of a tree and smack the tits off her before she gets near me!'

'What is it with you and people dropping out of trees? Look, you have to be prepared for any eventuality Aesop. I'm not going to be there every second of the day, am I? Come back.'

'Okay. Okay. But you better not hurt me. I need my arms to play the drums, right? Dónal's not paying you to put me in fucking traction a month before we go on tour.'

'Aesop, I won't touch you, okay? I won't even defend myself. I just want to show you how to get out of the way.'

'Okay then. Right. Okay. Right. Are you ready?'

They were standing opposite each other.

'Yep.'

'You don't look ready.'

'I'm ready.'

'I'm going to stab you in the head.'

'Off you go, so.'

'Right? Knife here, in the right hand. I'm going for your left ear.'

'I'm waiting.'

'I don't want to give you a clatter, Norman. By accident, like.'

'You won't.'

'Will I do it slowly first?'

'Will you just swing your hand Aesop? It doesn't matter how you do it.'

'Aren't you very sure of yourself?'

'Just come on.'

'You've your hands in your pockets, sure.'

'That's for your safety.'

'You really don't think I can hit you?'

'You want to make a bet now, is it?'

'Are you serious? Are you saying that even if I went full tit at you, I'd completely miss?'

'That's what I'm saying. And at the rate you're going, I'd have killed you five times at this stage if that's what I was trying to do.'

'A tenner says I connect.'

'A tenner? How about the fire? If you touch me at all, I'll clean the grate and set the fire every morning. If you miss, you do it. And in the morning, now, you hear me? Not bloody lunchtime or whenever you get around to it.'

'All right. It's a deal. Are you ready then, Sooty?'

Aesop went into a small crouch, one fist up like he was about to strike a hammer. He made a couple of feints. Norman didn't even flinch. Then Aesop let a roar out of him and jumped forward, the fist coming down in an arc towards Norman's head. There was a flash of movement and by the time Aesop's arm had come to a stop across his chest, Norman was getting to his feet right behind him and giving him a small poke into the back with his finger.

'You're dead.'

Aesop turned around.

'How the *fuck* did you get around there?'

'Sure Christ, I could've knit a jumper in the time it took that knife to come down on me.'

'But you were in the corner! There was no way past me!'

'The big blousey swing of you! I was gone under your arm, sure.'

'Show me how to do it!'

'Sorry man. Takes a bit of practice to get that one down. Anyway, that's not what I was going to show you. That was just for the bet.'

'Best of three!'

'No way! Sure you know what I did now. You can just keep your arm in.'

'So you only have one move then?'

'No Aesop. The bet was that you wouldn't be able to touch me. If it was a real situation, there would've been … contact.'

'What would've happened?'

'I'd have pulled your arm out of its socket and hit you in the mouth with the wet end.'

'Lovely. And are we going to be teaching me how to do that one?'

'Aesop, if this girl ever catches up with you, there's a good chance you'll be crying like a little girl and begging forgiveness, yeah?'

'Probably, yeah.'

'So we should probably concentrate on getting you to the point where you can do a runner with your trousers full of shite and leave advanced man-to-man combat techniques for another time.'

'Yeah. Yeah, that's fair enough.'

KAVANAGHS LOOKED like a gingerbread cottage to Aesop by the time they rounded the last bend in the road and he could finally see it.

'Oh thank fuck,' he said, through gritted teeth.

'Bit nippy all right,' said Norman.

'Nippy? There's icicles hanging off me nose!'

'Well we're just there now. Sure it was only twenty minutes. I'm telling you, you want to go on a rekky in Pakistan in the middle of winter.'

'Why would I fucking want to do that?'

'Freeze the mickey off you, so it would.'

'Oh hang on till I call me travel agent, so.'

'Up there for six weeks I was once, chasing a bollocks that wasn't even there.'

'Jesus. And did you boil up snow and ice to make hot beefy Bovril?'

'Far from Bovril we had. Sure, I saw one bloke piss on his flask once just to try and melt a drop out of it. Worked too.'

Norman chuckled at the memory.

Aesop looked sideways at him.

'Norman, do you realise how many of your Rambo stories involve going to the toilet?'

'It sticks in the mind, Aesop. You'd be amazed how much you'd kill for a civilised crapper when you're in certain parts of the world.'

'Yeah, well right now I'd kill for a bleedin' taxi. Do they not have them?'

'Of course they do. But won't you appreciate your pint more after your little stroll?'

'If I can hold it.'

'We'll get you a straw. Anyway, it's your own fault for coming down here with no decent clothes. Look at you. You'd swear you were about to go on stage.'

'Yeah, well, in case you don't remember, I was being hoofed out the door yesterday, half-asleep with no breakfast. I need a bit of time to get warmed up in the mornings, so I do.'

'You were chipper enough this morning.'

'That'll be the women that came to say hello.'

'Remember what I said earlier about that?'

'Norman, I'm sure they're old and mature enough to decide for themselves what they want.'

'Maybe they are. But you're not. Leave Helen alone. She's not like the girls in Dublin, okay? She's young and she's had a bit of a sheltered life. Don't even think of taking advantage of her.'

Aesop mumbled something.

'Did you hear what I said?'

'I heard you.'

'And?'

'And what?'

Norman held out his arm and they stopped right outside the door of the pub.

'Aesop, that girl is family. Make me a promise now that you won't touch her.'

'She's a grown woman, Norman!'

'I don't care. Promise me.'

'Fuck sake …'

'Aesop …'

'Okay, okay. Jesus, I promise.'

'Right so.'

'Can I ride Jessie?'

'I'd rather you didn't.'

'Cos I'd say she was the itchiest out of the two of them anyway.'

'Aesop!'

'I'm only bleedin' joking. Jesus. But she's no relation, is she?'

'No. Look Aesop, people down here know everything that goes on and they tell. Okay? It's not like Dublin. You start acting the slut down here and people will be dealing with it long after you fuck off back to the city. Okay?'

'I think you're underestimating your fellow culchies Norman. They're not babies.'

'Do we have to have a conversation about you calling them that too?'

'Sorry. Slipped out.'

Norman swung the door open and held it there for Aesop. As he went to step inside, Norman put a gloved hand on his shoulder.

'I'm serious Aesop. Mind your manners in here. Have a bit of respect and the locals will do likewise and everyone will get on grand and no problems.'

'You're making them out to be fuckin' eejits, Norman. I'm sure they're grand. They're not fucking aliens are they? We'll have a laugh tonight, watch.'

'Just don't take the piss.'

Aesop winked at him and then took a big breath and walked inside doing the Twilight Zone theme music.

Chapter Eleven

AESOP TRIED to be on his best behaviour. Norman seemed to be under the impression that just letting him out of doors down here was asking for trouble and if it was going to be like that for two weeks then Aesop wouldn't get to have any fun at all. After they collected two pints at the bar, Norman steered them back to a small table out of the way where they were pretty much on their own except for a middle-aged married couple quietly sipping a pint and a glass of wine next to them.

Aesop took a big pull on his drink.

'Nice pint,' he said, picking the glass back up to give it a closer look. 'Do you want a game of pool?'

Norman looked around. It was early enough and there was no one on the table.

'Eh …'

'What's the matter?'

'The boys down here take their pool very seriously Aesop.'

'What boys?'

'The local lads. Some great players there is too.'

'So what? Anyway, there's no one there now is there?'

'They'll be in soon enough.'

'They don't own the table, do they? They can have it when we're finished if they come in.'

'You're a bit handy yourself Aesop. I don't want any grief.'

'Why would there be grief? Jesus, is everyone down here just itching to stick the head on somebody? What's the matter with you? Will you relax?'

It was another half hour before two guys in their twenties came in and put some coins on the table. Norman and Aesop had just started their third game.

'Winners?' said one of the young fellas.

'Ah no,' said Norman. 'You can have the table.'

'Are you sure?'

'Yeah. We're finished anyway.'

'Thanks.'

They wandered off to the bar, leaving the lads to finish their game but looking over every now and again to see who these new guys on the pool block were and how their form was.

'Why didn't we play them Norman?'

'Ah, I've enough pool for tonight.'

'Chicken.'

'What?'

'You don't think we'd beat them?'

'It's not that. I'd rather just have a pint. And the band will be on in another bit anyway.'

Aesop bent over a shot and then looked up.

'You think I'm going to get us into trouble every time I open me mouth, don't you?'

'It's been known to happen.'

'Jesus man, all I'm doing is having a pint and a game of pool. You think I'm going to go out of my way just to annoy a few woolly-heads?'

'Look what you just said!'

'They can't hear me.'

'But I heard you. Anyway, they keep looking over.'

'Ah right. They lip-read, do they? Are they going to feel threatened and start throwing slaps around just because I'm all sophisticated and urbane and their women want to ride me?'

'Christ. Will you shut up and take your shot you langer? Sophisticated my arse.'

The game didn't even go the distance. Norman plugged the black with four of his balls left on the table.

'Pints on you, my big worried friend.'

'Right. Go on back to the table there and I'll bring them over.'

'The lads are coming back. You sure you don't want to play them?'

'Yes. Go on.'

Norman went to the bar as the two guys arrived with their own pints.

'Lads,' said Aesop.

They were looking at him a bit funny. One of them picked up a cue.

Oh fuck, thought Aesop. Here we go. They must have ears like rabbits, this pair. He looked past to them to see how far away Norman was.

'Are you that fella in The Grove? The drummer?'

Aesop relaxed. Thank fuck for that. He smiled and put his own cue down on the table.

'Yeah. Aesop Murray. How's it going?'

'Grand. What are you doing down here?'

'Ah, just taking a bit of time off. The band is on tour in a few weeks. That's me mate Norman. His Granny used to live down the road there, so we're staying in her gaff for a bit and seeing the sights.'

'Not many sights around here.'

'Have you not been to the holy well?'

They turned to check out Norman.

'I don't think I know him,' he said.

'Norman? He lives in Dublin now. I think he prefers it down here, but.'

Norman had the pints now and wasn't wasting his time getting back with them. He handed Aesop his, and then glanced around quickly to see what damage had been done.

'Hiya lads,' he said quickly. 'Enjoy your game.'

'Yeah,' said one of the guys. 'You sure you don't want to play? House rules. The table is yours till we knock you off it.'

'Nah, we're grand.'

'Fair enough.'

Norman made a beeline for their old seat.

'Talk to yis later lads,' said Aesop. He winked. 'Norman's shite at pool, but I'll give yis a game.'

He walked over to Norman and sat down, looking around the bar with a smile and saying nothing. Then he turned around.

'I told them you were shite at pool.'

'Good.'

'Set them up for later. Might snaffle a couple of pints off them.'

'I'm not in the humour Aesop.'

'Sure we'll see.'

He knocked back some of his pint.

'Anyway … so, c'mere, how is Helen your cousin?'

'Helen? She's Mikey Pat's daughter.'

'Oh. Right. But … hang on … I thought you said Mikey Pat was your cousin?'

'Yeah. His Dad was my Dad's brother.'

'But … then Helen isn't your cousin, is she? She's your … eh … second cousin or something.'

'So what?'

'Norman!' Aesop clapped his hands together. 'Sure, second cousins are grand! *You* could even ride her. The Pope says you can and everything, so he's hardly going to have a mickey-fit if I put one away, is he?'

'It's got nothing to do with the Pope, Aesop. And don't be talking about her like that or I'll give you a box. Second cousin or whatever she is, you promised you wouldn't go near her. She's still family.'

'I don't even know my second cousins, sure. I could have rode dozens of them already and I'd be none the wiser.'

'Jesus. And that doesn't bother you?'

'You can't be going around the place letting things bother you, Norman. Life is a fragile and fleeting thing. You never know when your next portion will be your last.'

'Will you ever … who are you waving at?'

'Next portion.'

Norman looked up at the two girls coming in the door.

'You better be fucking talking about Jessie.'

'Oh there's Jessie too, look.'

The two girls saw them and waved back with big smiles. Aesop felt Norman staring at him.

'I'm joking for fuck sake. Will you chill out?'

He turned to give the girls another poilite flash of the pearly whites and saw Helen's eyes widen just the tiniest bit. She said something to Jessie and they both laughed. Then she looked up at him again and gave it to him full-on, the smile dropping off a good bit but the eyes just scooping him up, green and shining even from thirty feet away. The flush in her cheek from the cold outside deepened ... and then back came the smile; pink lips and white teeth and the merest suggestion of the horniest fucking overbite that Aesop had ever seen.

He wondered if his own mouth was open. He'd never seen an entrance like it. She was stunning. Not that she was minging on her way out to work this morning when he was having his tea, but by fuck she was a goddess after a few pints. She unwrapped her head from a big shawl yoke as she stopped to say hello to someone, and her hair fell out of it, bouncing down around her shoulders in russet bundles like the whole arrangement was spring-loaded. She leaned to one side as she laughed at whatever the guy was saying to her and grabbed it by the fistful, shaking it and sweeping it out of her face until it seemed to run in rumpled bewilderment from one side of her chin right around her head to the other. Well, that was it. There was nothing else for it. He had to have her, didn't he? It was only manners. He wasn't even registering anything else that was happening in the pub, or who else was there. It was just Aesop and Helen and the ensuing chain reaction in Aesop's head was something he barely noticed shifting into first gear. Then they started to come over and his eyes flicked to Jessie.

Fuck. The mate.

'Okay Jimmy. Wingman. Wingman. I need a wingman.'

'What?' said Norman.

'I need a wingman. Get rid of Jessie.'

'What?'

'Get rid of Jessie. I'm going in. Jesus Christ almighty, would you look at her. Have you ever ...'

'Aesop, what are you doing?'

'What?'

'Did you call me Jimmy?'

'What?'

Aesop looked around and blinked.

'Oh.'

'What are you on about?'

'Eh … nothing. Sorry Norman. I was miles away.'

'What's wrong with your mouth?'

Aesop closed it.

'Nothing.'

The girls stopped at the table and started to unbutton coats and cast off hats and coats and gloves.

'Bloody freezing tonight!' said Helen. 'Hoosh up there Robert. Two pints?'

'No way,' said Aesop. 'Sit down there, the pair of you. I'll get them. What are you having?'

'Murphys for me,' said Jessie.

'Bacardi and diet Coke in a tall glass,' said Helen.

'Eh, right. A tall glass. Aren't you very precise? And a pint, is it Jessie?'

'Thanks.'

'Grand so.'

Aesop went up to the bar, slotting things into place in his head for later. Hmm … a tall glass. She must be a size queen, Helen. Mad for lad. And the heftier the better by the sounds of things. Aesop was a Freudian at heart.

He passed the pool table on the way.

'Howya lads. Still going strong?'

'So far, yeah. You ready for a game?'

'Sorry pal. A bit later. Entertaining.'

He nodded towards the corner where Norman and the girls were. The lads looked over and then looked at each other. Aesop caught a vibe of something, but just nodded and carried on to the bar. He didn't give a shite about pool any more. He gave the order to the barman and stood with his back to the bar, watching the girls talk to Norman. He had a bit of a problem there. Norman. Norman would freak. He looked at Helen again but could only see the side of her face. She turned suddenly to look over at him and out shone that smile again. He smiled back and then turned around to pay for the drinks. This wasn't right. She was barely related to Norman at all, and even if she was, what was wrong with Aesop giving her some rumpy pumpy if she was up for it?

He grabbed the drinks and started to make his way back, noticing another furtive glance from the two boys at the pool table. Aesop nodded again and kept going. Something was definitely up with this pair of muckers. Fuck it, he had other things on his mind. Back at the table he put down the drinks and sat beside Norman.

'That tall enough for you?' he said to Helen.

'That's grand, thanks. I like the extra Coke.'

'Ah right. C'mere, do you know those two lads playing pool?'

The two girls looked over and then quickly took up their glasses.

'Yeah,' said Jessie. 'They're from around here.'

That was all they said. Aesop nodded and finished his old pint. There was some history there. Did he have to sort that out too?

'Hey Aesop,' said Helen. 'Do you think you might play with the band for a bit? They're setting up over there, look. They'd be delighted for you to join in.'

Aesop turned around. There were about five guys setting up for a trad session.

'Ah, to be honest Helen, I don't really play that kind of stuff.'

'You could sing a song, sure.'

'Jaysis, no. I'm a shite singer. If Jimmy was here he'd get up all right, but you don't want me up there spoiling it for everyone.'

'Do you not do backing vocals? You do on the telly.'

'Nah. That's all Jimmy and Shiggy singing. My mike is just for show, I'm telling you. I do a bit in a few songs when we're playing live but, I swear, if I tried to do lead vocals on me own we'd all be asked to leave.'

'Norman, will you get up?'

'Ah sure I might in another few pints.'

Aesop looked around. Norman was worse than he was.

'What? Are you going to sing?'

'Not at all. I'll just play with the lads for a couple of songs.'

'Play what?'

Norman went red.

'Ah, I play a bit of oul' bones.'

'The bones? Are you serious? Since when?'

'I've always played them. Sure, it's only a laugh. It's nothing.'

'How come I never knew that?'

'Sure Christ, I'm hardly going to take them out when you and Jimmy are playing, am I? I'd look a right langer.'

'But … have you got them there?'

'In me pocket.'

'Give us a look.'

'Ah Aesop, don't start slagging me now.'

'I'm not slagging you. Take them out there.'

Norman reached into his coat and pulled out two flat sticks about six inches long and handed them to Aesop.

'How do you hold them?'

Norman showed him and Aesop gave them a quick shake. One of them immediately slipped loose and described a big arc over them before splashing off the top of his pint and skidding around the table. The girls roared laughing.

'Bollocks.'

He dried it on the seat and handed both of them to Norman.

'Here, you show me.'

Norman took the bones and demonstrated again how to hold them. Then he raised up his right hand to shoulder height and rattled off a rhythm to the Paul Brady song that was coming over the house system. Aesop clapped his hands together.

'That's brilliant! Jesus, when did you learn how to do that?'

'Ah, will you fuck off taking the piss Aesop,' said Norman. He put the bones down on the table and picked up his drink.

'I'm serious, man. Tell him girls. Jesus, you've been able to play all these years and you never said anything.'

'You should see him with two sets,' said Helen.

'Ah Helen, don't,' said Norman. 'He's only winding me up.'

'Do you have another set with you?' said Helen. She reached over into his pocket and found them. 'Here, show him.'

'He doesn't really want to see.'

'He does.'

'Ah …'

Norman took two bones in each hand and doubled up on the beat, one hand playing off the other for about five seconds. People started to look over. He put all the bones in his breast pocket and sat there with a head on him like a beetroot.

Aesop shook his head.

'I can't believe you never showed us that before. That was fucking deadly! Jaysis, it was like you had two tap dancers in your hands.'

'It's nothing, sure. It's only the bones.'

'It's percussion, Norman. Did you honestly think I'd have no interest in learning how to do that? Selfish bastard.'

Norman went even more red. He couldn't even count the times he'd have loved to whip them out when the lads were around jamming, but he'd been way too embarrassed. They were so cool and brilliant at their instruments, and it wasn't as though he didn't get enough slagging without producing something like the bones in the middle of the kind of stuff they played.

'If you want, I'll show you a bit.'

'Norman, I want you to show me everything you know.'

'It's not much.'

'You big modest gobshite, I know what I heard. You can really play them fuckers. We'll start tomorrow. No messing. First thing.'

'First thing? Now I know you're taking the piss.'

'We'll see about that. Now, your round I believe. My pint is wrecked from the little accident earlier.'

Norman looked around the table to see what the round was and then stood up.

'Helen likes a nice tall glass,' said Aesop, all kinds of images sprinting into his brain and firing memos off down to his underpants.

'I know, yeah,' said Norman, moving off to the bar.

Screams of laughter from Helen and Jessie followed him up there before the barman had even started pulling the first pint. He looked around and saw Aesop with his hand on Jessie's knee as he was telling them some story. As long as it was Jessie's feckin' knee there'd be no problems, he thought. The lads at the pool table didn't seem to know him, but he knew them. The tall one, Davey, and Helen had been engaged for a few months last year. That was why he didn't want to play pool. He wanted to stay away from them. That Davey bloke was a bit highly strung and a terrible prick on top of it with drink in him. If Aesop started in on Helen, you never knew what might happen. Norman didn't know the full story, but apparently Helen hadn't been with another guy since they broke up and the murmurs around the family were that it was because she was hoping Davey would find someone first and leave her alone. The whole thing annoyed Norman. He could deal with the situation in about five fucking minutes if he was let, but another one of the cousins told him he was better off out of it. Mikey Pat had apparently said something to Davey once and Helen got all upset and told him to just leave it. It wasn't Norman's place to get involved. And anyway, the last thing they needed was a scene down here.

His hands full of booze, he started to make his way over to the others. Just then the band started up and went into Fisherman's Blues.

AESOP HAD been steering his attentions carefully away from Jessie and onto Helen for about an hour when he suddenly found himself back where he started.

'I see we have a couple of Kellys in the house,' he heard one of the guys in the corner say over the sound system. All eyes turned to their table. It been happening all night actually, but for the most part they were looking at Aesop. Word had gotten around that he was there and everyone in the place had been doing their best to have a good gander without getting caught. Now, though, it was Norman that was getting the looks as he got to his feet to a big cheer.

'Come on Helen,' he said. 'We'll do a couple.'

'What?' said Aesop, looking at her. 'You as well?'

'Helen's the best singer in the place tonight, wait till you see,' said Norman.

'Really?'

Helen just blushed a beautiful shade of cerise and stood up, leaving Jessie and Aesop on their own clapping at the table.

Once she got over to a mike and turned around, still lovely and rosy about the face, she took a guitar off one of the guys and did a quick run on it as the guy adjusted the height of the mike stand for her. Ten seconds later she had the guitar in dropped D tuning and was strumming away on it. Aesop sat forward. This was getting fucking interesting.

'Thanks very much,' she said, into the mike. The crowd shut up cheering to let her sing. 'Here's a little song for a friend of mine.'

She looked out around the crowd and Aesop followed her eyes to see who the cunt was. Then she looked full at him and he copped on. Jesus. She was reeling him in, the slapper, and he was falling for it!

Off she went on the guitar, her hand going a mile a minute on the intro. A fiddle player came in after a bar or two and then a bodhrán and finally Norman, standing at the back so everyone would be able to see the rest of the band, started up with the bones. It was the Luka Bloom song, 'You Couldn't Have Come at a Better Time' and as Helen sang it she kept catching his eye. She didn't hang about staring at him though. She wasn't some hoor. She was being dead cool, pulling her face away from the mike and closing her eyes, her head cocked down as if to hear the bodhrán properly, for any of the short instrumental breaks. When she got to the 'me and you and me and you and me ...' line, up came those eyes again like searchlights to pick him out and nail him to his seat. Fuck sake! Aesop had watched Jimmy do this a thousand times. He'd done it himself sure, from behind the drums when he spotted some honey out among the punters, and here he was now grinning up at her like a fuckin' eejit and feeling special. He felt Jessie's hand on his arm and her voice in his ear as she leaned in to him.

'I think someone's got the hots for someone,' she said.

'She's great up there, isn't she?'

'She's been doing it for years. Everyone knows Helen Kelly around here.'

He nodded and turned back to the stage so she'd shut her hole and stop distracting him. This was great stuff. Everyone in the pub was clapping and singing along, punctuating the song with ye-hoo's and calling her name out. She got to the end of the last chorus and stopped singing so that Norman could step up and do a bones solo. Aesop roared laughing. He was fucking brilliant, the head down, the hands up and the bones flicking and bouncing off each other like he had one toe stuck in a socket behind him. Aesop had known Norman for over twenty years and he'd never seen him do anything like this. Trying to get him to sing at a party was like pulling teeth, and yet here he was up on a stage in front of a hundred people and standing next to a cracking bird while rattling out a percussion solo that Aesop knew you didn't just pull out of your arse. He was really good at those fuckers.

Helen took a bow and grinned.

'Thanks very much everyone.'

But she didn't look at Aesop this time and he felt a small jealous kick inside his belly. There were a few calls for another song and Helen nodded as she took off the guitar and handed it back to the guy behind her.

'Maybe one more,' she said, as they began to simmer down. One hand went into her back pocket and the other held the stand just in front of her with long slender fingers. The eyes closed, the hair got swept out of her face, and then she somehow shifted her body so that it glided right in, bringing the mike to her mouth and the rest of her a few inches closer to a rapt Aesop who was by now fit to mount the pint glass in front of him.

'Need a bit of hush for this one,' said Helen with an apologetic grin, and every gob in the place immediately snapped shut. One tool was on the phone, but his mate gave him a dig and a dirty look and the next thing the phone was back in his pocket.

The song was in Irish, and Aesop was hopeless at Irish, but it was sad and slow and full of heart-rending wretchedness the way any decent Irish ballad ought to be if it had any respect for itself. Her voice was low and full now, and the couple of people humming softly along with her lent it a resonance that was like a pulse that gently throbbed around the pub.

'What's the song?' Aesop whispered to Jessie next to him.

'It's called "An Cailín Álainn". The Beautiful Girl.'

'What's it about?'

'It's about being in love with a beautiful girl. But she's gone and all that's left is heartbreak and pain. If she ever came back, the singer would make music for her like a harp or the song of a bird in the dewy fog and never be sad again.'

'Fuck.'

'It's gorgeous isn't it?'

'Yeah.'

It was better than gorgeous. It was perfect. Helen. She was … she was just perfect. For fuck sake, she was up there singing a love song to another girl! Whatever lusty aspirations he had a minute ago, now she was playing right into his lesbian fantasies as well. Aesop held his pint glass to his mouth, gazing up at her. He wondered if she had a shaved minge too. That'd be fuckin' brilliant, so it would. He turned to Jessie.

'Yeah?' she asked.

'I don't s'pose … eh … ah, it doesn't matter.'

Jessie probably didn't know anyway.

Chapter Twelve

JIMMY WANDERED around his house, looking for things to do. But tonight all his clothes were washed and ironed, the place was spotless and there was half a lasagne in the fridge from yesterday so he didn't even have to cook. A quick flick through the channels revealed nothing but the usual shite on the telly. He sat looking at it, but thinking of Susan, and then he walked over to his laptop to check on flights. Fuck it. He needed a holiday. He could have her in his arms by lunchtime tomorrow.

He stood up and went out to the fridge to grab a can of Guinness and by the time it was in his belly he had his phone out, the contact list scrolled down to Susan's name. An hour later there were three more empty cans on the coffee table in front of him and he was still fingering the phone. Four cans was the sweet spot. He decided that he was being a big fucking girl. It was time to sort this out. He'd go over. First thing in the morning. Spend the weekend with her at least and before he came back again he'd know what they both wanted.

He pressed the green button, his heart hammering.

'THOSE TWO lads playing pool …' said Aesop.

It was some time after two and they were back in the cottage, sipping on a couple of fairly respectable Jamesons in front of the fire. They were both well oiled and there was no great urgency about sobering up.

'What about them?' said Norman.

'Well, maybe I was just imagining things …'

'You weren't.'

'So the big one fancied me then?'

Norman looked over at him.

'What?'

'Well, he kept looking at me. More than just the punters in the bar, like. They were just looking cos they knew I was in the band, but every time I saw yer man he was staring at me like he was on a promise.'

'Aesop, he doesn't fancy you. Langer. He's a big oaf called Davey Molloy and he was looking at you because he had a thing with Helen and reckoned you were moving in on his territory.'

'Ah. Right. Well that would've been me second guess.'

'Nasty one, that fella. Keep away from him. He only left the place early because he's got a match tomorrow and the manager of the team was in. I don't know him that well, but I've heard that he's a bit of an animal on the pitch and worse off it when he's tanked up. Put a bloke in hospital last year with a bottle.'

'Jaysis. So blowing him a kiss wasn't a good idea?'

'What? When did you do that?'

'When you were up on the stage with Helen. I was swept up in all that gorgeous music and when I caught him eyeballing me, all the love just came out.'

'You fucking eejit! What did he do?'

'Well, for a minute I thought he was going to come over and lamp me, but his mate grabbed him and said something to him and then they headed off a bit after that.'

'Aesop, it's no wonder everyone's trying to kill you. Why do you have to be such a cheeky bastard all the time? Jesus, for someone who couldn't box his way out of a paper bag, you've some knack for winding people up.'

'Sure aren't you here to protect me?'

'Not like that I amn't. Just because I'm here, that doesn't mean you can go about the place taunting big fuckers like him. You think I want to get involved with anyone down here where I'm known?'

'It was only a kiss. It's not like I was passing him notes to meet me out in the jacks or anything. Can we change the music?'

'No. Listen to me Aesop, it's not funny. Helen and that bloke were nearly married and he's having a hard time realising that it's not going to happen. If you see him again, you bloody ignore him, okay?'

'Do you not reckon you could take him?'

Aesop was grinning at him now, the eyes all bloodshot and droopy.

'That's got nothing to do with it. I'm not getting into stupid situations down here just because you're bored and feel like taking the piss.'

'Sure you're much bigger than him. I'd say you'd batter him. What is he … six foot? So in theory …'

Norman sighed and looked into the fire.

'He's six-foot one. Weighs about ninety-two kilos. Favours the right leg from an old knee injury and he was holding his cue tonight like he was after getting a belt of a hurley on the thumb some time in the last week. I'd say his reach is seventy-six inches give or take, but he's a southpaw. He leads with his right leg, so I'd stamp down on that, put the gammy knee out and that'd be the end of it. Two seconds. First round knockout. If he did try and get to his feet again he'd be a stupid bastard and it'd cost him the use of his shoulder for six months.'

He looked up, smiling.

'In theory, like.'

Aesop frowned at him.

'Fuck sake! Who told you all that stuff about him?'

'No one did. I can just do it. Used to box, remember?'

'Since when is stamping on some poor fucker's knee allowed in boxing?'

'Yeah, well … I did other stuff too.'

'You're a scary bastard sometimes, Norman.'

'The point is, Aesop, just because I can deal with Davey Molloy if I have to, if you start any shit with him I'll probably just apologise on your behalf and buy him a drink and if anyone will be getting a slap, it'll be you later on for being a tool.'

'Do me.'

'What?'

'Do me. Height and weight and all that. Fuck, and there's me for years saying you should be in the circus. Eh … I mean … a lion tamer, like.'

'You're five foot ten and about seventy-three kilos.'

'And how would you sort me out in a scrap?'

'You?' Norman chuckled and shook his head. 'Sure all I'd have to do is tell you what I *might* do to you and you'd faint down into a puddle of your own piss.'

Aesop roared laughing.

'Jaysis, what's Davey's number there? We'll get him around and I'll wind him up for you. Kevin Costner me bollix. Fuckin' Robocop I have here with me!'

'Just you keep away from Davey. You're in enough trouble.'

'Do Jimmy.'

'Ah stop messing. It's only knowing what to look out for. It's not that hard.'

'Yeah. Actually, you know what? I can do it too.'

'Can you?'

'Yeah. Well, with chicks I mean.'

'You can tell how to bate a girl? Christ, that must come in handy.'

'No no. Not fighting. When you walk into a place and it's wall-to-wall beaver, like. You're only going to leave the place with one bird, right? Most of the time. So you don't want any surprises later on when the kit comes off and you're committed.'

'What are you on about Aesop? If you're that concerned about a girl's body, can't you get a good enough idea of it just by looking at her in her clothes?'

'Exactly. That's what I'm saying. But if you pay attention to the details of all the different girls in the place, you can fine-tune the upcoming session, can't you?'

'Can't I what?'

'Take tits for instance.'

'Ah Jesus, Aesop …'

'Just for a minute. Jessie, right? Looks like a 34C. Sounds lovely, right? But she had a padded holster on her this evening. Now, I'm not saying that that's a bad thing. Shows that the girl is trying to make herself look nice before she goes out, fair play to her. You want

137

a girl that's going to put in a bit of effort, and the balcony's always a good place to start. This morning, though, she was a B. Sure, B is a lovely size too. Better on a 32-sized bird, but still. We can't all be perfect, right? Thing is, if you only saw her tonight and reckoned you knew what the day's specials were on the puppy menu, then you might well find yourself feeling hard done by, y'see? You'd have them out and you'd be wondering if your hands are after suddenly growing a bit bigger somewhere en route between the pub and the back of bus shelter. Y'know what I mean?'

'Aesop …'

'I, on the other hand, didn't even need to see her this morning to know she was giving the girls a little boost tonight. A top doesn't fall the same way across a bird wearing a padded bra. They keep coming up with better ones, but you can't fool Aesop. I've been at this game too long. Now, in Jessie's case it doesn't matter a bit. She's well-stacked either way and I'd be the first man to stick the head on them given the right circumstances. But it's still nice to know what you're letting yourself in for, is all I'm saying. Sure, once you get to know a girl you can tell what bra she likes to wear with what top, if she's not wearing a bra at all … for fuck sake, after a while you can even tell when she's got the painters in. Y'see, every month …'

'Okay Aesop! I don't want to hear any more.'

'Now … arses are a different story altogether …'

'Shut up, you fucking delinquent. Christ, this is your hobby, is it?'

'Jesus, no. It's much more important than that.'

'And you do it with every girl you see?'

'Just happens at this stage. Like noticing what colour her hair is.'

'So you were doing it with Helen?'

'Ah … well, I mean … it's not like I was …'

'And Trish? You want to tell me all about Trish's breasts?'

'I'd … rather not.'

'Good.'

'Right.'

They both sat looking into the fire for a couple of minutes.

'Norman, please. That music is doing me head in. Have you anything else?'

'It's grand. Stop moaning. And … anyway … I've seen them.'

'Seen what?'

'Trish's … breasts.'

'Yeah?'

'They're lovely.'

'Good stuff.'

'I like her, Aesop.'

'I'd say you do. She's a real honey.'

'Yeah. I think she likes you.'

Aesop leaned back in the chair and took a big gulp of whiskey.

'I doubt that.'

'She said she hasn't heard from you. I thought you were going to say sorry.'

'I am, Norman. I just feel like such a bleedin' eejit. I don't know what to say to her. Y'know, "Listen Trish, about the whole fucking-a-cup-of-tea-in-your-face-and-calling-you-a-psycho-cunt thing …"'

'You called her a …'

'Oh. Sorry. I didn't mention that bit before.'

'Fuck sake. Just call her, will you? Tomorrow.'

'I will.'

'Things are hard enough without …'

'What? What's hard?'

'Ah … nothing.'

'Tell me.'

'It's nothing Aesop. You wouldn't … know what it's like.'

'What what's like?'

'What it's like when a bird that you're mad about fancies your mate.'

'Who? Jimmy?'

'Jimmy? Jesus … Aesop, she fuckin' fancies you, you dope.'

'What? She does in her bollocks.'

'She does! It's obvious. You can see it in her. That night at the gig and all …'

'What are you talking about Norman?'

'You and her, and her breaking her shite laughing with you all night on the couch at the party afterwards. That's what I'm talking about.'

'Jesus, Norman, we were only chatting.'

'Yeah, but she never laughs like that with me.'

'So I'm a fucking comedian. So what? Doesn't mean she's into me.'

'Aesop, you were there being the fucking rockstar after your gig, with no shirt and a towel around your neck and your tight pants and those two stupid fucking studs in your eyebrow, people coming up to you and shaking your hand every five minutes, and I'm over the other side of the room talking to Sparky about his Mam's daffodils.'

'Fuck sake Norman, we were talking about you!'

'And that had her breaking her bollocks laughing? Brilliant …'

'No ye spa. I was making myself out to be a fuckin' eejit and telling her about all the times I'd have been in the shit if it wasn't for you. Remember the time that bloke thought I rode his wife? He would've killed me if you hadn't been there to calm him down.'

'You did ride his wife Aesop.'

'Yeah, but I didn't know she was his wife at the time, did I? It's not like I got her to fill out a questionnaire.'

'Anyway, women don't want the big hard case. They want someone who can make them laugh. Isn't that what they say in all the magazines?'

'That's bollocks! We're talking about real women, man. A giggle's all right now and again, but they want a lot fucking more than that. I'm telling you, the likes of me is the last thing they need. And they know it, thank Christ. Norman, they might want to fuck me, but they want to marry you; that's what they say in the magazines.'

'But I don't want her fucking you before she marries me!'

'Wh … hang on … are we still talking about Trish?'

'Yes!'

'Aw Jesus, listen man, I would never try and move in on your bird no matter what. Any bird! Ever. And anyway, I'd say we're safe enough as far as Trish is concerned. She thinks I'm a fuckin' weirdo.'

'But what was she doing in your gaff that night? Women don't forget their jewellery. You said that yourself, sure.'

'Wasn't she giving me that picture? She was just being nice. Getting in with your mates so that it'd be easier for you and her. She's fucking mad about you Norman. Really. It's all we talked about that night.'

'I don't know Aesop. There's something about her. I can't stop thinking about her but, it's like she's keeping something from me …'

'Norman, listen. I'm telling you that Trish is a great bird and all she wants is you. The only thing that'll change that is you fucking it up. Really. Chill out and stop looking for things to worry about. She's great and she wouldn't touch me with rubber gloves on. If she's keeping something back, it's probably because she sees that you're not sure and she doesn't want to get hurt.'

'I don't know …'

'You know how to bate the shite out of people, Norman. I know women. Trish is a fucking angel and she's all yours, so make the most of it.'

TRISH WAS in her bedroom on her own, very sober. It was two in the morning. The wardrobe door was open and she stood in front of the mirror stuck to the inside of it, just looking at herself. She was in her uniform still, even though she'd gotten in from work an hour ago. Only the bedside lamp was turned on and that was on a dimmer switch. Still, even in the rusty orange glow that seemed to seethe all around her, her uniform shone sharp and crisp. The way she liked it. She breathed deeply and closed the wardrobe door, stepping back to sit on her bed.

She was thinking about Aesop, remembering the fear and panic in his eyes that night. The way he'd bolted from her, flinging stinging obscenities in his wake, before she had a chance to stop him. She reached under the bed and patted around until her fingers touched the box and then she pulled it out and set it on her lap, just looking at it for a minute. The lid came away in her hands and she felt the catch in her chest when her eyes fell on what was inside. Something from another life.

'YOU RECKON?' said Norman, looking up.

'I'm telling you, man. I know women.'

Chapter Thirteen

IT WAS a beautiful Saturday morning in Cork. The sky was a brilliant pale blue and a fresh breeze was whooshing through the stripped trees behind the cottage, carrying with it in earthy wafts the musk of burning turf. The sun was low, but blinding bright, splashing long shadows across the fields from every ditch and bush and the rocks that pierced the earth like ancient broken teeth. A tractor and trailer crunched past on the road and then disappeared over the hill. A crow set down on the bench just outside the front door and looked around in jerks and twitches before taking off again and vanishing into a hedge. Inside the cottage, two figures sat at the kitchen table.

'Me fuckin' head,' said Aesop.

'What's left in the bottle?' said Norman. His chin was down on his chest, his hands folded demurely in his lap and his face scrunched up in pain.

Aesop opened his fingers and looked between them over to the small table in front of the fire. He closed them again.

'You don't want to know.'

'That's your fault. I wanted to go to bed when we came in from the pub.'

'I don't seem to recall having to break your arm to get you to have a small one.'

Norman turned to look at the bottle.

'Jesus. That was full when we started. No wonder I'm in this state. You're a bad influence on me. I was going down to the bog this morning and everything.'

'We're already there.'

'No. I mean the actual bog. I was going to cut some turf.'

'There's loads in the bin outside.'

'It was for the exercise. A bit of fresh air. I was going to show you how to cut peat.'

'That'd come in handy. All the times I've said to meself, if only you knew how to cut peat Aesop …'

'We'll go after lunch. A couple of hours. To sort out this hangover.'

'Or we could just take a load of tablets and not bother our bollocks. That gets my vote.'

'You don't have a vote. We can't stay in the house all day, Aesop.'

'Why not?'

'Because it's a gorgeous day. We should go out for a walk or something.'

'Norman, that's the kind of thing a girl says right between waking up in the morning and me pushing her into a taxi.'

'Well I'm not a girl Aesop.'

'Ah, you're a bit of a girl sometimes Norman, aren't you?'

'Is there eggs in the fridge?'

'Yeah. Helen brought loads over yesterday.'

'Right. Well I'll get started on the French toast, you sort out the fire.'

'Ah Jaysis. I don't want to. Can I make the French toast and you do the fire?'

'Do you know how to make French toast?'

'Eh … eggs, toast … em … garlic …'

Norman stood up.

'Don't use too many firelighters.'

'What the fuck is that on the radio? Listen man, is there any music at all in this house that isn't shite?'

'Granny's CDs are over there in the press.'

'I don't s'pose there's any chance Granny was a big Megadeth fan, is there?'

'Have a look.'

Aesop got down on his knees and started flicking through the selection.

'Dolly Parton?'

'Yeah.'

'I didn't know she sang.'

'What?'

'She has an album here. Oh, two albums. Did you know she sang?'

'What did you think she did?'

'Well … I thought she just had these massive knockers and … y'know …'

'She's a singer you fucking eejit.'

'Really?'

'Stop stalling and do the fire. I'm not doing it, Aesop.'

'I'm serious. What kind of music is she?'

'Country and Western.'

'Jaysis. Sorry Dolly, you can stay in there. Oh, look, "War of the Worlds"!'

'Yeah. Granny was mad into Richard Burton.'

'Excellent. That's my kind of granny. This is proper hangover music.'

'Aesop, get a move on, will you?'

'Who's Richard Burton?'

'Listen to me, you big …'

There was a knock on the door.

'Anyone awake in here?'

It was Helen.

'Oh thank fuck,' said Aesop. 'Saved.'

He ran over and opened the door.

'Helen!'

The arms went out and he gave her a big hug and a kiss on the cheek.

'Thank God you're here. Norman's being a terrible bully this morning. Will you tell him to leave me alone?'

Helen laughed and walked in.

'Morning, guys.' She stopped. 'Oh God … the smell in here.'

'That's him,' said Aesop, pointing at Norman. 'I keep telling him to see a doctor.'

'No. It's the cigarettes and booze. God, it reminds me of when Granny had one of her parties.'

'I'm beginning to like what I hear about your Granny.'

'She was great. So, what's up? Have you eaten yet?'

'Just putting on some French toast here,' said Norman. 'Do you want some?'

'I'm after bringing some sausages and bacon and pudding down. And Mam made a few loaves of bread for you. And butter. Here, Robert, let me do it.'

'Ah no, Jesus. I'll look after it.'

'You will not. Put on the kettle there and sit down before you fall down. Look at the state of the pair of you. Reeking of whiskey and bags under your eyes like pillows. What time did you go to bed?'

'I had to leave him asleep on the couch,' said Aesop. 'He can't hold his gargle.'

'Right. Well, the two of you sit down. Here's the paper, look. I'll make the tea. Robert, set the fire there.'

'But … that's Aesop's job.'

'Ah stop. He's our guest, sure. Go on. It'll only take you a minute.'

Aesop grinned at Norman and took the paper off Helen.

'Thanks Helen. You're very good. Norman had me doing everything.'

'Aesop …' said Norman. He looked fit to give him a box.

'Will you do what your cousin says and stop whinging?' said Aesop. 'Honestly, Helen, he's been like a bear with a sore arse all morning. I wanted to go out for a walk and everything but there was no shifting him.'

'Come on Robert. Get the fire going and we'll have our breakfast. You'll be grand then.'

'I'm grand now!'

'Can I do anything at all for you Helen?' said Aesop.

'Not at all,' she said, her head in the fridge. 'Sit down there and Robert will make the tea. Robert? The fire?'

Norman looked around and glared at Aesop. He opened his mouth to say something, but Aesop just made a show of flapping open the paper and sat on the couch.

'Will I put on some music Helen?' he said.

'Yeah, go on sure.'

'Do you like Dolly Parton?'

'I love her.'

'Really? Me too. Norman, can you stick on some sounds there while you're up. And Helen, are you sure I can't help?'

'Just sit down there Aesop and relax. Robert, I think that kettle is boiled.'

Norman gave one final dagger-glare in Aesop's direction and then knelt down to put a CD on. With 'Jolene' coming out of the speakers, he walked past Aesop and gave him a boot in the shin on his way out the back door to get some sticks.

'How do you like your eggs Aesop?'

'Actually, I love poached eggs Helen. But don't go to any trouble.'

'No trouble.'

'Ah, you're very good for coming down and making the brekkie like this.'

'Not at all. I wanted to say hello anyway. I don't get to see Robert much these days and he said you didn't know how long you'd be hanging around.'

'We'll be here for a couple of weeks probably, so you drop in to see him as often as you like.'

'Thanks.'

'Seriously. Drop in to see me too if you like.'

She stopped what she was doing for a second, but didn't turn around.

'Maybe I will.'

'Listen, I wanted to tell you last night, Helen, but I was pissed and didn't want to sound like a fuckin' eejit. You've got a beautiful voice. Man, last night you were absolutely … stunning … up there.'

'Thanks.'

'I'm serious. And, no, thank you. I had a brilliant time.'

'I did too.'

'Helen?'

'Yeah?'

'That Irish song you were singing …'

'Yeah.'

'Who is she?'

'Who's who?'

'The girl in the …'

There was a thump outside the front door, someone kicking muck off shoes. Then a knock.

'Hello?'

Aesop's head spun around in surprise.

'Jimmy?'

He went to the door and opened it. Jimmy was standing there, grinning.

'Howya Aesop. What's …'

'Did you bring your iPod?'

'What?'

'Your iPod.'

Jimmy tapped his jacket pocket.

'It's here.'

'Speakers?'

'They're out in the car.'

'Gimme your keys.'

'It's not locked.'

'Grand.'

Aesop bolted past him and out to Jimmy's car.

'Nice to see you too, Aesop. Fuck sake.'

Aesop ignored him, so Jimmy stepped inside and looked around. He saw Helen standing at the counter, looking at him.

'Hello.'

'Hi.'

'Eh … I'm Jimmy.'

She just nodded, a full black pudding in her hand, like she was seeing things.

'Where in the car?' shouted Aesop from outside.

'In the boot. There's a sports bag with me gear.'

Jimmy turned back to Helen.

'Is … Norman here?'

'He's out the back cutting up some sticks for the fire.'

'Right.'

'Jimmy, the boot won't open.'

'For fu … you need to lean on it with your knee. It gets stuck.'

He walked over to Helen and put his hand out.

'Nice to meet you, eh …'

'Helen.'

'Helen. Nice to meet you. Are you Aesop's … friend?'

'I'm Robert's cousin.'

'Oh right. Yeah. Helen. He mentioned you, yeah. Bridie's your Mam, isn't she? God, they have you making their breakfast for them? You should have told them to …'

There was a tremendous banging from the front garden.

'Sorry Helen, can you excuse me a minute?' He walked back to the door and looked out. 'Aesop, I said lean on it with your knee, not kick the fuck out of it.'

'It won't … fucking … the yoke is …'

'Christ, I'll do it. Hang … will you … Aesop, stop fuckin' kicking me car! Jesus …'

He went out and opened the boot and pointed at the bag, and then came back inside.

'Has he been listening to a lot of Norman's music?'

'And Dolly Parton.'

'Right,' he said looking back at Aesop rooting through his bag.

'Eh … will you have a cup of tea?' said Helen.

'I'd love one Helen, thanks. That was a long drive this morning.'

'Are you going to be staying?'

'Yeah. For a few days anyway.'

Aesop came in and went over to Jimmy, reaching into his pocket.

'What … Aesop … stop … will you … what are you doing for fuck sake?'

'Gimme your iPod. I need Zeppelin. It's an emergency.'

'Here. Jesus.'

Aesop took the iPod and speakers and went over to the counter to plug them in, the other two just watching. Ten seconds later Black Dog was blasting out through the kitchen. Aesop sighed and leaned back against the fridge like he was sinking into a hot bath.

'Ah Jaysis. Ah, that's grand now …'

'Aesop …' said Jimmy, shaking his head.

'Oh. Sorry. Yiz must think I'm very rude. Jimmy, this is Norman's stunningly beautiful cousin Helen, who's an amazing singer and a dab hand at the oul' fry in the mornings. Helen, this is my mate Jimmy Collins. He's a rockstar.'

A dishevelled and disgruntled figure stumbled into the kitchen through the back door, two arms full of broken sticks and his nose streaming blood.

'Head came off the axe,' he said, blinking at everyone and then staring at Jimmy with his mouth open.

'And of course, you know Norman,' said Aesop.

The lads were sitting on the low stone wall next to the holy well, smoking.

'A trout?' said Jimmy.

'Yeah,' said Norman, shrugging. He had toilet roll stuffed up one nostril.

'Fair enough.'

Aesop got up and peered into the well.

'Hello?' he shouted.

'Don't take the piss Aesop,' said Norman.

'I'm not. Just trying out the echo.'

'Sit down and have your smoke. And don't be flicking your butt into it either. Bring it with you back to the cottage.'

'And what did Saint Ita do for herself?' said Jimmy.

'Ah, I don't know all the stories. I think her Da wanted her to get married to some rich bloke, but she didn't want to because she wanted to live a simple life and go around helping people.'

'Typical Pisces,' said Aesop, sitting on the wall again and stubbing out his cigarette.

'Anyway,' said Norman. 'Are you going to tell us what you're doing down here? I thought you were busy in Dublin.'

'I was. But … well, I couldn't concentrate on what I was doing, y'know? I haven't been writing very much lately … figured I could do with a bit of time off. So I thought I'd come down here and see what you two were getting up to. So what have you been up to?'

'Not much,' said Aesop. 'Met Helen and her mate Jessie yesterday. Then Norman showed me some karate. Went to a trad gig last night and fell in love with Helen, God bless her sweet voice like honey and eyes the size of dinner plates, but Norman made me promise not to touch her which I think is totally fucking out of line. I nearly got into a fight with a bloke called Davey, who's Helen's ex-fiancé, for blowing him a kiss across the bar, but his mate pulled him away before I could batter him. Then Norman got up and played the bones with the band. Came home, drank a bottle of whiskey, told Norman I called his bird a cunt, and then passed out upside down in the bed. Oh, by the way, apparently Jessie is mad for your cock, Jimmy. You haven't met her yet, but you will. A couple of nice handfuls on her and the deadly accent and everything. All I did was mention your name and next thing she's there shifting around on the seat trying to get comfortable, y'know? The bullets out and everything just thinking about you.'

Jimmy just blinked at him and looked around at Norman.

'Aesop,' said Norman, pointing at the well. 'Do you know where we are? This is s'posed to be a holy place. Can you not have a bit of respect?'

'Sorry man. I keep forgetting.'

'Anyway Jimmy,' said Norman. 'Why didn't you go across to England to see Susan if you had a bit of time off?'

'Well …' said Jimmy. 'I was going to. But it didn't work out.'

'What didn't work out?' said Aesop.

'I called her but … I think it's over.'

'Ah no,' said Norman, turning to him. 'Why? What happened?'

'I don't know to be honest. But she just told me it wasn't working and she'd prefer it if I didn't call again.'

'Really? Why, for fuck sake? I thought you two were going to sort out all the stuff between you.'

'Well I was hoping we could. Man, she wouldn't even talk to me. She just said she'd had enough and wanted to move on. To be honest, I can't really say I blame her. It was too hard. I was working my arse off on the record, and I'll be on tour in a few weeks. And …'

Jimmy drifted off and looked out over the fields.

'Are you all right?' said Norman.

'Yeah. I s'pose. It was a tough one though. Tears and everything. I only talked to her for five minutes, but she was all upset. Worse than that. She sounded really angry or something. Like she suddenly realised that I've only been wasting her time.'

'Do you think it's worth trying again with her?' said Norman.

Jimmy sighed.

'Yeah. But I'm a selfish bastard. I only want to do it my way. Wait until I had everything cleared up and could concentrate on the two of us.'

'Jimmy?' said Aesop.

'What? And before you say anything, I'm not in the humour for listening to any of your shite about riding someone else to get over it. This only happened last night, right?'

'All right. But I was just going to say that this was always going to happen and that you're a fuckin' eejit.'

'Thanks.'

'Seriously man. You're like a fuckin' book I've read already.'

'What fuckin' book have you ever read?'

'I'm just saying, like. You've a head full of piss and if you want this bird so much, why don't you just go over there and sweep her off her feet and tell her you love her and that no matter what happens with the band or any other shite in your life, she's the most important thing and you'll do whatever it takes to make it all okay. Tell her to come to Dublin, move in with you, get a job if that's what she wants and then the two of you can fuck like rabbits and make babies and build a castle and be the coolest fucking rock and roll couple on the planet.'

They other two looked over at him.

'What are you looking at?' he said. 'It's simple! It's not what I'd do, but I'm taking into consideration the fact that you're a handbag. If you don't do all that because it's not what you want, well then that's grand. Drop it, leave her alone, stop whinging, get on with your shit and ride the arse off Jessie tonight. But if you don't do it because you're too busy doing all that complicated poet bollocks in your mind again, then your head is full of piss and I don't want to fucking hear any more about it.'

'Jesus … isn't life simple Aesop?'

'Yes! You fucking … langer. Norman, call him a langer. I can't do the accent.'

'He's not a langer Aesop.'

'You're both fucking langers then.'

'What do you know about it, Aesop?' said Jimmy. 'You don't give a shit about any girl.'

'I know you love this Susan bird. Whatever that means. I know that fucking Kleenex dispenser over there loves his Trish bird. What's the problem? You're always telling me I'm a waster and I should cop on and settle down and get serious about a girl. Well, the pair of you are hardly fucking brilliant advertisements for it, are you? Look at you. You want to know what it all means, Jimmy, even though it means fuck all except for what you've got here and now. And you, fucking … Mr Bean on steroids … are so happy that all you can think of is the whole thing going to shit. What are you fucking like? I'm not allowed ask Helen out, but I'll tell you, if I did bring her out at least she'd have a good time and neither of us would come out of the experience fucking traumatised.'

No one spoke for a minute.

'Well … maybe you have a point,' said Jimmy.

'You know I have a point. Norman? Am I right?'

'You're not totally wrong. Maybe.'

'And can I ask Helen out?'

'Only if you want your bollocks fed to you.'

'Bastard. Well, listen, if I'm going to be imprisoned in this bleedin' hellhole for the next two weeks with the pair of you, I don't want any more of this shite, ye here me? Fuck this …'

He stood up and started walking around the well. After three circles, he reached into his pocket and then fired a handful of coins down into it.

'Aesop,' said Norman, reaching out to grab him. 'What the fuck …'

'Shut up a minute. I'm not finished. Is there a special prayer, or what's the story?'

'I don't know. I think there's a prayer, but …'

'And does it work if you talk out loud, or is it like blowing out birthday candles?'

'I don't know Aesop. And I don't think …'

'Well I'll try anything if it means you two aren't a drippy couple of homos for the next two weeks. Actually, y'know something, I feel better already. I think me hangover's gone.' He leaned over the well again and shouted. 'Thanks Ita! Seeya tomorrow.'

He sat back on the wall and lit up again. The others were laughing.

'That's more like it,' said Aesop.

'Aesop, why did you throw money into the well?' said Norman.

'You said people made an offering.'

'They do. See that box over there?'

Norman pointed to a metal box chained to a small post.

'Ah. Right. Well …'

'It's not a wishing well.'

'We'll find out about that won't we? So where does the money go?'

'I don't know. I think it goes to some charity or something. Listen, I've to have a crap. Are you coming in or will you be out here?'

'Ah, we'll stay a minute,' said Jimmy. 'It's nice out here.'

'Grand. Seeya in a bit. I think there's a few beers in the fridge. I'll bring them out.'

'Any word on Shiggy?' said Aesop, once Norman had set off for the cottage.

'I talked to him the other day. He might have a business trip here coming up soon. We can talk properly about it then. You know he's been working for Kyotosei for twenty years?'

'Really? Jaysis, he looks about twelve.'

'Yeah. Well, it'd be a big thing for him to just drop it all.'

'That's fair enough I s'pose. Still, it'd be deadly to have him back.'

'I know. Sparky said he'd fill in for the Irish tour, but when we go over to England, it'd be too hard. He's got enough shit on his plate in Sin Bin. If Shiggy isn't back, we'll have to get someone else by then.'

'Fuck that. We're a good band with Shiggy. Starting all over again with … y'know …'

A car drove past on the road. A knackered thing that roared as the driver gave them a wave. They waved back.

'Hang on a minute Jimmy,' said Aesop, watching the car drive vanish.

'What?'

'Keep sketch for Norman, right?'

'What? Aesop, what are you doing?'

'Nothing. Just keep an eye out. Hang on …'

He ran off towards the ditch at the side of the road and came back a minute later with a straight broken branch about six foot long. He started stripping all the twigs and smaller branches off it.

'What are you going to do with that?'

'Nothing. It's grand.'

'Aesop, what are …'

'Here we go,' said Aesop, after a couple of minutes, holding up his stick and grinning at Jimmy.

'What are you going to do with that?'

'Watch …'

He walked over to the well and looked down into it.

'Aesop, that stick is nowhere near long enough to get your money back. And anyway, you'd need a scoop or something on the end of it.'

'You reckon?'

'Of course, you dope.'

'Is that a car coming?'

Jimmy looked off down the road. There was another car approaching, coming into view and then disappearing as it came towards them over the dips in the road.

'Yeah. Why?'

'Are you ready?' said Aesop.

'For fucking what?' said Jimmy, looking around quickly. He was starting to panic. You never knew what the mad fucker was going to do. 'Aesop, what are you up to?'

'Hush a minute. Hang on … hang on …'

Just then the car came over the last dip and Aesop immediately stood back and held his stick in two hands over the opening of the well. It suddenly looked very much like a fishing rod.

'Aesop …'

Aesop's shoulders were already starting to shake with the laughing. Jimmy could see the driver of the car slow down and look at the pair of them, her mouth open in a big O. Aesop gave her a big smile and a wave and then turned back to his rod. He suddenly gave it a jerk upwards and leaned back like he was trying to land a whopper. Jimmy put his face in his hands and turned away. When he managed to look back over his shoulder, the driver of the car, a woman of about fifty, was still staring in horror at the sight in front of her. Aesop gave a final pull on his stick and jumped backwards, landing on the ground with the stick still jerking. The car finally trundled out of site behind a hedge.

Aesop got up and came over to Jimmy, one hand still clutching the branch and the other on his belly. He was roaring laughing.

'Ah, man … did you … did you see her face?'

He pointed out at the road and then doubled over.

'Ah Jesus … ah Christ … that was fucking brilliant that was …'

'What's he laughing at?' called Norman, coming over the field towards them with a sixpack of Guinness bottles.

'Eh …' said Jimmy. 'He , eh … we were just laughing about something Shiggy said once.'

'Ah right. Gas man, Shiggy. What's with the stick, Aesop?'

But Aesop couldn't talk. He just bent over, cackling, shaking his head and pointing at the road. Eventually he straightened up and took a bottle off Norman.

'We should go to Dingle.'

'Now?'

'Yeah.'

'It's nearly two o'clock.'

'So what? Come on. We'll head off now, have a few pints tonight and then be ready in the morning to get out on the harbour.'

'Me bollocks,' said Jimmy. 'I'm not driving to Dingle now to look at a fucking dolphin after driving down here this morning already.'

'Ah go on.'

'No.'

'Tomorrow?'

'We'll see.'

'We'll see? I'm not fucking seven, Jimmy.'

'Look at that sky, Aesop. It's going to rain.'

'But we'll be in the water.'

'We will in our fuck. It's freezing.'

'But they get you in a wet suit.'

'They'll be lucky to get me in a boat. We'll talk about it tomorrow.'

'I want to go today!'

'Tough.'

'That's not fair! You said we'd go to see Fungi.'

'Another day, Aesop.'

'But Jimmy, you said …'

'Jesus, Aesop,' said Jimmy, rubbing his head. 'I thought you weren't fucking seven? Will you shut up? Anyway, he's probably hibernating.'

Aesop tutted in disgust and crushed his can under his foot.

'Hibernating … fuck sake. I'm getting more beer.'

He walked off back to the cottage, muttering to himself.

Norman and Jimmy didn't say anything for a bit. Then Norman looked up.

'I don't think dolphins hibernate, Jimmy.'

'Yeah? Why not?'

'I think there might be a danger of them ... y'know ... drowning.'

Jimmy thought about that for a minute and then nodded.

'I s'pose they'd need to be careful about that all right.'

Chapter Fourteen

'THERE HE is!' shouted Jimmy, pointing. 'Look at him!'

It was the next morning. Cold and dark under heavy clouds and the boat was rolling all over the sea.

'I see him,' said Norman, laughing. 'Jesus, he's massive. Aesop! Look!'

But Aesop wasn't looking. He was at the back of the boat puking his guts up. He raised one hand in acknowledgment and then up came some more of his breakfast and he bent over fully again, grabbing the rail with both fists and roaring.

There were about a dozen people on the boat. Three Americans, a couple from Germany or somewhere, and the rest Irish. It was fairly choppy out in the harbour, but only Aesop was suffering to the point where he couldn't even stand up without feeling the huge fry he'd eaten that morning squirm and boil in his stomach.

'Aesop, you're missing it,' shouted Jimmy.

'I'll be grand … ugh … I'll be grand in a minute, Jimmy. Just … I'll be …'

'We've been out here for an hour, man. We'll be heading back soon.'

Jimmy walked back to him.

'Come on over here. At least if you're puking out the side of the boat, you'll be able to see him when he comes up.'

Aesop stood up straight. He was green, blobs of old food on his chin and his eyes red and streaming. He put one hand on Jimmy's shoulder.

'I don't want him to see me like this,' he said.

'I don't think he gives a shite, Aesop.'

'He does. Jimmy, I've been … aw … aw Jesus … wait … wait a minute Jimmy.' He belched. 'Ah, that's better … I've been waiting for years to meet him and look at the state of me now.'

'He's a dolphin, Aesop.'

'Dolphins are more intelligent than people, Jimmy.'

'Some people, yeah, I can see that. Nothing would do you only to eat all them fried eggs this morning, would it?'

'She said she was after making too many.'

'You could've just said no.'

'To food?'

'Well anyway, I'm sure you're not the first person Fungi's seen vomit out here.'

'You don't understand.'

'Well … why don't you sit down and just peek over the side.'

'He's not fucking stupid, Jimmy. He'll know I'm …'

'Hi guys!'

It was one of the Amercian blokes. He was standing there in a bright luminous orange raincoat and beaming out of a tanned face with teeth like a mouthful of snow.

'Howya,' said Jimmy.

'Nice camera,' said Aesop, glancing up. It was about the size of fax machine.

'Thanks! Hey, I guess you're not feeling too good, are you?'

'What makes you say that, Inspector?'

'Well … I noticed that you've been throwing up. Are you okay?'

'I'm fine. Here, look … high five …'

He put up one hand, but before the other guy could do anything, Aesop was spraying the sea again.

'Hey buddy, what you need is some toast. Dry toast.'

'Is that what I need?'

'Sure is. That'll sort you right out. We've been having problems with the food over here too. But when your stomach is upset like that? It's the only thing that works. Dry toast. Guaranteed.'

"I see. And, c'mere, do you have any dry toast?'

'No. Sorry.'

'I see. Right. Jimmy, what did we do with all that dry toast we had?'

'I think I left it in the car, Aesop.'

'Shite. Ah well. But, listen, thanks anyway, man. It was a cracking idea.'

'You're welcome. Are you guys English?'

'No,' said Jimmy. He could see that Aesop had had enough already. 'We're from Dublin.'

'Really? It's hard to tell. Everyone we meet has all these crazy accents. We don't have an accent in the States.'

'Is that a fact?' said Aesop. At least he was distracted now from his vomiting. 'Aren't yis brilliant?'

'Yeah. I guess we're lucky. Hey, I think we're turning around. I should get some more pictures of Fungi. I gotta tell you though, I'm a bit disappointed.'

'Why's that?'

'Well, he doesn't do any tricks. He just kinds of swims along with the boat, doesn't he? I guess he's not so smart.'

'He jumped up out of the water a few times,' said Jimmy, looking at Aesop quickly.

'Yeah, I guess. But they'd make a lot more money if they put him in a pool and taught him some tricks. That's what we do at home.'

'Where's home?' said Jimmy. He gave Aesop a small kick in the shin.

'South Beach, Florida.'

'Florida, right. God. You must be loving the weather here so, are you?'

'Y'know, actually, I prefer the sun.'

'Oh. Do you? Right so.'

'Anyway, we're heading to Dublin on Tuesday. We've been in the countryside for a few weeks now. Looking forward to some excitement. Is there anywhere you'd recommend? We've heard about Temple Bar and Grafton Street and …'

'Have you ever heard of Ballyfermot?' said Aesop.

'No. What's there?'

'Great nightlife. You'd like it. Ballyfermot. Just ask the taximan.'

'Ballyfermot. Right. Well, we'll be sure to check it out.'

'Do. Bring your camera.'

'Yeah? Okay.'

'And that raincoat.'

'Sure. Well, I'll see you guys later. Thanks for the tip.'

'And you.'

He went back to his mates, and Jimmy turned around to Aesop.

'Ballyfermot?'

'Did you hear what he said about Fungi? Fungi's not a fuckin' clown Jimmy. We're lucky that he shows up here at all and lets us get close to him. You can't capture him and put him in a pool. There'd be a riot.'

'Jesus. The bloke was only making conversation.'

'Yeah. And slagging Irish food he was, too. Well, anyway it doesn't matter. He won't remember Ballyfermot.'

'But he's writing it down, look.'

Aesop gave a small laugh and looked over.

'Is he? Well he said they were looking for some excitement. Ah Jimmy ... I'm just a bit depressed. I was really looking forward to seeing Fungi.'

'Well he's still out there. Come on. Give him a wave anyway.'

'All right.'

They went back to Norman who had moved over to the other side of the boat now that they were heading back in.

'Hang on,' said Norman, putting his arm out. 'Get down wind from me, you.'

'I'm finished.'

'I don't care.'

'Believe me Norman, there's nothing left. I think the last thing that came up was something I'm going to miss later on.'

'I'm not taking any chances.'

'Is he still out there?'

'He was there a minute ago. He must be getting tired though. He was lepping out of the water like it was scalding. It was brilliant. Did you not see him at all?'

'No. Fuck it. I don't believe this shit. All this way ...'

'That's what happens when you make a savage of yourself at breakfast. How many eggs have you eaten in the last two days?'

'They're nicer down here.'

'Why didn't you tell the landlady you were full?'

'Don't you bleedin' start.'

'Well we're going back in now.'

'Thanks, I can see that Norman.'

'Jesus, it's not my fault you didn't see him. Don't be getting snotty with me.'

'Where was he?'

'Over there. Next to the head.'

Aesop looked out but there was no sign. Just the waves, which seemed to just be getting rougher and higher, the spray flying off crests in sheets.

The boat carried on into the harbour and just five minutes later they were pulling up to the pier. Aesop sighed and started to walk off back up the boat.

'Where are you going?' said Jimmy.

'I'm getting me money back.'

'What?'

'He said you get your money back if you don't see the dolphin on his boat trip.'

'You're going to go and get your money back, are you?' said Norman. 'From a Kerryman?'

He roared laughing.

'C'mon, Jimmy, this'll be good …'

'DO YOU want another pint Norman?' said Jimmy, getting up.

'I'll go,' said Aesop.

'You got the last one.'

'Yeah, I know. But I'll get this one too.'

He stood up and went to the bar. Jimmy looked and saw that two hotties were after coming in and were standing there wondering what to order. Aesop was making a beeline for them.

'He never stops, does he?' he said to Norman.

'Ah, feck him. We know him well enough at this stage.'

Aesop came back from the bar with three pints, a packet of peanuts and a grin like a Christmas tree.

'Stockholm,' he said.

'Yeah?' said Jimmy, finishing the last of his old one. 'On holliers in February?'

'Nah. They live here. Well they live in Athlone, but just came down for the weekend. They work for some phone company or something.'

'Ericsson?'

'I didn't catch their names.'

'Do they work for Ericsson?'

'Fuck, I don't know. Anyway, who's up for it?'

The two lads said nothing.

'C'mon, you useless fuckers. Do I have to do everything around here?'

'Aesop, I've got a girlfriend,' said Norman.

'Ah … okay then. That's allowed. Jimmy? You just got your marching orders. Are you on?'

'No, Aesop. I'm not on. I'm just having a pint here.'

'Ah Jesus lads, come on! Do you not feel the Need for Swede? Are you going to make me go over there and ride both of them? Have you never had a Swedish bird? It's like being strapped to a kangaroo.'

'Off you go, so. Enjoy yourself.'

'Are you sure you don't want to spoil yourself? Don't say I didn't offer.'

'I'm grand.'

Aesop opened his wallet and pulled out two sets of the earplugs he used when he was playing drums and put them on the table next to the pints.

'In case they're a pair of screamers later. Who's always looking out for you?'

He picked up his pint and turned around to go back to the bar.

'And he wonders why I won't let him near Helen,' said Norman to Jimmy.

Aesop turned around.

'What?'

Norman put down his glass.

'I'm just saying. This is exactly why you're to keep the fuck away from Helen.'

Aesop looked back at the bar quickly and then sat down.

'Are you saying that if I don't go over there, I can ask Helen out?'

'No.'

'Well ... well what are you saying, then?'

'I'm just saying you're a prick with ears and that's why you're not going near her.'

'But ... hang on a minute, Norman. You said I wasn't to touch her.'

'That's right.'

'Well I'm only thinking of riding that pair because you said I'd no chance with Helen. I'd never do that if I was with Helen.'

'So Helen would be more like one of your prolonged and happy relationships?'

'But ... wait a minute Norman. That's not fair. Didn't I say that I thought Helen was great. What do you take me for? If I thought ... if I thought that ...'

'She'd be like strapping yourself to a kangaroo?'

'No! Jesus, Helen isn't like that. Helen's totally cool. I mean it, man. There's something there, I'm telling you.'

'No there isn't.'

'There is!'

'And so this is how you display your affection for my cousin?'

'Look ... look ... hang on a minute ...'

Aesop was scratching his head.

'What do you want me to do for fuck sake?'

'Just be yourself.'

'Norman, I really like her. If I thought I'd get a chance with her, I'd never go near the Swedish birds.'

'Prove it.'

'So ... okay ... if I don't ride them, you'll let me ... y'know?'

'I didn't say that. Did I say that Jimmy?'

'Ah fuck sakes,' said Aesop. 'You're only messing with me head now, Norman.'

'Well, let's just say that as far as I can see, you're still the same gobshite you always were, following your cock everywhere it takes you. And it's not going to happen with my cousin.'

'Okay. Okay. I won't ride them.'

'Good.'

'I'm not sick, Norman. I can say no. All right lads, you're about to witness something special. I'm staying put here. No sex for me tonight. I can do this.'

'Well, you're about to be put to the test,' said Jimmy.

'What?'

'I think they got bored waiting for you. They're coming over.'

'Shit. Itchy Swedish bastards …'

NORMAN WAS in the jacks about two hours later. The Swedish girls were long gone. Aesop had sat there fingering his pint and going out for a smoke every five minutes and had barely opened his mouth the whole time they were sitting down with the lads. Jimmy and Norman had a laugh with them, but they eventually wandered away.

'Aesop?'

'Yeah?'

'You did very well.'

'Thanks.'

'Although I think they might have been be wondering what your problem was.'

'They're not the only ones.'

'You really like Helen?'

'Yeah. It's like … eh … ah, I don't know …'

'Yeah. It's been puzzling me too.'

'No. I mean, I haven't done anything about it. But she's looked at me a few times and I know she's up for it.'

'Up for it? Aesop, that's just the kind of expression Norman wants to hear out of you.'

'I didn't mean up for *it*. I just meant that I think she likes me too. Man, there's something about her and I just … will you say something to Norman for me?'

'What am I s'posed to say?'

'Tell him I'm serious about her.'

'Aesop, will you fuck off!'

'What?'

'You're not serious about her! You're just gagging for it because you can't have her.'

'No. No, it's not that at all!'

'It fucking is. Cop on and leave the girl alone.'

'Didn't I not just show him that I was serious?'

'No. You sat there for an hour and said nothing with your foot tapping and your hands shaking like one of them was going to fly off your pint at any minute and land on a big Swedish tit. Helen is just another girl, Aesop. You should have gone off with the two honeys tonight.'

'Aw Jesus. Don't say that Jimmy. I'm all … I'm all …'

'They were fucking gorgeous. They only came over here for you and then you left them hanging. They're probably lapping champagne out of some other bloke's belly button right now.'

'Stop! Will you shut up?'

Aesop had his eyes scrunched up now and looked like he was in pain.

'Look Aesop, Norman is right. Just be yourself. This lark doesn't suit you. Look at the fucking state of you. You're sweating for fuck sake. Hey, why don't you go off and find them. They're probably in one of the pubs. Go on.'

Aesop looked up.

'You think?'

'Yeah. Sure it's still early. Isn't there a session in that other place you were in yesterday? Maybe they're in there. Go on. Do us all a favour.'

'Well …'

Aesop picked up his smokes and his phone and started to stand up.

'I could … I could just … but … but Helen …'

He plonked down again, closing his eyes tightly and putting his fists up to his forehead.

'Jimmy, me head is fucked.'

'But what's your prick telling you to do?'

'Will you shush! I'm trying to ignore it …'

Chapter Fifteen

AESOP STILL wasn't himself the next morning. Even the land-lady was worried about him.

'Will you not have another sausage Aesop?' she said.

'I'm grand thanks, Mrs Kennedy. Really.'

'I have more rashers on.'

'Ah, I'll leave it. We were out on the sea yesterday and it was awful rough. I'm still feeling a bit ropey so I am.'

'Ah you poor thing. Have a cup of tea just, so, and let me know if you want anything before ye head off. I can put some rashers in a sandwich for you.'

Jimmy and Norman looked at each other and shook their heads. Oul' ones were always like this with Aesop. If only they knew.

'Thanks very much Mrs Kennedy. You're very good.'

The old lady smiled and wobbled off back into the kitchen.

'You weren't feeling too ropey to down eight pints last night,' said Jimmy.

'Aw, I had to make her go away, man. She's minging.'

'I can't believe you're not eating.'

'With the pissy smell off her? And anyway I didn't sleep very well.'

'Thinking about the Swedish pair?'

'No. This fucker honking and groaning all night long.'

'I have been known to snore all right, it has to be said,' said Norman, a huge forkful of beans on its way into his mouth.

'I can deal with snoring, Norman. Snoring has a rhythm. It's when you sit up out of the blue and start roaring and punching the fuck out of the pillow that I get a bit nervous. Jesus, what happens when you've a bird in the bed? If you can remember what that's like. Does she have to wear a crash helmet?'

'I slept like a baby, I don't know what you're on about.'

'Some fuckin' baby. At one stage you stopped in mid-dig and looked over at my bed with your fist in the air and only one eye open. I nearly shat meself. So, no Jimmy, I wasn't thinking about the Swedish birds. I spent most of the night afraid of going asleep and keeping an eye on Freddy fuckin' Krueger over there.'

Jimmy laughed.

'Well anyway, are we right then? We'll head back to the cottage?'

'Yeah. Fuck it.'

'Do you want to have another go at seeing at Fungi?'

'No Jimmy. Sure the weather's worse today. I'll come back again.'

'You sure?'

'Yeah.'

'Right. Come on. Are you eating them mushrooms Norman?'

'No. I'd a bad experience with mushrooms once. Bangladesh. Christ, never again.'

Jimmy reached over and stuck his fork into about five of them, put them in his mouth and then stood up, nodding upstairs with his head.

THEY LOADED up the car quickly, sorted out Mrs Kennedy with her money and took off for Cork again. There wasn't much talking after the drink the previous night and the only sounds were the occasional belch out of Jimmy's Peugeot on gear changes, and 'Live and Dangerous' coming out of the speakers.

'Is there any word from the cops?' said Aesop.

'I talked to Garda Ní Mhurchú last night,' said Norman. 'She gave me a ring.'

'Any news?'

'Nah. Not really. The note was just from a diary yoke, but that's about all they know. The flowers could've come from anywhere. Nothing's been robbed, so they can't trace anything that way. And nothing's come up from the prints they took. A lot of prints, she said, considering that it's a brand new gaff that's only had one bloke living in it.'

'That'll be all the new special friends I've made since I moved into town.'

'Yeah. Well, anyway they're keeping an eye on the place. She was just checking up on things with you.'

'Why didn't she call me then?'

'She probably didn't want to waste her time talking to a fuckin' eejit.'

'Fuck sake. It's my bollocks we're talking about.'

'I rang her last week and told her I'd be in charge of things. And to talk to me with any news.'

Aeosp sat back in the seat and sighed.

'I do actually have a fucking brain you know. Didn't I beat you at chess the other night?'

'That was drafts Aesop. And I could barely see with the bottle of whiskey I had in me. And you a cheating bastard robbing three of me men when I went to the jacks. Yeah. Don't think I didn't notice that. I just wanted the game to be over so I could get some kip. And … hey … hey Jimmy, slow down.'

'What's up?'

'Can you back up a bit?'

'What?'

'What was on that sign we just went past?'

'I didn't see it.'

'Back up,' said Norman, looking out the back window. 'It's grand. There's nothing coming. About fifty metres.'

The car was stopped now and Jimmy turned around in his seat to reverse the car back up the empty road. They got to the sign, which was tied to a tree. They all read it, and then Norman looked at the other two with a big grin.

'Are yis on?'

Jimmy and Aesop turned to each other

'Eh …'

'Come on. It'll be a laugh.'

'Norman, I'm not sure … eh …'

'C'mon to fuck. Live a little.'

'That's the problem,' said Aesop. 'I'd like to.'

'You dragged us down to see Fungi Aesop, didn't you?'

'There was more than a fifty-fifty chance of us surviving that experience Norman.'

'Don't be such a big blouse, Jimmy?'

'Eh … I s'pose we could go and have a look anyway.'

'Grand. Let's go so. Next left Jimmy …'

Jimmy looked out the windscreen for a minute and then put the car into first. It farted a couple of times and then took off down the road with Aesop already biting his fingernails in the back seat and looking worried. Norman's idea of a good time usually meant doing something that normal people associated with mortal injury. It was always a bad sign when he was excited about an outdoor activity.

THEY PULLED up into the car park and got out. The wind had dropped off and the sun was making an effort, but it was still freezing. Aesop walked between the other few cars that were there and over to a notice board.

'Jaysis. Lads, according to this yoke, Slieve Mish is eight hundred fucking metres high.'

'Yeah,' said Norman. 'Jesus, it's gorgeous here, isn't it? Look at that view. A man could go walking here for a week and never see it from the same angle twice. You can see the rain down in Kilshannig, look. I've a good mind to leave you here and walk home.'

'Right so Jimmy,' said Aesop. 'Back in the car, c'mon.'

'Can you see the sea boiling up down there?'

'Would you ever stop beating your big farmer's chest for a minute,' said Aesop. 'Did you hear what I said?'

'I heard you.'

'Eight hundred metres.'

'Right.'

'Jimmy, I'm assuming that you haven't lost the will to live. Can we just go?'

'Hang on Aesop. I want to have a look at this.'

'But it says …'

'Aesop, I'm pretty sure you don't jump off the top of the mountain and go all the way to the bottom. Come on. We'll see what it's like anyway.'

They started walking up a rocky pathway that curved around a bend in front of them. A half hour later, one which consisted of more leg exercise than either Aesop or Jimmy had had in about ten years, and they finally reached a cabin. They could see the platform about a hundred metres further on, a few people standing around.

'Hi, I'm Shauna,' said a smiling girl at a desk inside the cabin door. 'Welcome to the Mish Mash Experience.'

'Mish Mash? Jaysis ...' said Jimmy, stepping into the room. 'Ooh, it's lovely and warm in here.'

'You guys here to jump? We've just started going again. It was too windy this morning.'

The other two stepped into the cabin behind Jimmy. Aesop went straight over to the electric heater.

'Ah, that's better. Jaysis, you've a little kitchen and everything in here.'

'Yeah. Well we're up here all day,' said the girl. 'So ... three for a jump?'

'Two,' said Aesop.

'Or ... maybe just one,' said Jimmy.

'Don't mind this pair,' said Norman. 'I'll go anyway.'

'Ah, a Cork man. We've had nothing but foreigners today so far. Would you like to see the platform first?'

'No. I'm grand. How high is the drop?'

'Exactly two hundred and ninety-five feet. About a hundred metres.'

'To the ground?'

'Yeah. Although we try and fix it so you don't do the full ton.'

Norman laughed.

'What's the closest you've come?'

'Well, there's no water down there, so around seventy-five is about right before the snap.'

'Sounds cool. How much?'

'Seventy-five euro please.'

'One euro per metre? Sounds fair. Credit card?'

'No problem. And you'll have to sign this disclaimer.'

'Of course.'

Aesop was watching all this, his head going between the girl and Norman.

'Norman?'

'Yeah?'

'Are you off your bleedin' trolley?'

'What?'

'You're going to jump off a cliff with a rubber band tied to your feet?'

'Yeah. Always wanted to do one. It'll be great. Will you not have a go?'

'I will in me brown. Sorry love, but do you get many nutters doing this?'

'Well, we've only been here since the summer. First permanent one in Ireland. There's a few people out there now. Americans they are, or Canadians.'

'Mad foreign bastards.'

'Okay. Well, if you go out to the platform, you'll meet Robbo. He's the boss and he'll sort you out.'

'Grand,' said Norman, striding out of the cabin.

The other two looked at Shauna, who was still smiling.

'Not too late,' she said, waving Norman's disclaimer form.

'Sorry,' said Aesop. 'There's this thing I've to do later on this afternoon and I kind of have to be alive for it.'

She looked at them again, tapping her pen against her cheek.

'Are you … are you guys … ?'

Jimmy nodded.

'Oh brilliant! I thought I knew your face all right? Can I have an autograph?'

'No problem.'

'And can I take a picture on me phone?'

A couple of minutes later, the lads left her beaming at her phone and went out to find Norman. He was talking to Robbo, who was showing him all the gear.

'What do you think?' said Norman when he saw them coming over. He was holding up a big roll of bungee cord and grinning.

'I think you need to sit down and have a cup of tea for yourself and think this through,' said Aesop.

'Did you look over the edge?'

Aesop gripped the railing in front of them and slowly leaned towards it. Then he looked out and down.

'Oh holy Jesus,' he said, leaning back quickly and pushing himself up against the opposite wall.

'Safe as,' said Robbo. Australian accent.

'Safe as what?' said Aesop, still running his hands along the wall behind him for something to grab onto.

'Safe as you like!' said Robbo.

'Me bollocks.'

'You're not jumping?'

'Correct.'

'Mate, what would I have to do to convince you that it's totally safe?'

'Well, you'd have to move the whole fucking thing about two hundred and ninety-four feet closer to the ground for starters. And I still probably wouldn't do it.'

'Come on, ya poof. I have cords for every size. What do you weigh?'

'Twenty-seven stone. Sorry Robbo. It's not going to happen.'

'What about your mate there?'

'Ah …' said Jimmy. 'I don't think so. My insurance wouldn't cover this.'

'Mate, it's all included in the seventy-five euro.'

'Is it? Still …'

He looked over the side and then edged back next to Aesop.

'I don't think so. Did you know there's a sheep down there?'

'That's "Woolly the Jumper". If you can grab a handful of wool, you get your money back.'

'Right. Yeah. Anyone ever done it?'

'Not yet mate.'

'I'll give it a go,' said Norman.

'Norman …' said Jimmy.

'Seriously,' said Norman to Robbo. 'Can you get me that close to her?'

Robbo looked at him.

'I was joking mate.'

'Come on. I can do it.'

'Eh … sorry mate. I can't do that.'

'Ah c'mon to fuck. It'll be a laugh.'

Robbo looked at the other two, but they were staring at Norman.

'Norman,' said Jimmy. 'Don't be fucking stupid. Robbo was only messing.'

'Hey Norman,' said Aesop, pulling cigarettes out of his pocket. 'I'll give you another seventy-five on top of it if you can check whether she's been squeezed.'

'Remember how we established that we only squeeze the boys, Aesop?' said Norman. 'Anyway Jimmy, if you get the measurements right, it should be no problem. That right Robbo?'

'Sorry mate. No facking way. It took me three years to get permission to open this place.'

'Well, can you put me down further than seventy-five metres? Say, eight-five? Ninety?'

'Mate, if you really want to, I'll get you down to eighty metres. That's it.'

'Okay so. That'll do. Lads? Are you sure you won't do it?'

'Positive,' said Jimmy, swallowing. He didn't like being up here in this cage thing. He was already starting to hum a happy tune from his childhood in his head.

'There's a couple of girls over there that are thinking of giving it a go,' said Robbo, pointing over to the other group, twenty metres away and trying on harnesses. 'You don't want to look like a couple of poofs now, do you?'

'I don't mind,' said Aesop, looking around. He frowned. 'Jimmy, is that who I think it is? There can't be more than one raincoat like that in Kerry.'

Jimmy looked over. It was. The guy turned around and they could see his shiny choppers from here.

'Hi guys!' he shouted, and started to come over, waving.

'Hiya,' said Jimmy.

'Going to give it a go? By the way, I'm Bill. I don't think we introduced ourselves on the boat yesterday.'

'Howya Bill. Jimmy. And Aesop.'

'Hi guys. So … you going to jump? It's smaller than the ones I've done before but, hell, a jump is a jump, right?'

Jimmy nodded.

'Speaking of jumps,' said Bill, leaning in and whispering. 'My buddy and I got real lucky last night with two chicks from Sweden. Ya know what I mean?'

Aesop's eyes doubled in size.

'From Sweden?'

'Yeah. Met them in some bar last night. Wow! Talk about a couple of honeys! I don't usually go for blondes but … oh man …'

Aesop looked over. There they were, the Ericsson sisters, laughing with the other two Americans.

'So are you guys going to jump?' said Bill again.

'Eh … yeah. We are,' said Aesop.

'Great! Hey, we should get some pictures together. Come over when you're ready, why doncha.'

They both watched him walk back over to the group.

'You're going to jump now, are you?' said Jimmy.

'I said "we",' said Aesop.

'I heard what you said. And I'm not doing it.'

'What'll we look like if he jumps and we don't?'

'I don't give a fuck what we look like. I wouldn't jump off this mountain if I was bleedin' Spiderman and I'm certainly not doing it just so you can impress some tart.'

'It's not the girl, man. It's that Yank. He thinks he's brilliant. The fucking jump isn't high enough for him now, did you hear that? We're jumping for Ireland here, sure.'

'Ask me arse Aesop. I'm going to watch Norman jump, from a nice safe distance, and then I'm heading back down to the car and getting some lunch. There's a pub down the road with a singing dog according to Norman.'

'Yeah? What does he sing?'

'Who the fuck knows.'

'We'll do that so. But the jump first, yeah?'

'No.'

'Well I'm doing it. Look, come on over to this crowd for a minute. I have to know if he rode them.'

'He said he did, didn't he? One of them anyway.'

'Blokes are full of shit. You have to go to the source.'

'They're hardly going to tell you what they …'

'They won't have to,' said Aesop, walking away.

Jimmy followed him over and Bill introduced them all round. Aesop turned around at one point and gave Jimmy a solemn nod. It seemed that Bill had indeed scored, although Jimmy had no idea how Aesop knew this. He didn't even want to know.

'So,' said Aesop. 'You don't reckon it's high enough?'

'Nah,' said Bill. 'I did a five hundred footer in Costa Rica last year. Now *that* was scary.'

'Jaysis. You should be on the telly.'

'This is only a small one. For kids.'

'And you don't reckon you'll be scared at all? Did you not look over the side? It looked scary to me.'

'Nah. Should be cool. Hey Elina, you want to help me with this thing?'

One of the Swedish girls came up and kissed him before helping him step into his harness. She gave Aesop a nice smile, one hand on her hip and one on Bill's shoulder.

'Hello again,' said Aesop. He cleared his throat. 'Okay, well I'll seeya in a bit, Bill. My mate is itching to go, so we're going to have a look at him first.'

'No problem. We'll see you in five.'

Aesop and Jimmy started walking back over towards Norman.

'Did you see that?' said Aesop. He was fuming, fists clenched. Jimmy had never seen him look so upset.

'See what?'

'Kissing her in front of me and everything. Cheeky fucker … coming over here like that, robbing our women …'

'She's fucking Swedish, Aesop.'

'It doesn't matter. This is *my* turf, Jimmy!'

'What? Your turf? We're in bleedin' Kerry, Aesop. You might as well have stepped out of a fucking spaceship, the head on you.'

'He doesn't even like blondes he said! What does that mean? What's wrong with him? He's just winding me up now, man.'

'Will you give over, Aesop. He doesn't even know you were talking to her last night.'

'Me bollix Jimmy. And anyway, that pair are s'posed to be back in Athlone by now.'

'Maybe he gave her such a good looking-after last night that she didn't want to go back.'

'Ah shut up Jimmy. That's just being rude, now, so it is.'

'You're not really going to do it, are you?'

'Someone has to put manners on the fucker.'

'He doesn't give a shite if you jump or not. How will that teach him manners?'

'He's been rising me for two days, Jimmy. Taking advantage of me when I'm sick on the boat and then when I'm trying to do the right thing by Norman with Helen. Then he's snogging that gorgeous bundle right in front of me, and laughing in me face. And now you want me to let him think I'm a chickeny bastard who won't even jump off a mountain?'

'Look, Aesop, you do what you want. You fuckin' eejit. But I'm not doing it.' They were back at the main platform now. 'Hey Norman, that didn't take long.'

'Sure I've done me share of this kind of thing. The gear's the same.'

'Are you ready to go?'

'Yeah. Robbo, are we ready?'

'Sure Norman. Are you ready?'

'Yeah. Let's go.'

'Okay mate. You need to hop to the edge there. That's right. Until your toes are just over the edge. Don't look down.'

'How will I be able to grab hold of Hilda if I don't look down?'

'Eh …'

'It's grand Robbo. I'm only messing. Okay?'

'Right. Now I'll go one, two, three, BUNGEE! All right? You dive off like you're diving into a pool.'

'Grand. Lads, will you take a picture?'

'Eh …' said Jimmy. 'You mean lean over and …'

'It's okay guys,' said Robbo. 'We have a guy over on that ridge. He'll get some good shots and we can email them on to you, no charge. And then Phil on the winch here will go down and pull you back up.'

Phil gave them a wave. He looked cold and bored.

'Lovely. Can I go so?'

'Wait till I give you the countdown.'

'Okay. Lads, you're not going to see anything from back there.'

Jimmy and Aesop slowly moved to the railing again and clung onto the top of it.

'One … two … three … BUNNNNGEEEEEE …'

Norman let a whoop out of him and executed a beautiful dipping arc before the angle they needed to lean out at to see him became too much for the lads.

'Faaack,' said Robbo. 'Nice dive. Has Norman really not done this before?'

'Eh … well he's done similar stuff,' said Jimmy.

'Facking mad as.'

'Mad as what?' said Aesop from up against the back wall again.

'Mad as you like!' said Robbo.

'Does everyone talk like you in Australia Robbo?' said Aesop.

'Straylia? Faack. I'm a Kiwi, mate. Aussies are poofs!'

'Oh right. Sorry.'

'You poofs going to jump?'

'I'm thinking about it,' said Aesop.

'Beauty. Okay, wait till I get Norman back up here and then I'll go and check on the other guys.'

Phil was already en route down to Norman and a couple of minutes later the two of them appeared at the platform.

'Holy fuck,' said Norman, when he saw the lads. 'That was fucking deadly!'

'You're mental,' said Jimmy, shaking his head.

'Lads you have to do it!'

'Aesop is thinking about it.'

'Good stuff out of you Aesop! You'll love it!'

He detached himself from all the cables, wires and his harness and then thanked Robbo and Phil.

'Man, I'd do that again in a flash. I can't wait to see the pictures.'

'We email them on to you Norman. You left your address with Shauna?'

'Yeah, she has it. Thanks a lot.'

'Right guys, I'm going to check on the others. Aesop, you want to start trying on harnesses there?' He handed him one. 'I reckon this one will do you.'

'Thanks.'

A couple of minutes later Bill and his mates and the girls came over. Only the guys were doing the jump. Bill gave Elina another kiss right in front of Aesop and they both grinned at him. Now even Jimmy was sure that he was taking the piss. She must have said something to Bill about last night. Well, Aesop was the one that decided Helen was more important. He couldn't exactly complain about it now that they were with Bill and his mate, could he? Still, Bill was being a bit of a prick about it.

'How was that?' said Bill.

'You'll love it,' said Norman, still flushed and high as a kite. 'It's a right mad buzz!'

'Thanks man. Pity it's such a lame one though. Still it's for the video blog, right? But I've done much tougher jumps.'

Norman nodded and looked a bit bemused.

'I've done a few meself.'

'Anyway Robbo, let's go. If this is the only Irish bungee, then I guess I might as well do it.'

Once he was all strapped up and ready to go, he bunny-hopped to the edge.

'Well,' said Jimmy to Aesop. 'He's doing it. You're up after him. Does your harness fit?'

'Yeah, it's grand,' said Aesop.

'Are you nervous?'

'Actually Jimmy, I feel strangely calm.'

'I think you're a looper doing this just to prove some stupid point that he probably won't even get anyway.'

'Hey Aesop?' called Bill, turning around from the very edge. 'How do I look?'

'You look brilliant, Bill.'

'Elina? You ready with the video?'

'Yes.'

Aesop pulled out another smoke and lit it up.

Robbo stood with one hand on Bill's back.

'Hey Aesop ...' said Jimmy.

'One, two, three ...' said Robbo.

'Just a second Jimmy,' said Aesop.

'BUNNNGEEEEE ...' yelled Robbo.

Bill leapt into the air, arms out, one hand on top of the other, his body turning into an A-shape, bent at the waist, before he straightened out and hung for a split second right in front of them.

Aesop pulled the smoke out of his mouth, took a step forward and roared.

'No Bill! No! Not yet! Jesus Christ, not yet!!'

But Bill was gone. Screaming and tumbling, his perfectly formed dive a distant memory as his arms and legs tried to flap their way back up to safety and his underpants quickly filled with urine. For a second, that's all anyone could hear. Bill's frantic screams of terror. Then they all turned to Aesop, who was taking off his harness, the smoke back in his mouth so he could use both hands. He looked up.

'Jaysis, I'd say that'll look deadly on his video blog,' he said out of the corner of his mouth.

'Aesop …' said Jimmy and Norman together, mouths open.

'Aw … mate,' said Robbo, shaking his head. 'That was …'

Elina was just looking at him in horror.

'You evil, evil …' said Jimmy.

'Later Jimmy. Listen, I think the best thing to do would be to get the fuck out of here, yeah?'

Norman nodded. He couldn't speak.

'Grand. Well, thanks for everything Robbo,' said Aesop, handing him the harness.

'You … and you're not even going to jump?'

Aesop roared laughing.

'I am in me bollix. I'm going for a pint. Lads? Seeya in the car.'

He took off away from the platform in a half jog. He went straight past the cabin and then stopped and walked back, sticking his head in the door.

'Hey Shauna.'

'Oh. Hi Aesop. You want to jump now?'

'Nah. Listen, did I see a … ah. There it is. Will you do me a favour Shauna?'

'Of course.'

'HOW MUCH is that doggie in the window?' sang the man with the guitar.

'Woof woof!' went the little mutt.

'The one with the waggly tail …'

'Woof woof!'

The lads were breaking their bollocks laughing.

Four miles back up the road, Bill had recovered sufficiently so that his shaking legs were able to carry him slowly to the cabin to pick up his keys and phone from the basket. He was dazed, dishevelled, queasy and very uncomfortable. He'd never relieved himself upside-down before and gravity had made shite of his t-shirt. Tear marks still stained his cheeks.

'Hi Bill,' said Shauna, all sweet and innocence. 'Your mate Aesop told me you'd want this.'

Bill looked down at the saucer she was holding out.

'I have butter and marmalade, but he said you preferred it dry?'

Chapter Sixteen

'OKAY MUPPET,' said Norman, standing over Aesop the next day. 'Two things ...'

'What?' said Aesop through the chocolate bikkie in his mouth. He'd been flicking through an old Hello magazine on the armchair.

'You've to call Trish tonight and say sorry.'

'Ah Norman ...'

'You said you would ages ago and you haven't yet. You have to Aesop.'

'She's probably forgotten all about it.'

'She has in her arse. After dinner you give her a call. Okay? And you're to apologise properly, you hear me? I don't want any of your bollocks-acting on the phone. You're to ...'

'Okay okay. I'll bleedin' call her. And?'

'And it's your turn to make the dinner.'

'Me?!'

'Yes, Aesop. You're making the dinner. You think we're all going to be waiting on you hand and foot for the rest of your life? There's no women here now for you to *plámás* into feeding and watering you.'

'But ... but we had that big feed at lunchtime. Are you hungry again already, you big gorilla?'

'Who's stuffing his face with rubbish in front of me? It's five o'clock now. What are we having? You don't have to go mad. I'll go out to the shop now and get whatever you need. Check the fridge there.'

'But Norman ...'

'Go on.'

Aesop sighed and walked over to the fridge.

'Jesus, it's packed.'

'Grand. So what are we having?'

'Hang on a minute.'

Aesop rooted around in there, pushing things aside so he could get a good look at his options. He held up a plastic bag.

'What's this?'

'Lettuce.'

'Lettuce. Right. And how does that work?'

'Come on Aesop, it's frosting up out there already.'

'All right, all right. Okay. I think we have everything. Will you just get some salad cream? Not mayonnaise or anything. Proper salad cream I need, right?'

'What are we having?'

'A surprise.'

'Right. Is that it?'

'Yeah. That should cover it. Get some smokes too. And we're out of beer.'

'Okay. Give me money.'

'I've to pay for it too?'

'That's the rules.'

'Fuck sake. Okay. Here ...'

'Grand. I'll see you in a bit. Jimmy, do you need anything?'

'What?' Jimmy was on the couch with his guitar, doing his warm-up exercises. 'No. No I'm grand thanks. Or, actually, will you get some Ribena? I don't want to get a cold with the tour coming up.'

'No problem.'

Norman grabbed his coat and went to the door. The whole roof seemed to shift and creak when he opened it and stepped outside.

'Christ, there's a fair wind coming up,' he said, pulling up his collar and closing the door after him.

The lads could hear his heavy footsteps walking to the car.

'So what's for dinner then?' said Jimmy, looking over.

'I'm going to make me signature dish.'

'I didn't know you had one.'

'It's bleedin' magic. Wait till you see. What are you playing there?'

'Ah, I'm just practising. A few scales and modes. Good for the fingers. This is a Dorian mode. Y'see, the Dorian mode comes from a minor scale ...'

Aesop held up his hand.

'Hang on a minute Jimmy. Will we wait till Norman comes back before you explain? Because maybe he gives a bollocks.'

'Nothing wrong with learning a bit of theory, Aesop.'

'Ah, it's all a load of me arse. Who gives a wank about the difference between diatonic scales and minor scales and all that bollocks?'

'The minor scale is a diatonic scale, Aesop.'

'Well I managed to become a rockstar without knowing that or giving a flying fuck, didn't I? So it can't be that important.'

'Whatever, Aesop. But the Dorian mode is one of the …'

'I knew a Doreen once. She was good for the fingers. But, Christ, she'd some gob on her.'

'At least you remember her name.'

'It's buried in me brain! She had this mad habit of talking to herself as you were lashing into her. Mental. I mean, I'm all on for a girl knowing what she wants in the leaba, but … well, it's only manners to direct it at the bloke that's on top of her, right? But this one used to be cheering herself on. "That's it … good girl Doreen … come on Doreen … oh, oh, we nearly had it that time … come on pet, that's it, we'll get the next one … concentrate now, Doreen …" You'd swear she was coming for Ireland, the scrunched-up head on her, and didn't want to disappoint the folks back home. Sure I was getting all caught up in it too, nearly joining in and everything, just to wish her all the best. After about an hour she told me to wait a minute, and disappeared out of the room. I thought she was going to come back in with a plate of oranges for fuck sake. But she was just changing her frillies. "It works better when I'm wearing this one," she says. Bleedin' spacer. It took another hour. I swear, by the time she got there I didn't know whether to give her a kiss or a medal.'

Jimmy laughed.

'Gold?'

'Jaysis yeah. After all that? Fuck sake, I spent the next week waiting for an invitation to the Mansion House.'

'So c'mere. Are you going to phone Trish?'

'Yeah. Jesus, I have to, don't I? He'll go fuckin' spare if I don't. But what are you s'posed to do in a situation like this.'

'A situation like this? Aesop, this is a unique situation. Look, just talk to her. The longer you leave it, the harder it'll be.'

'But what am I meant to say to her?'

'Just tell her the truth. Tell her you're a fuckin' eejit.'

'She knows that.'

'But she wants to hear it from you, doesn't she? Just do it and then Norman will chill out and I won't have to be fucking mortified the next time I see her.'

'Yeah. I s'pose. But I don't care what anyone says, she was acting all fucked up that night.'

'As opposed to your own performance?'

'She gave me the willies, man.'

'Well I'm pretty sure she'll be careful not to do that again. Now will you try not to talk for the next twenty minutes so I can finish this?'

'Ah play something else Jimmy. Scales are boring.'

'I have to do them for me tendonitis, don't I? Go and start the dinner or something.'

'It doesn't take that long. I'll wait till Norman gets back. Go on. Play something cool.'

'Like what?'

Aesop grinned.

'Do "Cat Scratch Fever"!'

'What? Fuck off! On an acoustic?'

'Yeah, come on. I'll sing. For the craic.'

Jimmy laughed.

'Okay. Okay. I'll give it a go … hang on a minute till I get a key for you. And c'mere, if I get a blister trying to bend these strings, you're dead.'

'You won't. C'mon.'

Aesop watched Jimmy work it out and start the intro. This was brilliant. This was how they'd started, all those years ago. Two fuckin' eejits and a guitar. Aesop watched Jimmy effortlessly find the right chords and notes. He probably hadn't played this song in years but it was right there, like he'd written it himself only yesterday. How the fuck did he do it? Aesop had no idea. He loved the guitar, but he was shite at it. Compared to Jimmy anyway. The drums were easy. He couldn't remember a time when he wasn't able to play whatever he wanted on them. But Jimmy … Aesop would never be so gay as to actually admit it, even to himself, but he thought Jimmy was fucking deadly.

AESOP BROUGHT two big dinner plates over to the kitchen table, where the other two were waiting with something approaching trepidation. He held them up in the air over them.

'Are yis ready?'

'We're ready. Come on, will you? I'd eat a scabby babby through a tennis racquet.'

'Right, here ya go.'

He plonked the two plates down on the table with a big grin.

'Tuck in lads.'

They looked at the plates in front of them and then up at each other.

'Sandwiches?' said Norman.

'Yep.'

'We're having sandwiches for our dinner?'

'Not just sandwiches, Norman. My special sandwiches.'

'What's in them?' said Jimmy, picking one up.

'Ah ah!' said Aeosp. 'No looking. You have to close your eyes and tell me what's in them.'

Norman had a sandwich in his hand now too.

'Close your eyes!' said Aesop again.

'You're not taking the piss now?' said Jimmy. 'There's not fucking ash from the fire or something in them, is there?'

'No! I'm telling you, they're bleedin' gorgeous. I came up with the recipe when I moved into the new gaff and had to start feeding meself.'

'Are you sure?' said Norman. 'Cos if I break a tooth or something … I'm telling you …'

'Will you relax? Okay. Eyes closed? Right. What do you think?'

They both took bites out of their sandwiches.

'Aesop …'

'Eyes closed Jimmy!'

'They are closed.'

'What do you taste?'

'Salad cream.'

'And?'

'Onions.'

'And?'

'That's all I fuckin' taste Aesop. Salad cream and onions.'

'And salt?'

'Eh … I s'pose. Maybe.'

Norman opened his eyes as he swallowed the first bite.

'Aesop, are you after making salad cream sandwiches for the dinner?'

'You don't like them?'

'Fuck sake … you useless prick.'

'They're bleedin' gorgeous! What's the matter with you?'

'How is this dinner?'

'I eat this all the time!'

'Well that would explain the pasty face of you. Jesus, there's half a bloody pig in the fridge and cheese and eggs and all kinds of stuff for a proper salad, and this is what you serve up to us? And you wasted a whole sliced pan on them too, you fucking langer.'

They'd both thrown down their sandwiches at this stage and were looking up at Aesop.

'Lads this is gourmet shit, I'm telling you …' he said.

'It's not, Aesop. It's just shit,' said Norman.

He stood up and went to the fridge, pulling out the huge leg of ham and getting a chopping board and knife.

'What are you doing?' said Aesop.

'I'm making proper sandwiches.'

'But you'll ruin them.'

'Aesop, has anyone – anyone in your life – given you salad cream sandwiches for dinner.'

'I eat them every day! Twice a day if there's no beans in the house.'

'Do you never eat fruit or vegetables?'

'What do you call onions?'

'Fuck sake. Jimmy, do you want some of this?'

'Please Norman.'

'Right. Do you, you fucking eejit, while I'm cutting it?'

'No! I'm grand with the salad cream.'

'This doesn't get you out of making meals, Aesop. And you better start coming up with some new recipes or there'll be trouble in this house, I'm telling you. And you can do the dishes and put everything away after you talk to Trish.'

'Who put you in charge, you big bullying bastard?'

'Dónal did.'

'You're only getting paid to make sure no one kills me.'

'And you're making me earn it too, aren't you? Blowing kisses at Davey and winding me up about Helen, making that poor American lad cry like that …'

'Well … you don't have to go around slagging the dinner I made for you.'

'Oh, you're going to start sulking now, are you? We're the ones who should be sulking Aesop, and the stomachs hanging out of us with the hunger at half past seven. Salad cream sandwiches …'

'Well, if it's such a stupid idea, why did they write it on the bottle then?'

Aesop went over to the fridge, found the bottle and pulled it out, clearing his throat and reading.

'See? It says it right here. "Perfect for Sandwiches". Where do you think I came up with the idea?'

Norman turned back to the chopping board.

'Do you know the aerial sticking out of the roof of my van, Aesop?'

'Yeah.'

'Well, will you ever go out and hang your bollocks on it?'

'YEAH … yeah, he is … no, he's doing the dishes. Okay … okay … here he is.'

Norman handed the phone to Aesop, who was standing there with a teacloth and a wet plate. Aesop gave him one more pleading look, but Norman just frowned and jerked the phone at him. Aesop mouthed the word 'fucker' at him and took it.

'Eh … hello?' he said.

'Hello.'

'It's Aesop.'

'Yeah, I know. How are you, Aesop?'

'I'm grand. How are you?'

'Okay.'

'Listen, I … I … eh … hang on a minute …'

He took the phone away from his face.

'What are you two fuckers looking at?'

Jimmy laughed and started playing the guitar again. Norman turned away and started to put away the dishes.

'Sorry about that.'

'That's okay. What can I do for you?'

'Well, for starters, you can tell me that you weren't hurt when I … did that awful thing that time in my gaff.'

'You mean physically?'

'Yeah.'

'I wasn't. It was mostly milk, sure.'

'Really? Oh. Well anyway, the other thing you can do is tell me that you forgive me for being a total muppet. I'm so fucking sorry I scared you like that. I was a bit on edge that night and I don't know what I was thinking. I was all …'

'Aesop, it's fine.'

'Really?'

'Really. Don't worry about it. Norman told me that there's been someone following you. I suppose I can see how that might … get you all uptight.'

'Ah, thanks Tracy. You're very good.'

'Trish.'

'Oh fuck, yeah. Sorry. Trish.'

'Anyway, is he looking after you down there?'

'He is, yeah. Sure I'm no trouble anyway. Isn't that right Norman?'

Norman just raised his eyes to heaven.

'We went to see Fungi yesterday.'

'Yeah, Norman said that. How was he?'

'Well, I didn't actually see him meself. I had a bit of food poisoning and the boat was terrible rough. Every time I tried to look over the side, I kind of . . . puked.'

'Oh. That's a pity. You should go again. Hey, I'll be down home in Sneem next week. Maybe we can hook up and go together?'

'Yeah, deadly. I'm not sure if Norman wants to go again though. He's seen him loads of times. And Jimmy's hopeless. He's got no interest in aquatic mammals.

'Well, we can go and see Fungi just the two of us then. I haven't seen him in years.'

'Eh, yeah. Great. Well anyway, I don't want to keep you. I just wanted to say sorry for wrecking your dress and giving you a fright. Can I pay for the cleaning?'

'Not at all. Sure it just needed a soaking. It's not the first time, believe me. You have to get used to it in my job.'

'Right. Ah, listen, thanks very much for not giving me shit over it.'

'Forget about it Aesop. I already have. Hey, do I hear Ted Nugent in the background?'

'Yeah! Jesus. That's Jimmy messing. How do you know Ted Nugent?'

'Sure don't I have two big brothers? Mad rockers they were, when I was growing up.'

Aesop laughed.

'Yeah, me and Jimmy were just messing about earlier on the guitar.'

'Cool. Well anyway Aesop, just forget about what happened before. Okay?'

'Thanks. Well, look, how about I buy you and Norman dinner then? Can I do that at least?'

'You don't have to, Aesop. Really.'

'Ah, I want to. Just to say sorry properly. Please?'

'Well … okay. If you like. But … Aesop?'

'Yeah?'

'I … I was kind of hoping for a chance to see you alone. I want to just have a chat with you about something. In private, like.'

'You want to … eh …'

Aesop changed the phone to the other ear and lowered his voice.

'You want …'

'How about you buy just me and you dinner instead? Just the two of us? Or we could even meet somewhere? No need to mention it to Norman. He can be a bit … y'know …'

Aesop swallowed and looked around. Jimmy was de-tuning to play some Foo Fighters and Norman was poking at the fire.

Fuck. This wasn't good.

He moved towards the bedroom quietly and went in, closing the door behind him.

'Just us?' he said. 'And … what do you want to talk about?'

'I'd rather just meet with you. If that's okay? There's something I want to show you. Or … well, give you.'

Aesop's head was whizzing. What the fuck did that mean? Did she want to ride him again? Or … or …

'Is it the picture from the Baggot? Because you can do that any time. You don't have to go out of your way or …'

'No, it's not that. But it's something to do with it all right.'

'Sounds very mysterious.'

Aesop tried a little laugh. Jesus, he was getting a headache. Why couldn't this mad tart just leave him alone?

'God,' he said. 'We don't want Norman to get jealous, do we? Ha ha …'

OUT IN the living room, Norman turned away from the fire.

'Where's he gone?'

'I think he's in the bedroom.'

'What's he in there for? Is he finished talking to her? Where's me phone?'

'I don't know.'

Norman stood up and looked at the table and the counter. No phone.

What was he gone into the bedroom for? What were they talking about?

He went over to the door and listened. He could hear Aesop talking in there, but he couldn't make out what he was saying. He was practically whispering. What the fuck?

Suddenly Norman could feel it. Like a bit of bread he'd swallowed before it was properly chewed, stuck in his gullet. He felt it like a faint nausea that hit the pit of his belly and started to move through him until he could nearly taste it in the back of his throat. Jealousy didn't feel green to Norman. It was a roaring, thumping red. It was a blazing inferno. It was a vicious storm on the ocean. It was a boiling cauldron of something that twisted and squirmed, and it mocked him. He stepped away from the door and took a big slow breath.

'More tea Jimmy?'

'Hmm? Yeah, okay. Is it after getting a bit chilly in here?'

'I put another log on the fire. It'll catch in a minute.'

'Grand so.'

'Oh, I got coffee earlier. Coffee?'

'Lovely. I'll have a Wagon Wheel too if Aesop didn't eat them all.'

'Yeah, there's a couple left.'

'Is he still talking to Trish?'

'He must be.'

'Jaysis. Is that a good thing or is she reading him the riot act?'

'Don't know.'

'I hope she's giving him a right bollo ...'

Jimmy didn't get to finish. There was a sudden roaring scream from the bedroom.

'*Arrghhh! Arrgh!! Jesus fucking … argghhh!! Hoh-leeeee fuuuuuuck!*'

A crashing sound followed by another quick bout of swearing exploded through the house.

'What the fu … ?'

Jimmy and Norman's faces were locked onto each other for a split second and then Norman dropped the kettle onto the floor and before Jimmy could even register what was happening, he was at the bedroom door. He slammed down on the handle, but the door wouldn't budge. There was another bang from inside.

'*Arggh*! Help! Help! *Norman*!!'

'Aesop, what's going on?'

'There's a … a … ah Jesus! *Quick*!'

'Oh fuck,' said Norman. He rattled the handle again and when it didn't move he took a step back.

'*Norman*!'

'I'm coming Aesop. Hang on …'

'Jesus fucking Christ! Norman! *Arggh* …'

The screaming was becoming more and more high-pitched and frantic and then Norman could hear one more crash and Aesop scrabbling at the door on the other side.

'It won't … it's … it won't …'

'Stand back.'

'What?'

'Get back from the door Aesop.'

Norman shifted backwards again and then propelled his body into the heavy old timber. It exploded into the room. Before he even had a chance to get his bearings, a figure pushed past him, through the kitchen and out the front door. Footsteps pounded on the gravel outside and then faded into the night. Norman straightened up and looked around. The room was empty. He looked at the window. It was closed. Under the bed. Nothing.

'He's gone!' he said, looking out at Jimmy, who was now clutching his knees and his guitar to his chest, completely white on the couch.

Jimmy nodded.

'He just ran out the door. Who the fuck is in there?'

'No one.'

'At all?'

'No one. Look …'

Jimmy got to his feet very slowly and put his guitar down. He grabbed the poker from the fire and peeked around what was left of the doorframe. Norman pulled the wardrobe open, Jimmy standing by ready to split anyone that might be hiding in there, but that was empty too.

'What the fuck?'

The both went back out to the kitchen. The only sound now was the wind howling in the front door.

'Where did he go?' said Jimmy.

'Come on.'

Norman led them out to the garden. There was no sign of Aesop.

'Can you see him?'

'Maybe he's hiding.'

'Aesop?' called Norman. 'Aesop, where are you?'

Nothing. It was hard to hear anyway with the whistling and banging from the wind.

'Aesop!' shouted Jimmy. 'Aesop!'

'Out here!'

It was faint, but it was coming from the road. They walked out through the gate and saw a shadowy figure standing about thirty metres down the road. It waved.

'Is he gone?'

'Who?' said Norman. 'Come back for fuck sake. Is who gone? There's no one in there.'

'Are you sure?'

'Will you come over here, Aesop. What the fuck happened?'

Aesop started to walk towards them. He was shivering, dressed in only a t-shirt and jeans, no shoes and his arms wrapped around him. But he didn't look like a man who was in the process of being butchered alive, which is exactly what he'd sounded like two minutes before.

'Is he gone?'

'Who? Who was in there, man?'

'Did you go right into the room?'

'Yes!'

'He must have run out past you.'

'Who? You were the only one who ran out.'

Aesop stopped at the doorway and looked in.

'Gimme that poker,' he said to Jimmy.

Jimmy handed it to him.

'Okay. Nice and slow.'

'Please Aesop,' said Norman, when they were in the living room again with the front door shut. He wiped the sweat off his face, even though the house was cold now. 'Jesus, you're after scaring the shite out of us. What the fuck happened?'

'A fucking big badger was in there.'

'A what?'

'Badger. I was talking to Trish and it just ran out from under the bed. I nearly fucking died.'

Jimmy let a huge sigh out of him and sat down on the couch again. For fuck sake.

'A badger?' said Norman, looking at the splintered door into the bedroom. 'Is that all, you prick?'

'Yeah.'

'A fucking badger?'

'Yes, Norman!'

'In February?'

'Would you fuck off? I know what I saw.'

'Aesop, badgers don't be running about the place in February.'

'Well someone needs to tell this fucker, because he was running around that bedroom a minute ago.'

'You made me break a hundred-year-old door off its hinges because of a small little furry animal?'

'Little? It was like a fat hairy child with a tail!'

Norman walked over to the bedroom.

'You fucking langer.' He had his arms out in front of him.

'Look what you made me do! I thought you were being attacked in there!'

'I was! He came running out from under the bed, ran across me feet before I could even shit my pants, and then he started doing laps of the room and screeching.'

'The only screeching I heard was from you. It was like a pig being slaughtered.'

Jimmy looked over.

'Jesus, Aesop, you fucking scared the crap out of us.'

'How do you think I bleedin' felt?'

'Are you sure it was a badger?' said Norman.

'What?'

'Did it have a stripey head?'

'Did it have a stripey head? I was running for me life, Norman, not giving the cunt a shampoo.'

'The door was locked. What did you lock the door for?'

'I must have knocked the stupid fucking culchie latch thing down when I was trying to get out. Why can't you have proper doors?'

'And what were you doing in the room in the first place? Could you not talk to Trish out here?'

'I ... well ... Jimmy was playing the guitar and I couldn't hear her properly.'

Norman turned around again, shaking his head.

'Look at the fucking door!'

Aesop looked.

'You're after wrecking your Granny's door Norman,' he said.

'Am I?'

'Your Ma's going to batter you.'

'We'll have to get it fixed. Fuck ye anyway.'

'And where am I meant to sleep tonight?'

Norman pointed into the room.

'In there. Why?'

'I am in my fuck.'

'What?'

'With that fucking thing on the loose?'

'He's gone.'

'I don't give a wank. I'm not sleeping in there.'

'Aesop, he's gone.'

'You show me his twitching corpse, and I'll sleep in there tonight.'

'He must have …'

Norman bent over and looked under the bed again.

'There. There's a hole in the floorboard. That's where he got in. Look …'

Aesop leaned over very carefully.

'See?' said Norman. 'Up against the wall …'

'No. He didn't come in there.'

'How do you know?'

'Sure that hole is only two inches across.'

'Well that brings me onto the other thing I was going to say. It wasn't a badger, Aesop. It was a mouse. And it wasn't the size of a child either. It was the size of a mouse.'

'My bouncy bollocks it was.'

'Aesop, you're a dozy prick and you're paying for that door.'

'I didn't break it, did I?'

'You scared the living daylights out of all of us, and it's your fault the door is broken. Look at the face of poor Jimmy still. Come on, look at him …'

Norman led Aesop back into the kitchen and pointed over to the couch.

'Look at him! He's fit to puke with the fright you gave us. And I thought I'd be going back to Dónal with you in a casket. Fuck sake. *And* the mess on the floor as well. I dropped the fucking kettle too, with you, you fool. What if it had been boiled already?'

He sat on the armchair and ran his hands over his head.

'Christ. I'll have to talk to Mikey Pat about the door and … where's me phone?'

'Your phone?'

'Yeah. Give it to me and I'll call him now to see if he has any timber or will I have to drive to Millstreet.'

'I … eh … I think I left it in the room.'

'Well get it so.'

'Norman?'

'Yes Aesop?'

'It might be broken.'

'What?'

'I kind of threw it at the badger.'

'You what?'

'I threw it at the badger. I nearly got him! But he … well, he ducked and …'

'Where's my phone Aesop?'

Aesop went into the bedroom again.

'Norman?' he called.

'Yeah?'

'It doesn't look good.'

'Jesus.'

Norman got up and went into the bedroom. Aesop was pointing at a mess of broken plastic in the corner.

'Man, can you imagine if I'd hit him? He'd have been fucked. Look at the state of it!'

'You total bastard Aesop. I only got that last month. It's one of the new …'

He stopped picking up pieces of it and looked around at Aesop, frowning.

'You were still on the phone when the mouse ran out from under the bed?'

'Badger. Yeah. We were just chatting, like.'

'And what happened then? Did you say goodbye?'

'Say goodbye? No. Sure I nearly pissed me pants! I started yelling and … oh. I see your point.'

'So you're telling me that you're in the middle of a phone call to Trish, apologising for scaring her the last time you spoke to her, and then this mouse appears and you lose your fucking mind? *Again*?'

'Maybe … maybe it didn't sound so bad over the phone?'

'Aesop, me and Jimmy thought you were being flayed alive! At what point in the proceedings did you throw the phone at the mouse?'

'Badger. Right before you broke the door down. I was too freaked out before that to do anything except jump up and down.'

'So one minute she's shooting the breeze, everything's cool, and the next minute all she hears is you screaming and yelling for help. That's all she hears. She doesn't know it's only a mouse you saw. All she gets is a load of roaring and bangs and crashes and my name being shouted. All this and then the phone goes dead from you hopping it off the wall? Is that what you're telling me happened? Is it? Aesop, is that a fair fucking description of the course of events?'

'Well ... except that it was a badger, and ...'

'I don't care if it was a charging fucking elephant! You're after doing it again, aren't you? Christ, what did that girl ever do to you? What did I ever do to you that you can't just let me have a girlfriend for a change?'

'I ... I didn't mean to frighten her again, Norman. It was ... the badger's fault.'

'Jesus man, are you trying to put the poor girl in therapy, is it? I have to call her.'

He looked at the bits of phone he'd put on the bed.

'It's fucked, look,' he said.

'Use my phone,' said Aesop.

'And what number will I call?'

'You don't know it?'

'Who remembers numbers any more, you langer? It was on the phone, sure!'

'Is it not on the little card?'

'No! I put them all onto the phone when I was swapping over from the old one. I've a whole new card and everything. There's nothing on it at all!'

'Sorry man. I don't know what to do so.'

'There's nowhere open to even drive to at this hour to send her an email!'

'Sure who reads emails at this hour?'

'What are we going to do? She thinks we've all been murdered by your fucking stalker!'

Norman sat on the bed next to the smashed phone, his head in his hands.

Aesop stood there, trying to think of something to say.

'Well …' he said eventually. 'Well, at least the badger didn't spray the place with that smelly stuff they shoot out of their arses.'

Norman just shook his head.

'Christ, will you go away from me now, Aesop, will you? Before I do something terrible to you.'

Chapter Seventeen

JIMMY WOKE up to Norman knocking on the door.

'Jimmy? You awake? I'm going over to Mikey Pat about the timber. You want to get up and get the breakfast going?'

'Yeah. Yeah. What time is it?'

'Half eight.'

'Right.'

'I'll be back in half an hour.'

'Grand.'

'Tell Aesop to set the fire.'

'Yeah. Seeya.'

'Good luck.'

Jimmy heard him go out the front door and then the van started up. He lay there with his eyes closed, frowning when he stretched and smacked one foot off the wall. Bloody bunk bed. This was the room where Norman's young cousins slept and since he was the last one to arrive, he was stuck here. He'd forgotten to close the curtains and the sun was coming right in the window. The wind last night must have blown all the clouds away. There was no sound at all in the house. Not even in his head. The few days off hadn't done much yet to set a spark to any of the latent music he hoped was buried in him somewhere. He'd had a laugh last night playing a few of his old favourites with Aesop, but his own holy well was still bone dry.

He tried to stretch again in the cramped little single bed and got a sudden feeling of having lost his bearings. Like vertigo. Like the room was spinning. It wasn't right. The bed seemed to be moving on its own or something. Earthquake? He opened his eyes and was greeted by the sight of two white legs and a bollocks hanging off the top bunk and dangling right in front of his face.

'Jesus!' he shouted, pulling his head back and lashing it off the wall. 'Aw …'

'Morning Jimmy.'

'What the fuck are you doing up there?'

204

'Well, I couldn't sleep in the other room. And I thought, hey, maybe badgers can't climb, so …'

'Me fuckin' head.'

'What?'

'I'm after banging me … will you either get up or down off that bunk? Do you think that's what I want to see first thing in the morning when I open me eyes?'

'Am I near the ground? There's no ladder on this yoke.'

'Yeah. Just get down, you fucking tool.'

Aesop dropped onto the floor and walked over to the window.

'It's nice this morning, isn't it?'

'Lovely. Any chance you could put a pair of jocks on? And get away from the window before someone sees you.'

'Who's going to see me out here?'

'Well I don't want to see you. Put some clothes on.'

Aesop turned around.

'They're in the other room.'

'Well fuck off and get them then. And Norman says that you're to … what are you after doing to yourself?'

'What?'

'Did you shave your … self?'

Aesop looked down.

'Ah yeah. Sure that's all the rage now. Chicks don't dig foliage these days, Jimmy. You need to take a trimmers across the chest, and then from the belly button down to the bean bag. And that's a special job in itself. Do you not do it?'

Jimmy just stared at him. Aesop came over, grinning.

'Do you not do it?'

He started grabbing at Jimmy quilt.

'Give us a look.'

'Go away Aesop.'

'Ah c'mon. Show us your bush Jimmy.' He had a fistful of quilt now and was trying to yank it away.

'Will you … stop … will you fuck off, Aesop? Go away …'

'Just a quick look …'

'No! Fuck off. I don't shave, only me face.'

'You dirty big ape. Women are mad for shaved minges now on blokes. Sure they're all doing it themselves and everything. It feels deadly man. Well, once you keep doing it. Cos if you let it come back … aw man, the itchies will drive you up the wall. You should try it. But, c'mere, make sure and grab a hold of your balls up and out of the way when you're doing your hole, right? You don't want to catch them, I'm telling you.'

Jimmy still had his quilt wrapped around both hands and pulled up to his chin.

'Thanks. Will you go and get dressed now? And you've to set the fire, Norman says.'

'Yeah yeah. But do you want to borrow me trimmers? I swear, Jessie will be down on you like a felled tree. I have it with me. Do you want to try it?'

'No.'

'Are you sure?'

'After you shaving your hole with it? I'm grand, thanks.'

'But Jessie …'

'I've never even met Jessie, Aesop. Is that how I should introduce meself to her? Walk up, stick her hand down me pants and tell her I heard she likes them glossy?'

Aesop looked off to one side for a minute.

'I don't think she'd like that, Jimmy. She'd probably rather just … happen upon them, y'know? In her own time, like.'

'If you don't put jocks on right now, Aesop, I'm telling Norman you slept in the kids' bed in the complete nip.'

'What's wrong with that?'

'Do you want to see if Norman thinks there's anything wrong with it?'

'Eh … no. Not really. He's already pissed off at me over last night. Jaysis. He's like eggshells these days.'

Aesop moved to the door.

'Don't forget the fire.'

'What's for breakfast? I can't eat any more eggs. I think I'm after making meself allergic.'

'Fruit salad. We're in training from now on, Aesop. The tour's in less than a month.'

'Do we have any papayas?'

'Papayas? In Cork? In the middle of winter? Of course we do. Isn't there a field of papaya trees next door. Go out and pick a few and I'll throw them in.'

'I do like papayas. Ever since Thailand. Remember that? You never see them here.'

'It's far from fucking papayas you were rared.'

'I used to love the way they were all juicy and …'

'Aesop …' said Jimmy, pointing. 'Jocks? Please? Go away and let me get dressed and then I'll see what exotic delicacies from the Far East Norman picked up with the salad cream last night.'

'IS HE still out there?' said Aesop from the couch. 'Is he not freezing?'

Jimmy was doing the dishes and could see out the window.

'Yeah. Actually, I think he's enjoying himself. I asked him could we help, but he just said he was grand. And that you'd only get in the way.'

'How does he know how to make a door anyway?'

'Ah, Norman learned all kinds of stuff in the army.'

'Oh that's what they do in the army, is it? Ah, right. Well that's good. I was worried that if we were ever in a war we'd have to make do with guns and tanks and helicopters. But woodworking skills … Jaysis, that can be the difference between defending our borders against invasion and all of us having to learn Swahili.'

'We're going to be invaded by Uganda, are we?'

'You can't trust them Ugandans, Jimmy. South American bastards …'

'Anyway, wasn't Norman in Turkey that time? Remember when they had to help rebuilding a village or something after the earthquake? Villages need doors.'

'I don't remember that.'

207

'He was gone for four months, Aesop.'

'Ah, I could never keep up with the mad places that fucker used to go. I only remember the ones where he brought me back a pressie.'

'Well anyway, he's grand out there, look. It nearly looks like a door already.'

'Will we go out and take the piss out of him? He's far too happy out there with his hammer and his bucket of nails. C'mon …'

Aesop walked out the door and Jimmy saw him through the window lighting up a smoke and saying something to Norman and Norman giving him the finger back.

His phone rang. Dónal.

'Heya man, what's the story?' said Jimmy. 'Were you able to get hold of Norman's bird?'

'Yeah, no problem. She was in the book, so I just called her and told her that everything was grand and no one was hurt or anything.'

'Brilliant. I'll tell Norman. She must have been freaked out, was she?'

'Well, when I told her who I was she went a bit quiet. I think she's a bit suspicious about anything to do with Aesop at this stage. A mouse was it?'

'So Norman reckons. He didn't see it, but I'd still take his word for it over Aesop.'

'He's some gobshite.'

'Stop. You should have seen him. You'd swear Norman's Granny was back from the grave and chasing him around the room.'

'Well Trish sounded okay after a bit. She's working this afternoon she said, but I gave her your number so that she can ring when she gets a minute.

'Cheers man.'

'No problem. So anyway, how's Cork. Relaxing?'

'As much as it can be with Aesop around. Do you miss me?'

'I do, yeah. But c'mere, I've a job for us.'

'What's that?'

'We need to go to London. All of us.'

'For what?'

'Senturion want to start talking about extending the contract. They've a few ideas on the marketing side, and they said they want the bass-player thing sorted out too. And they want to talk about America. Plus, we sent over the Leet EP and they're interested in that as well. Oh, and before I forget, I got a mail from Shiggy.'

'Yeah, he mailed me too. He's in Dublin next week for work.'

'Well, we'll see what Senturion have to say and then we can talk to him.'

'Cool. So, when do we need to go?'

'I'm thinking Thursday. Can you get back here? Or you could just fly straight from Cork or Shannon if you want and I'll meet you there. Up to you.'

'Well we'll see what the craic is. All of us … you mean Aesop too?'

'Yeah. We should all get together in the same room. If it's contract stuff, he should be in on it. Anyway, it'd be good for him to meet everyone. He's only met the head honchos once.'

'Okay, I'll tell him.'

'Will you ask Norman to come too? Maybe he can keep the other bollocks out of trouble.'

'I don't know if anyone can do that Dónal. But he's probably our best bet all right. Right. That's grand so. I'll book flights for Thursday morning?'

'Grand. I'll email you the details and the hotel and all.'

'Cool. All the best, man.

'Jimmy, before you go, there's something else … eh …'

Jimmy caught something in his voice.

'What's up Dónal?'

'You and that girl in London … Susan, right?'

'Yeah. But I don't think that's happening any more. I talked to her a few days ago and I think she's had enough. Wasn't a happy camper.'

'Oh. Right. Did she say why?'

'No. Not really. She sounded pissed off though. Wasn't like her.

I s'pose it just sunk in that being with me was going to be a pain in the arse. With the band and all, y'know? She probably had the hump that she'd been wasting her time. It's a bit of a … what about her anyway?'

'Jimmy, I … I think I know what her problem might have been.'

'What? What are you talking about?'

'You know we have that clippings company working for us?'

'Yeah.'

'Well this morning they sent me all the latest reviews and stuff for the album, the tour dates, all that, right?'

'Yeah.'

'So they sent me a clip from one of the English papers.'

Jimmy was getting uneasy now. He sat down at the kitchen table.

'Yeah.'

'Jimmy there's a photo of you in there. With Aesop's sister.'

'Jennifer? From where?'

'I don't know. I think it was just after the Vicar Street gig. You have your arm around her and she's kind of reaching up to kiss you.'

'What the fuck?! She was just thanking me for "More Than Me". Marco was right next to her!'

'Yeah, but he's not in the shot. And the caption … eh …'

'Oh fuck. What about the caption, Dónal?'

'Well, it kind of says …'

'Yeah?'

'Will I just read it to you?'

'Yeah.'

'It says … "Collins' new friend".'

'Jesus …'

'Friend is in quotes. And then underneath, it has … "Jimmy Collins of Irish rockers The Grove is seen above leaving a popular Dublin nightspot with an unidentified brunette. Collins had been dating Susan Plester (27) of Kent since their meeting on idyllic Thai island Koh Samui last Summer, but is this the end of their whirlwind romance? A source close to the band says that Collins and Paul 'Aesop' Murray, drummer with The Grove, have been thoroughly enjoying the trappings of their new-found fame. Ms. Plester (below) was unavailable for comment." It's only a small little thing in the gossip section, Jimmy, but ...'

'Fucking hell! Bastards! Dirty fucking scumbag cun ...'

'And then there's a picture of Susan and you underneath.'

'What?! Where the fuck did they get a picture of Susan and me?'

'I don't know. But she's not smiling or anything and the caption under it says, "Plester ... not amused".'

'But Dónal ... but ... and what source close to the band is telling them this shit?'

'No one is, Jimmy. It's just a way for them to say any oul' shite. They make it up.'

'Pricks! I've known Jennifer for twenty bleedin' years! What paper is it? We have to get on to them and ... and ...'

'Jimmy, I know you're pissed off, but even though it's all bollocks it's the kind of thing that happens. You're not to go mad or anything.'

'But it's not even true! We have to sue them or something. Can we? Is that ... eh ... libel or ... ?'

'Probably not. They didn't actually say anything that isn't true, except for the bit about the source and they can easily get away with that. And anyway, something like this is tiny compared to some of the shit they can pull. It's not worth it. I'm only telling you because I didn't want you to see it first. And I know how you feel about Susan.'

'Jesus.' Jimmy had his free hand on his face. 'Bastards ...'

'Yeah. Well anyway, you might want to give her a call. I'm very sorry about this, man. I hope it doesn't mess things up for the two of you, but it sounds like she already saw it.'

'Well it would explain the last bleedin' phone call I got anyway.'

'Man, I have to run. I'll scan the piece and email it to you. Or I'll just bring it to London?'

'Can you email it? Now. I'll go into town and find an Internet café or something. We're in the middle of nowhere out here.'

'Okay. I'll do it when I hang up. Listen, I'll catch you later, right?'

'Yeah. Thanks Dónal. Seeya.'

'Seeya Jimmy.'

Jimmy put the phone down and looked at it for a minute, biting at his knuckle. Then he picked it up again and put on his coat. She probably hated his guts now but he had to call her and apologise. To tell her it wasn't the way they made it out too, of course, but more importantly to apologise for scandalising her on the pages of some crap rag. But he wasn't going to do it here where the other two were hanging around. She had every right to be absolutely livid. Of course she did. Christ, at least Jimmy was getting used to being in the public eye. But Susan didn't deserve this.

He went out of the house and looked over at the others. He had to tell them about London and about Dónal getting in touch with Trish earlier.

'No Aesop,' Norman was saying. 'Along the grain.'

'I am.'

'You're not. Here, I'll show you again.'

'I can do it.'

'You're making a balls of it.'

'Leave me alone Norman. I can do it.'

'You're going around in circles!'

'Will you fuck off! I can paint a bleedin' door.'

'I keep telling you, it's not paint. Here … just let me …'

Jimmy sighed and went over to his car. He'd talk to them later.

'Lads, I'm going out for a bit,' he called back.

'Can I come?' said Aesop.

'Yeah, Jesus,' said Norman. 'Will you bring him, Jimmy? Please. He has me tormented here.'

'Sorry man. I have to sort something out. Seeya in an hour or so.'

While Norman was distracted, Aesop made another grab at the paintbrush. The can of wood stainer went flying off the bench and spilled onto the ground.

'Oops.'

'You fuckin' little …'

Norman was looking down at his ruined shoes.

'Norman … now Norman … deep breaths …'

Jimmy shook his head and sat into the car. In the back window he could see Norman chasing Aesop down the garden.

Twenty minutes later, he pulled in and parked on the main road of Kanturk. His head was still going a million miles a minute, so he decided to walk back down to the river and sit down for a smoke. It was lovely there, with the water folding over the rocks and clouds racing in the sky. When he was sure the email would be in from Dónal, he went back and found an Internet café. Two minutes later he was fuming again, the small scanned article on the screen in front of him.

'Bastards …' he muttered. He sighed and pulled out his phone. He had to call her. Had to.

'Hello?'

'Hey Susan. It's Jimmy.'

'Oh. Jimmy. Jimmy, I'm in work.'

'Can you talk? Is there somewhere you can … eh …'

'Well … look, just hang on a minute, can you? I'll see if the conference room is free.'

'No problem Susan.'

He heard a few muffled clicks and scrapes as she moved and used the time to take a couple of big breaths. That seemed to go okay. She didn't sound like she was going to read him the riot act anyway.

'Jimmy?'

'Yep. Still here.'

'Good. I wanted to talk to you.'

'Yeah? Great. I really wanted to talk to you too. The last time we …'

'It's not about us Jimmy,' she said. She was trying to sound all business-like. 'I was just wondering if you or Aesop had heard from Amanda.'

'Amanda? No. I don't think so. Why?'

'Well, it's just that I haven't heard from her for a few weeks and she said she'd keep in touch.'

'She's in Paris, isn't she?'

'I think she was, but she might be in Ireland now.'

'Right. Well, I haven't heard from her. And Aesop hasn't been on email for a few days. We're down in Cork taking a little break. Norman's Granny's old house.'

'Oh.'

'Why do you think she's in Ireland?'

'Well it's just that the last time she called me, I could hear all these people swearing in the background, so … y'know …'

'Eh … okay. Well I'll ask Aesop to check his messages and let you know.'

'Thanks. I'm sure she's fine and all, but I just wanted to ask you if she'd been onto you. She was talking about Aesop a lot before she left. I think she's still hung up on him.'

'God. Listen Susan, you should probably tell her that he's not worth getting hung up on, y'know?'

'I know. I have. But she's kind of got it in her head. And she really wasn't herself before she left. She might have the idea that, well, there might be something there and try to see him. It was all, "I must send Paul an email" and "I wonder how Paul is getting on" and all that. She never calls him Aesop. It's like a special thing they have between them.'

'They don't have a special thing, Susan, sorry. And it's nothing to do with Amanda. She's just barking up the wrong tree with that fella.'

'So I gathered. Okay. Well anyway … what did you want to talk about? Jimmy, I kind of said everything I had to say last time.'

'Yeah. I understand. But I just got off the phone with Dónal. Remember Dónal? Our manager?'

'I remember.'

'Well he told me about what they put in that newspaper over there. And he emailed it to me. I'm looking at it right now.'

She didn't say anything.

'Susan, I don't know what to say. I can't believe those bastards did that. I'm so sorry. I understand now why … y'know … the last time we spoke …'

Nothing.

'Listen … I mean I'm only starting to get used to all this stuff myself, but I do know how you must have felt. Please, I … it was a horrible thing to have happen to you. And I'm sorry. Really sorry. Susan? Are … are you still there?'

'Yes.'

She was crying. He could hear the sniffles. Fuck.

'I got such a shock Jimmy.'

'I know.'

'I felt so … God, it was like the Twilight Zone, but there I was on the page.'

'I'm sorry. If there's any way to get the pricks for doing that, I'll find it. I swear.'

'Everyone knew. Everyone knew I was seeing you. I know it was hard, with you being in Ireland and all, but I was so proud, Jimmy. You'd come on the telly or they'd play your songs in the pub and everyone would look at me and give a big cheer. I was so proud of you. Like a bloody fool. Thought I'd bagged a real live rockstar! God, I'm so stupid …'

'Listen Susan, before you say anything else … listen, right?'

'What?'

'That girl in the picture was Aesop's sister. Jennifer. Remember I told you …'

'Oh Jimmy don't. Please …'

'I swear to God, Susan. It was Jennifer. I've known her all my life. I'm going to be the best man at her wedding this year. Marco is my mate. We worked together for years. He'd be right next to her in the picture if the bastard that took it didn't cut him out. You would have met her in Dublin except she's in Galway every other week for work. Really, Susan. That whole bullshit article was nothing only some idiot's idea of a gossip column.'

'She's kissing you.'

'She's like my sister, Susan. I'd just given her a wedding present and she was kissing me to say thanks. I don't know what fucking hole the photographer crawled out of at that particular moment, but that's the picture he published. And I don't know where the other one came from either. Jesus, they must really hide behind hedges or something, the fu …'

'Jimmy …'

'Yeah.'

'I … how many girls have there been since I was in Dublin?'

'One. You.'

'Please Jimmy … don't …'

'I swear.'

'But why? For God's sake, we're not even together! We were just … barely clinging onto it.'

'I know that. And I know that it's my fault. Susan, I'm going to be on the road for at least six months this year. I'll be in the studio for four at least when we get back. How can I ask you to …'

'But you haven't asked me, Jimmy! You just figured it all out on your own and decided what was best.'

Now it was Jimmy's turn to say nothing.

'Jimmy, I had my mother in tears on the phone over that newspaper piece.'

'Aw fuck. I'm sorry.'

'My twelve year old niece was crying because I promised her that she could meet you when you came over to visit. My Dad wants to murder you and you don't want to know the things my sister says about you. These are people I love, Jimmy. Do you understand what this last week has been like for me?'

'Yeah. I do.'

'Jimmy, I can't wait around for twelve months so you can sort yourself out. I actually thought I might be able to, but I can't. After this? What would happen? I fly over to see you for a few days, get snapped leaving your hotel some morning? Another notch on the rockstar's bedpost?'

'What?! It wouldn't be like that at all Susan. I'm not like that.'

'Well, maybe *I* can believe that, Jimmy. But you're public property now and I've got other people to think about. What would your Mum have thought if it had been an Irish paper? Smutty stories about her darling son. Well I've got a family too, Jimmy. I'm not putting them through that. I haven't been able to go out for a week since that picture came out. I go home from work and watch the TV. That's it. I was so embarrassed. The groupie. That's what they all think I am now.'

'No one thinks that, Susan. That's only ...'

'Jimmy, please. I'm sorry I gave you a hard time last time we spoke. I thought ... well, I s'pose you know what I was thinking. And I'm sorry for thinking it. But no more newspapers for me. It's not who I am. I don't do socialite slut and I won't be your half girlfriend either. I'm sorry Jimmy.'

'Susan, listen, I'll be in London this weekend. For work. Why don't we ...'

'No! Jimmy, please don't call. Please. I've made up my mind. This isn't working and we need to let it go before it gets worse.'

'But if we just ... this weekend ...'

'No Jimmy. No. God, I can't see you now.'

She was crying again.

'But why? Susan, listen, we can have the whole weekend. I don't have to be back until ...'

'Bloody hell, Jimmy, can you not ... not just leave me alone?'

'No. I don't want to.'

'Please. Don't call when you get here.'

'Why?'

'It's too hard. It's too hard.'

'But it's just a weekend. We can talk ... why does that have to be hard?'

She was barely audible now through the sobbing, but Jimmy heard the next thing she said and it was like a punch in the chest.

'Because I love you Jimmy!'

And then pinpricks of cold marched up his back and into his hair.

Chapter Eighteen

'AMANDA WHO?' said Aesop.

Jimmy put his face into his hands and looked through his fingers.

'Fuck sakes ... Susan's friend, Aesop.'

Aesop's face was totally blank.

'Susan ...' he said, rubbing his chin.

Jimmy sighed.

'Yeah. My girlfriend, you fucking waste of space. Amanda is her friend. With the GT-R?'

'The GT ... ? Ah yeah. I remember now. English bird. I rode her in Japan.'

'Well at least you got the continent right.'

'And she's gone AWOL, is she?'

'Well Susan hasn't heard from her for a bit and she was just wondering if you had.'

'Why would I have heard from her?'

'Because the poor insane girl still has a thing for you.'

'I see. A cling-on? Phasers on stun, like?'

'Just check your email when you can and let me know if she's been onto you, okay?'

'No problem. But does she not know that I'm engaged to Helen now?'

'Does Helen know?'

Norman turned around from the sink where he was peeling spuds.

'I've a sharp knife over here in me hand, Aesop. Shut your hole. You're on probation until I hear from Trish later. And by the way, you owe me a pair of work boots.'

'Paint on the shoes is an occupational hazard for clod-hoppers like that, Norman. And anyway, if you'd let me have a proper go it never would've spilt.'

'Well I want a new pair, Aesop. These are your clod-hoppers now.'

'Mine? What am I meant to do with a pair of size seventeen boots? Jesus, me and Jimmy could make matching jackets out of them.'

'I don't give a shite what you do with them. Hey Jimmy, Susan reckons that Amanda is over here, is it?'

'Yeah. Why?'

'Ah just wondering. I never met her, but I heard all the stories. Nice girl?'

'Grand, yeah. But she was a bit down. She was after getting dumped and all and thought that this degenerate over here might be her new Prince Charming.'

'God. Talk about being wide of the mark.'

'Yeah. Anyway, she's off travelling now and Susan was wondering why she hadn't been in touch.'

'Right.'

Norman got back to peeling the spuds. He didn't want to say anything yet.

'Do you still have all them photos on your laptop?' he said over his shoulder. 'From the holiday, like?'

'Yeah, they're in me room. Do you want to have a look at them?'

'Sure why not. It's raining out now. Something to do. I only saw them for a minute when you got back.'

'Yeah, well they're in there. Hang on and I'll get them.'

Aesop yawned.

'Jesus, is this what we're reduced to now, is it? A slide show from the holliers? Isn't the country great? So much more fun than Dublin. I've always said it.'

'Would you rather finish the potatoes?'

'Peel potatoes? Man, you don't want me peeling your spuds. You'll end up with marbles.'

'So you've nothing at all to contribute. And yet here you are … still flapping your gob.'

'What are we having anyway?'

'I'm making a curry.'

'A curry? I'm not great with spicy stuff, Norman.'

'It won't be too bad.'

'What kind of curry?'

'Beef vindaloo.'

'Is that a hot one?'

'Nah. You'll be fine.'

'Are you sure, now?'

'Aesop, what kind of a whinging fucking child are you? It's only a bit of spice. It won't kill you.'

'I'm just saying, like …'

Jimmy came back with his computer and fired it up.

'Actually, I haven't looked at these in ages.'

They crowded around him at the coffee table.

'Look! There's Johnny!' laughed Aesop. 'He doesn't know I'm after robbing his pint, look.'

It was a on a slideshow setting, each new picture fading into the last one.

'That's the band in Tokyo is it?' said Norman. 'In that pub?'

'What the Dickens, yeah. Remember that bloke in the rubber gimp suit Aesop?'

'Now *that* I do remember. He fancied me as well. Madame Tina, wasn't it?'

'Jaysis, he remembers the name and all. Yeah, Madame Tina. Mad fucker.'

'Oh there's Shiggy. Nice pose man.'

'He was showing off his new hair cut.'

They all laughed at the next one.

'That's Samui. Prem must have taken that one out in the garden.'

Then up came a picture of Jimmy, Susan, Aesop and Amanda, the four of them standing together just at the edge of the sea. The lads all stopped laughing and bent in very slightly closer for a better look.

Jimmy gazed at Susan's melting eyes and that perfect smile. He felt a small thump in his stomach.

Aesop blew a quiet whistle at the blonde chick coming out of the sea in the background, off to the side. He hadn't noticed her before.

And Norman stared at the picture of Amanda, frowning and biting at his thumbnail. He wanted to remember that face.

AFTER DINNER, the lads headed to Kavanaghs. Helen had called and said there was an open mike session and it'd be a good laugh. Jimmy wasn't sure it was a brilliant idea. For starters, what were the chances that he'd be able to just sit there and enjoy his pint? Fuck all probably. He'd be cajoled onto the stage at some point in the evening. And anyway, he wasn't really in the mood for the pub. At the end of the phone call earlier to Susan, he'd spent five minutes just shushing her and telling her it'd be okay – whatever that meant – and then she said she had to go. He could see her sniffling back to her desk, eyes and nose red, make-up running down her face and every fucker looking at her. Well, okay, she'd probably go to the jacks first to sort herself out, but still. He was after doing that to her. He – Mr fucking Nice Guy Jimmy – had rung off and left a girl he was crazy about to sort out her own shit without saying anything to make it right, or even knowing what right was.

'Jesus, it's jammers,' said Aesop, looking around the pub when they pushed open the door.

'They must like their sessions down here,' said Jimmy.

Helen and Jessie were sitting at a table with a few other girls and Jessie waved over, gesturing to a few spare seats.

The lads waved back and Norman and Aesop made their way over to the girls, as Jimmy prepared to push his way to the bar to get a round in.

'Anyway, you're some cunt,' said Aesop.

'It was only a curry, Aesop,' said Norman.

'I'm afraid to fart.'

'You didn't have to eat it.'

'I did!'

'Well then you're a gobshite.'

'Fuck sake, I had to put a roll of toilet paper in the fridge for later …'

As their conversation faded out, Jimmy found that he didn't actually have to do much pushing to get to the bar. The crowd parted before him like he was carrying a staff and wearing a long flowing cloak. By the time he actually pulled up in front of the taps he was puce. Everyone was staring at him and the pub was nearly silent. Bollocks anyway.

The barman grinned at him.

'Now, yes please,' he said.

'I'll have, eh, three pints of Murphys and ...'

He looked over to the table. Aesop was standing and holding up the various drinks and giving him the count with his fingers.

' ... eh, one white wine ... eh ... is that Becks? ... eh ...'

'Is it for the girls?'

'Yeah. Just over there.'

'No problem. I know the round.'

'Good man. Thanks.'

Jimmy started poking around in his pocket for his wallet and got a tap on the shoulder. He turned around.

'You're Jimmy Collins.'

The guy was about twenty and looked like he'd been in the pub since lunchtime.

'Yeah. Howsit goin'?'

'Grand. You look like yourself, so you do.'

'Do I? Yeah ...'

'I play the guitar as well.'

'Oh right.'

The guy just grinned at him, swaying a little bit, what looked like a JD and Coke making small circles in the air in front of Jimmy.

'And ... eh ... what kind of music do you play?' said Jimmy. He hated these ones the worst. Someone makes a point of coming up to talk to you and then has fuck all to say.

'Ah ... y'know.'

'Right, yeah. Nice pub, isn't it?'

'That black girl in the video ...'

'The Strut video?'

'Where's she from?'

'Eh, Longford I think.'

'Yeah? Fuck off! What's her name?'

The bloke wasn't making any great effort to keep his spittle in his mouth and Jimmy was trying to lean back without knocking the setting pints off the counter behind him.

'I can't remember. We weren't really talking.'

'She was all over you, sure!'

'Ah, they were just dancers.'

'Lucky bastard.'

The smile on Jimmy's dial was under pressure. He did remember her name. It was Shamari and she danced when she wasn't studying at the Royal College of Surgeons. She was from Somalia. But this muppet didn't need to know any of that.

Another salvo of silvery flecks were launched at him from the USS Arsehole. Christ. Where was the bloody barman with the rest of the drinks?

'I'd say you rode the arse off her, boy, didn't you?'

He started cackling now, like he was after coming out with a classic. Jimmy smiled as best he could.

'Sorry pal, I just need to get these drinks. I'll seeya later.'

He started to turn around.

'You will indeed. Up there,' said the other bloke, pointing back at the stage. 'Sure we'll be seeing you as well, won't we?'

'Well, I'm only really out for a pint with me mates, so ...'

He followed the guy's thumb and stopped talking. There was a big sign on the wall behind the piano.

Tuesday Night
Open Mike Night!
9pm – Late
Featuring Special Guest Performance by ...
!! The Grove !!

'Oh bollocks,' said Jimmy, quietly. How the fuck had that happened?

His new pal was gone now, knocking elbows and apologising his way back to his mates. Jimmy paid the barman and picked up the tray of drinks. The throng parted for him again and then he was sitting down and Aesop was introducing him to all the girls at the table.

'Aesop?' he said, leaning in, once he had his pint in his hand.

'Yeah?'

'Did you see that sign up on the stage?'

'What sign?'

'The one that says we're doing a gig tonight in here.'

'What?'

'That's what it says.'

Aesop half stood up and looked up at the stage.

'But there's no drums. We need drums.'

'We need a fucking bass player too, Aesop, remember?'

'Well why did you say we'd play?'

'I didn't say anything! I don't know where …'

'Guys …'

It was Helen. She was sitting opposite Aesop and leaned forward.

'Listen, I'm really sorry. I think I know what happened. I said to Mam that you'd be here tonight and … well, she must have gotten straight on the phone. Packie Kavanagh owns this place and Nuala his wife is in the choir with Mam.'

'Is the pub usually like this for the Open Mike?' said Jimmy, looking around.

Helen gave a little grimace.

'Sorry. No. This is like a Saturday night, sure.'

'So they're here to see us?'

She nodded.

'Lads, I'm sorry. Really. I can go up and talk to Packie if you like?'

'Nah. It's all right.'

'Are you sure?'

'I'll talk to him. Which one is he?'

'The red tie.'

'Okay.'

He took a big pull on his pint.

'Back in a minute.'

Aesop watched Jimmy go up to the bar. Jessie was between him and Norman, so the coast was relatively clear. He turned to Helen.

'So are you singing tonight Helen?'

'Ah yeah. One or two, maybe.'

'You were really ... great the other night.'

'Would you stop.'

'Really, Helen. I don't usually go for trad sessions and all, but you were brilliant. And you looked deadly up there too. But I told you all that already, didn't I? You were made for the stage, I'm telling you.'

'God. What's all this? You must be trying to seduce me now, are you?'

'Me? Jesus, no. What gave you that idea?'

She laughed.

'Aesop, do you not read the stuff they write about you in the papers?'

'Eh, well, some of it I do. I don't go looking for stuff though. Why? What are they saying?'

'Let's just say you have a bit of a reputation.'

'Right. A sterling one, like? Fine upstanding young gentleman? That kind of reputation?'

'Depends on your point of view. And everyone around here now has got one. Since the two of you arrived, it's all anyone's talking about.'

'What about your point of view? How's my reputation there?'

She gave a little shrug.

'Well ... I like to make up my own mind about things.'

'And, so what do you ... eh ...'

She laughed and put a hand on his knee. Christ she was fucking smashing. He wanted to gobble her up.

'Someone's getting the evil eye,' she whispered. 'Look.'

Aesop turned around. Norman was leaning over so he could see past Jessie.

'All right there Aesop?'

'Couldn't be better, man. How's trix with you?'

'Grand, grand. Are you going up to the bar?'

'Jimmy's up there.'

'I think he needs a hand.'

'He's grand.'

'He's not.'

'He is, look.'

'I think I heard him calling you.'

'Ah … all right, all right. Fuck sake …'

'Hey Aesop,' said Helen, when he stood up, pulling at his jeans.

He sat down again.

'Tell me something. While we're on the subject of your escapades. Did you really spend a whole weekend in bed with two of the dancers in that video?'

Aesop swallowed. He wasn't expecting that. Technically, he could say no without lying. Obviously, they'd had to get out of the bed to eat and use the bathroom and all. Grand. He'd just say no.

'Eh …'

She gave him a good slap on the wrist.

'I'm a schoolteacher Aesop. Don't lie to me now.'

'Eh … Christ, Helen … I mean …'

'Yeah? I'm waiting …'

'Well, y'see, sometimes in the papers … they …'

She laughed.

'That's okay Aesop. Off you go and help Jimmy. I was just seeing if I could make a rockstar go red.'

He put a hand to his face.

'Did I?'

'Maybe a little bit pink, just.'

'Ah, that's just the curry Norman made earlier. Me tongue was like a balloon after it.'

At the bar Jimmy was waiting for drinks.

'How's it going?' he said to Aesop.

'Not sure.'

'What?'

'Ah, I've been talking to Helen … well, I mean I've been trying to talk to her. I swear Jimmy, I don't know what's going on. I'm like a fuckin' eejit. I sound like Norman trying to get laid.'

'She's not falling for your lines, is she?'

'What lines? Jimmy, it's not like talking to a bird at all with her. It's like talking to a real person or something, y'know? I couldn't even tell her a lie a minute ago about the marathon I ran with that "Strut" pair. Christ, normally at this stage I'd be getting the keys to the car off you.'

'Maybe you're losing your touch.'

'It's not fuckin' funny, man. It's like she's actually not that bothered about me riding her. Last week she's singing me dirty songs in Irish and now she's over there playing hard to get, or some fucking thing … ah … I don't know what the fuck …'

'Dirty songs in Irish?'

'Yeah. Real carpet-muncher stuff, y'know?'

'Carpet-mun … in Irish? But … oh, fuckin' whatever. Aesop, I thought you liked this girl.'

'I do.'

'Do you just want to shag her?'

'Well … I don't not want to shag her.'

'Yeah, I can see how all this is new for you. Why don't you try this, okay? Talk to her. Have a laugh. Get to know her. See what happens.'

'Sounds complicated. That's all that bollocks you go on with.'

'Me and the rest of the humans, yeah.'

'It's kind of a load of me arse, though, isn't it? I don't think …'

'So you're right and the other six billion of us are wrong.'

'Wouldn't be the first time, Jimmy.'

'Yeah, well why don't you give it a go? Anyway, your biggest complication isn't in your head. It's sitting next to Jessie with fists like breeze blocks.'

'Don't remind me. He's like a wart on me arse. Every time I turn around he's there.'

'He's meant to be there. He's your bodyguard, Aesop.'

'Yeah, but it's not my body he's worried about, is it? Jesus, just talking to her is like trying to cheat in the Leaving without getting caught. And I'm telling you, his curry isn't helping the situation either. I'm trying to be cool and charming and all, but I'm sitting there with a hole on me like a stab wound.'

The round of drinks arrived and Aesop reached into his pocket.

'It's grand Aesop.'

'You got the last one Jimmy.'

'These are on the house. I had a chat with Packie. He's all apologies. Says his missus must have gotten it wrong. Me bollix. Anyway, the gargle's free.'

'Brilliant.'

'Yeah, but we have to stay sober now.'

'What? Why?'

'Because all these people are here to see us. If we're going to get up there, we can't be shite. We've an album coming out, y'know?'

'But …'

'Aesop, we're professional musicians. We don't go to work pissed. And we're working tonight.'

'But it's only an amateur night. It's not like …'

'Listen man, there's no such thing as an amateur night for us any more. I told him we'd do five acoustic songs and I want to make sure we sound good. I'm worried about the sound system as well. I've no idea what the mikes are like or anything. So the last thing we need is the two of us wobbling up there shitfaced on top of things, okay?'

'Yeah. All right.'

'Five or six pints and that's it. Right?'

'Okay okay.'

'Okay.'

Aesop looked at him.

'Have you got the shits now because we're playing?' he said.

'What? No. Well, a little bit I s'pose. And I was talking to Susan earlier after Dónal told me about London.'

'Oh. Right. How did it go?'

'Not great. There was a thing in one of the English newspapers about us and she was all upset.'

'What did they say?'

'Ah, it doesn't matter. Anyway, I don't think I'll be seeing her in London this weekend.'

'So she doesn't love you any more?'

Jimmy grabbed half the drinks and turned away from the bar.

'Something like that.'

TWO HOURS later the pub was even more wedged. A dozen or so people had already been up there, either accompanied by a few core players or doing the job themselves on the guitar. Most of them were doing classic covers rather than trad, but a few ballads came out as well. The lads that made up the 'band' were brilliant, swapping instruments around and lashing out a few tunes or songs if the next punter needed an extra pint before getting up in front of everyone. The bloke on the uilleann pipes especially was incredible when he got into it. Jimmy was watching him closely. He'd never really paid attention before, but the pipes were one mad bastard of an instrument, the drones shifting under the melody and sliding, bending notes being coaxed from the chanter. The guy was very impressive on the runs, but when he played a slow air, to the respectful hush, the pipes seemed to throw up layered, mournful voices that twisted around each other, hanging back or stepping forward as though waiting in turn to offer condolence. Hmm. Jimmy put down his pint. He'd probably had enough for the moment.

'What?' he said. Aesop had said something into his ear.

'I want to sing,' said Aesop. 'And play.'

'Here? Tonight?'

'Yeah.'

'Aesop, remember what I said about not being shite tonight?'

'I won't be shite.'

'What do you want to sing? The only one you can do properly like that for a crowd is … oh no. Don't tell me …'

Aesop shrugged.

'It's worth a go.'

'C'mon Aesop, she's not fucking sixteen.'

'But I'm out of ideas, man! She keeps saying stuff to me in that Cork accent. I'm going mad. Jimmy, it's the magic song. We must have scored dozens of chicks singing it.'

'When we were kids, yeah. Aesop, she's a grown woman. She's not stupid. And anyway, Norman will beat the piss into you before you get to the chorus.'

'He won't. In a pub full of people?'

Jimmy sighed.

'How many pints have you had?'

'Four. And a half. I'm grand.'

'Can you still play it?'

'Yeah. Jesus, I'll never forget that song. All that gee …'

'Christ. Okay. But I'm singing seconds, right? And take it easy on the falsettos. Are you sure you don't want me to play the guitar, Aesop?'

'No man. I'm giving it the whole shebang.'

'Well … for fuck sake, don't try the run at the outro.'

'I won't. Thanks Jimmy.'

'God … he'll fucking kill me too, probably.'

'He won't. I'll just say I sprung it on you on the sly when we got to the stage.'

'Yeah. Christ, the sooner this poor girl tells you to fuck off with yourself the better. I think I prefered it when you were a trollop.'

'I haven't had a bounce in ages, Jimmy. I'm going spare. Fuck sake, I keep finding teethmarks on the headboard when I wake up and everything.'

'But … Aesop, you either really like this girl or you just want to fuck her. Which is it?'

'Both. What's wrong with that?'

'Well … nothing. But you need to calm the fuck down. Listen, I know you're only a visitor here on planet Earth, but some girls want more than for you to shag them. I think she's one of those girls.'

'But that's what I want too!'

'Are you sure?'

'Yes! Man, she's fucking beautiful and she sings great and she has the accent and she's dead-on. And all night talking to her I've had this funny feeling in me belly ...'

'Aesop ...'

' ... although that might be the curry ...'

'Aesop, there's plenty of nice young ones in here. Are you sure you wouldn't rather just be yourself and grab one of them? It's not like they won't be up for it. Then you'd have your pipes cleaned and your brain might get a look-in.'

'Not interested Jimmy.'

'What about Olga?'

'Who?'

'The girl sitting next to Norman.'

'The little fat yoke?'

'What? No, next to Norman.'

'Oh. Nah ... me bollocks.'

'She keeps gawking at you. Your type of bird. And she's all right looking Aesop.'

'She is not.'

'She is!'

'She's not Jimmy. She's a disgrace.'

'But she ...'

'If I had a garden full of mickeys, Jimmy, I wouldn't let her look over the wall.'

'Oh fuckin whatever. Look, sing your bleedin song. But if Helen breaks her bollocks laughing, it's not my fault.'

Another thirty minutes went by and the open mike thing was starting to wind down. People were starting to get a bit pissed anyway and a lot of them were looking over at Jimmy and Aesop, waiting for the real show to start. Jimmy looked around. Aesop and

Helen were talking to Norman. He caught Jessie's eye and gave her a smile. She'd had a few pints and looked like she might be trying to muster up a bit of courage to make a move on him. He turned away and looked around the bar. He didn't need to be encouraging that shite. He had enough on his plate tonight, landed with an impromptu gig here and his head full of a broken-hearted girl in England.

Eventually Packie got up to the mike and called for a bit of quiet.

'Now, ladies and gentlemen, we're very lucky to have a couple of lads in tonight …'

There was a roar.

' … now, now, hush a minute. Jimmy and Aesop from The Grove are going to give us a couple of songs now, fair play to them. And I hope you're all going to support them when they're playing in Cork in a couple of months?'

Clapping and shouting.

'Grand. So … Jimmy, are you right?'

Jimmy gave him a wave and stood up.

'Right Aesop,' he said, when the guitar was strapped on and the mike fixed in front of his face. 'Just me on this one, right?'

Aesop nodded and took the other guitar, sitting down behind Jimmy and winking out at Helen.

Jimmy started into 'Big Love' by Fleetwood Mac. It was the mental version for solo guitar that he'd seen Lindsay Buckingham do on that video. It had taken Jimmy six weeks before he was happy with his own version, and that was with the help of the transcription he'd found in Total Guitar. Perfect for a venue like this. He didn't want there to be any confusion about who was the fucking best guitar player in the place tonight, and the pub half-full of musicians. But he needn't have worried. The punters shut up and stared at his fingers, their mouths open. They all knew that they wouldn't be able to do what Jimmy was doing in a blind mickey fit. Not that Jimmy was trying to be a cunt or anything. This was business. He couldn't have them walking home going, 'ah, sure he was only all right, like'.

He followed with a nice fiddly version of 'Wish You Were Here' and then stopped to look out and see how he was doing. It was grand. They were all over him, beaming and taking pictures.

'Thanks very much. And thanks for having us here tonight. I s'pose a few of you have met Aesop?'

He looked behind and Aesop stood up and bowed.

'Aesop's been practising the bodhrán. Do you want to hear him?'

They all yelled, the girls whooping and whistling.

Actually, Aesop was pretty good on any percussion instrument and the bodhrán was no exception. But they didn't know that.

'Okay. Here's the version Jagger wished he recorded ...'

Aesop led them into 'Sympathy for the Devil'. It would've been a bit mad in any other venue in the world, bodhrán instead of bongos, but with the versions of songs Jimmy had heard tonight, it'd fit right in. Christ, the lads had done a bluegrass rendition of some Oasis songs earlier. Better than the originals they were too. Not that that was saying much ...

This was a good one to get the crowd going, because they could all do the Woo Woo's near the end. Jimmy wanted them in his pocket before Aesop sang.

All too soon the song was over and then Jimmy took a deep breath and smiled out.

'Right, thanks very much. Eh ... I'm afraid Aesop's been pestering me to sing a song as well. Is that okay?'

He grinned at the reaction and stepped to the other mike to make way for Aesop. Aesop stood up to the mike and gave it a tap.

'Thanks Jimmy. Thanks for that. Eh ... actually, I'm not the singer in the band. As you'll find out in a minute. But I heard all these people getting up earlier and it sounded like a good laugh, so I thought I'd give it a go. I only know one song on the guitar anyway, and Jimmy's going to help me out, so hopefully it won't be too bad.'

The punters were right in their faces now, the first four or five rows consisting of some very excited girls. Jimmy closed his eyes. They hadn't done this one in ages and the last time they'd done it, it was with two very definite purposes in mind ... called Aoife and

Angela if his memory served him correctly. He heard Aesop get his fingering right on the guitar and barely opened one eye. Helen was right there, a huge, faintly curious, smile on her. Jimmy leaned in to him.

'Can we get this over with before I bottle out?'

Aesop winked and started the intro. Almost immediately the hundred or so girls in the place started screaming, so much so that he had to go around twice before he could start singing. By then it didn't even matter. Two hundred breasts were suddenly pointing straight at him like he was the North Pole and they had magnetic nipples. The last time they'd heard this song they were teenagers in love, or just out of love, or wondering what it might be like to be in love.

It was 'More Than Words', by Extreme … Aesop's magic song.

As Jimmy sang his first harmony line and the two hundred breasts swung around in unison to pick him out, he relaxed a bit. It sounded pretty cool. Cheesy as all fuck, but Aesop was getting away with it. Sometimes you got lucky with a crowd or a venue or a vibe, and it was working now. Jimmy put his right hand up to the side of his head so that he could close his ear and hear himself properly. Everything was grand. And then he saw Norman, right at the back of the crowd, towering over everyone and staring at Aesop like green fire was about to come out of his eyes and reduce the man to a charred cinder. Norman knew all about the magic song. He'd heard all the stories. He'd even been there for a few of them. Everything was grand … except that Aesop was a dead man for trying this on Helen.

Jimmy finished out the mini-gig with 'Caillte'. That was a no brainer for the punters. It was the reason they'd all turned up. Normally someone would have sung it already by now in the Open Mike, but no one had had the balls to do it tonight. They lapped it up when Jimmy sang it. For an encore he decided to go out on a limb, just to see.

'I wrote this next song a few weeks ago for a friend of mine. I haven't actually played it with just me and a guitar, so … eh … I'd appreciate it if you let me know what you think. Aesop?'

Aesop was playing the bass line on the other acoustic and started it up.

'This is a new one called "More Than Me". It's about ... well, it's about knowing when you've got it good. Hope you like it ...'

THE PUNTERS mostly cleared out of the place by one in the morning. Everyone had work the next day. There were a few people still there and Packie didn't seem to be too bothered about shifting them. The lads were still on free booze and now that the gig was over they could relax and have a proper few pints in the lock-in. Jimmy was signing autographs at the bar and chatting to Helen and Jessie. Norman and Aesop were on their own at a table down the back of the pub.

'You dirty shite, you made me a promise.'

'I didn't touch her!'

'Bollocks! I know what you were at with your fucking smoochy song.'

'Jesus man, it's the only song I can sing properly on an acoustic. All the way through, y'know? To a crowd like this. It was either "More Than Words", "He's Got the Whole World in His Hands", or "Swallow Every Drop of My Love". What was I meant to do?'

'Why didn't you just let Jimmy sing?'

'It was an Open Mike night!'

'Not for the likes of you.'

'Listen man, you need to chill your boots.'

'What fucking boots? Didn't you destroy them earlier today on me.'

'Look Norman, I know you think I'm a scumbag with women. I know you think I'm immature and that I don't respect women's feelings. I know you think all I'm after is a quick ride and that I'd no more make an effort to get to know a woman than I would eat me own toenails. And that to me, women are just ... Jesus, Norman, stop me if you think I'm talking shite ...'

'I will. Go on.'

'Look ... Norman, I really, really like Helen. That's it. All I want is a chance. Jesus, it's not like she's throwing herself at me, is it? She might even give me the red card. But I can't even talk to her properly if you're giving me the hairy eyeball across the room every time. It's very fucking unnerving.'

'Good.'

'Man, she's nearly thirty. You can't stop her from seeing who she likes.'

'I can stop you.'

'But that's bollocks! And it's not fair. Norman, all the shit you've given me down the years about women. And now here I am, balls fit to fucking explode from not riding the whole of the last week, turning down a threesome with a couple of Swedish chicks, trying to watch me language, waving off a pub full of women tonight … and why? Because I keep asking meself what Helen would think. Does that not tell you something?'

'Only that the country air is doing you some good and it's about time you started copping yourself on. Congratulations on not being fifteen any more.'

'So?'

'So what?'

'If I'm not fifteen any more, will you ever fuck off and let me at least talk to Helen alone without breathing down me neck like a fucking mountain gorilla whose banana I'm after robbing. You're fucking up my chances of getting to know …'

'You don't have a chance, Aesop. Helen is my cousin and I'm not leaving you alone with her for five minutes. This pub was full of girls that would be more than happy to attend to your exploding balls for you tonight, but she's not one of them.'

'Helen and my balls are not the issue here, Norman, you're the …'

'Hi guys.'

They both looked up.

'What are you talking about? Sounds serious.'

'Hiya Helen,' said Aesop. 'I was just explaining to Norman that I like … it down here in the country.'

'Great. You should come down more often.'

'Yeah. I think I'd like that.'

'Do you want to come outside for a minute with me? We've never really had a proper chance to chat and it's a bit stuffy in here. The stars are out and everything.'

'Well ...'

'It's cold out there,' said Norman. 'You should stay in in the warm.'

'Come on, Aesop. Unless you're in the middle of something? Robert? Do you mind?'

'Eh ... I'm not sure. I'm meant to be keeping an eye on him and ...'

'Oh, I'll keep an eye on him for you.'

'Yeah, but ...'

'Come on Aesop.'

Aesop started to slowly slide out from behind the table, grabbing his coat and smokes and looking sideways at Norman. Norman put his hand on Aesop's arm.

'Helen, I think you should just stay in here and ...'

'We'll be fine.'

'But Helen ...'

'Robert!'

Norman and Aesop both stopped dead and looked at her. Then she smiled.

'Come on Aesop.'

They both walked out together into the car park.

'How the fuck did you do that?' said Aesop.

'What?'

'That voice you did ... Jesus, I felt about six years old!'

'I'm a schoolteacher, remember?'

'Christ, I'd say you don't have many problems in the classroom, do you?'

She laughed.

'Not too many.'

'I think Norman's still probably stuck to his seat in there. I've never seen real fear in that man's eyes in twenty-five years until just now.'

'Ah, Robert's a dote. Gentle as a lamb.'

'A lamb. Right. You've obviously never seen him eat a lamb, then, have you?'

She laughed again, leading the two of them past the tarmac car park and into a field. There were picnic tables and benches set up, and a small playground for kids. Further along there was a gate into another field. This one was a rose garden, but the bushes were bare now except for the coats of frost that each one wore, glistening under the moonlight. As she closed the gate behind them, she put her hand in his. It felt warm. They went on along the path between the rows of shrubbery and eventually came to another bench. She tucked her long coat under her legs behind her and sat down. His coat only came to his waist but he sat down next to her anyway, immediately feeling a slight dampness and a rush of freezing cold seep into his jeans. He didn't give a fuck. He was too busy being mesmerised by the way her eyes seemed to give out a light of their own.

And anyway, it actually felt kind of nice on his curry-damaged arsehole.

Chapter Nineteen

'HOW PISSED off was he on the phone?' said Aesop, when they were settled into their seats.

'Well, I've heard him worse …'

'Right.'

'But not by much. Did you ride her?'

'A gentleman doesn't say.'

'Right. So, did you ride her?'

'I'm not messing Jimmy, what happened is between me and Helen.'

'So you're not going to fill me in on all the details?'

'I'm saying nothing about it.'

'Give us a look at your passport for a minute.'

'For what?'

'I want to make sure it's you.'

'Listen Jimmy, forget about it. If it'll shut you up, let's just say my feelings haven't changed, okay? Are you eating them nuts?'

'Here.'

'So who's going to be looking after me in London if Norman's in Dublin having a sulk?'

'Dónal and Norman reckon you'll be grand. Your stalker doesn't know where you'll be. Anyway, it'll give Norman a chance to cool down. And he misses his bird he says.'

'Yeah … his bird …'

'What?'

'Hmm?'

'Every time anyone mentions Trish, you get all quiet. Is it the shame of it?'

'No. It's just … listen Jimmy, if I say something, will you do your best to listen to it without calling me a fuckin' eejit?'

'Can I just think it?'

'Yeah … I s'pose so.'

'Go on so.'

'When I was talking to Trish that time ... y'know, with the badger and all ... she wasn't fuckin' normal?'

'What do you mean normal?'

'She said she wanted to talk to me. She needed to show me something. Not the picture, something else. And she said not to tell Norman about it. She wanted to meet me for dinner. Just the two of us, like.'

'What? That's a bit fucked.'

'I know. I don't know what she's after, but I'm not into doing all this behind-the-scenes shite. Norman is my mate and if she wants me to shag her or something, then I don't know what to do.'

'You mean about shagging her? Because ...'

'No, you fuckin' dipstick. I'm not shagging her either way. But what do I do about the psycho fuckin' vibes I'm getting?'

'Did you tell Norman what she said?'

'Jesus, no. I already broke his door, wrecked his shoes, scared the bejaysis out of his girlfriend twice, served him up salad cream sandwiches for his dinner, smashed his phone, and then I disappear into the night with his cousin. If he's anywhere near breaking point, do you think I want to tell him his bird is looking for me to throw a length into her on top of everything else?'

'Fair point. So what are you going to do?'

'I don't know. Maybe I can get her on her own for two minutes and tell her to fuck off and leave me alone.'

'Maybe the curious incident of the badger in the night did the trick?'

'Maybe it did. But I don't know man. She's a bit mental, that one.'

'Are you sure she said all that stuff about meeting her privately? You know the way you're an awful dopey cunt sometimes ...'

'I'm telling you man it wasn't right, the stuff she was coming out with. The girl was saying all this shit to me, and Norman's in the next room. That's why I was in the bedroom at all that night. I didn't want him hearing what was going on.'

'Look, just give her a call. See what she wants, okay? If she wants you instead of Norman, you're going to have to say something. Unless she just accepts that it's not going to happen and never mentions it again to either of you. Then it can just be a little secret between the two of you. Or, well, the three of us.'

'Ah … fuck this shit anyway. Who needs all this crap when I'm already after telling Helen that … eh …'

'Yeah? What did you tell Helen, Aesop?'

'Nothing.'

An airhostess came by with champagne for them.

'Thanks very much,' said Jimmy, taking one for each of them.

'How long is this flight?' said Aesop.

'It's just over an hour, Mr Murray.'

'Oh right. Thanks.'

The girl moved on to the next row.

'She recognised us,' said Aesop.

'Yeah. Well, she has a list of all her passengers too. So maybe …'

'Nah. Did you see that look?'

'She wanted to ride you as well I s'pose, is it?'

'It's a cross I have to bear Jimmy. I'm mad for gee and women can sense it.'

'Oh, okay.'

'It's the way God made me.'

'God made you mad for gee?'

Aesop nodded.

'Right,' said Jimmy. 'I didn't know that was his department.'

'Yeah, well it doesn't matter. I'm retired now anyway.'

Jimmy looked at him.

'Over Helen?'

Aesop said nothing.

'Aesop, are you and Helen a full-time thing now or what's the fuckin' story?'

'You wouldn't understand.'

'You're not answering me, Aesop.'

'Well stop asking then, Jimmy.'

'Fuck sake.'

'DÓNAL!'

'Great to see you lads. Jaysis, Aesop, I think you're after putting on a bit of weight, are you?'

'You should see the size of the dinners Norman was making, Dónal. The things that man can do with a spud.'

'Well it suits you anyway. A bit of colour in the cheeks and everything.'

'Yeah, well I've been taking these morning walks and all y'know? A few miles across the bogs, just to get the heart going.'

'Jesus, don't mind him,' said Jimmy. 'You have to empty him out of the bed.'

'Lads, we'll go and grab a bite for lunch, right? We're meeting with Senturian at two.'

'Grand,' said Jimmy. 'Do you already know what the story is with them?'

'Only that they want to talk about the next album. And they've got something on the cards for America. They were talking about a support slot for you.'

'Cool. With who?'

'Don't know yet. C'mon.'

The bellhop signalled a taxi just outside the main door and they got in. Dónal told the guy where they wanted to go and then they all sat back and gazed at the sights going past.

'Do you know what I love about English women?' said Aesop, when they stopped at a traffic light and a pile of pedestrians started walking in front of the car.

'What?' said Dónal.

Jimmy had more sense.

'I love the way they're posh and dirty at the same time,' said Aesop.

'I'm not with you.'

'English women can do posh and make it sound dirty. Liz Hurley, now. I could see her spanking the arse off you.'

'Off me?'

'Off anyone.'

'And that'd be brilliant, would it?'

'Oh Jaysis yeah. Smacking you on the arse and telling you you're very bold. I'd say she'd be deadly at that.'

'Based on what?'

'Are you not listening to me? Her accent.'

'So you've decided that Liz Hurley, a woman you've never met, is into smacking people on the arse. And you're basing this revelation on her accent.'

'I know women, Dónal.'

'Jimmy, what's he on about?'

'Ah, don't listen to him, Dónal. It's not worth it.'

'Do you know what else I love about English women?' said Aesop.

Silence.

'Lads?'

Nothing.

'Lads? Do you know what else I love about English women?'

'Christ. What do you love, Aesop?'

'Knickers. Well, underwear in general. Do you ever notice that English birds have the coolest jocks?'

'I've been married for fourteen years, Aesop,' said Dónal.

'Yeah, but you can still look, can't you?'

'At their jocks? How, for fuck sake?'

'Magazines or on the telly or whatever. They have some good gear over here, I'm telling you. I don't know where they get it. Do you?'

'Do I know where English women get their underwear?'

'Yeah.'

'No I don't.'

'That'd be a good business to be in. Bringing English girls' scanties over to Ireland and selling it.'

'I'm sure it's the same stuff at home as here.'

'Well maybe they just don't buy it as much. It's all about marketing, y'know?'

'Is it? Okay, right. That's enough, Aesop, please.'

'Oh, by the way, that reminds me … I'm after having a brilliant idea.'

Dónal was rooting in his briefcase now. Jimmy was still looking out the window.

'Lads? Lads, me brilliant idea … do you want to hear it? Lads?'

Jimmy looked around.

'Aesop, if we listen to your idea, will you shut fuckin' up until we get out of the car?'

'Yeah.'

'Okay. What's your idea?'

'It's a band. A trad band, right? But it's an all-girl band. A female trad supergroup. I betcha a few of them Riverdance babes play instruments and …'

Dónal looked up.

'An all-girl trad band?'

'Yeah. I was watching Helen singing the other night, right? And this other young one, Cathleen, was on the whistle and another one was on the guitar, y'see? Dónal … Dónal, do you see?'

'Yes, Aesop. I don't know the girls, but what about them?'

'They were all gorgeous!'

'Good. Great. And so you rode them all and everyone lived happily ever after …'

'No, no. I'm just saying, there were these three top birds and they were all playing trad music. No hairy jumpers on them, no moustaches, no beer bellies. We're talking top-shelf gee, right? You don't normally get that in trad. So my idea was, right, you get four or five birds that look like the Corrs. Sexy Irish country accents, good singers, good musicians, the whole nine yards, right? But proper trad. Dress them up properly in lovely black dresses, proper make-up, English jocks … and all of a sudden you've got a new type of girl band. Like a normal girl band, except trad. Trad needs more sexy birds, lads. The Yanks would lap it up. I'm telling you, it'd be a goldmine.'

Jimmy and Dónal were just looking at each other.

'Wouldn't it be deadly?' said Aesop.

Dónal sighed.

'I s'pose it might have a market.'

'Might?! They'd be gagging for it! Can I do it?'

'What?' said Dónal.

'Can I do it? For Sin Bin, like. Can I start auditioning young ones for it? We could have different troupes, y'know? Touring and all, like Riverdance.'

'I'm not having you use Sin Bin so you can collect yourself stables of pretty young trad musicians to scandalise.'

'It'd be a good name for the band, though,' said Jimmy, looking around. Aesop's Stables.'

Dónal laughed.

'Yeah. True.'

'I'm serious lads. Youse are always talking about other bands and all. I'd like to give it a go. Be a manager and all, y'know? And anyway, I'm not scandalising anyone at the moment. Amn't I not Jimmy?'

'So you say.'

'So anyway, Dónal. What do you think?'

'Aesop, if you're serious about managing a band, we'll talk about it again. There's a lot to learn, y'know?'

'I can learn stuff.'

'Well, there's a lot to know before you can go hand-picking a group of musicians anyway.'

'But this band will be sexy. That's their thing.'

'That's not enough, Aesop.'

'Ah cop on, Dónal. Do you think The Corrs would be The Corrs if they all looked like the brother?'

'Look, the restaurant is just there. We'll talk about it again. There's a lot of thought needs to go into something like this.'

'I've already given it a lot of thought.'

'Have you?'

'Yeah. I've already got a name for the band and everything. It's sexy girl band, but it's trad sexy girl band. Irish, sexy, trad, girls …'

'Okay okay, Aesop. So what are you going to call them, then?'

'B*Jaysis.'

Jimmy started laughing out the window.

'Fuck sake …' said Dónal, shaking his head. He got back to the contents of his briefcase.

'Wotcha think? Lads? B*Jaysis. Lads, what do you think of that? Lads?'

THE SENTURION offices were very sexy.

'So you like your hotel?' said Alison, leaning back in a huge leather armchair.

She was the boss. A tall beautiful black woman with some kind of Caribbean accent. They'd met her before in Dublin, but Jimmy and Aesop had both forgotten just how stunning she was.

'It's brilliant, thanks,' said Jimmy.

'You have us spoilt, Alison,' said Aesop. 'You could play Twister on the bed, sure.'

She laughed.

'Really? You'll have to make some friends then, Aesop, while you're here.'

Jimmy immediately gave him a boot under the table. He knew Aesop well enough to know that he was about to say something dirty to her and Dónal had warned them about ten times that she went spare when blokes thought they had a chance at getting the cacks off her.

She went on for another fifteen minutes or so, telling them they were brilliant and how happy everyone was. The singles, the tour, the album … everything was going great. There was even some interest in the US in the whole thing. She was pretty sure that a tour over there would be on the cards as soon as they were done in Europe. Jimmy and Aesop were beaming. A US tour. That would be the absolute mutt's nuts. Then Alison leaned in again to the table and put on a pair of glasses.

'I guess we should talk a little business now?' she said.

'Why don't we start on the album contract?' said Dónal.

'Sure,' said Alison. She looked at the guy next to her and he pulled some pages out of a folder. She passed them out. 'What we have here is a four-album contract to replace the single-album one we're working to at the moment. As you'll see, we've got some very exciting ideas about where all this will go.'

The lads all looked at the documents for a few minutes. Dónal skimmed through his copy and glanced up at Jimmy. Jimmy was frowning at his. Aesop was still on the first page, bending down to try and read it. He hadn't gotten used to the controls on his own armchair and it was at its full height. He seemed to be miles above the table.

'As you know,' said Alison, 'we're extremely excited about you two guys and can see great potential for upcoming projects. This document and your talent will make all of us a lot of money over the next two years.'

'Two years?' said Jimmy.

Dónal put a hand on his arm and looked at Alison.

'Go on …'

Alison pointed to a graph on the overhead projector.

'Well, as you can see, the next twelve months are going to see some movement in the industry. We'll be striving to maximise all the leverage we can within that calendar.'

Jimmy swallowed. They'd be striving to maximise their leverage? He was used to hearing this type of nonsensical bollocks when he worked in an office, but he wasn't expecting to have to listen to it here. And what was that about two years?

'So, if no one has any questions, we'll move on to some of the details … eh, yes Aesop?'

Aesop had his hand up.

'What does "whereon" mean?'

'Em … well it doesn't really mean anything. It's just a word for … em …'

'Oh. Okay. Can I have a lend of your pen?'

She passed it across and he started crossing out words on his contract.

'Eh, okay, so moving on … are you … okay Aesop?'

'Sorry. I'm just … I can't get this chair to go down. Look at me. I feel like I should be eating a bowl of Liga up here.'

'There's a little lever just at the side. You need to push it down. But be careful …'

There was whoosh and then a bang.

'Ow! Aw … me fuckin' mouth …'

'Are you okay Aesop?'

'Bit me tongue. Aw man, that hurts like a bastard. Look, it's bleeding … don't be looking at me like that Jimmy … Oh God … look at that … aw, I … I don't feel well Alison …'

He was looking at the blood on his finger, the other hand steadying himself on the table.

Alison barked a few instructions and one of the guys next to her went around to Aesop to help him to his feet.

'Maybe you could show Aesop to the bathroom please Phil?'

Dónal looked at her.

'And maybe then Phil could introduce him to a few people around the office?'

'Good idea. Why don't you do that, Aesop, when you've got yourself cleaned up?'

'Okay. Sorry for all this trouble Alison,' said Aesop, taking his contract and moving towards the door, leaning on Phil's arm.

'It's no trouble. These chairs can take a bit of getting used to.'

When the door closed behind them, Jimmy turned around to Alison.

'Sorry about that. Usually he waits until all the chocolate biscuits are gone before he gets bored and starts annoying everyone.'

'That's okay Jimmy. Now, where were we?'

'The album contract,' said Dónal. He hadn't been distracted at all by Aesop. He was still frowning and looking down at a particular part of it.

'Right. Yes. Well, the way we see this working, going forward, is that …'

AESOP THOROUGHLY enjoyed himself for the afternoon. Once he was done in the bathroom, Phil led him through the office, stopping at all the girls' desks and introducing Aesop as the drummer with The Grove. They all knew exactly who he was. Each one stood and smiled at him in turn and he bowed and shook their hands and grinned at them like his whole life was a complete fucking waste of time until about five minutes ago. He concentrated on cramming as many names as would fit into the special mental vault he used for people he wasn't planning on shagging but wanted to charm anyway. It was usually reserved for mammies and table staff in pubs. But these girls were the ones who'd be working on the album; making calls, sorting out the publicity, making sure the shops were stocked and the CDs properly displayed. They'd be putting out the press releases and contacting journos and setting up interviews and promotions. Never mind all that shite going on in Alison's office, this was where the real work was done and he wanted to make a good impression.

Phil was a bit of a tit though. He showed Aesop some of the latest reviews.

'One magazine two weeks ago said you were easily the most exciting new drummer in England, Aesop. What do you think of that?'

'I wasn't in England two weeks ago, Phil.'

'I'm sorry?'

'I'm from Dublin.'

'Oh of course, sorry. Maybe it said the UK, not England.'

Aesop nodded at him slowly.

'Did you get The Muppets on the telly over here, Phil?'

About an hour later he saw Jimmy coming out of the meeting room and going into the lift without a word to anyone. Then Dónal came out and followed him. Aesop frowned and said his goodbyes to the girl he was talking to. Dónal and Jimmy were waiting for him on the street outside.

'C'mon,' said Dónal, before Aesop could open his mouth. 'There's a pub just down here.'

They all started walking down the road.

'Anyone want to fill me in on what the fuck happened up there?'

'Wait till we have a pint in front of us, Aesop. That got a bit heated, so it did.'

'But I thought we were all mates, Alison and us?'

'We're business partners, Aesop. Not always the same thing.'

'Were you having a row?'

'Discussion. In loud voices.'

'Yis bleedin' eejits. See what happens when I leave you alone? You need my unique brand of charm and can-do attitude in these situations.'

'Yeah. How's your tongue?'

'I think a bit came off. Feels funny. Bumpy.'

'Doesn't affect your appetite though. What's that you're eating?'

'Yorkie. Do you want one? I have a Turkish Delight too.'

'I'm grand thanks.'

'Murray Mint?'

'Where did you get all that stuff Aesop. Were you robbing their fridge?'

'There's a fridge? Bollocks. No, that Phil bloke was annoying me so I had to get rid of him out to the shops a couple of times.'

'How did he annoy you for God sake?'

'Ah, he's a dope. He thinks Ireland is part of the UK.'

'For the first time, Jimmy looked over.

'You weren't exactly the best geography student yourself that Brother Patrick ever had, were you Aesop?'

'Jesus Jimmy, at least I know where me own country starts and finishes.'

'Yeah,' said Jimmy. 'Dublin.'

'Ah, not any more Jimmy. Sure I've a whole new appreciation for bog-warriors now. I mean, when you get right down to it, most of them are only a decent haircut and a change of jocks away from being like the rest of us.'

'Very magnanimous of you, Aesop.'

'Sticks and stones, Jimmy.'

They were outside the pub now and Jimmy pushed open the door and led them inside. At the bar, Dónal called for three pints.

'Okay then,' said Aesop, picking up his glass. 'What's up? Why did this fella come barrelling out of Alison's office like a man with the trots?'

'Right Aesop,' said Dónal. 'This is what's after happening, right?

Are you listening?'

'I am.'

'Okay. Basically, they want us to sign a four-album deal. For a lot of money.'

'The bastards.'

'No, listen. The new album will be out in a couple of weeks, right?'

'Right.'

'Then you go on tour.'

'Yeah.'

'Well it seems that Alison and her team have come up with an ingenious solution to the problem of us not having a bass player.'

'Deadly! What is it?'

'Well, it's a bit complicated. But, what they want to do is for us to tour with Leet.'

'Sure that's grand. It'll be a laugh having young fellas like that around the place.'

'Yeah, well we tour Ireland, then the UK. We use Leet's bass player in The Grove. He plays with us every night when Leet come off. We just pay him a session fee.'

'Okay.'

'Now, here's where it gets a bit fucked.'

Jimmy put down his empty glass. He nodded to the barman for three more, even though the other two had barely touched theirs.

'You can fucking say that again,' he said.

Dónal went on.

'Senturion aren't sure about us being headline material in the States.'

'Well that's all right, isn't it? Nothing's even been released over there yet.'

'Yeah. But they think Leet might be.'

'What?'

'The Grove would be supporting Leet in the States.'

'But they haven't even recorded anything yet! They're only kids.'

'I know. But they have the makings of an album and Senturion are ready to put a huge amount of money behind it, based on what they've heard. They'll have songwriters working on it straight away on the side, and they'll come up with a production sound for us to work to in the studio. They're looking for something new and they've decided that Leet is it. They're going full tilt, man. They have some big American friends on board with the whole thing. It's time for a new biggest-band-in-the-world and Leet are in the right place at the right time. Could've been anyone, but it's Leet.'

'But could it not have been us?'

'Well, that's what we were kind of hoping for, Aesop. Unfortunately, they basically think you're too old. You and Jimmy. Great musicians, great songwriters … but a bit long in the tooth to attract the kids in the US. Kids who don't want to see their Dads up there on the stage. They need a new Green Day, now that Green Day are getting all serious.'

Aesop looked in the mirror behind the bar and flicked at his hair.

'Me? Look at me, for fuck sake. I'm gorgeous! I could pass as twenty-two no bother.'

'Maybe not any more Aesop.'

Aesop looked over at Jimmy.

'Is this what has you like this, grandad?'

Jimmy nodded.

'It gets better, man. Go on Dónal.'

'Right. Aesop, do you understand what's happening so far?'

'Yeah. Jesus, it's not like I've no brain at all Dónal.'

'I know that. I just want to make sure you know where we are. We'll all need to be able to discuss it later, the three of us.'

'I'm grand. Go on.'

'Right. So, we release The Grove album, go on tour around Ireland and the UK with Leet as support. The Leet album is recorded on the road. Not easily done, but the timing means it has to happen that way. When it's ready, your album and Leet's album *both* go out in the US, a shed load of money behind theirs and fuck all behind yours. But you'll get the run-off because you're touring together over there

– except with The Grove supporting Leet this time. All the kids over there run out and buy the Leet album because MTV tells them to, some of them buy yours too.'

'Okay. I'm starting to not like it as much now.'

'Right. But that's not all.'

'What do you mean?'

'Senturion are after having another great idea. What they're basically saying is, The Grove is too old to really sell records from a standing start. But Leet don't have the musicianship in the studio to cut it. Or the songwriting. So … after the US tour we all come back here and get back here to work on our second album.'

'Yeah …'

'Except, it's a Leet album.'

'We work on a Leet album? But …'

'The drummer and guitar player in Leet get fired. You and Jimmy join Leet for the other three albums in the contract. What you have in your hand there is really a contract for Leet not The Grove. You see the problem now?'

Aesop nodded.

'One contract, two bands.'

'No. One band Aesop. That's the problem. The Grove is no more. You can take the songs into Leet with you, almost everything else stays the same, except the front man of the band isn't Jimmy. Eamonn does the singing. Jimmy gets to hang back and become a guitar hero. You do what you've always done. You're Jimmy's rhythm section.'

'And … The Grove is gone?'

'Except for the songs. Yeah.'

'Jimmy?'

'Yeah?'

'You all right?'

'No.'

Aesop looked back at his pint for a minute.

'Dónal, it'll never happen.'

'Why not?'

'Man, them lads in Leet have been mates since they were kids.'

'I know.'

'Well, they're not going to just fire the drummer and the guitar player, are they?'

'Well, I don't know. But when there's money involved, Aesop, people can surprise you.'

'Well … okay. But we can just say fuck off, right? We don't want to be in Leet. We want to be in The Grove. Right Jimmy?'

'Right.'

'And anyway, what are they on about? We're huge in Ireland! Everyone loves us.'

'Ireland is a piss-splash Aesop. This is a whole different game we're playing. There's no money in Ireland. Not like that anyway. It's too small.'

Aesop had caught up to Jimmy at this stage and waved at the barman.

'So,' he said, turning back to Dónal. 'We sign this contract, tour, and then come back and join Leet?'

'Right.'

'And if we tell them to fuck off?'

'We tour the UK and Ireland. With Leet if we want. Then we're on our own. The album is released at home and here. Anywhere else, it's only on export. End of story. We go looking for another deal unless the album really breaks. Then Senturion will probably get behind us again. But, Aesop, the album won't break unless they're behind us in the first place. And their plan is to pull money out from under us and put it into Leet. Do you understand?'

'Yeah. I think so. But we can still get another deal, right? We got the first one easy enough, didn't we?'

'Well, in retrospect, the first one was probably all about getting some exposure for you and Jimmy. They wanted you to become known in your own right while they looked for another band that you could join. Kids that will fit the image of this new vibe they're trying to put together. They probably never intended for The Grove to be it. The Grove was just a vehicle for putting you guys on the map, but they need someone else to complete the line-up they have in mind. And then when we came up with Leet, there it all was. A package deal. What they basically want to do is hand-pick a new version of Leet that they think will do the job. So anyway, maybe The Grove could get another deal. We'll still be big in Ireland. We can always pay the bills that way. Maybe the UK fan base from this album would give us a bunt up to something bigger … but no one's making any promises.'

'So what do you think we should do?'

'I think we should think about it.'

'You mean you want to go for it?'

'I mean we should think about it. It's a lot of money. A lot, Aesop.'

'Come on then, how much?'

'You sign that document and commit to the next three albums with Leet – and by the way, you can sign it on your own if you want – and one million will go into your account tomorrow. Sterling.'

Aesop's glass went crashing to the floor.

'Are you all right Aesop?'

He was pale.

'Aesop?'

Aesop stood up and then sat down again.

'You okay?' said Dónal.

'Yeah man. Sorry. When you said one million I got such a shock that I thought I was after having an accident. I could feel it sliding around back there and everything.'

He pulled a melted Curly Wurly out of his back pocket and grinned.

'False alarm.'

Chapter Twenty

'SO YOU'RE really thinking about it?' said Aesop. They were sitting in his hotel room the next night, drinking beer, having gone another round of meetings with Alison and her lads over at Senturion. 'I'd have put money on you telling them to fuck off.'

'Well that was what I nearly did straight away. But I've sat around enough tables like that in me life, Aesop. The best thing to do is chill out and think about it. The worst thing you can do is go flying off the handle and telling people to get fucked.'

'But ... joining Leet? I mean, we've come this far on our own, haven't we? Why do we need to do that? I just don't understand why they're doing it. One minute everyone thinks we're brilliant, songs in the charts and everything, and the next minute we're a couple of oul' fellas and we won't sell records. How the fuck did that happen?'

'We're selling those records because Senturion want us to, Aesop. They're pushing them. It all depends on how many records we want to sell. We keep going the way we're going, without Senturion, and there's a good chance that we end up being just another band that a few people like. She's got loads of them bands. She wants U2.'

'But, Jesus, we can't all be U2.'

'I know.'

'Well ... listen, Jimmy, this is all a bit mad for me to be making decisions. I don't know what to do. Whatever you do, I'll go along with it okay?'

'Aesop, it's too big for that. You need to make your own mind up this time. Really.'

'But I'm not doing it on me own, man. Joining Leet, y'know? Without you? It wouldn't be any fun.'

'Fun? Being rich and famous and touring the world and having every chick on the planet trying to give you ball-hummers wouldn't be fun? Since when?'

'Ah Jaysis, Jimmy. Sure that's practically happening already, isn't it? I've only two balls and I can't keep up with the girls as it is. And

I'm not really there in me head anyway these days, with Helen and all. But c'mere, I meant to ask you ... what about me gaff? That'll still be paid off, won't it? Even if we don't go ahead with the contract.'

'Yeah, that should be grand based on the album. But that might be all you ever have out of it.'

'But it's *more* than I ever had. I'd still be up on the deal. And we'd still get money touring as The Grove. Even if we're only playing Vicar Street and all that. And there's always the chance that we might get another record deal. Y'know? So it's not like we're bollixed if we don't sign.'

'Yeah, I know all that Aesop. And you're right. But ...'

'But you don't want it any more?'

'No, I do. But not like this. Just handed to us, y'know? This way they just press a few buttons and the next thing we're headlining Reading, y'know? Out of the blue.'

'But Jimmy ...'

'Yeah, yeah. I know, I'm never happy. You think I'm a fussy bastard, don't you?'

'You are a fussy bastard, Jimmy.'

'I s'pose. But this'll be like joining another company, Aesop. I just got out of all that shite. I did it for years and I don't want to go back to it now. Y'know what I mean? That contract went into a lot of details, and all the control goes to Senturion. I'd just be back being someone's gimp.'

'But you'd be a gimp with a fleet of Ferraris.'

'And no self-respect.'

'Ah, fuck self-respect. And you don't know it'll be all that bad.'

'I've an idea how it'll be. And it's different for me as well, man. I'm a partner in Sin Bin, okay?'

'Yeah.'

'So, either way, I get a pay out. Join Leet, and it's the big time. Don't join Leet and I'm still getting my cut of Sin Bin's twenty percent. Plus production credits on the albums. I'll probably play a bit on them too. Maybe even contribute a song or two along the way. Y'know what I mean? I'm sorted. Whatever about The Grove,

I'm looking good on the business side whichever way this works out. It's not the same thing at all for you. If you don't join Leet, you've got this album and whatever The Grove can come up with down the line.'

'And that's grand, sure.'

'But Aesop, who the fuck knows where The Grove will go? You need to think about that.'

'Where's it going to go?'

'I'm just saying, Aesop. What happens if me working for Sin Bin takes over? Say we have a rake of bands that we're managing, producing, all that. Say I'm called over to LA to produce a Leet album this time next year, and I'm gone for six months. That's six months with The Grove doing fuck all, y'know? You scratching your bollocks.'

'So … are you saying that you're going to be giving it up? Packing in The Grove? Either way?'

'No I'm not. But it might happen some time. You never know, that's all. In fact, it will happen some day. Aesop, the fuckers are right about one thing. We aren't kids any more. No one does this lark forever.'

'But we're only getting bleedin' started!'

'I know, I know. All I'm saying man, is that this is an opportunity for you to clean up while you can. You sign that deal and you never have to worry about another fucking meal for the rest of your life. You need to think about that.'

'But …'

'Dónal and me are going to advise Leet to sign on. As their business managers, this is fucking huge for them. And us. Right place, right time, jammy bastards, but that's the way it goes sometimes. And c'mere, I'm not just your mate or your bandmate. I'm *your* business manager too.'

'Me bollix.'

'Yeah, well I am. And purely as your business manager, I'd tell you to sign it.'

'What? Without you signing it?'

'Yeah. Listen Aesop, I'm not trying to insult you here, but playing drums is what you do. You're not exactly going to be Ireland's first astronaut, are you?'

'I don't like heights.'

'You're too good a drummer to starve, man, but this chance is once-in-a-lifetime to go way past that. You need to think about it. Sober.'

'A bit late for that.'

'Well, you don't have to give your decision tonight.'

'And what about you?'

'I'm leaning towards no.'

'Not signing it.'

'No. I don't think so.'

'Because. ...'

'I don't know. Because I'm a fuckin' eejit, probably.'

'So the way you're leaning, and what you're advising me to do … it all means no more Grove. No more Aesop and Jimmy keeping it real.'

Jimmy stood up and went to the fridge. He grabbed the last two beers and threw one to Aesop.

'Aesop, you should sign it.'

'But …'

'Really man. I'm not just saying this. You need to sign it. This is a lot bigger than The Grove. This is your chance. Sign it.'

Aesop opened his beer.

'And what happens to Jimmy Collins if I sign it?'

'Jimmy Collins becomes a famous producer.'

'Is that what he wants?'

Jimmy took some of his own beer and shrugged.

'At least working for Sin Bin means doing things my way. That's always better than being a gimp.'

'Ah right. But it's okay for me to be a gimp, is it?'

Jimmy laughed.

'They don't want *you* to be a gimp, Aesop. That's the point.'

'What do they want me to be then?'

'They want you to be Aesop! Why mess with perfection, right?'

'But … so I'd just be kind of a hoor then?'

'Yeah. Your dream job.'

'But … ah, fuck sake, this is hard. Are we out of beer?'

'Yeah.'

Aesop leaned over to the bedside table and picked up the phone.

'Ah yeah. Hello. Is Jonathon there? Tell him it's Aesop … right, thanks.'

'I'm a bit full of beer Aesop,' said Jimmy.

Aesop nodded.

'Jonathon? How's it goin'? Listen, what whiskey do you have? Ah, I don't know where the menu is, just tell me. Right … right … okay … is that all? Hang on …'

Aesop put a hand to the receiver.

'Jimmy, they only have Tullamore Dew.'

Jimmy shook his head.

'Okay Jonathon, Plan B. We'll have to go with scotch. Can you just send us up a bottle of Glenfiddich? Grand. Yeah. That's grand. I'll seeya in a minute so. Cheers … oh c'mere, can you get us a couple of hookers as well?'

Jimmy looked up.

'Aesop …'

Aesop held up a hand at him and kept talking.

'Yeah. Grand. I'll have something dark. Not mad hairy though. I'm not in the mood for cross-country this evening. Yeah. No, that's fine. And … hang on … Jimmy?'

'Will you fuck off Aesop, I don't want a hooker! What are you doing?'

'Ah … no, he's just a bit shy Jonathon. Why don't you just call Julie from last night? She was nice. Yeah. That's lovely, man. Yeah. And the Glenfiddich. Seeya in a minute so.'

Aesop hung up.

'Sorted.'

'Aesop, what the fuck are you doing?'

'You don't have to ride them, Jimmy. It's just a bit of company.

You want to sit here just the two of us all night?'

'Aesop, you can't charge two brazzers to the room. Alison will have a canary. And anyway, I'm not into that. And since when are you into paying for it?'

'Sure, I'm paying for fuck all.'

'But … and what about Helen?'

'Amn't I after saying that you don't have to ride them? Hookers know how to have a good time, that's all. We'll have a laugh, watch. And they don't let skangers into this place. They'll be classy.'

'Classy hoors? I'm getting the fuck out of here, you mad bastard. And who the fuck is Julie?'

'Don't be such a big girl, Jimmy. We're rockstars now.'

'I don't care, you can fuck off.'

Jimmy stood up and grabbed his room key from the bed.

'I don't know what kind of …'

Aesop couldn't keep it in any longer. He started breaking his bollocks laughing.

'Look at the fuckin' face on you!'

'What?'

'There's no hookers, Jimmy. Jonathon was already after hanging up. I was only having a laugh.'

'What? Are you sure?'

'Yes! And don't I keep telling you that I'm in love?'

'Bastard.'

'How could you think I'd be ordering hookers on room service after all the things I keep saying about Helen?'

'Prick.'

Chapter Twenty-one

THE CHAMBERMAID turned up at around ten the following morning, the noise of the doorbell like an air-raid siren in Jimmy's head. He sat up straight, confused and stiff and not knowing where the fuck he was. Then the pain hit him. It was like there was a little man in his head and he was trying to push Jimmy's left eyeball out with the back of a spoon.

'Fuckin' ... hell ...'

The bell rang again and Jimmy winced and went to the door so he could tell whoever it was to fuck off. It opened before he got there and a foreign lady in a uniform started to walk in. When she saw Jimmy she said something that might have been 'House keeping' or 'Sorry' or 'I'll come back later' or even 'Look at the state of your pissed-up head'. Or anything at all, really. Jimmy's brain was only starting to slowly piece stuff together and understanding mad accents was way down on its list of priorities. She backed out of the room again and the door closed, leaving him standing in the middle of the floor with his two hands pressed against his temples. He looked around. Aesop was still lying on the bed, absolutely motionless, one hand down his jeans and the other up his t-shirt. Jimmy didn't want to even think about the dream he might be having.

'Aesop?'

Nothing happened.

'Aesop? Wake up.'

He walked over to the bed.

'Aesop. It's ten o'clock. Wake up.'

Jimmy grabbed a pillow and smacked Aesop on the head. He didn't budge.

'Fuck sake. Will you wake up?'

It wasn't working. He'd have to try something else. He found the remote and flicked through the iPod until he arrived at an old Bronski Beat song and then he turned the volume way up. That did it.

'What the fuck?' said Aesop, one eye open wide and scanning the ceiling, the other one glued shut.

'Get up.'

'Is that … ?'

'Yeah.'

'Make it go away.'

'Are you going to get up?'

'I'm up. Please Jimmy, turn it off … I'm up.'

'You're not. Come on. We said we'd meet Dónal at ten downstairs. We're late.'

'Jimmy?'

'Yeah.'

'You know Clerys clock?'

'Come on Aesop. I'm going next door to have a shower. You're to be up when I get back, okay?'

'No problem.'

Jimmy went to the door.

'Aesop?'

The eyes were closed again.

'Aesop, are you asleep?'

'Culchie. Normansculchie … ssh …'

'Bollocks to this,' said Jimmy. He went into the bathroom and came back with a tall glass of water.

'Last chance, Aesop.'

'Mmm-ffhp-fuckinfuck … twominutes …'

Jimmy poured the water slowly onto Aesop's head and then, when he was nicely teed up, spluttering and looking around in shock, Jimmy gave him two massive smacks in the face with the pillow that sent him toppling off the bed and onto the floor. Aesop bounced up and stood there, dripping.

'Ye fuckin' bastard!'

'Are you awake yet?'

'Mean *fucker*!' He was rubbing the side of his head. 'I was only resting me eyes.'

Aesop went for Jimmy across the bed, but Jimmy just backed up towards the door and escaped out into the corridor. He held the door handle. Aesop was rattling it on the other side.

'You're dead, you bastard. Let me out till I batter you.'

'Go in and have a shower. Dónal is downstairs waiting for us.'

'Fuck'm.'

'Come on. I'll give you a knock in ten minutes right? You're up now. Don't go back to bed, okay?'

'The bed is soaked!'

'Ten minutes.'

'Evil bastard … I'll fuckin' get you for that, Collins.'

THEY WERE both wearing shades going down in the lift to the restaurant. From the outside, if you didn't look really closely, they could've been just another pair of posers going down for their breakfast. Inside, though, they were dying. They weren't used to scotch. It fucked you up slightly differently to Irish whiskey and most of their insides seemed to be writhing in confusion. Aesop had the gargle sweats and his hands were trembling. Jimmy was as sick as a small hospital.

'She'll think I pissed the bed,' said Aesop. 'That lady who does the rooms. She'll think I'm after pissing all over meself. How come I keep ending up with a pissy bed this weather? That's fucking twice now and it wasn't me either time.'

'I wouldn't worry about it.'

'Says the man with the dry bed.'

'I'd say she comes across a lot worse than a wet bed in her job.'

'I don't care. She shouldn't have to clean up my piss. That's not on.'

'It's not your piss, Aesop. It's water from the tap.'

'But she'll think it's my piss. Like the bloke that delivered me new mattress and took away the pissy one after yer woman had a squirt on it. The head on him when he sniffed it. Mortified, so I was.'

'Just leave her a big tip.'

'Me? You were the one that drownded the place.'

'You wouldn't get up.'

'So what? That's no reason to go around firing water at people that are just trying to …'

Jimmy took out his wallet and slapped a twenty into Aesop's hand.

'Here,' he said. 'Now shut up till I get a cup of coffee, will ye? I've a head like a kick in the bollocks.'

The doors of the lift opened and Jimmy and Aesop walked out and down the corridor to the restaurant.

'Good morning gentlemen,' said a bloke in a uniform standing behind a kind of pulpit thing.

'Howya,' said Jimmy.

'Would you care for breakfast? Our buffet is just finished I'm afraid, but you can still order from the à la carte menu?'

'Grand.'

'Is the bar open?' said Aesop, stopping.

'Of course sir. I can call through for you, if you like.'

'Aesop,' said Jimmy. 'Don't …'

'You know it'll work man,' said Aesop. He turned back to the pulpit and squinted at the guy's chest. 'Right … eh … Michael. Can I get two Bloody Marys please? Do they come in pints?'

'Yes. Yes, of course, if Sir would like a pint that should be no problem.'

'No tabasco.'

'I see.'

'And I don't like tomato juice.'

'I'm sorry?'

'Tell the barman to use Guinness instead, okay?'

'Okay. So … eh … that will be: Guinness, vodka …'

'Jesus no. No vodka. What are you trying to do to me? Just Guinness.'

'Just Guinness. Okay. And … Worcestershire sauce … ?'

'In me pint? Are you mad?'

'So … would … would Sir like two pints of Guinness?'

'Ah Jaysis no. It's a bit early for that, Michael. Just the Bloody Marys is grand.'

'I see. Em … very good. I'll … I'll … have them brought to your table.'

He picked up his phone.

'Good man,' said Aesop.

He turned around.

'Jimmy, do you want anything?'

But Jimmy was just shaking his head and walking off.

'Just the two then,' said Aesop and followed him.

'What did you do that for?' said Jimmy, looking around when Aesop caught up.

'Ah, a bit of fucking around in the morning helps me get going for the day. Did you see the head on him? Very polite though. Wasn't he very polite? I'd have told me to fuck off.'

'Just leave him alone, will you? There he is, look.'

They saw Dónal sitting on his own with a newspaper and a cup of coffee.

'Morning, Dónal,' said Jimmy.

Dónal looked up.

'Good Christ. Look at the state of the pair of you. Take off your glasses there and give us a look at you.'

Aesop and Jimmy took the shades off and stood in front of Dónal with their heads down, like they were about to get a bollocking off the headmaster.

'What were you up to last night?' said Dónal, scanning them.

'Ah, we just got talking and then when the beer ran out we started into a bottle of … eh … scotch,' said Jimmy.

'A bottle of scotch. You pair of eejits. Why didn't you come out with me and meet some of my old mates? We had a great night.'

'Man, by the time you rang we were well past being let out among strangers.'

'Well anyway, sit down there. Do you want breakfast?'

He gestured for the waiter.

'Just coffee for me,' said Jimmy.

'Mine's on the way already,' said Aesop.

Dónal ordered coffee for them all and looked at them again.

'Christ. The whole city of London out there waiting for you and you sit in your room on your own and get pissed. Were you talking about the contract?'

'A bit, yeah,' said Jimmy.

'And?'

'Well ... ah, I don't know. I need to think some more about it. Ask me again.'

'Aesop?'

'Are you eating them beans?' said Aesop.

Dónal looked down.

'No. I'm finished.'

Aesop pulled the plate over.

'Do you want to order something?' said Dónal.

'Nah. I need to go easy. The few beans is grand.'

'And the contract?'

'Well ... I'm just thinking about Helen, Dónal. Norman's cousin, y'know? I'm not sure it would work. Me being in Leet and her back in Cork.'

Dónal nodded slowly.

'I didn't realise it was that serious with her.'

'Yeah, well. She's a great bird, man.'

'Okay. But ... you haven't decided for sure yet?'

'No. But I don't think it would work.'

'Right,' said Dónal, sitting back and putting his hands together and looking at them both. 'Well, look, there's no point in talking about it now, is there? With the two of you stinking of ... good fuck. Are they yours?'

A waiter was standing behind Aesop with two pints of Guinness.

'Two Bloody Marys?'

'Just here, thanks,' said Aesop, tapping the table in front of him.

'Enjoy your breakfast Sir.'

'Thanks.'

Dónal looked at the pints and then up at Aesop.

'Bloody Marys?'

'Yeah. Meant to be good for a hangover. Do you want one?'

'No thanks.'

Aesop pushed a pint over to Jimmy.

'I'm not drinking that, Aesop,' said Jimmy.

'Are you not? Why are you pulling it towards you then?'

'That's just a reflex.'

'Cheers lads,' said Aesop. 'Here's to a pain-free afternoon.'

He took up one of the pints and sank half of it. Then he put it down again as a series of expressions ranging from confusion through nausea and on to disgust passed over his features. He shuddered.

'What the fuck …'

'What's wrong?'

'Nothing. I just forgot we were in London. Tastes like he dipped his bollocks in it before bringing it out.'

Jimmy pushed his pint away back towards Aesop.

'And on that note …'

'Lads,' said Dónal, checking his watch. 'I've to make a call outside in the lobby. I'll be back in a minute, okay?'

'No problem.'

Jimmy watched him go and then turned around to look at Aesop.

'Aesop, I think we … Jesus … what are you doing?'

Aesop put down the empty pint glass and gave a little burp.

'Taking my medicine like a man.'

'You'll be sick.'

'But I won't be in the horrors, will I? I'm starting to feel better already. Drink yours, look. Cast out the evil.'

'I'll be grand with the coffee there.'

The waiter had arrived back with a pot of coffee.

'Thanks.'

'You're very welcome, Mr Collins. Have a wonderful morning.'

'Eh … right. Thanks. You too.'

Off he went again.

'Would you say he's gay?' said Aesop, staring into the second pint.

268

'Who?'

'Yer man. The waiter.'

'I don't know. Why?'

'He's all happy and all. And his little walk, look. Would you say he likes mickey?'

'I don't know.'

'Maybe he's just Italian.'

'Are you drunk again?'

'Again?'

'Here, gimme that, will you? Before you get us barred.'

Jimmy took the pint and started to take a few big pulls on it. Then he stopped and slowly took it away from his face, his mouth still open and his eyes staring.

'You have to imagine you're in Mulligans, Jimmy, in the back room. It's not that bad if you just drink it up quickly.'

Jimmy shook his head and pointed over Aesop's shoulder.

Aesop turned around.

Dónal was walking back into the restaurant, grinning his head off. Next to him, a small bag on his shoulder and with an equally beaming smile, was the last person Jimmy expected to see. The small guy laughed when he saw their faces and gave a big wave.

'Supplies!'

ONCE SHIGGY'S bags were safely ensconced in Jimmy's room, the four of them congregated around one of the low tables in the lobby.

'I thought you weren't coming in till next week?' said Jimmy. He was sitting forward in his armchair, all excited now to see Shiggy.

'I called him,' said Dónal. 'He had to come through London anyway, so I asked him to come over a couple of days early.'

'Brillliant! So what's the story Shiggy. How's things?'

'Berry good Jimmy. So busy! I sink Kyotosei and Eirotech ready to do big deal again.'

Jimmy's old company, Eirotech Systems, had been in the process of being taken over by Shiggy's company, Kyotosei, when Jimmy had left the whole corporate scene to concentrate on The Grove. In fact, Jimmy's leaving had a big part in the reason for the deal not going through at the time. It wasn't even a year ago, but it felt like another lifetime to Jimmy. There had been ... complications. Around the time the whole thing was meant to have taken place, Jimmy had gone through a rough time trying to work out if a great job and a secure future were more important than his music. By the time the thing came to a head, drastic actions had to be taken. But Jimmy didn't want to think about that any more. It was such a mental time. Jesus, he could probably write a book about it only no one would believe it.

'So it's going to happen?' he said. 'Great! Will you be coming to take over the operation in Ireland?'

'Probabry. If I want.'

'Do you not want to?'

'Ah Jimmy. Maybe. But different from before. When I go to Ireland before, meet with you guys and Marco, play in Grove ... great fun. But new job will be work work work and you guys not around. Marco getting married, even. Fuck sake, you know?'

'I do, yeah,' laughed Jimmy. 'Nice to see you've been practising your Dublin accent.'

Shiggy smiled.

'Only happens when I see Aesop. Hey Aesop, you okay?'

Aesop was smiling too, but his eyes were half-closed and his head lolling at an unnatural angle for someone who was following a conversation.

'Grand, Shiggy. Just a bit drowsy.'

'He had two pints for his breakfast,' said Jimmy.

'Two pints only? No plobrem for Aesop.'

'Yeah, but he was topping up from last night. We were on the piss a bit.'

'Ah. Always the same with Jimmy and Aesop. How is Norman?'

'He's brilliant. Gave up the bank. He's a landscape gardener now.'

'Randscape ... ?'

'He looks after people's gardens. Y'know … flowers and the grass and all that.'

'Ah. I see. Good job for culchie Norman, *desho*?'

They all laughed.

'Yeah,' said Jimmy. 'He loves it.'

'He is in Daburin? Will I see him?'

'Actually, he's in Cork at the moment. He has a girlfriend now.'

'Great! Nice?'

'Eh … yeah, she's lovely.'

Jimmy glanced at Aesop, but Aesop was starting to fade out.

'So what are we going to do today, lads?' said Dónal. 'The flights home aren't till tomorrow lunchtime, so we can do whatever for the afternoon and then go out properly tonight.'

'What's there to do?' said Jimmy.

'In London? Are you mad?'

'Okay. Whatever. You be in charge. I don't want to use me brain today. Aesop?'

Aesop raised his eyebrows, but didn't open his eyes.

'Aesop, what do you want to do tonight?'

'Gig,' said Aesop.

The lads looked at each other.

'Cool,' said Jimmy. 'Do you know who's playing London at the moment, Dónal?'

'Not really … well, actually, I know that the Bolshoi are here. Could be a once in a lifetime chance, lads. What do you reckon?'

Jimmy frowned at him.

'That's ballet, isn't it?'

'Yep.'

'I'm not really a big fan, Dónal.'

'Have you ever been?'

'No. Have you?'

'No. But it's something I'd like to see once before I croak. And it's the *Bolshoi*, man, y'know?'

'Ah, I'm not sure about ballet. Shiggy?'

'Sure. I go. Which one they do, Dónal?'

271

'They're doing Sleeping Beauty. Tchaikovsky.'

'Right … yeah …' said Jimmy, scratching his chin. 'Is there no proper gigs on, but?'

'What does Aesop want to do?' said Dónal.

'Well, I don't think we'd have to wake him up to find out what he'll think of the ballet idea.'

Dónal gave him a shove beside him on the sofa.

'Aesop?'

'Yeah?'

'Do you want to go to the ballet tonight?'

Aesop opened his eyes and frowned at the three of them in turn.

'Hmm?'

'Do you want to go and see the ballet tonight? Sleeping Beauty …'

'I'm just resting me eyes.'

'No, that's not … Aesop. Aesop, look at me.'

Aesop looked at him again and straightened himself up.

'Are we there yet?'

'Do you want to go to the ballet tonight?'

'The ballet?'

'Yeah.'

'What? Ballet?'

'Yes, Aesop, the bleedin' ballet.'

'In the tights?'

'Yeah.'

'Why would I fuckin' want to do that?'

'Just to see it.'

Aesop tried to point to his nose.

'Does this look like the face of a man who wants to see the ballet, Dónal?'

'Not really, no.'

'Is Liz Hurley in it?'

'I doubt it.'

'Ask me bollix, so.'

He looked across the table and grinned, pointing.

'There's Shiggy.'

Then he drifted off again.

'Yeah, anyway I don't think so Dónal,' said Jimmy. 'Sounds a bit heavy.'

'All right. Actually, y'know what? I'm going to call Mags and get her to fly over. She can leave the kids with her sister. She's been up to her bollocks with Cian the last couple of weeks. Did I tell you he got an awful dose in his chest and wouldn't sleep? Why don't you three head off and do something else and I'll seeya in the morning?'

'Grand,' said Jimmy. 'There'll be a gig on somewhere. Well, have a good night then. Seeya tomorrow. Tell Mags I said hello.'

'Will do. Cheers lads.'

'Seeya.'

Dónal left the three of them there and walked off to make the arrangements.

'So Shiggy, what do you want to do this afternoon?'

'Never been to Rondon before, Jimmy.'

'Me neither. Not properly, like. I'll have a chat with the concierge over there and see what he recommends.'

'What about Aesop?'

Aesop was fast asleep now.

'The bleedin' state of him. He can sleep it off and we'll pick him up later. He's in love by the way, did you know that?'

'Aesop? But … how?'

'Yeah I know. He's in love with Norman's cousin. They met in Cork and this idiot wants to marry her now.'

'Oh oh. Norman not rike that.'

'No, man. He doesn't. Not one fuckin' little bit.'

Chapter Twenty-two

'WAS THIS the best you could do, Collins?' said Aesop, flapping his arms against the cold as Jimmy leaned in to pay the taximan.

'They're fuckin' brilliant. I seen them a couple of times at home.'

'We just left the bleedin' bog behind us, and now that we're all the way over here in the middle of London, you drag me out to see a poxy trad band?'

'What happened to your new-found love for Irish culture, Aesop?'

'Fuck sake. Baby steps, Jimmy, y'know?'

'Anyway, it's not exactly trad. It's more of ...'

'It's not exactly Marilyn Manson either, is it?'

'Ah, Marilyn Manson me hole.'

'Shiggy doesn't want to see a trad band.'

'Is okay, Aesop,' said Shiggy. 'I love Irish trad.'

'What? Since when?'

'Live music, Aesop. Any live music is cool.'

'Fuck sake. Is Clapton or something not playing anywhere?'

'If you wanted in on the voting, Aesop, you shouldn't have gotten shitfaced at breakfast, should you?'

'I had to!'

'Well there you go. That's what happens.'

'Why are we here so early?'

'They do food. I haven't eaten all day.'

'They better not be shite.'

'They're not shite. And stop whinging. They'll have beer inside for you.'

'I'm not drinking tonight.'

'Really?'

'After last night? No bleedin' way. Sure, my body is a temple.'

'Yeah, right,' said Jimmy, walking off towards the venue. 'The fuckin' Temple of Doom.'

The place hadn't really gotten going yet. All the house lights were on and staff were still moving between the few punters who'd turned up early for a feed. Aesop and Shiggy found a spot with a high table near a window off the main concert space, which would hold about three or four hundred punters, and Jimmy went to the bar to order the food and some drinks.

'Two Carlsberg, a Coke and three steaks please,' he said.

'No problem mate,' said the barman, getting to work. 'How do you want the steaks?'

'Eh … ah, well-done is grand.'

There was a guy standing next to him and they nodded to each other.

'Howya. Have you seen the lads before?' said Jimmy, flicking his head in to the stage area.

'Kíla? A few times, yeah,' said the other bloke, smiling. He was Irish.

He took out his wallet to pay for his drinks. Then he looked up again, with a small frown.

'Are you … Jimmy Collins?'

Christ. Here we fuckin' go again, thought Jimmy. He wouldn't have bothered his bollocks saying anything if he'd thought this was going to happen.

'Yeah. Howsit goin'?'

'Grand. Colm Ó'Snodaigh,' he said, putting out his hand.

'Nice to meet you,' said Jimmy, shaking it.

'And you.'

'So … are you living in London?'

The barman would be back in a minute. He could put up with it till then if he had to.

'Nah. Just over for the gig.'

'Oh right. Jaysis, you must like them, so.'

'Ah, they can be a shower of pricks a lot of the time, but you get used to it,' said Colm with a grin.

Jimmy blinked at him.

Colm laughed.

'I'm in the band, Jimmy.'

'Wha … oh fuck, I'm sorry. Ó'Snodaigh, of course. Jesus, I forgot. I didn't recognise you with the beard.'

'Don't worry about it, man.'

'I haven't see yiz play since Croke Park that time.'

'Were you at the game?'

'Nah. Me mate's from Cork. He dragged us all down the pub to watch it.'

'Cork? God. And how was he after the game?'

'Did they not win?'

'Kilkenny did by three points.'

'Well, I don't remember the game, but I've a fair idea of what he was like if they didn't win. A fuckin' bull probably. But, c'mere, playing to eighty thousand people. Jaysis. What was that like?'

'Mental.'

'I'd say, yeah.'

'Your own band is going great guns, though. Fair play.'

'Thanks, yeah.'

'What are yiz up to now?'

'Eh, well we'll be touring Ireland in a few weeks. Then the UK. Then probably over to the States. The lads are over there, look.'

Colm looked over.

'That's brilliant, Jesus. Great stuff. Are you still writing in Irish?'

'Ah, not really. "Caillte" just happened. It might happen again, but … y'know …'

'Yeah. That one was a good one though, Jimmy. Made a lot of people take notice. Lovely tune.'

'Thanks. So … what time are yiz on tonight?'

Colm checked his watch.

'Won't be for a few hours yet. There's a local lad on first and then we'll go on about half nine.'

'Well, I'm looking forward to it anyway. I saw you during "Tóg Go Bog É", in the Olympia I think it was. Jaysis, you had the roof shaking, I swear.'

'Cheers Jimmy. Listen, I might talk to you later, right? Need to get these back to the lads.'

'Yeah, seeya. Good luck.'

'Thanks.'

Jimmy paid the barman and walked back to Aesop and Shiggy.

'Who's yer man?' said Aesop.

'Colm. He's in the band.'

'Right. And did he say … what's that?'

'Coke.'

'Coke?'

'You said you weren't drinking.'

'I'm not *drinking*. I'm having a few pints though, Jesus.'

'Well drink your Coke and you can get a round in when you're done.'

'Where's the steaks?'

'Fuck sake, he doesn't keep them up his jumper, Aesop. They'll be out when they're cooked.'

'Did you get mine rare?'

'Yeah.'

An hour later the lads were mostly finished their dinner. Aesop was still pushing pieces of steak around his plate and scowling at Jimmy now and again. The place was starting to fill up a bit and a buzz was kicking in around the venue. There were a lot of Irish people around, and hearing all the different accents made Jimmy laugh. He looked over at Aesop.

'Are you nearly done with your dinner? We should head in and grab a good spot.'

Aesop sighed and looked back down at his plate.

'Jimmy, didn't I tell you …'

'Heya Jimmy.'

They all looked around. Colm from Kíla was standing there.

'Oh, hiya Colm. Eh, Colm, this is Aesop and this is Shiggy. Lads, this is Colm Ó'Snodaigh. Plays the flute and a few other things with Kíla.'

They all shook hands with each other and then Colm turned back to Jimmy.

'Listen Jimmy, I have …'

'Colm,' said Aesop. 'Does this look rare to you?'

He had his fork with a piece of steak held out in front of Colm's face. Colm looked at it.

'Eh … no, Aesop. I wouldn't say so.'

'Now. See, Jimmy? I bleedin' told you, didn't I? I'm fuckin' losing fillings over here.'

'Jesus. Will you ever get back in your box, Aesop? Sorry Colm …'

'Eh … no bother Jimmy. Listen, I was just wondering … we were back there and I mentioned to the lads that you were here tonight. Would you be interested in getting up to sing "Caillte" during the gig?'

Jimmy wasn't expecting that.

'Ah Jaysis, Colm … I don't know. Kíla plays all these big arrangements and all, already worked out. I wouldn't want you to have to try and ad-lib something at your own gig.'

'It's no problem, Jimmy. Rossa and myself are already after putting something together back there. It'll be nice and loose. Just a jam with the rest of the band, but me and Rossa will keep it together for you to sing over. Eoin plays this lovely slow air on the pipes called "The Moon on my Back", right? And then as it's finishing up, he'll start the melody to "Caillte" and you walk up and take the mike. No intro or anything. What do you reckon? The place will go spare.'

'Aw man … it's very nice of you to offer, but … I don't know. Are you sure?'

'Absolutely Jimmy. Listen, no pressure at all, right? We just thought it'd be cool.'

'Well …'

'Listen, if you're not up for it then no problem. But would you mind if we did it anyway? Rónán loves the song.'

'Yeah, yeah. Jesus, no problem. Does he know the lyrics?'

'He thinks he knows most of them, yeah. Could you write them out anyway?'

'Of course. The Irish ones, right? Here, I'll get some paper off the barman and scribble them down for you.'

'Grand. And listen, I'll give you a nod during the gig, right? If you want to sing, just give me a wink and I'll let Rónán know that you're going to do it yourself.'

'Yeah. Right. Jaysis, it's very nice of you Colm …'

'Ah stop. The crowd will lose their minds, sure.'

'Right. Eh … well, hang on a minute and I'll get a pen and stuff …'

Jimmy went back up to the bar to get something to write on.

Aesop tapped Colm on the arm.

'Colm?'

'Yeah?'

'I don't s'pose you'll be playing any Metallica tonight, will you?'

'Of course we will Aesop. Sure, isn't the last half of the gig mostly stuff from "Master of Puppets".'

'You're only telling me lies now, aren't you Colm?'

'I am.'

'You're some bollocks.'

BY THE time the lights came up later for the main attraction, the lads had a cool table up near the front and to the side. There was some movement in the wings and Jimmy sat forward. He was looking forward to this. He'd been a bit pissed the last time he saw them live, but he remembered the vibe in the place.

'Hey Jimmy,' said Aesop. 'How come they only want you up there later?'

'What?'

'I'm the pretty one. I could've played one of the bodhráns or something. Done a battle of the bodhráns thing with one of them. Y'know … the two of us, seeing who was the best.'

Jimmy looked over at him.

'Have you ever seen their bodhrán player play?'

'No.'

'Well if I were you I'd sit there and shut me hole and be thankful I'm not up there with him.'

'What? Are you saying he's better than me?'

'Aesop …'

'Jimmy, I'm the best drummer in the country. Isn't that what the paper said last week?'

'Yeah. I'm sure they meant rock drummer. It doesn't mean you're the ultimate bodhrán fighting champion.'

'Fuck off. I am.'

'Okay then. You are.'

They didn't say anything for a minute.

'Do you not think I am?'

'Aesop, let's just say it's not your main instrument, okay?'

'Me bollix.'

'Right. Well have a look at this bloke then, and see what you think. Hey Shiggy, you're very quiet there are you okay?'

Shiggy just nodded. Almost as soon as he'd seen the stage, he'd just sat back and sipped on his pint. He'd spotted an instrument up there that he hadn't seen in a very long time.

'Are you sure?'

'Yes Jimmy. No plobrem. Excited.'

'Good stuff. You'll like them, watch.'

'Diddely-diddely-dee,' said Aesop, sighing and looking down at his pint. 'Fucking marvellous way to spend a Saturday evening.'

The band came out to roars and cheers and took up their spots. There were seven of them, all dressed casually. No leather pants or wraparound shades or strutting about the place. It wasn't a Grove gig. The singer wasn't even wearing shoes for fuck sake, and it didn't look like he'd spent the afternoon around at Vidal Sassoon's either. The stage was covered in instruments. Tons of them. Jimmy didn't even know what half of them were called. Typical trad. Bloody talented bastards, this lot.

Aesop leaned forward to take the piss out of them.

'Hey Jimmy, do y'know what? I betcha …'

Then he saw the fiddle player who'd just walked on. A gorgeous tall blonde with a magic dimply smile. Up went one eyebrow. He closed his mouth and leaned back again with his arms folded. He was here now, wasn't he? Sure, he might as well give it a chance.

'Yeah, what?' said Jimmy.

'Eh … nothing. Shut up a minute.'

'Shut up? I wasn't the one …'

'Jimmy, please!'

'Fuck sake …'

They turned to the stage again as the band started into their first piece.

Almost immediately, Jimmy was enthralled. Yeah, he'd seen them before, but he'd just been one of crowd then. He was really listening to them this time, watching them. And not just enjoying the music. He was taking it apart, following the swells and peaks not with his ears but with that other part of him that he'd almost forgotten he had. By the second or third song he was barely even in the room with everyone else. Kíla songs were huge and lush one minute, haunting and lingering the next. Playful or thunderous. Sometimes playful *and* thunderous in the same song. It was nothing like rock music. When they were in full flight, it was like seven people keeping seven footballs in the air by passing them around between them.

As the gig went on and Jimmy shifted his attention around the various performances of the people on the stage, he found himself getting faintly embarrassed. Here was this band, virtuoso musicians painting canvas after vivid canvas in sound and sending them soaring through the air out to the rapt audience; no pretension, no posturing, no fucking about … each one supplying their own colour and texture so that each picture would emerge whole and perfect.

'Fuck sake,' said Aesop at one stage, shaking his head as another tune reached a shaking, shrieking summit before disappearing into the roars of the delighted audience.

'What?' said Jimmy.

'How is this trad, you lying bastard? Some of this stuff is heavy as fuck! Maiden weren't that loud in The Point. Me ears! What was that one called again?'

'"Glanfaidh Mé". Didn't I tell you it wasn't just trad?'

'Jesus. It sounds like trad being locked in a barrel and thrown down a hill. How come I never heard this stuff before?'

'You wouldn't come with me and Norman the last time. Remember? You said you'd rather be run over. Anyway, do you like it?'

'Yeah, it's deadly. I mean, it's not like jazz or anything, but … eh … it's kind of … y'know?'

Jimmy nodded. It had the same kind of interaction between the different instruments, but without that straight-edged structure. No one was trying to fill any corners, because there weren't any. The music was rolling and organic and if one performer took a lead, the new focus seemed to grow out of what was happening already instead of suddenly appearing in the piece like a stuck-out elbow. Everyone in the place was part of the gig and the stage seemed to extend out into them, past the fetch of the lights and back to all the walls.

'And Rónán?'

'Rónán?'

'On the bodhrán.'

'Eh … yeah. Right. I want to talk to him about that. Can we go backstage afterwards?'

'I'll say it to Colm.'

'Did you see the little skinny yoke he's using as a tipper? And the way he holds it? There's something going on there, man. I need a word with him before we leave. Can't have that shite going on and me not knowing how it's done, the fucker.'

'So you're not the best bodhrán player in the country any more?'

Aesop shook his head. He looked up at the stage, where the guy was rounding off a solo percussion bit, and bit at his knuckles and frowned for a minute as he watched. Then he turned around to Jimmy again.

'Still the prettiest, though.'

The piper's drones started to wail on their own, a low desolate voice, before his fingers started to pick out another slow air. The lads hushed up with everyone else and watched. It was beautiful and eerie. Outside was the city of London, all lights and bustle and energy, but in here it was dark and close. They could have been hunched over the fire in Norman's cottage in Cork, a moonlit bog at their door.

Jimmy got a tap on the arm from Aesop. He looked around and Aesop pointed up to the stage. Colm was standing back in the shadows, but he was looking down at their table and giving Jimmy big eyes. Did he want to sing 'Caillte'?

Jesus. He'd been so wrapped up in the gig that he'd forgotten completely about this. He didn't know what to do. This was like no gig he'd ever sang at before. A session down the pub was one thing, but he wasn't prepared for this. It wasn't a different league, it was a different game. It wasn't about haircuts and standing with your legs apart and throwing big sultry eyes at the chicks in the front row. It was about the song. That was the only reason you were there. Not to play or sing it … to channel it.

Jimmy closed his eyes and thanked Christ he'd written 'Caillte'. He very suddenly and very badly wanted to get onto that stage and grab some of the vibe that was floating around up there. It wasn't like what he got with The Grove. This gig was a completely different animal. It wasn't his scene but he wanted a sup, just to see. He'd been feeling funny ever since the gig had started. Something had been nagging at him. Tugging his sleeve. He didn't know what it was, but he might find out up there. He swallowed. Okay Jimmy. No leather pants. No Strat or Les Paul. No effects pedals. No mates in the audience. No posing. No Dónal or Sparky. No rehearsal. No intro. No soundcheck. No fucking idea what key they're going to play it in, even.

Just the song.

He gave Colm a wave and got a nod in return. He was on.

He wiped his hands on his jeans and drank the last couple of inches of Aesop's Coke to wet his throat.

'Ugh,' he said, pushing the glass away. 'There's vodka in that, you bollocks.'

'I didn't ask you to drink it, did I?'

'Bastard.'

'Go on, look. Colm's waving at you.'

The piper was after easing out of his own tune and the main melody of 'Caillte' was now recognisable. To the lads, at least, because

283

they knew it was coming. The punters probably just thought it was part of the air he'd be playing anyway. Then the piper looked up from his hands and over at Jimmy, giving him a small nod. Jimmy took a big breath and stood up, walking over to the right side of the stage. A couple of people in the crowd looked over but they still didn't know what was going on. A few heads had seemed to recognise him earlier, but himself and Aesop had pretty much kept their own heads down all night. Now he could have just been one of the crew fixing something.

But when he stepped up onto the stage and walked over to the mike in the middle, everyone twigged. That was Jimmy Collins up there, and it was 'Caillte' they were suddenly hearing out of the pipes. A huge clamor of roaring and clapping started up, everyone turning to their neighbour and pointing. Jimmy gave a little smile and adjusted the angle of the mike to his mouth. This wasn't the time or place to be acting the Jagger, stomping around and sopping up the love like a needy, greedy fucker. He just stood there with his hands in his pockets and his eyes closed until they hushed up again.

As soon as they did, Jimmy heard the sound filling out. The bass was in now. A couple of guitars. Rónán was clicking gently around the rim of the bodhrán. Jesus. They'd put this together in a few minutes backstage? The piper had put down his uilleann pipes and now the low whistle was blowing across the stage. The released version of the song was about four minutes long, and they'd nearly played that long already just as an intro. It was gorgeous. Jimmy found his way in and started singing, opening his eyes briefly to take it in. Four hundred upturned faces were like moons out in the blackness. He closed his eyes again and just let it come. Rónán knew the harmonies and sung them softly with him, adding a few of his own. Long bowed notes that seemed to go on forever were coming out of the fiddle. Somebody was playing a beautiful countermelody on a bouzouki or some fucking thing. Christ, they were good. It was like he was guesting on their song. It was still 'Caillte', but it was different. The version Alice might have heard down her rabbit hole. Jimmy had never been so immersed in sound. He was blown away.

At the end he just stood back from the mike and waited until the others brought the song down. The crowd bellowed and cheered but Jimmy just nodded and gave a little smile and a wave. He'd done fuck all, really. It was all them.

Rónán leaned into his ear.

'Seeya later Jimmy, right?'

'Yeah. Thanks man.'

Rónán nodded and stepped to the mike.

'Jimmy Collins from The Grove,' he said, clapping over to Jimmy who waved again on his way off the stage. The crowd yelled louder.

Then Jimmy was back in his seat, getting clapped on the back from Shiggy and having a pint thrust towards him by Aesop.

'Great!' said Shiggy. 'Wow. So great Jimmy …'

'Man,' said Aesop, laughing. 'You looked stoned off your tits up there.'

'I was. How did it sound, but?'

'Sounded deadly.'

'Sure?'

'Yeah, it was fuckin' great.'

'Cheers.'

The band were already barreling away into their next tune. A couple of people at tables next to them were catching Jimmy's eye and saying well done and stuff, but for the most part he was just leaning back in his chair and trying not to notice his heart banging the shite out of his chest. That had been amazing. What they'd done to his song … how the fuck would he ever be able to sing it again with The Grove. His version sounded like it was in the nip.

He barely registered what was going on for the rest of the gig, except just to sit there and listen. Another guy, a Japanese guy, got up later on and played with them for a few songs. Shiggy was riveted to the stage for that part. Then they played some more and then it was over. Lights up, the crowd finishing their drinks and making their way out into the London night and staff cleaning the place down. Colm came out and brought the lads backstage. It was mad back there, the band and a load of other people just mixing and having a laugh. Jimmy shook about a hundred hands and talked with loads of people, but he was still high from singing and wasn't taking much in. Shiggy was talking with the Japanese guy who'd played earlier and Aesop hadn't wasted any time in collaring Rónán. Jimmy walked past at one stage and heard them arguing. Rónán was beating out a rhythm on a conga drum and Aesop was trying to follow him on the bodhrán.

'That's not what you played a minute ago,' Aesop was saying, frowning at Rónán's hands.

'It is! That's twice now I've played it.'

'It fuckin' is not Rónán. It's a slip jig, sure.'

'It was a slip jig the last bleedin' time I played it as well.'

'It wasn't! Look, play "Double Knuckle Shuffle" again. Here, take the bodhrán. What are you doing with your left hand again? I don't remember.'

'Christ. That's four times now. If I play it on your dopey head will you remember?'

'I was drinking for Ireland last night, Rónán, piss off. You're lucky I'm here at all. Only for Jimmy nagging me I'd be home in bed.'

'Jesus, I must remember to thank him. Okay, now are you watching? It's in four-four ...'

Later on in the taxi back to the hotel, Jimmy sat in the back with Aesop, just staring out the window.

'What's up?' said Aesop.

'Hmm?'

'What's with the big cheesy grin on you?'

'Have I? Oh, nothing. Just ... eh, nothing.'

But it was something. Jimmy's eyes were flying back and forth, following the scenes outside, but inside he was still. Aesop wouldn't get how happy he was right now. No one would. He leaned back against the seat and listened, relieved and excited.

His head was filled with music. At long fucking last.

LATER ON, unable to sleep with the torrents of ideas now filling him, he called Susan. He got her voicemail.

'Hey Susan. Sorry, I know it's late. Look, I just wanted to say hello. I'm still in London, but we're heading back at lunchtime tomorrow. I could meet you for breakfast or coffee if you have time? The flight is at one-thirty, but call me any time in the morning, or even tonight if you get this? I'd love to see you, if it's okay. Right, eh … I'll go so. Hope you're okay. Seeya …'

He put down the phone and stripped to his jocks. He thought he heard his phone ringing when he was brushing his teeth, but when he went back into the room and looked at it lying on his bed, it showed nothing. He went back into the bathroom and finished up. She'd be asleep. Or she didn't answer when she saw his name flash up on the screen of her phone. Again he heard the ringing. He was on his way back to the bed when he realised that the noise was just in his head, writhing around with jigs and reels and huge Celtic-inspired Lizzy and Big Country and Frames riffs.

Chapter Twenty-three

NORMAN WAS waiting for them at the airport, all smiles. When he saw Shiggy, he let a yell out of him and ran up to give him a hug.

'Bloody hell, Shiggy, what are you doing here? I thought you weren't coming in till later in the week?'

Shiggy extracted himself from the tentacled mountain that was clinging onto him and shook his head a few times until his neck cracked back into place.

'Fry in early to see you guys,' he said, smiling.

'Magic! We'll have a great oul' laugh. Are you working or what's the story?'

'Working from Thursday. Horiday now.'

'Brilliant. Well it's great to see you.'

He turned to the other two.

'How was London?'

'A bit mental,' said Jimmy. 'Mostly on the piss once the meetings were over.'

'How did it go with the record company lot?'

'Ah, long story. I'll tell you later. Hey, we went to see Kíla last night.'

'Yeah, were they over there? How was it?'

'Brilliant, man. You'd have loved it. I sang "Caillte" with them and everything.'

'Deadly! How did that go?'

'Man, it was cool. You should have heard the version they did. I'm telling you, I'm after getting a load of ideas.'

'Yeah. You look pretty happy. A good trip so? Did you hook up with Susan?'

'Nah. Left her a message, but it was pretty late last night so she probably didn't get it. Anyway, you look pretty happy yourself. What did you get up to?'

'Jimmy, you wouldn't believe the few days I'm after having with

Trish. We just drove up this morning from Granny's. She's in work now. But it was so cool down there just the two of us. We just stayed in the house the whole time, with the weather the way it was. But, God, it was magic all the same.'

'Great.'

'Ah Jimmy, she's some girl. She's … Christ …'

Jimmy laughed.

'Jaysis, look at the head on you. Wedding bells, is it?'

'Don't be messing. Well … ah no, I'm saying nothing …'

But he didn't have to. It was all over his face.

Aesop didn't say anything but Norman eventually turned around to him.

'Well, Aesop.'

'Howya Norman.'

'Did you have a good time in London?'

'Was grand, yeah.'

'Grand.'

'Listen Norman, about the other night in Cork …'

'I don't want to hear it Aesop.'

'No, listen a minute. Just … if it'll make you feel any better, nothing went on between me and Helen, okay? We were just talking. Okay? That's it. No big deal. Can we forget about it? Your family honour is intact.'

Norman nodded and didn't say anything. Aesop went on.

'I know what you think of me when it comes to that kind of thing. I s'pose I deserve it. But I can't do anything about the fact that I like her, okay? If me and you are going to keep having rows about it …'

'So how many English slappers did you pick up in London?'

'None.'

'Jimmy?'

'He didn't, Norman.'

Norman nodded again.

'Well this isn't the place to talk about it anyway. C'mon and we'll get you all sorted out.'

The four lads made their way out to the bitterly cold concourse. Jimmy and Shiggy turned left to head down to the taxis. Norman and Aesop crossed the road into the car park.

A girl stepped out of the airport building and the doors whooshed closed behind her. She stood and watched Norman and Aesop disappear into the car park lift and then she crossed the road after them.

JIMMY COULD see that Dónal wasn't exactly chuffed, but that he probably wasn't all that surprised either. He was nodding slowly. He always did that when he was negotiating or otherwise engaged in a conversation that wasn't going exactly the way he'd hoped. The nodding made you keep talking when really the best thing to do was probably shut your hole.

'So that's why, Dónal,' said Jimmy. 'I've been thinking about it since last week and the bottom line is that Senturion just want my guitar and the fact that I've got more cop-on than Eamonn and the lads because I'm older. I'd just be the consultant, only there to keep the lads on an even keel.'

Nod. Nod.

'So … well … when it comes down to it, I'd be a session musician, wouldn't I? Well-paid and all that, but that's not why I want to be in this game. I'd just be working for a company again.'

Nod.

'And I'm saying no. Sorry man. I know what it means to Sin Bin, but …'

'Yeah,' said Dónal, flicking something off his shirt.

'Are you pissed off?'

Dónal shrugged.

'With you? Nah. You're a stubborn bastard, Jimmy, and you have your own ideas about how you want things to go. I knew that the first time I met you. If you were eighteen, this'd be a doddle, but you're not. Hey Aesop? Anything to say to us?'

Aesop had just been sitting there on the couch in the meeting room, watching them. He'd already told both of them that he was going to stick with Jimmy and no amount of cajoling was going to change his mind. If being a huge rockstar meant no more playing with Jimmy, no more craic in Dublin, so much travelling that he'd hardly ever get to have dinner in Peggy's or call around to see his nephews or go for a pint in the Fluther … or get a chance with Helen … then he didn't want to do it. He didn't need that much money and he'd already convinced himself that the Old Aesop and his debauchery were a thing of the past and being surrounded by all that carry-on when Leet were on tour would only disgust him.

'Told you man,' he said. 'I'm with Jimmy.'

Dónal sighed and gave a final nod.

'Okay then.'

'You are pissed off,' said Jimmy. 'Look at the head on you.'

'I'm not Jimmy. This was just … this business is like a skyscraper, right? You walk into the lobby and usually the guard fucks you out on your ear. Assuming he doesn't, every now and then an elevator door opens and you jump in and see how far you get.'

'There'll be other elevators Dónal,' said Jimmy.

'Yeah. I know. But you're not going to fucking make it easy for me, are you, ye bollocks? Jesus, you won't even let me make you into a bloody superstar!'

'Sorry man.'

'Forget about it. If that's the way it is, then fuck it. I'll talk to them later in the week. And we've still got a lot of work ahead of us. If the tour goes well and the album goes well, maybe The Grove will still hit big. And it'll be the hard way, Jimmy. The way you like it, right?'

Jimmy laughed and put his hands over his face.

'Jesus, am I that bad?'

'Let's just say there aren't too many people in this game that would turn their nose up at what's on the table here. Man, you're the least greedy person I've ever met.'

'But it's not about greed, Dónal. Is it? I mean, it's about … freedom.'

Aesop stood up and belched.

'Ah, fuck this. Freedom? Will you ever ask me bollix. Are we done Dónal, or you … fuckin' … William Wallace … do you have any more words of inspiration for us before lunch?'

'It's only eleven o'clock Aesop,' said Jimmy.

'I'm starving. Norman had me up at half-six, the prick.'

'For what?'

'The lying shite said it was half-nine and we were late for this.'

'What did you do at that hour?'

'He's mad. First of all he was after making a fruit salad for breakfast. Fruit! For breakfast! And then we got in the van to come here. Of course, I fell asleep and when I woke up we were at Dollymount. The first thing I see out the windscreen when I open me eyes is Norman in a pair of jocks running into the sea. Me fuckin' heart. I thought I was after eating a bad prune.'

The lads were laughing.

'I'm telling yis, it's not funny. He comes out and is standing there in front of the van, grinning and drying himself and singing some fucking song about a Red Rose Café at the top of his voice. It's about minus fifty degrees out there and he's in the nip with a delighted head on him, like he's getting a rub and tug off six dancing cowgirls. I'm morto, looking around to see if anyone else is watching this. Of course, then I realise that it's barely even bright and no one's about. The clock on the dashboard says it's only half-seven. The fucker laughing at me then. Dónal, I want a new bodyguard.'

'Sorry man. He's doing a great job. You're still with us, aren't you?'

'He was bad enough when he was just a big culchie with shite taste in music and always calling me names, but now he's in love and he won't stop singing and laughing. And every time he sees me, he shouts me name and thumps me on the back like he thinks I'm fuckin' choking. It's like getting hit by a telephone book, I'm telling you. And I'm only small.'

'He's just happy, Aesop.'

'Well I'm getting a pain in my hole, so I am. I want a decent bodyguard, Dónal. A proper big scary shaved-headed fucker with

292

tattoos, not that dizzy, lovesick, overgrown fuckin'... leprechaun.'

'Where is he now?' said Jimmy, laughing.

'He's helping Sparky,' said Dónal. 'They're gone off to pick up some new gear.'

'Right. Well, anyway it's too early for lunch, Aesop.'

'But I'm dizzy with the hunger.'

'Jesus. Have a banana. Sparky keeps a stash in the kitchen.'

'I don't want a bleedin' banana! I want a burger. The bleedin' jolly green giant has been feeding me nothing but fruit and vegetables all week. He said I could have a chicken breast last night, and then he goes and he fucking *boils* it. No salt or fuck all was I allowed put on it.'

'He's only looking out for your health. God knows, a bit of de-tox would be good for you before we go on tour.'

'There'll be nothing left of me to go on tour! You'll have to wheel me out onto the stage.'

Dónal suddenly frowned and started rooting in his inside pocket. He pulled out a small Milky Bar and held it up.

'It's a bit melt ...'

Aesop grabbed it off him and had the wrapper scrunched up on the table in about half a second.

'I meant to give that to Molly last night,' said Dónal, looking at it disappear whole into Aesop's mouth. 'But she was in bed when I got in.'

'Ah'll ge ha an udder un,' said Aesop, his mouth full of white gloop.

Jimmy and Dónal watched him swallow and wipe the dribble off his chin.

'You're after eating the child's Milky Bar,' said Jimmy, shaking his head.

'Emergency Jimmy,' said Aesop. 'Don't tell Norman, right? He said he wouldn't wake me up before nine from now on if I promised not to eat shite until the tour.'

Jimmy sighed.

'Whatever.'

'That was nice, actually,' said Aesop, looking at them in surprise and licking his lips.

'Okay,' said Dónal, picking up his pencil and looking down at his notes. 'Can we get on with the meeting now?'

'I don't know when I last had a Milky Bar.'

'Aesop … please?'

'Yeah, no problem. What's next?'

'Bass player. We're going out in three weeks and we've no one. Do we use Ryan from Leet, do we stick with Sparky, or is Shiggy going to play.'

'I talked to Shiggy,' said Jimmy. 'He'd love to play, but he can't. He can't walk away from his job. I told him what'd probably happen with Senturion and that I wasn't going to go for it. If he'd been in on the big bucks deal, then he might have done it. But he's not going to drop everything to play with us on one tour around Ireland and Britain when no one knows what'll happen after that. It's fair enough.'

'Ah bollocks,' said Aesop.

'C'mon, Aesop,' said Jimmy. 'He'd be stupid to do it.'

'You did it.'

'Yeah. Well there you go.'

'So …' said Dónal. 'Ryan or Sparky?'

'We should probably use Ryan,' said Jimmy, looking around. 'Right?'

Aesop nodded.

'I s'pose.'

'Will Sparky be all right with that?' said Jimmy.

'He'll be delighted!' said Dónal, laughing. 'Reckons he's too old for rocking it out with you guys at this stage. He'll do it if you ask him, but it probably wouldn't be good for his … demeanour.'

'Jaysis, well that seals it,' said Aesop. 'Anything that makes that fucker any crankier is something we should steer clear of. Some kid will get all excited and slag his beard or something and he'll hop off the stage and cream him with the bass.'

'Will Ryan know the parts in time though?' said Jimmy.

'I think so,' said Dónal. 'It won't be easy, but he's a good lad and he likes the sound of the extra dosh.'

'Shiggy said he'd be okay about coming in here in the evenings and going over it all with him.'

'Ah, that's cool. Fair play to him. We'll give him a few quid.'

'I said that. He doesn't want it.'

'Will he be here for any of the gigs?'

'Nah,' said Jimmy. 'He finishes up a couple of days before The Point gig. How are the sales going for that, by the way?'

'Brilliant,' said Dónal. 'Nearly three thousand so far. Should be full. Pity Shiggy can't guest though.'

'Yeah. Ah well.'

'Okay. So, we've got to get some serious rehearsals in. You two good to go?'

'Yeah. No problem.'

'Aesop?'

'Yeah. I'm easy.'

'Norman happy that you're going to be in Dublin? There's been no news of the quare one, has there?'

'No. Not since she stopped going around the place pissing on people's beds and robbing their favourite t-shirts. But anyway, to answer your question, me being in Dublin doesn't seem to be bothering Norman very much all of a sudden. He's all happy once his bird is here too.'

'Grand so.'

'Yeah. Nice to see I'm on top of his list of priorities, isn't it? Fuck sake.'

'I'm sure he knows what he's doing.'

'You didn't see him splashing around in the sea this morning like a fucking two-year-old in the bath. If yer woman catches up with me I'm fucked. I'll be running for me life and he'll be sitting in a field somewhere singing Cliff Richard songs and pulling the petals off daisies.'

'You're grand,' said Jimmy.

'Okay. So the next thing …' said Dónal.

'Oh, that's all sorted out so,' said Aesop. 'Thanks lads.'

'Next thing. Look, I know we've all been busy with other stuff, but we need to start at least getting an idea of what we're going to do after "Brazen Songs and Stories".'

'It's not even out yet,' said Aesop.

'I know. But we need something to aim for. Jimmy, I know you've been struggling a bit with all the things that were going on, but I need to know … do you have any ideas?'

He was expecting this to be tough. Jimmy had hit a wall and Dónal knew all the signs. He figured that this was where the meeting was going to get hard and he was pretty much expecting Jimmy to get all pissed off and defensive. What he didn't expect was for Jimmy to jump off the couch and run in to get a guitar before coming back out to them grinning like he had a coathanger in his mouth.

Dónal sat back and folded his hands against his belly, waiting.

Did this mean … ?

'Okay lads … I'm after having an idea.'

'Brilliant,' said Dónal. He looked over at Aesop to see if he knew what was up, but Aesop seemed just as surprised as he was. 'What is it?'

'Okay,' said Jimmy. 'What's this?'

Jimmy played the main lick of Thin Lizzy's version of 'Whiskey in the Jar'. No one said anything. It was a rhetorical question. That was the most recognisable guitar lick in Ireland.

'Lads?'

'It's Lizzy,' said Aesop. 'What about it?'

'Eleven notes,' said Jimmy. 'Eleven notes that changed the world.'

Aesop looked over at Dónal and sat back into the sofa with a small sigh. He knew Jimmy. Whatever the fuck this was, it wasn't going to be short and sweet.

'How do you mean?' said Dónal.

'Lizzy were like any other band. Looking for a break, right? "Whiskey" was s'posed to be a B-side and, whatever happened, it ended up being the A-side. Bang. Next thing they're on Top of the Pops. Philo's up there. Black, Irish, sexy, cool-as-fuck. Singing a rock version of a folk song. Do you have any idea how old the lyrics are, for fuck sake?'

Dónal was nodding again now, although this time it was more out of confusion than any great desire for Jimmy to keep talking.

'So, do you see lads? One song. Lizzy are on the map. Ireland is on the map. We were after having a generation of show bands and céilí music that went nowhere. All that talent disappearing into nothing. You had Van Morrison over in the States wanking out "Astral Weeks" and you had Rory playing the blues because that's what was in his bones, but nothing had ever come out of *Ireland* before that meant anything. Then there was Lizzy. You think the Rats would've gotten a look-in if Lizzy hadn't gone to England and made them all realise we weren't just a bunch of dopey spud-farmers? Would U2 even have bothered their bollocks only for "Jailbreak" and "Bad Reputation"? Ireland had nothing to offer the world except drinking songs and set dancing and the world didn't give a fuck about either of them. Then Eric Bell pulls those eleven notes out of his hole and everything changed.'

He looked at Aesop.

'What are you fucking nodding at?'

'Hmm? Nothing. Just … eh, sorry Jimmy, but I'm not sure what you're bleedin' on about.'

'Right. Well this is what I'm on about. I'm sick to the back fucking teeth of playing songs that sound like they were written for American teenagers. MTV my hole. That's not who I am. It's not who *we* are. We're meant to be Celts for fuck sake! All the kids care about these days is Paris Hilton and her bleedin' chihuahua. What's that? Pop Idol and Fashion Idol and Model Idol and Build a Better Gaff and Sell if for Loads of Fucking Money Idol. This country needs to remember who we are before we're all talking in American accents and drinking coffee out of buckets. That's what I'm on about.'

'And the next album …' said Dónal, carefully, hoping to prompt Jimmy in at least that general direction before he started ranting again.

Jimmy looked down at the guitar again and played another clutch of notes.

'"When You Were Sweet Sixteen",' said Dónal.

'Yeah. I can't do it properly on this, but you know how the banjo sounds on it, don't you? It's sounds like it's fucking *crying*. Now *that's* an Irish love song. A beautiful melody, poetry for lyrics and sung by a big mad fucker with electric hair, a red scraggly beard and the special voice he uses when he's singing you tender ballads instead of kicking the fuck out of you in the pub. When I write a love song, that's what I want it to be.'

He played the intro to 'Black Rose'.

'And when I write a rock song I want it to sound like that. Like I *am* kicking the fuck out of you in the pub.'

'Jesus, Jimmy,' said Dónal, rubbing his head. 'We're not all about milling the shite out of each other in pubs.'

'No, we're not. But at least we're passionate about stuff. Or we used to be, anyway. Remember Sinéad O'Connor? Never happier than when she was winding people up. Mad as a brush one minute and she'd have you weeping into your pint the next. And Geldof. Look what he did! Just by being a belligerent cantankerous Irish fucker who thought it was all a pile of shite and decided to tell them all to go fuck themselves and cop-on. They were *Celts*, man. Irate, livid, loopers the pair of them. Or Ronnie Drew with them mad eyes and a voice so gravelly you could park your bleedin' car on it. Or Shane McGowan and the locked head on him with no teeth, or Moving Hearts saying fuck you to the Brits and the Yanks. We're losing it, man. And I don't want to lose it. I've been looking in the wrong place for months and now I know what I have to do. That's our next album.'

'That's our …' said Dónal.

'And by the way, Aesop, that idea you had for the girl trad band was a fucking brilliant idea. We should do that as well. That's *exactly* what I'm talking about. A trad band of total honeys? Well that's your baby. You can be fucking *Mister* B*Jaysis, right?'

'Can I?' said Aesop, who looked like he'd just been woken up. He turned to Dónal all grins. 'Mister B*Jaysis … deadly.'

'Because *that's* what we're about. Fuck sensible skirts below the knee and big woolly jumpers. It's about time a trad musician can say "yeah, I'm a chick up here playing a reel on the fiddle, but I'm all tits and legs and rage too and maybe I might shag you or maybe I might tell you to piss off, but before any of that happens you're going to come with me and this tune to wherever it takes us and we're going to get lost there for a while and if there's going to be any riding going on then we'll talk about it when I'm done playing, maybe".'

'Jesus …' said Dónal. He rubbing with both hands now. 'What the fu …'

'And another thing …' said Jimmy.

Aesop was sitting forward in the sofa now, smiling at the two of them.

'I'm starting to get into this,' he said, jiggling his legs. 'Go on Jimmy. Let it all out, son. What's the other thing?'

'It's not just about …'

'Howya lads.'

Sparky had just walked in with Norman.

'Will yis have a cup of tea?' he said.

'Good Jesus no,' said Dónal. 'Tea is the last fucking thing we need over here at the moment.'

'Okay so. Be out in a minute.'

'How's it going?' said Norman, taking off his coat and sitting down beside Jimmy.

'It's going great,' said Jimmy. 'Actually, I'm glad you're here Norman. Now. You're a culchie, right?'

'Christ Jimmy, I'm only in the door. Will you ever fuck off with yourself and let me warm up a bit?'

'No Norman, listen, I'm not slagg …'

'Jimmy's having a revelation Norman,' said Aesop. 'Sit back there and listen to this. He's gone mad.'

'Norman,' said Jimmy. 'Who would you say is your favourite musician in the world?'

'Eh …' said Norman. He didn't know what was wanted here.

'You, Jimmy?'

'No, fuck that. Seriously.'

'Oh. Okay. Probably Dónal Lunny then.'

'Yes!' shouted Jimmy, making Norman jump backwards and almost punch him in the head as a reflex.

'Exactly!' said Jimmy. 'And why is he, Norman?'

'Eh …' said Norman, moving away up the couch a bit for both their sakes. 'I s'pose it's because of the Bothy Band and Planxty first. And then … well, he just always had these brilliant bands around him, didn't he? And musicians. Christy, Davy Spillane, Liam O'Flynn … Christ, did you ever hear Liam Óg playing 'An Buach-aill Caol Dubh'? It'd set the hairs jumping off your neck … but anyway, yeah, Dónal Lunny I'd say, Jimmy. He's always there when something's happening.'

'That's right. And he did more than just be in a band, didn't he? Planxty had the purists pulling their hair out, and then Moving Hearts had them in conniptions. But did he care? He did in his bollocks. So, I'm getting back to me roots. Horslips, Hearts and Lizzy all did their bit. Now it's my turn.'

'Okay, okay,' said Dónal, sitting up. 'Jimmy, listen to me man, Lizzy were a rock band. They'd a few rocked-up Irish tunes, yeah, but everyone remembers "The Boys are Back in Town", not "Emerald". Philo was the man, but he wasn't on some big mission, y'know? "Whiskey in the Jar" was thirty years ago. You can't say it had this huge lasting influence on …'

'Can I not? Cos I heard Metallica playing it two days ago on the radio and it sounded brilliant.'

'All right. Bad example. But, man, you still haven't told us what you're planning here. Do you want to make a trad album? Trad rock? What are we fucking talking about? It sounds like a sharp left from everything we've ever talked about for The Grove. You put out a trad album and, I'm telling you, you can just about kiss every arse in Senturion goodbye as they're walking out the door.'

'I bags Alison's,' said Aesop quickly, putting up his hand.

'I'm telling you, man,' said Dónal, ignoring him. 'Tell me what you have in mind, will you? And c'mere, keep in mind that Sin Bin isn't just here so you can indulge any Celtic Twilight fantasies you might be having at the moment, right? Sorry Jimmy, but this is a business meeting we're having, and Sin Bin is a business. If you're going to go off the bleedin' wall on us, I need to know now. This isn't shifting the goalposts, man, this is putting them in the back of a lorry and driving them to the west coast of Clare.'

'I have to do this Dónal,' said Jimmy, quietly. 'And I'm doing it. One way or the other.'

A weird tension suddenly filled the space between them. It had never happened before in all their time working together. Norman got up and went into the kitchen without a word. Aesop sat back and starting biting a knuckle, just watching.

'Are you?' said Dónal. 'And what are you doing?'

'Who are we?' said Jimmy, staring at him. 'I mean who *are* we?'

Dónal said nothing. He didn't even nod. He just stared back at Jimmy over the table.

'That's what it's all about,' said Jimmy again, shaking his head this time. 'Who are we?'

Aesop looked at both of them. This was getting a bit hairy. No one was saying anything and he'd never seen that expression on Dónal's face before. He sat forward.

'Well, I'm Mister B*Jaysis,' he said into the silence, folding his arms.

They both turned to him. He looked like someone was trying to take away his ice-cream on him. That did it.

Dónal gave a big sigh and started laughing, and then Jimmy joined in. Aesop followed when he couldn't keep a straight face any more.

'Jimmy, seriously,' said Dónal, wiping his eyes. 'Please tell me you have some real ideas. Musical ones. Give me something, man.'

'I do,' said Jimmy, clapping his hands down on his legs. 'C'mon inside.'

He stood up and led them into the main rehearsal room. He plugged in his guitar and stepped on a few pedals, making a few tweaks until he was happy with the sound and the tuning.

'You right?' he said.

The others nodded. Sparky and Norman were in the control room now, sipping on tea and watching through the glass.

'Okay. Right, this is only new, right? I'm only getting started. But listen to this …'

He started playing a solo, way up on the guitar. High and piercing, but creamy too through the neck pickup of his Strat, like David Gilmour weaving one of his big stadium-fillers. It sounded vaguely trad, but a lot more intricate than any kind of basic jig or reel. It was also way faster than any trad the lads had ever heard. Jimmy's eyes were closed and his fingers were flicking between frets and strings like they were being drawn into position rather than his consciously putting them there. Once he'd gone around the body of the solo twice, he played a thunderous rhythm part for a few bars, low and growling, and then flicked onto the bridge pickup for the second solo and changed the key. Now the creaminess was gone, the space filled instead with howls and dives. This one sounded even less trad. It had a kind of classical vibe, like Strauss on pills or something. The whole thing certainly rocked though. It was just guitar playing, not real songs or anything, but as a piece of music it was all there.

Aesop was sitting down on a stool and tapping his feet. As far as he was concerned, it was kick-to-the-goolies metal he was after hearing. He'd have no problems with that. Dónal looked into Sparky. They both kind of shrugged at each other. Norman was just keeping out of the way. This wasn't really any of his business.

Jimmy stopped playing and looked up.

'Well?'

'Jimmy, smashing guitar playing, but … eh … what was it?' said Dónal. 'I thought you were going to be giving us some Chieftains.'

'Nah. A bit different.'

'Was the second bit classical? Sounded a bit like Richie Blackmore going off or something.'

'Yep. But not Richie.'

Jimmy smiled at them all.

'Any more guesses?'

They all looked at each other. No one had a clue.

'Did you write it yourself?' said Dónal.

'No. It's Irish though.'

'Irish? Even the second bit?'

'Yeah. Lads, I was playing Carolan. Speeded it up, gave it some welly. But it was Carolan.'

'Caroline who?' said Aesop.

'You don't know Carolan?'

'No. Who is she?'

'Turlough O'Carolan, Aesop. He was a composer. And a harper.'

'A harper? What's a bleedin' harper?'

'He played the harp.'

'Who plays the fuckin' harp?'

'A lot of people played it in the seventeenth century.'

'What?! What you just played is that old?'

'Yeah. Well, I took a few liberties with it … but basically, yeah.'

'I s'pose the second bit sounded a bit … what was it called?'

'The second part? That's a piece called "Fanny Power".'

'Right, yeah. Women's libber, this bloke, was he?'

'What? No. No, Jesus, he wrote it for a woman called Fanny Power. Most of his music is named after the people he wrote it for. It's not Fanny as in … fuck sake, Aesop, it's three hundred bleedin' years old …'

'Jimmy,' said Dónal. 'Are you telling me you want to do an album of Carolan music? Because …'

'No. I'm just saying that I wanted to go back as far back as I was able. I found some sheet music for Carolan on the web and learned a couple of bits quickly for today. But the album … I want to see what's out there for me to draw on. I want to do an album of Irish music. But a different way. I don't know exactly what it'll sound like yet, but … imagine something like "Dark Side of the Moon". Except it's Irish. We haven't got a Dark Side, man. I want to write it.'

'An Irish Dark Side of the Moon,' said Dónal, pursing his lips. He ran a hand through his hair. 'And would I be right in thinking that there'll be fuck all three-minute songs on it that I can put out there as singles?'

'You never know,' said Jimmy. 'But ... eh ... I doubt it.'

'I see.'

'What do you think?'

Dónal walked over to the drumkit and tapped a finger on one of the cymbals a few times. Then he looked up.

'And what exactly are you trying to do with this album, Jimmy?'

Jimmy put the guitar down onto a stand.

'I'm ... I want to put it all together. Everything from Carolan through Percy fuckin' French, right through to Planxty, The Pogues and Kíla.'

'Right.'

'I want to grab it now before it's too late, show the kids who we are before they all disappear up Justin Timberlake's arsehole.'

'I see. And you're going to do all this on one album? Hundreds of years of musical influence and you're going to squeeze it onto a CD?'

'Eh ...' Jimmy went a little bit red. 'Well, not exactly. I was thinking that this would be an on-going project.'

'Figures,' said Dónal, wearily.

'There's just so much out there, man. Everything. The first album will be like an aria. A snapshot of everything we have. That's Dark Side. Then I want to dig a little deeper. Maybe do an album of Carolan stuff. Look up the old ballads. Rework some *sean nós* pieces. Pipe music. Stuff from all over the country, y'know? The whole lot, mixed up. Aesop there playing a Lambeg drum over a slow air from West Cork, that kind of thing, y'know? And then get into full Celtic rock for a bit and see where that goes.'

'But Jimmy, okay so you seem to be having some kind of identity crisis, but you're talking about music that's ... *old*. What about looking forward?'

'But I am looking forward, Dónal! This whole thing is just the start. Because Irish music is going to change and it's going to change right fucking now. I want to nail down something of what we have first and then get started on what's coming.'

'What's coming?'

'Look around man. The country is full of Africans and Poles and fuckin' Romanians! Their kids are going to be Irish but their families won't have forgotten where they came from, no more than the Irish did in America. Irish music twenty years from now is going to have African beats and Romanian gypsy tunes and … eh … Polish stuff all over it. It's going to be fucking great, and I want in on it. But first I want to be able to hold me head up and say I know where *I* came from before I see where I'm going. This is what I want to do man. Sorry, but "Meatloaf's Underpants" is not me any more. If it ever was. No offence Aesop.'

'Don't give a fuck,' said Aesop, waving a hand absently. 'But c'mere, what about me new band of sexy trad musicians? Were you just saying that to get me to shut up?'

'No man. We should do that. The name is fucking stupid, but the rest of the plan makes sense. Doesn't it Dónal?'

'What? Oh, yeah … I s'pose. It's not a … but lads we're a bit busy here talking about The Grove, y'know? I mean, one minute this bollocks hasn't got a single song in his head, and now he's got a twenty-year vocation lined up in front of him. Fuck sake, can we focus a bit?'

'Sorry Dónal,' said Jimmy. 'But what do you think? Just in general, like.'

'I … Jimmy, this is all a bit sudden, right? Look, just … describe the next album for me, will you? Can you do that?'

'Irish influence. No set structure. I'm not writing songs necessarily, I'm writing … well, call it a concept album if you like.'

'But will it have something on it I can bloody *sell*, Jimmy? You're the one who hates it when bands start taking themselves too seriously. Remember what you said about that Radiohead album?'

'I know. Dónal, I've got something here, I promise. People are going to dig it.'

Dónal stood up and looked in a Sparky again. Sparky might have given a little nod, but it was hard to see him properly in the dark of the control room. Dónal sighed and turned back to Jimmy.

'Look, I'll make a deal with you Jimmy. Right?'

'Right.'

'First of all, Senturion are going to tell you piss off with this idea. That's a given. We're losing out there. So it's just us, unless you write this thing and suddenly everyone thinks it's the new "Tubular Bells". But assuming that's not going to happen, we're back to square one and trying to market you as a totally different kind of band after the tour. Ye bastard. So I'll agree to do it on two conditions, right? First of all, never mind Justin Timberlake, there's to be no disappearing up your own arsehole, right? Promise me you'll take a step back if me and Sparky ever tell you it's not working.'

'Right.'

'Right. And the second thing is, you're to promise me you'll keep one eye on the balance sheet in here, okay? We're just talking about a one-off with Sin Bin on this next album you want to do. I'm saying nothing about recording Lithuanian banjo music down the line, so don't be getting distracted by all that shite for the moment. Give me Dark Side of the Moon and we'll go from there. If it falls on its arse, then you need to promise me here and now that you'll make me a proper rock record afterwards. Okay? A real album with songs. They don't have to be about teenagers in love, but I need to be able to sell them to someone or else we're all fucked.'

'No problem.'

'Deal?'

'Yeah.'

'Really?'

'Yeah.'

'Jaysis, you agreed to that very quick.'

'It was easy, Dónal,' said Jimmy smiling. 'Wait till you see the album I'm going to write. I'm going to blow everyone away. It's going to be huge. It's going to be the biggest fucking thing that's ever happened.'

'Well good. Glad to hear it. Right. Well we'll see.'

'Aesop?' said Jimmy.

'Yeah?'

'You cool with all this?'

'Well I'm only half following you, to be honest. But if your new stuff sounds like what you were playing earlier, then I'm cool with it. Can we go and eat now before I chew the arm of this chair? If there's more to talk about, can we do it over food?'

'Dónal?' said Jimmy.

'Sure. Why not?'

'Okay. Let's go, then.'

Aesop jumped up suddenly, laughing, and ran to get his coat.

'Jaysis, man, you can't be that hungry,' said Jimmy, looking over at him.

'What? Oh I am. But it's not that. I just thought of something brilliant.'

'What?'

'The head on your Da when I go on the telly playing the Lambeg drum. I must get meself a Rangers jersey.'

Chapter Twenty-four

'NOW YOU'RE just taking the piss,' said Aesop, looking down at his plate.

'I'm not,' said Norman.

'It's ten o'clock in the morning!'

'I know. Eat up now before it gets cold, boy.'

'In the name of all that's holy, Norman, who eats fish for breakfast?'

'Half the planet does, Aesop.'

'Half what planet? The Planet of the fuckin' Mermaids?'

'Aesop, why do you think the Yanks are having heart attacks all over the gaff? It's because they have a kilo of pancakes first thing in the morning before they wobble out to work.'

'I'd murder a pancake right now. This ... it's still got its skin on and everything, look.'

'Just pull it off and eat up the flesh. It's all protein. The rice is fresh made and everything'

'Good fuck. Do I look like Shiggy to you? What ever happened to a bowl of poxy cornflakes?'

'Cornflakes are only shite. And anyway, I've seen the way you pour fistfuls of sugar on them.'

'But Norman ...'

'Will you shush up whinging and let me listen to the news? That's what you call a healthy breakfast there.'

Aesop frowned down at his plate and poked the fish in the head with his fork for a minute. He looked up at Norman again.

'If it was healthy, it'd still be swimming around in the bleedin' sea, wouldn't it?'

'Aesop ...'

'Poor little fuck. You frying the bollocks off him at this hour of the morning.'

'He's grilled.'

'Look at him. He's all sad.'

'He's dead, Aesop. Eat him up like a good man, will you? And let me alone for five minutes to hear the headlines, just.'

Norman turned the radio up and left Aesop to his muttering.

'Fish … all I wanted was a bit of toast … boiled egg, even … smelly all day now I'll be, watch … probably choke on a bone as well … fucker keeps hiding the salt … poxy green tea … Charlie Bird me bollix …'

Once they were done eating and everything was cleared away, Norman sat down opposite Aesop at the kitchen table.

'Listen Aesop, me and Dónal were talking last night. There's been no news of your stalker now in a long time. No dead flowers through the letterbox or wetting the bed on you, or even a message or anything. We think she's probably going to leave you alone. I talked to Garda Ní Mhurchú this morning as well. She reckons the same thing. If the girl was really obsessed, she'd still be hounding us. It was probably just some young one that got a bit carried away with herself and now she's after copping on.'

'So we're done? You being me bodyguard?'

'No. I wouldn't say that. I'm still going to be around, but there's no need for me to be with you every minute of the day, like.'

'Oh thank Jaysis. Well, that'll do for starters.'

'There's new deadbolt locks on all the windows and doors in this place, and the new alarm was put in while you were in London. You'll be grand in the house, once you're careful about who you open the door to. Of course, that won't matter much if you bring every girl you meet back here to …'

'Haven't done that in weeks, man. No interest.'

'Yeah. Well, anyway, the story now is that I'll be with you a lot of the time when you're out and about, but I don't need to shadow you when you're with Jimmy or whatever, okay?'

'Grand.'

'But I still need to know where you are. You have me on speed dial on your phone, right? And the panic button next to your bed and in the hall will have the Guards here in five minutes as well.'

'It's all very exciting, isn't it?'

'Don't be messing now, Aesop. All we're doing is easing you back into your normal life. As normal as that is, anyway. And no walking down dark alleys or through parks on your own.'

'Jesus … what about hanging around playgrounds?'

'Just listen to me. This is important, okay? Make sure I always know where you are. And Jimmy too, just so as we can be sure. Keep an eye out when you're on your own, especially at night, and just try not to be … y'know … fuckin' stupid. In general, like.'

'I'll do me best. So you're not sleeping here any more?'

'I will sometimes, probably. For a little while anyway. But we'll try it out tonight. I'm meeting Trish this afternoon. I'll be with her for the day and I'll be staying in hers tonight.'

'Rumpy pumpy?'

'Will you shut up acting the langer? Now, I'm not keen on you being alone the first night I'm not around, so you're to stay in Jimmy's tonight okay? Can you ask him if that's okay? If there's no sign of anyone messing with the door or anything here tomorrow, then maybe you can stay here tomorrow on your own.'

'Okay. I'll talk to Jimmy this afternoon, then. We're rehearsing at one.'

'Grand. I'll drop you over before I meet Trish.'

'There's no need, Norman. I can walk it in ten minutes.'

'No. I'll drop you over in the van.'

'But Norman, I'm not …'

'Will you shut your hole arguing with me? I'll drop you over and I'll talk to you tomorrow afternoon.'

'Okay, Christ. Well can we go now, then? I like to get there early so as to get warmed up before Jimmy gets in.'

Half an hour later they pulled up outside Sin Bin. Aesop went to get out of the van and Norman held his arm.

'Are you okay?'

'What?' said Aesop.

'Are you all right?'

'I'm grand. Eh … how are you?'

'You're okay with me not being around?'

'I'm very fucking okay with you not being around, Norman. Already looking forward to beans on toast for me tea tonight.'

'Yeah. Remember what I told you about butter?'

'I know, I know. Rots your teeth and gives you brain cancer, right?'

'Gobshite. And you'll keep an eye out?'

'I'll keep an eye out. Norman, there's a car behind us.'

'Okay then. Well … be careful, right? Anything happens, or even if you're just worried, give me a call and I'll be there.'

'Grand. Talk to you tomorrow then.'

'Right. Seeya.'

'Eh … tell Trish I said hello.'

Norman shook his head.

'Maybe I won't bother just yet.'

'She still arsey?'

'She says you might be the most unbalanced person she's ever met. And this is coming from a woman that's surrounded by fucking Alzheimers patients all day.'

The car behind them beeped.

'Well … tell her I'm sorry then? Again, like …'

'Seeya tomorrow, Aesop,' said Norman. He checked his watch. 'Go on. I might as well head round to Mam's now for an hour.'

'Okay cheers, Norman. Watch the trams.'

'Yeah.'

Aesop watched him pull away and disappear around a corner. He pulled out a smoke to have a think for a minute. That mad fucking tart Norman was going out with had called him again last night. She still wanted to meet him for dinner. Said nothing at all about that previous call where he'd broken the phone off the wall. If she thought he was unbalanced, she wasn't letting on to Aesop. That shit was obviously just for Norman's benefit. She was the one with the problem. She wouldn't leave him alone. Aesop was pretty sure that he'd been right the first time. It had nothing to do with wanting to kill him or anything. She was after a good shagging, so she was. Christ, how could she want it that badly that she'd keep at him and at him? Was Norman saving it for their wedding night or something? Aesop had never come across itchiness like it in his life. It was disgraceful. Very un-ladylike. And it wasn't as though Aesop had been giving her ideas, even. Fuck sake, surely she knew from Norman that Aesop was after Helen? What was her fucking problem?

His life never used to be this complicated. He sighed and stubbed the cigarette out against the wall, flinging the butt into a litterbin with a curse and sniffing at his fingers. Now he couldn't even enjoy a bloody smoke, the fishy fucking taste of everything. He took out his phone. He was going to sort her out now before he did anything else. He'd gotten rid of Norman and now he could do it properly. He went to his logged calls, and pressed her number. He had talk to her once and for all before he got on with the rest of his day. It was a pain in the arse but … well, what was the worse thing that could happen?

NORMAN HAD lunch with his Mam and was walking out the door to go back into town when his phone rang.

'Hello?'

'Hiya Norman.'

'Trish! How's it going. I'm at Mam's. I'm just heading in now to meet you.'

'Oh. Listen Norman, you're not going to believe this. I have to work.'

'What? Oh no.'

'Yeah. You remember Nuala?'

'Eh …'

'Remember I told you? She's one of the girls.'

'Oh, your mate, yeah. She's a nurse as well, right?'

'Yeah. Well she called me and asked me to cover for her. She's after coming down with a cold and she thought she'd be okay to work, but it's been getting worse all morning now and she can't go in.'

'Oh. Okay. Ah well.'

'I'm really sorry Norman. I'd have told her I can't, but you should have heard her on the phone. She could barely talk. And she covered for me a couple of weeks ago when we ... remember you and me ...'

'I do remember. God, of course I do ...'

'I'm sorry. I'll make it up to you, I swear.'

'Ah don't be silly. If she's your friend and she's in a fix ...'

'If there was anyone else ... but it's such late notice and the weekend and all.'

'Of course. Listen, don't be worrying about it. Will you be working tomorrow too?'

'Looks like it. But I'll give you call if Nuala's better, okay. Sorry about this Norman.'

'Will you stop. It's grand. I'll talk to you tomorrow sure.'

'Are you sure it's okay?'

'Trish, it's grand. All right? Go on. Give me a call when you have a minute.'

'I'll make it up to you, Norman. Promise.'

'There's no need ...'

'There is. And I will. I know how to make it up to you too, don't I?'

Norman was standing in his driveway on his own. No one was out on the street. His Mam was in the back room with a cup of tea and could no more hear or see him than the man on the moon. But he still went absolutely puce and turned his back on the house. He wasn't used to this sort of talk at all. His jocks suddenly felt tight and uncomfortable.

'Ah ... now ...'

'You just be thinking of me making it up to you, okay? And I'll talk to you tomorrow. And when I see you I'm going to be badly in need of a big Corkman. Do you know where I might find one?'

'I ... I might have an idea ...'

'Well you tell that Corkman that I've got something special for him. Just for him. I think he's going to like it. Okay? Will you do that for me?'

'Eh ... oh ... oh ... okay. Seeya so.'

'Seeya. My man.'

Jesus. He was all in a tizzy, the disappointment of not being able to see her for the weekend tempered by the images she was after painting in his head. It took a few seconds to realise that she'd hung up. Norman turned to go back into the house. He might as well. There wasn't much else for him to do was there? His plans were fairly scuppered. But he couldn't go in yet. He'd have to give it five minutes and let the freezing wind do its work. His Mam would call him in to ask him why he was back so soon, and how was he meant to explain to her that his plans had suddenly changed, and him standing there with a big bugle on him.

THE NEXT day was Saturday, and they were booked into the studio for the whole day. Leet finished up at lunchtime, and then Ryan hung back with The Grove and they carried on from where they'd left off the previous night, showing him the ropes for the tour. Jimmy was pretty relentless, but he tried to make sure the poor bloke wasn't too wrecked by calling regular breaks. There was no point in burning him out. He could have Monday off, when Shiggy was back in work.

Jimmy skipped out with Shiggy in the late afternoon to get some coffee and buns, leaving the others in the studio to listen to some tapes. He hadn't wanted to take from the work at hand for the tour, but he was desperate to know what Shiggy thought of his Irish Dark Side idea. Shiggy played three or four instruments expertly and was no slouch on about another half a dozen. He was also great in the studio. He appreciated how instruments fit together in the ensemble. What sounded good off each other, when a piece needed something extra and when restraint was probably the way to go. Jimmy was essentially going to try and compose a whole work this time, not just write songs, and he was just starting to get an idea of how much he'd told everyone he wanted to bite off. He went over the whole thing for Shiggy as they ambled down the south bank of the Liffey to Jimmy's favourite coffee shop on Wood Quay.

Shiggy didn't say much, but eventually he nodded and looked up at Jimmy.

'Jimmy, my grandmother is Ainu.'

'Ainu? What's that?'

Shiggy sighed.

'Ainu is ... rike ... eh, different flom Japanese.'

'What? What do you mean? You're not Japanese?'

'Yes. But, no, I am Japanese. Now. Of course. But Ainu is rike ... you know Indian in America?'

'Yeah.'

'Indian is rike Ainu. Ainu was in Japan before Japanese.'

'Oh. So ... and are they still there? I mean, like the Indians living in America have their own, y'know, places where they live and all.'

'Yes. In Hokkaido. North in Japan. Still there. Have Ainu language, Ainu foods, Ainu clothes ...'

'I thought yis were all just Japanese over there.'

'Yes. Everybody sink that. But still there.'

'Well, okay. And so what about it anyway.'

'Jimmy, Ainu also have Ainu music. Remember gig in Rondon rast week?'

'Yeah. Oh right, the Japanese guy that ...'

'Ainu guy.'

'Ah.'

'When I see *tonkori* on stage ...'

'Tonkori?'

'Guy play it, remember?'

'Oh right. The Japanese harp yoke.'

'Ainu harp yoke. First time I see it in thirty years. My grandmother pray tonkori for me, but grandfather get berry angry.'

'Why?'

'Ah ... berry compricated, Jimmy. Ainu in Japan rike ... gypsy in Ireland.'

'You mean like ... discrimination and all that?'

'Yeah. Kind of. But, *ne*, too difficult to exprain in Engrish. Anyway, in Rondon, guy pray Ainu music with Kira, remember?'

'I didn't realise. I though it was just Japanese music.'

'Rónán say on stage, before guy come on.'

'I wasn't really listening, sorry. I was kind of zonked after singing "Caillte".'

'Anyway, I talk to guy after gig. So cool. To hear Ainu music over here. First time to see Ainu rike this. So many people crapping and cheering. Sound great with Irish instruments too. I berry proud.'

'Well, that's brilliant. I'm glad.'

'Point is, Jimmy, I rearise that Ainu is me. I rike to study Ainu music, I sink. For my grandmother. I don't want to forget music. Forget her. Is in me.'

'Deadly. You should do that.'

'Yeah. But what is in *you*, Jimmy? You tell me so many ideas.'

'Well, I'm from Dublin. The suburbs. That's where I come from, where I've always lived. But that's not … we've had the Brits and their influence right on our arses for hundreds of years. And anyway, in any big city there's a different … it's down the country that all the …'

'Peggy and Seán flom Dublin?'

'Yeah.'

'Grandparents?'

'Yeah. Well, me Ma's Ma was born in Kerry. But she moved up when she was small.'

'So. Kerry then. Start in Kerry. Have music in Kerry?'

'Yeah. Jaysis, some of the best trad musicians are down there.'

'Okay. Great. Start there maybe. But Jimmy, prease, can't write music for whole country and all history. Three hundred years? Write music for Jimmy first. Then see.'

Jimmy nodded. Shiggy was probably right. Typical Jimmy, getting all excited about his new project. It was just so long since he'd had a proper grasp on any idea at all, that he hadn't had the chance yet to piece it together in his mind. It was all still just a bag of ideas, mixed-up plans and designs and excitement. He needed to sort through it. Chill out a bit.

'I s'pose,' he said. 'Cheers.'

'No plobrem.'

'We should do something together one day, man. Irish and Ainu.'

'Rike Kira?'

'Yeah. But us. I know I keep talking about Irish music and all, but the last few days going over stuff with Ryan, I can't help loving rock music too. I can't help it. I fucking just love it. I s'pose I went off the wall a bit, thinking I was done with all that.'

They were standing in the queue now for their coffee.

'You think we could mix rock and Ainu, Shiggy?' said Jimmy.

'Sure. Why not.'

'What's it sound like?'

'Ainu music? You hear in Rondon!'

'Sorry man. I was kind of tuned out for the last hour of that gig.'

'Dopey bastard, Jimmy.'

Jimmy gave the order and looked back at Shiggy, shaking his head.

'We really need to do something about your cursing, Shiggy. It's getting fuckin' worse, so it is. I'll have to talk to Aesop later.'

They hurried back to the studio so that the lads' coffee wouldn't get cold on them and then they all sat around chatting and having a laugh, slagging Ryan about the women he'd meet on the tour and stuff. He was more of a Norman than an Aesop and just kept going red and telling them to give over. When they were done with the rehearsal, Ryan gone off blushing and excited, Norman tapped on the door and came in.

'Lads. Sorry. Don't mean to interrupt yis. I'll just wait in with Sparky while you're working. I won't get in the way.'

'No problem Norman. We're done,' said Jimmy. 'Do you want a bun?'

'I'm grand thanks,' said Norman. He walked over to them and sat down for a minute. 'Just had a big feed over in Mam's before I came out.'

'Okay so,' said Jimmy. 'How'd you get on last night? You were out with Trish, right?'

317

'Well, I was meant to be all right. But she called me yesterday afternoon to say she couldn't make it. She has to work for the weekend.'

'What? Tonight as well?'

'Yeah.'

'Ah, that's a pain in the hole. You should've given us a call. We had a couple of scoops in Mulligans last night.'

'Nah. Sure I haven't seen too much of Mam in the last while, so I just stayed in with her. Had an oul' chat, y'know? Watched a bit of telly. What are ye doing tonight?'

Dónal was just putting down the paper.

'I'm heading off after this, but there's meant to be a session on in Whelans later. Why don't you go around to that? Jimmy can soak up some of the vibe for his new masterpiece.'

'Sounds like a plan,' said Jimmy. 'Are yis up for that?'

Nods all round.

'Yeah, grand,' said Norman. 'Where's himself?'

'Hmm?' said Jimmy.

'Is he in the jacks?'

'Who?'

'Aesop.'

'Aesop? Aesop's not here today, man. We were concentrating on teaching Ryan the set for the tour.'

'He's not here?' said Norman, frowning. 'The langer. I told him he needed to let me know where he is and he said he'd be here.'

'Nah. He must've made a mistake.'

'The eejit. So he's in your place still, is he?'

'My place? Why would he be in my place?'

'What? Didn't he stay there last night?'

'No.'

'What?!'

'What are you on about, man?' said Jimmy. 'Why would he have stayed in my place?'

Chapter Twenty-five

NORMAN STOOD up.

'He said he'd stay with you after rehearsals yesterday!'

'Norman, Aesop wasn't rehearsing yesterday either. What are you on about? He's not coming in till Monday, I told you. We're working with Ryan for the weekend. While we have Shiggy. What makes you think …'

'But … he was here yesterday. Didn't I drop him outside the door myself at eleven o'clock.'

They were all looking at each other now. Dónal stood up and put his hands in his pockets, scowling.

'He said he liked to get here early so as to get a warm-up done,' said Norman.

'Norman, Aesop has never been early for a rehearsal in his life. He's always wandering in half an hour late, the fucker.'

'Are you telling me you haven't seen him today or yesterday?'

'No, Norman, I haven't. I haven't seen him since the other night.'

Almost at the same moment, they all pulled out their phones.

'I'll do it,' said Norman, and clicked the number. After a few seconds, he took the phone away from his ear again. 'It's not ringing. Says it's turned off.'

'Jesus fu … what the fuck is going on?' said Jimmy, he was standing up now too and trying Aesop's phone. He shook his head. 'Nothing. Fuck! What now? Do we call the cops, or … I mean …'

'Hang on a minute, Jimmy,' said Dónal. 'Let's just think for a minute. Norman?'

'Jimmy, call Jennifer, Marco and his Da, will you? Call your Ma too. Don't get anyone all worked up or anything, okay? Just say he's late for a rehearsal and you were wondering where he is.'

'Right,' said Jimmy, taking out his phone again.

'Then check your email.'

'Okay.'

'Dónal, go in there and check your email as well. And you Shiggy.

Dónal, when you're done with that, send him a text and get him to call you or me as soon as he gets it.'

'Yeah.'

'Tell him it's important. You know what he's like. It's possible that the gobshite doesn't realise what he's after doing.'

'Right.'

'I'm going over to his place now, just to check. He probably is asleep, the eejit.'

'Why did he say he was rehearsing with us yesterday?' said Jimmy, waiting for Jennifer to answer her phone. 'That's what he told you, right? He didn't come in here. We were here at eleven with Leet.'

'I don't know. But I left him standing outside the door downstairs and he said he was coming up here.'

'But …'

'I don't know Jimmy. Look, I'll be back in half an hour, okay? Keep trying his number there and call me if you get anything.'

'Okay.'

Norman went outside and started down to the Ha'penny Bridge. It'd be quicker just to go on foot with the traffic the way it was, although he nearly broke his fucking ankle on the bridge, jumping over a couple of buskers. He picked up the pace at the other side of the river and was outside Aesop's front door less than ten minutes later.

He stood panting for a minute before he took out the keys. Something felt wrong. A hint of it had struck him when he left the studio, and it had taken hold as he ran across the city. This was his responsibility. He was the one that was meant to be looking out for Aesop, and now there was no sign of him. The bollocks had obviously lied yesterday about the rehearsal, but that didn't change the fact that Norman's job was to make sure nothing happened to him. But none of that was what felt wrong now. He took out his phone and looked at it, his breathing back to normal now but his stomach squirming. Fuck. He had to check.

He dialled her number first. The phone was off. Well that wasn't unusual. They weren't allowed take calls when they were on duty. Still. He pulled a business card out of his wallet to get the number of the office. He'd never actually called her this way, but he had the number from when he'd been doing the gardening work there. Should he? Well, he had to, didn't he? It was in his head now and nothing would shake it until he knew.

And he had to know. The fucking pain and heartbreak would be better than wondering. Probably.

He dialled.

It took less than a minute and then he knew. Certainly he could leave a message for Patricia Sweeney. She'd get it on Monday when she came into work. Were they sure she wasn't in there covering for someone today? They were absolutely positive. Everyone who was supposed to be working today, was working.

Norman thanked the girl and hung up. Anger, confusion and hurt milled through him, each new thought and picture in his head causing him to clench his jaw and his fists. He fingered the keys to Aesop's house for a minute and unlocked the deadbolt. Then he turned the other key in the latch and went in. There was no buzzing from the house alarm. Someone had been back here since he and Aesop had left yesterday. Well … not someone. Only Aesop and himself knew the key combination to turn it off. Checking downstairs just took a few seconds. There was no sign of anyone. They must have been in such a hurry that they didn't hang about down here. He went quietly up the stairs and stood in front of Aesop's bedroom door. He paused for a second. The fury was building in him, burning. There was still time to walk away. Because if he saw what he knew he was going to see …

But he couldn't walk away. He'd lost control now. Totally. He was practically someone else. The person he'd been trying for years not to be any more. His hand went out on its own and gripped the doorhandle. Then, drops of despair and rage starting to well in his eyes, he took a big breath and pushed the door open.

JIMMY AND Dónal had done everything that Norman had told them to do, but there was no news. No one knew where he was and he hadn't been in touch on email, texts or voicemail. They sat on the couches with Sparky and Shiggy, no one saying anything, just waiting for Norman to come back, hopefully with an apologetic and sleepy Aesop.

'Tea?' said Shiggy eventually.

Jimmy just nodded.

Shiggy went off into the kitchen and Dónal turned to Jimmy.

'It's fine, man. You know what he's like.'

'Yeah. But he's a bloody idiot for doing this after everything that's been going on.'

'I know. But, look, at least we know that he never intended to come in here yesterday, right? It's not like we haven't got a clue at all. He was up to something. So none of this means that he's in trouble with … y'know.'

'That was yesterday Dónal. Whatever he was up to, he'd be finished by now. And what's up with his phone? Why isn't he answering it?'

'I don't know. Maybe he's out of battery.'

'Me bollix.'

'It happens man. Especially to a dizzy muppet like Aesop. He just forgot to charge it.'

'How long is Norman gone?'

'Twenty minutes. Just … just try and take it easy, okay? He'll be back in a little bit.'

'Where did Sparky go?'

'He's calling a few of the pubs. He knows half the landlords in Dublin. Just to see if Aesop's been around the place, last night or whatever.'

'Okay.'

'Can you think of anywhere else he might be?'

'No. But that's not the point! He wouldn't just piss off like that without saying anything.'

Jimmy tapped his pockets. He wanted a cigarette, but he had none.

'Anyone have any smokes?' he said.

Dónal shook he head and Shiggy called out from the kitchen that he didn't.

'Is there any in the control room?'

'There might be. Maybe one of the Leet lads left some lying around.'

Jimmy walked through the doors and started pulling open drawers and searching under bits of equipment. Eventually he found two half-crushed cigarettes in a box behind the mixing desk. He grabbed them and started down the stairs to go outside. Hunched over with his back to the wind, the smoke tasted a bit stale, but Jimmy didn't care. Whatever toxins and poisons were in the thing, he needed them right now. He stared down at the cobbled street as he pulled on it. A guy and a girl walked past holding hands, making him look up so he could get out of their way, and they caught his eye, grinning in recognition. He didn't respond at all. He barely registered that there were other people on the street. His mind felt dulled and numb but at least that was probably better than letting it get to work on what might be going on here.

AESOP'S EYES snapped open and jerked around the room. What was that? A noise. What … where … ? The empty bottle of Jameson on the bedside table brought it all back. What he'd done last night. Oh bollocks. He was a fucking idiot. He knew he was fucked. He was in the wrong place in the wrong time with the wrong person. He was fucked. Big time. He tried to sit up quickly in the bed, pushing himself against the headboard. Blinding pain shot through him. Why did he have to drink all that whiskey last night? He looked down at the sleeping figure beside him and cursed again before looking up to see the door swing open.

This was what happened to fucking idiots.

'Okay …' he said, his hand trembling out in front of him. 'Just … listen, let's just fuckin' relax for a minute before we do anything, right? Okay? Let's just …'

Chapter Twenty-six

JIMMY WAS starting to pace frantically.

'Jimmy, please,' said Dónal. 'Will you sit down for God sake?'

'I can't man. Where the fuck is Norman?'

'He'll be here soon.'

'It's been an hour, nearly. I'm calling him.'

'He knows what he's doing. Just let him …'

'Bollocks. I'm calling him.'

'Okay Jimmy. Okay.'

Jimmy dialled Norman's number, but there was no answer. It rang out and went to voice mail.

'Jesus Christ, now *he's* not answering his bleedin' phone!'

'Jimmy, in the name of God, sit bloody down for five minutes and leave him alone, will you?'

'He should have been back ages ago, Dónal. Either Aesop is at home or he isn't.'

'Norman will want to check the place over. This is his thing, Jimmy. Let him get on with it.'

'But Dónal, why …'

'Jimmy!'

It was Sparky, and his face was good and purple.

'Sit fucking down and wait for Norman to come back. It's bad enough in here without you losing the plot on top of everything, okay? We're all worried, right? Having you throwing a wobbler about the place and talking shite is only making it worse. My doctor says I'm to avoid stress at all costs and I'm only holding on here by the skin of me teeth, I'm fucking telling you. I've got too much blood pressure, not enough liver, a hypnotist that's afraid to put me under after the last time, and the shrink in the hospital is convinced I have an anti-social personality disorder as well, the cunt. So I don't need you making me all fucking jumpy too, ye hear me? Will you ever relax the head before I have a bleedin' heart attack on us.'

Jimmy opened his mouth to say something, but then he just sat down and stared at the table.

'Okay, Sparky,' said Dónal. 'Okay. Look, we're all stressed. Sit down yourself, sure. There's no point in getting all worked up until we know what's what, is there? Can I get you something?'

'No,' said Sparky. He looked around and sighed. 'Well ... where's me bananas?'

'I'll get one for you,' said Dónal. 'Sit down there.'

'I'm not hungry, but I need ... I have to make sure ...'

'I know, pal. Potassium. You're grand. Hang on a minute.'

Shiggy arrived in the door.

'Anything?' said Jimmy.

'No Jimmy. No sign.'

He'd been out checking a few of the music shops. Aesop loved to window shop for instruments and yap with the staff. Most of them were into the same music as he was and he'd spend hours just shooting the breeze and getting the latest from the metal scene.

'Well it was a long shot I s'pose,' said Jimmy.

It was another half an hour before Norman arrived back. He looked awful.

'What's the story?' said Jimmy, jumping up.

'He wasn't there,' said Norman.

'Fuck! Was there any sign of him at all?'

'The alarm wasn't on when I went in, so he must have gone back after I dropped him off here yesterday.'

'Jesus. What was he up to?'

'I don't know, Jimmy.'

'And there was no note or anything? Did it look like there'd been ... anyone else in there?'

'No. Nothing.'

'Are you sure?'

Norman looked over at him.

'Do you want to fucking check it yourself, Jimmy?'

'What? No! No ... I was just ... sorry man. I'm a bit ...'

'It's okay lads,' said Dónal, handing a banana to Sparky. 'Last thing we need is to be getting annoyed with each other.'

He looked at Norman.

'Okay. So what now?'

Norman shrugged.

'We've checked everywhere, right? Pubs, email, voicemail …'

'Yeah. Shiggy was out checking the music shops,' said Jimmy.

'And there's been nothing.'

'Nothing.'

Norman nodded and sat down.

'Norman,' said Jimmy. 'Are you all right?'

'What?'

'You look a bit …'

'So do you.'

'Yeah, but you just seem a bit kind of … angry or something.'

'I am angry.'

'Aw, listen man, it's not your fault. He disappeared on his own, right? It's not like you were there or whatever, was it? He said he was coming in here yesterday. You dropped him right outside the …'

'Not now, Jimmy. This isn't the time for that shit.'

'Okay. All right man.'

Jimmy sat opposite Norman and tried to calm himself down so as he could think clearly. Aesop wasn't anywhere obvious and no one who he might have been in contact with knew where he was. It wasn't looking good.

'The zoo?' he said, suddenly.

Norman didn't even look up.

'He's been in the zoo since yesterday afternoon, has he?'

'I s'pose not.'

'Well … fuck it, it might be worth checking anyway.'

'I'll go,' said Sparky. 'I need to get the fuck out of here.'

'I go too,' said Shiggy, standing up. 'Better than stay here.' Then he looked all confused. 'Eh … zoo? Why the fu …'

'Okay lads,' said Dónal. 'Give us a call when you get there, right?'

'Yeah,' said Sparky. 'C'mon Shiggy.'

'But …'

'I'll explain on the way.'

The others watched them head out the door and then turned back to one another.

'So is it time to call the cops?' said Dónal. 'Because …'

'No,' said Norman. 'No cops.'

They looked at him.

'Not yet. Just … let me alone for a minute … to think.'

Jimmy sat back in the couch and looked over at him. He knew he wasn't a picture of happiness and contentment himself, but Norman was the colour of dishwater, his foot dancing up and down off his toes on the floor. He looked like he was going to be sick, wiping his face with his hands every minute or so and then looking at them. His hair was wet too. His hair … Jimmy looked at him properly again. What? What was …

'Did you change?' he said.

'What?'

'Your clothes. You weren't wearing that when you went to Aesop's.'

'Oh. Yeah. I had a quick shower and changed my clothes. A load of me stuff is over there still.'

'Why did you change, but.'

'Jimmy, I sprinted from here to Smithfield in ten minutes. By the time I got there and tore through the gaff I was in a state. When I saw he wasn't there, I knew we might be in for a long day. I needed to change and calm down before I came back here. I had a quick shower.'

'I called you and you didn't answer.'

'Must have been in the shower. Sorry.'

'Oh. Eh … okay.'

He could understand why Norman would be upset – Christ, they were all upset – but there seemed to be something else going on. A weird shudder suddenly ran up Jimmy's back, but he didn't know why.

Norman's foot stopped jiggling and he stood up. His face had changed again. He looked like he'd decided something.

'Look, I'm going to check something. I'll be back in an hour or two and if nothing's turned up by then we can call the Guards. Okay?'

Jimmy and Dónal looked at each other and then at Norman.

'Eh … where are you going?'

'I won't be long.'

He grabbed the keys to his van.

'Right? I'll have my phone with me Jimmy.'

'Okay. I s'pose. What'll we do while you're gone?'

'Just keep doing what you're doing. Keep trying his number and if you think of anyone else to call, then go ahead and call them. Okay?'

'Yeah. Okay. You don't think we should call the cops now? Because Garda Ní Mhurchú said that if anything at all …'

'When I come back, Jimmy. I need to check one more thing and then we can call her.'

'But …'

'Jimmy, Aesop is famous. Once you start this, you won't be able to stop it. It'll be all over the radio and the telly. Okay? We'll have every dope in the country calling us to say Aesop was seen wherever and … and if he's in trouble … well, you don't want anyone panicking, do you?'

'No. Jesus. I s'pose not.'

'So just give me a bit of time and when I come back we'll do what we have to do.'

'Okay then. Yeah. Okay.'

Norman walked out without another word.

Dónal's phone rang over on the coffee table. He ran to get it and picked it up, frowning at the screen.

'Is it him?'

'No.'

'Sparky?'

Dónal shook his head.

328

'Well who is it then, for fuck sake?' said Jimmy, walking over to him.

'It's … Alison.'

WHEN NORMAN got back a couple of hours later, he found Jimmy and Dónal sitting opposite each other across the table. Jimmy looked up when he came into the room.

'Anything?'

'No. You?'

'Maybe.' said Jimmy.

'What?! Why … why … didn't you call me? What is it?'

'Alison called. Alison's from the record company in London.'

'What about her?'

'She called to ask us had we spoken to Aesop. She was worried about him.'

'What? Why?'

'Because he called her late last night.'

'He called her? From where? Where was he?'

'She doesn't know. But he called because he wanted to tell her that he was leaving The Grove and joining Leet. Remember that deal I told you about? Well Aesop apparently had second thoughts.'

'And you didn't know anything about this?'

'Of course not. Norman, me and Aesop talked about all this. He was sticking with The Grove. He didn't want to join Leet on his own and I wasn't going to do it.'

'But he'd never leave The Grove. Certainly not without talking to you two about it.'

'I know. Something bad's after happening, man. Can we call the fuckin' cops now? Please?'

'What did Alison say?'

'She just said that he sounded a bit drunk or something and that he asked her not to say anything to me or Dónal. We'd find out soon enough.'

'He didn't say where he was or who he was with or anything?'

'No. Just that he was after changing his mind.'

Norman, started biting his thumbnail.

'Okay. So … this doesn't tell us anything then, does it?'

'It tells us a bit.'

'What? What does it tell us, Jimmy?'

Jimmy frowned at him. What the fuck was going on with Norman?

'Just that he was okay last night. Norman, what …'

Before Jimmy could say anything else, they heard a knock on the studio door.

'What now?' said Dónal. 'Jesus …'

He went over to it and pulled the door open.

It was Trish standing there.

Chapter Twenty-seven

SHE WALKED in.

'Hi guys,' she said, smiling. She gave a little wave.

Jimmy just blinked at her and looked over at Norman, whose mouth was hanging open.

'Eh …' said Trish, looking at them uneasily now. 'Oops. Did I come at a bad time?'

'Trish …' said Norman. He looked like he'd seen about eleven ghosts. 'What are you doing here?'

'Jesus. I'm sorry Norman. You said you'd be here today. I thought I'd surprise you. I'm sorry. Look, I'll just go …'

'No,' said Norman. 'No, come in a minute.'

She walked slowly into the room, her hands pulling her coat tightly across her.

'What's going on?'

'Where have you been?' said Norman.

'I've been working. I told you. But Nuala called me this afternoon to say she was coming in, so I was able to get away.'

'I called Baldoyle, Trish. They said you weren't there.'

'What? You called Baldoyle? Why?'

'I … I wanted to talk to you.'

'About what?'

'About … because … Aesop is gone missing. I was wondering if … you'd heard from him at all.'

'What do you mean he's gone missing? Where?'

'We don't know. We haven't heard from him since yesterday.'

'Oh no! That's awful! But listen, I talked to him yesterday.'

'What? When?'

'I don't know. In the afternoon. Just before I called you to say I was working.'

'Why didn't you say anything?'

'I only spoke to him for a minute, Norman. I had to phone you and run out the door or I'd be late.'

'What did you talk about?'

'Nothing really. I think he was just apologising about the other time, y'know, when you lot were in Cork. I told him I'd talk to him later.'

'But … but … and did he say where he was or anything?'

'No. I was on the phone for a minute, just. He didn't say anything.'

'Fuck,' said Norman. He ran a hand over his head, staring at the floor.

'Norman, you look awful. Do you think Aesop …'

'We don't know where he is, Trish,' said Dónal. 'Look, will you ever come in properly and take off your coat.'

They all made their way over to the couches by the coffee table, saying nothing. When they were sitting down, Norman looked up suddenly.

'Trish, where the fuck were you yesterday and today? Tell me the truth now.'

Dónal and Jimmy didn't even have to look at each other. They both got up and went into the control room. This sounded like a job for inch-thick soundproofed glass. Christ, as if there wasn't enough going on around here.

'What?' said Trish, once the door was closed behind them.

'Where were you? I called Baldoyle. You weren't there. They said you wouldn't be in till Monday. What the hell is going on?'

Trish shook her head slightly.

'Norman … why are you being like this?'

'Like what? You tell me one thing and then I find out something else. What way am I meant to be?'

'Where do you bloody think I was?'

'I don't know. I don't even want to think about it.'

'So you think I'm lying to you?'

'What am I meant to think? I just drove over to your place and the girls haven't seen you.'

'I was at work!'

She opened her coat.

'Look! I stayed in the dorm last night because it was snowing by the time I finished and I knew I wouldn't get a taxi. I haven't been home yet to change. I was hoping we could go together and then go out for the night. Jesus, what's the matter with you?'

Norman looked at her uniform. But … well that didn't necessarily mean that what she was saying was true, did it?

'I don't know!' said Norman. 'They said in Baldoyle that …'

'Baldoyle?'

'Yes!'

'Christ, Norman, Nuala doesn't work in Baldoyle. She works in the hospice in Raheny. I told you that ten times. I was nowhere near Baldoyle.'

'Wh … what?'

Norman blinked. Had she? He spent so much time just gazing at her that sometimes he couldn't even hear what she was saying.

'But … but … I thought …'

'What, Norman? What did you think?'

'Just that … well, when Aesop went missing all of a sudden, and then the next thing you're called in to work out of the blue … Jesus, I've been so freaked out. I was sure …'

He was staring at his shoes. She didn't say anything. When he looked up, he saw a tear trickle down her cheek.

'I thought we were past that,' she said quietly.

'I couldn't get hold of you!' said Norman. 'I tried everything. No one knew where you were. No one knows where Aesop is. All at the same time. I didn't know what … what …'

'I told you where I was, Norman.'

'But I … I called your work and …'

She had a tissue out and wiped at her eyes. Then she sniffed her nose and looked over at him.

'So it's like that, then, is it? That's the kind of person I am to you.'

'No, Trish. Please. I was … I just made a mistake. I was worried about Aesop but I was sure his stalker was finished with all that shit. So when you call me to say you were working, all I could think of was …'

'I know what you were thinking, Norman. And I'm sorry.'

'For what?'

'For making you think those things about me.'

'You don't.'

'I obviously do. But we can fix that.'

'No, Trish. No …'

She was crying properly again now.

'I hope Aesop is okay,' she said, standing up and starting to button her coat again. 'I really do. Let me know if I can do anything to help.'

'Where are you going?'

'Home.'

'I … I'll call you later.'

'Please don't.'

'What?'

'Norman, I can't deal with people freaking out on me. Not people I want to … be with. I needed you to be steady for me. I really needed …'

'But I am … I want to be.'

'I know. Maybe you do.'

She put a hand on his arm.

'But I can't tip-toe around you. No matter how I feel about you. To know that that's what you think of me … what's going on inside you every time I'm not around. I just can't do that. It's not worth it.'

She walked to the door and Norman ran over to her, taking her arm.

'But Trish …'

'I'm sorry Norman. Please, go and find Aesop. I hope to God he's okay.'

'Can I not …'

'Please Norman,' she shook her arm away from him, her eyes red and streaming. 'Don't do this to me. I really thought … I thought that we might …'

'Trish,' said Norman. 'Don't … don't go.'

'I have to. I'm sorry.'

'Please Trish. I … I love you. You're all I have, Jesus. I love you. Please don't. Please don't.'

He was whispering now.

She squeezed her eyes shut and shook her head, pulling the door open.

'You don't, Norman. That's not love. It's something else and I can't deal with it.'

JIMMY AND Dónal had watched all this through the glass. You didn't need subtitles to know what was going on.

'Poor cunt,' said Jimmy, watching Norman go off to the toilet.

'Yeah. That didn't go well, whatever it was.'

'It was about Trish and Aesop.'

'What? He wasn't … was he? With her?'

'No. Of course not. But Norman got it into his head that she was up for it. So did Aesop actually. Ah, it was just something stupid. She wanted to meet Aesop to tell him something. There was probably nothing in it, but you know what Aesop's like. Fucking drama queen that he is, he was sure she wanted him to shag her. Norman must have picked up on it too.'

'So … Norman thought the two of them were off shagging the last two days?'

'Looks like it. And it looks like she didn't appreciate him thinking that.'

'Fuck.'

Back in the main room, Norman was back from the toilet.

'Sorry man,' said Jimmy. 'Whatever that was, I hope it works out.'

Norman ignored him.

'We know he talked to Trish at lunchtime,' he said. 'But we don't know where he was when he was talking to her. We know he called that one, Alison, at some stage last night. But we don't know where he was then either. Do we know any fucking thing else at all?'

'No,' said Jimmy. 'Except that something happened to make him want to leave the band and join Leet.'

'What would make that happen?'

'I don't know.'

'Well think. Cos that's all we've got to go on.'

'He was always against stopping The Grove. Even after I told him I might not be able to play much with everything going on here, he still said he didn't want to join Leet. It'd mean he was always away and he'd miss home and … and …'

'Yeah?'

'Fuck,' said Jimmy, understanding breaking across his face.

'What?'

'Helen.'

'What? My Helen? What about her?'

'He said … he wanted …'

'What Jimmy?'

'I know where he is. Fuck! Why didn't I think of it before?'

'What about Helen, Jimmy?'

'He's fucking mad about her, Norman.'

'I told him I'd fucking throttle him if he so much as …'

'I know! That's why he spoofed you yesterday about rehearsals. He was trying to get away from you so he could go down there and try and hook up with her! That's where the fucker is!'

'Are you sure?!'

'Yes! Call her. Call her now. Quick.'

Chapter Twenty-eight

NORMAN GAVE the other two a thumbs-up. Jimmy felt the weight dropping off him like a sodden coat.

Aesop was in Cork.

'So come on,' said Jimmy, as soon as Norman rang off. He was jiggling about. 'What's the story? He's down there? He's okay? What happened yesterday?'

'He called Helen yesterday around lunchtime and told her he was coming down. She told him not to go to all that trouble, because it wasn't going to work out between them. She'd made up her mind.'

'Fuck.'

'Yeah, well he must have flown down, cos he met her anyway at about seven in Kavanaghs. He didn't want to hear it over the phone.'

'Right. And then?'

'And then she told him that she was after hooking up again with Davey Molloy. That's the ex, remember? Apparently he's on the wagon now after seeing Aesop on the stage that time and the way Helen was with him. So he's going to the meetings, off the drink completely, working hard in his job and playing out of his skin on the park without losing the rag with every fucker that comes near him. Anyway, they all reckon he's a new man. She wants to give it another go with him.'

'Jesus. Aesop must be fucking gutted.'

'He wasn't happy. Stayed back in the pub on his own and got trolleyed for two hours. Then he got a bottle of Jameson and went back to the cottage.'

'How did he get in?'

'He had keys, didn't he? From the last time. I don't remember him giving them back.'

'So that's where he is, then? Dying with a heartbroken hangover in your Granny's place?'

'Yeah. Probably.'

'So call him.'

'There's no land line there, Jimmy. Sure the house isn't used that much. It'd only be a waste of money to have a line active. We're stuck with his mobile, and the langer has it turned off, doesn't he?'

'Right. Yeah. Well anyway, Jesus, that's good, right? We know where he is.'

'Yeah. We know where he is. But it's not good. He's on his own down there with no one around.'

'But sure, wasn't that the reason yiz went down there in the first place? No one knows about it. He's grand. He just needs to sober up and turn his phone on. He's might even be on his way back up here right now.'

'Yeah, probably.'

'Aw … thank fuck. I'm telling you, I'll bleedin' kill him when I see him. The bloody idiot doing that to us. I'll kick the arse off him.'

'You'll have to get in line,' said Dónal. 'Because I've got a new pair of walking boots that I need to break in. And I don't even want to think about what Sparky's going to do to him.'

The tension was gone out of the room now. It was all deep breaths, shaking heads and sheepish grins. Except for Norman. He was still quiet and the colour hadn't come back to his face yet.

'You all right man?' said Jimmy.

'Not really, Jimmy. I fucked up. She's gone.'

'She just needs to cool down. I'm telling you man, you should have heard me and Sandra back when I was going out with her. I don't even know how many rows we had over stupid stuff, but then we'd both calm down and everything would be grand after a bit. Everyone needs to let off a bit of steam. It's probably only your first row, isn't it? Just give her a bit of time.'

'Time won't do it, Jimmy. Because she's right. I am a fucking freak. I couldn't just be happy that everything was going great. I have this fucking … thing in me that gets all mental and has to go looking for things to mess it up. I mean, once I got it in me head that her and Aesop … I just couldn't let it go. It didn't matter what anyone said. It didn't matter that I knew she really liked me or that

Aesop knew I'd pull his head off his shoulders and punch the fuck out of it. Didn't matter. I *knew* nothing was going on. I knew it and then I decided that something was going on anyway. Ran over to his gaff expecting to see them at it. Then I went over to her place. And this is what happens. She's better off.'

'Ah, shut up, will you?' said Jimmy, 'Look, you were a bit jealous. Who the fuck doesn't get a bit jealous?'

'You don't.'

'What? Of course I do! Jesus. Everyone does. You were just a bit thrown because Aesop was gone and then Trish turned up at the wrong time when we're all trying to figure out what was happening. It's nothing, man. Call her later. I know what happened. She turns up here to surprise you and then finds you all bent out of shape. She wasn't expecting to walk in on all the shit that was going on here, was she? She thought you'd be chuffed to see her. She was just upset.'

'Yeah. And then I go and accuse her of lying to me and riding Aesop on the sly. Like she hasn't put up with enough shit from me and fucking Aesop? She's better off. I'm bad news, so I am.'

'Will you shut fucking up, Norman? She's lucky to have you and she knows that. Go over with a bottle of wine and a big apology and tell her you're a gobshite and you'll never do it again.'

'But I will!'

'You won't! After this? Jesus, Norman, the next time the little green bastard taps you on the shoulder, you just keep your fucking trap shut and you'll be grand!'

'But how am I meant to do that when I'm going mad inside?'

'You practise! Christ man, if you give vent to every thought that occurs to you when you're with a bird, you'll never get a minute's peace! Dónal, tell him!'

'Aw Jesus, lads, don't involve me in all this,' said Dónal, backing away with his hands up.

'But you're married.'

'Yeah.'

'And am I right?'

'About what?'

'About keeping your gob shut sometimes when you're with your woman.'

'Oh fuck, yeah,' said Dónal. 'You're right about that. Absolutely.'

'See?' said Jimmy to Norman. 'And he knows what he's talking about.'

'Wha … hang on,' said Dónal, frowning. 'What's that s'posed to mean, Jimmy?'

'Hmm? Oh. Nothing. Just that you've had a lot of experience with being in a relationship.'

'What's wrong with Mags?'

'Nothing! What? Nothing's wrong with Mags, Dónal. I'm just saying, sometimes when you're with a person, it's better to keep quiet than say every little thing that pops into your head.'

Dónal nodded slowly, looking at him.

'Right.'

'It's probably the same for women, Norman. What kind of home life would Dónal here have if all he ever got all day long was "take your shoes off … I saw you looking at her tits … what's wrong with the steak … turn off the football … is that you I smell … why do you hate my Ma … I wonder how much beer went into the size of that belly … but *why* do you love me … distinguished my arse – fat and bald, more like … you're wearing *that* jumper …" Y'know what I mean? No one would ever last more than a fortnight, Norman. Okay? So the next time …

'Hang on a fucking minute now, Jimmy,' said Dónal. 'What are you on about?'

'What? Nothing. I'm just saying, like.'

'Saying what?'

'Just that, y'know, sometimes you need to keep quiet.'

'Right. I think this might be one of those times, Jimmy.'

'Oh.'

'Fuck sake.'

'Sorry.'

'Mags does a great steak.'

'No, Dónal, I wasn't talking about Mags.'

'You were!'

'I wasn't.'

'And I've always had thin hair.'

'It was just an example of the kind of …'

Norman stood up.

'Yeah, thanks for that lads. But I need to get to Cork.'

'What?' said Jimmy. 'Now?'

'Yeah. Now.'

'Why?'

'Because I need to know he's all right and I don't know that yet.'

'But … you think there could be a problem in Cork?'

'Not really. But it's not my job to play odds. I'll drive down. You call me if he calls and I'll turn around.'

'But … are you sure?'

'Yeah.'

'I thought things were grand now.'

'They're better. But not grand. Not yet.'

Jimmy checked his watch.

'What time will you get there?'

'I know the roads well. I'll be grand.'

Dónal walked over to the window.

'I don't think so, Norman.'

'What?'

'Look out there.'

Norman and Jimmy went over to him and looked out the window. It had finally started. The snow that everyone had been talking about for ages was finally putting in an appearance. An inch of fluff already covered everything and it was coming down in huge thick waves now, blocking out anything that wasn't just a couple of metres away.

'Look at it,' said Jimmy. 'But … it's not that deep yet. It's only starting.'

Norman shook his head.

'I'd never make it. That's down for a while.'

'Could you fly?'

'Maybe. I'd get to Shannon or Cork if the airports were open, but the roads down around Granny's are … I wouldn't get much further than the airport.'

'What are you going to do?'

'Hang on. I'll check the forecast on the computer in there.'

He went off into the control room and was gone for five minutes. When he came back he was scratching his cheek.

'No good. It's down until about midnight they say. Fuck.'

'So what do we do?'

'Two things. First thing is that we hope he calls. Second thing …'

Out came the phone again.

'I'm calling Mikey Pat to look in on him. He only lives a couple of miles down the road. At least we'll know then that he's safe before we go down there and kick the bollocks off him.'

'Is it snowing in Cork too? Did you check?'

'Started two hours ago. Hang on …'

When he was done he put the phone back in his pocket.

'Mikey's up in Charleville. It'll take a few hours now with the weather to get home, but he said he'll drop in to Granny's on his way past.'

'Okay. Well, there's nothing else we can do now, is there?'

'Not really,' said Norman. 'Except go home. Because getting out of the city is going to be murder if we don't go now.'

'Yeah. Okay,' said Jimmy. 'You're probably right. I'll call Shiggy and Sparky and tell them we'll lock up here and we'll call them tomorrow. I'll tell them what's going on. And I'll cancel with Leet for the morning too until we sort this out. That okay with you Dónal?'

Dónal wasn't listening.

'Dónal?'

'Hmm?' said Dónal.

He was looking down at himself and rubbing one hand up and down his belly.

'Fuck sake, Dónal,' said Jimmy. 'I never said you were fat!'

NORMAN CALLED Jimmy at home at around eight that night.

'Jimmy?'

'Heya. What's the story? Is Aesop okay?'

'Listen man, Mikey Pat got stranded in Kanturk. He's staying in a mate's tonight. The roads are shocking he said and he can't get home. He probably went a bit further than he should have as it is.'

'Bollocks.'

'Yeah. He said he'd try in the morning. It's meant to clear up a bit by then he'll give me a call when he gets there.'

'Okay. Well, fuck, there's nothing we can do, is there?'

'No. Not really. We just have to wait. But at least Aesop'll have to stay put wherever he is. He won't be able to get about either.'

'Yeah. All right. Well look, I'll be up early. Just call me when you hear from Mikey.'

'Will do man. Seeya tomorrow.'

'Good luck. Eh … Norman?'

'Yeah?'

'Any word from Trish?'

'I haven't talked to her.'

'Right. Listen, give her a bell.'

'Ah, I don't know …'

'Norman, I know what I'm talking about. Believe me, I've spent enough of me life staring at a phone and not picking it up. Just call her. Right? You two are good together. You'll sort this out.'

'Yeah. Well thanks Jimmy. I'll think about it.'

'Okay. Seeya so.'

'Cheers.'

Norman had been thinking about little else. Now that they had a good idea of what had happened to Aesop, all he could do was curse himself and the fucked-up bit of him that made him lose all reason. It had probably always been there. Losing his Dad and then moving to Dublin hadn't exactly been a barrel of laughs. Putting up with being called names over his size and his accent almost from the day he'd arrived in the city had made him liable to get angry the odd time, but then he'd become a soldier and the next ten years had seen what used to be a fringe part of his make-up become honed and sharp. It had probably saved his life a few times back then, but it was nothing but a fucking awful hindrance back in the real world where everyone lived their lives by different rules.

Jealousy was a new aspect of it. He'd never really been in a position to be jealous before. It's not like he'd had loads of girlfriends. But Norman recognised it as all being part of the same thing. Mollified by a few pints, surrounded by friends, occupied by his job or immersed in the daily goings-on of his life, no one would have suspected it. But inside him was a tight red coal of anger. Always. It never went away. The day he stepped off the plane after coming home from Afghanistan he thought that would be the end of it. He'd seen enough of what feeling like that could do to people and he was sure he'd made some kind of peace. But he'd had dreams that very night and it was still there the next day, only worse.

Only Trish had cooled it. Those times when there was nothing in his head only her and how lucky he was. He couldn't feel it then.

He called her. It took half an hour to push the button, but he did it.

'Trish?'

'Hi.'

'It's Norman.'

'Yeah. I know.'

'You got home okay? The snow started soon after you left.'

'Yeah. The buses were still running then. Did you find Aesop?'

'No. Well, he's in Cork, so we kind of found him, yeah. But we haven't talked to him yet. I'm going to head down tomorrow. So you're okay?'

'Not really. But I'm not stuck out in the snow, if that's what you mean.'

'Well that's good.'

'What did you want?'

'Only … to say that I'm sorry, Trish. I'm a bloody idiot for think-

344

ing what I did. I don't deserve a chance, but I'm hoping you'll give me one.'

'Do you know how much you hurt me?'

'I can guess. If it's anything like how I feel right now then I should be shot.'

'I'd never do that, what you were thinking. Never. I never have. I was with you, not Aesop or anyone else.'

'I know. I'm sorry. Trish, I'm not good at this. I've never felt like this about anyone, and when I thought … I just went mad. It's stupid, but I couldn't help it. I just went mad.'

'But I can't deal with that, Norman.'

'It'll never happen again. I swear to God it won't.'

'Will it not? Not even when I'm out with mates or working late? If I'm just talking to a guy in the pub. Or even if Aesop's around and we're all having a laugh? I can't always be worrying about what's going on in your mind, Norman. Trying to make sure I don't upset you.'

'I know.'

'There's meant to be trust. Respect.'

'I know that.'

She didn't say anything for a while.

'Trish?'

'Yeah?'

'Just checking you're still there.'

'I'm here.'

'Can I come over?'

Silence again.

'Please?'

'Norman no. Not tonight. Look, I've had a bloody long couple of days. I'm wrecked.'

'Okay. Well … can I see you tomorrow?'

He heard her sigh.

'Norman, I'm not sure that …'

'Trish, I fucked up. I know that. It won't happen again. I'm sorry.'

'But you're going to Cork tomorrow.'

'I'll … fuck. Yeah. I have to. I have to get that bloody fool Aesop. Christ, that man needs the hiding of a lifetime.'

'Okay, listen. Call me in the morning okay? I need to get the car down to Dad anyway. His other one is on the blink. He said he didn't need it, but I know him. He'll have Mam tormented if he's stuck in the house. I'll drive you down to Cork and head on to Sneem. We can talk on the way. The weather here says the roads should be better by tomorrow. In the afternoon anyway. How did Aesop get down there?'

'I think he flew.'

'Right. Well I s'pose you'll have to fly back with him. I'll get the six o'clock back up from Killarney on Monday morning for work.'

'Okay. Okay, that's great. Thanks Trish.'

'We'll talk in the morning okay?'

'Yeah. But thanks for even …'

'Shush. Norman?

'Yeah?'

'You told me you loved me today.'

'I did.'

'Do you?'

'I do.'

'Say it again.'

He swallowed.

'I love you.'

'Do you really?'

'Yeah. I do. Really.'

'Because if you ever do that to me again …'

'I won't. Jesus Christ, I never will. I swear to God. I'd cut my throat first.'

'Okay. You need to work on your imagery, Norman. You've already had your throat cut and been shot so far in this conversation. And Aesop's getting a hiding.'

'Sorry.'

'And me here trying to convince myself you're not deranged.'

'Eh … well …'

'I'm joking, Norman. Look, call me tomorrow, okay?'

'As soon as I'm up.'

'Bye.'

'Seeya.'

'Norman?'

'Yeah?'

'Tell me again.'

'I love you, Trish.'

'Good,' she said.

And then she was gone.

Norman fell back onto his bed, every nerve in his body tingling. He made a mental note to buy Jimmy a barrel of porter for telling him he should call her. Who'd have thought it? That a conversation between him and a girl could actually make a shite situation better?

He lay there, just watching the snow fly past his window.

NORMAN WENT to Mass with his Mam at half eight the next morning. He rarely actually went into the church with her these days, but this morning he had a lot to be thankful for. Trish had called to say that she'd be over at about twelve and they could head down to Cork then.

Back in the house from the church, Norman put on the kettle as his Mam started preparing the dinner.

'Will you be here for dinner?'

'No Mam. I'm heading back down to Cork to pick Aesop up.'

'What? In this weather?'

'Sure the worst of it is over now. There'll be no more snow now till later in the week, they're saying.'

'What's he doing down there? And can he not pick himself up?'

'Ah … he just went down to see a girl. I said I'd pick him up.'

He didn't know if she was biting all this, but she just shrugged and turned back to the cabbage she was stripping.

'A girl?' she said, over her shoulder.

'Eh … yeah.'

'Anyone we know?'

'Not … sure.'

'Robert, what kind of an eejit do you think I am? Didn't I have Bridie on the phone to me yesterday. I know all about himself and Helen.'

'Oh. Well, I didn't want you to get all … y'know …'

'She's a big girl. She can do what she wants.'

'Yeah. Well, apparently she isn't interested in Aesop.'

'Good for her.'

'I think she's going back with that Molloy young fella.'

'Molloy,' said his Mam. 'God. All belonging to that crowd are mad for drink.'

'Well he's off it now, he says.'

'And he better stay off it. Because if Mikey Pat hears he's acting the maggot again, there'll be trouble.'

'Yeah. Anyway, I'm going to collect Aesop. I'll probably be back tonight, assuming the weather holds.'

'Grand so. Well be careful.'

'I will of course. Listen … Mam …'

'Yes love?'

'Eh … I've been meaning to tell you something.'

'What's that?'

'Well, it's just that I've … I've been kind of seeing a girl.'

She stopped what she was doing and turned around to him.

'Have you now?'

'Yeah.'

Norman had his hands in his pockets in case they started shaking on him.

'What girl?'

'Ah, a girl I met in work. A nurse. She's lovely Mam.'

'Really? Lovely, is it?'

'Yeah. She's great. Anyway, I've been seeing her now for a good while, and I'd like you to meet her.'

'That sounds very serious.'

'Ah no … well, maybe a little bit. We, eh, we … we're getting on grand. She's coming down to Cork with me this afternoon. She's picking me up here, so you can meet her then.'

'You're bringing her to Cork? Again? God, it must serious, so.'

'Well, she has to go down anyway, so she'll drop me off at Granny's and then … eh … what?'

'Hmm?'

'What do you mean "again"?'

His Mam laughed.

'What do you take me for, you gom? Don't I know you were down there with her a couple of weeks ago.'

'What?'

'Yes! You think your oul' Mam's gone soft? Robert, there's nothing goes on down there that I don't hear about.'

'Bridie told you?'

'Bridie. And a few others. Sure I've known about that little trip you took for ages. But you weren't exactly showing her off, were you? Cooped up in the house the whole weekend, so you were.'

Norman was crimson.

'Well, the weather wasn't great, so …'

'Ah, I don't want to hear all that. So you like her then?'

'Yeah. I do. A lot.'

'Good.'

She smiled at him and turned back to the counter.

'So do I.'

'You … what?'

'I like her too.'

'Wha … I mean … how do you …'

'Bridie isn't the only one I've been talking to, you know. Didn't your new girlfriend call here herself? I was bit surprised, I have to say, given that my son doesn't tell me a thing these days, but she seemed like a very nice girl. She was looking for you and we ended up having a great chat. Sure at that stage I already knew her name anyway from Bridie, so it was nice to talk to her finally. I'd be a long time waiting for you to introduce me. Patricia, isn't it?'

Norman laughed.

'Yeah. Trish. She never mentioned it.'

'Sure why would she? We were just a couple of girls having an oul' chinwag.'

'What did you talk about?'

'Don't you mind. Two can play at that game, Robert. Hand me up the sieve there.'

Norman bent down to get it out of the press.

'God. Well anyway, she'll be here soon, so you can put a face to the name.'

'I'll look forward to that so. What time is she coming?'

'About twelve.'

She looked at the clock over the table.

'Grand. Well can you finish this then, and I'll go up and give meself a touch-up.'

'You don't have to Ma. You look grand.'

'You just put that cabbage on and get started on the carrots. You think I'm going to meet this girl in an apron?'

'No, but …'

She was disappearing up the stairs now.

'We want to make a good impression, don't we? God knows, it's not like they've been banging down the door all these years …'

That was for fucking sure, thought Norman, smiling and picking up a carrot. And where was this version of his Mam all through his youth? There might have been a few more knocks on the door if it wasn't for her putting the fear of God into everyone he ever brought into the house.

An hour later, Norman's phone rang. When he hung up, he turned to his Mam. He was all nervous now.

'Okay, that was Trish. She's at the roundabout and just checking where the house is. She'll be here in five minutes.'

'Grand so. Put the kettle on there.'

He started fidgeting around the kitchen, folding the J-cloth and checking to see that there was enough milk for a cup of tea.

'Will you ever relax, Robert? God, you do like her don't you?'

'Yeah, Mam.'

'Well stop fussing or she'll think there's a want in you.'

'I know. I'm grand.'

She smiled at him from the kitchen table.

'Actually, she's not what I would have expected for you. Nice and all as she is, like.'

'How's that?'

'Well. God, I wasn't expecting her to have the accent and all. I know what you're like.'

'Ah Mam, she's not one of those Kerrywomen. She doesn't even like football.'

'What are you talking about?'

'Ah, her brothers were mad footballers at home in Sneem. Put her off completely when she was small. She can't watch it at all now, only big games.'

'Sneem? What do you mean, Robert?'

'What?'

'Sure, isn't the girl English?'

Chapter Twenty-nine

'IN THE name of God, Norman, will you slow down?' said Trish.

'I'm under the limit.'

'But look at the roads! We won't get as far as the M50 at the rate you're going, never mind Cork.'

'Will you try Jimmy again?'

'Yeah. Hang on …'

She handed him the phone when he answered.

'Jimmy?'

'Yeah Norman. Sorry man. In the shower. What's up?'

'Listen Jimmy, it was Amanda.'

'What? What are you on about?'

'Amanda. The English girl. She's the one that's been after Aesop. And she's either in Cork now, or else she's on the way there.'

'What? Norman, what are you bleedin' talking about?'

'She called my Mam. Pretended she was Trish. Found out about the cottage in Cork. She must be gone to find him.'

'Wha … what'll we do? Jesus. What … where are you?'

'I'm on the road. We'll be there in a couple of hours. Mikey's on the way there too. He left Kanturk and he'll be there in half an hour.'

'Fuck. What about the coppers?'

'Mikey's going to sort that out when he checks the house.'

'Jesus. How … how did you find all this out?'

'I'm telling you. Amanda called my Mam. Mam thought it was Trish and they started talking. She must have been following us or something. Or maybe your Susan bird in London was telling her what we're up to. Who I am and everything.'

'But … man, Amanda was lovely. She was a bit upset over that bloke, but she never came across as some kind of … y'know …'

'You can't tell with some people, Jimmy. Look I have to go. It's hard enough this morning without trying to drive with one hand.'

'Yeah. Yeah. But … but Norman, listen. It can't be her.'

'Why not?'

'Because she's Amanda! We need a P, remember? That's what she wrote on the door! A P and an A. It can't be her. We don't have a P.'

'We have a P, Jimmy.'

'What? Who?'

'Paul. Isn't that what she calls him?'

'Oh … oh fuck! I never thought of that!'

'Yeah, well …'

'Christ, I don't believe it!'

'Jimmy, I have to go.'

'Okay. But … well … can I do anything? Call someone or …'

'No man. And listen, don't call Susan either. Just in case.'

'In case what?'

'Just in case. We don't know what we're dealing with here.'

'What?! Norman, you don't think …'

'Jimmy I don't think anything. I just don't want any more people sticking their oar in until I find him.'

'Okay. Jesus. Okay.'

'I'll call you, right? Keep your phone with you.'

'Right. Thanks.'

'Okay.'

Norman hung up and handed the phone to Trish, gripping the wheel with both hands now and speeding up again. Trish put a hand on her seatbelt for about the fifth time to make sure that it was safely clicked. Norman tore through a yellow light and gunned across an intersection.

'Jesus,' said Trish, a hand clapped to her face. 'Did you not see the truck?'

'I saw it.'

'Feck sake. And so this is what's it going to be like going out with you, is it? Rock concerts and VIP rooms and mad dashes across the country to save your friend from a mad stalker? Is that what I'm after signing up for, is it? And me thinking you were a gardener.'

'No Trish. I'm sorry about all this. This is a one-off.'

'Me father's poor car.'

'I won't hurt it.'

'It's bad enough.'

'It's grand.'

She sighed and sat back against the seat as they got onto a motorway ramp. She needed to try and take her mind off his driving.

'Your Mam seemed nice.'

'She's great.'

'Although she was a bit worried when we bundled into the car and tore off without telling her anything.'

'I'll call her later.'

'Right. So, have you ever met this Amanda one?'

'No.'

'But you're sure it was her that pretended to be me?'

'Yeah.'

'You really think she's in Cork?'

'Yeah.'

'How would she find the place? It's in the middle of nowhere.'

'Mam told her.'

'Eh ... Norman?'

'Yeah?'

'Am I annoying you with all the questions?'

He cleared his throat.

'Of course not.'

'Are you sure?'

'Positive.'

She put a hand on his arm.

'Okay. Well, I'll stop anyway and let you drive.'

'Thanks. And ... and thanks for being here.'

She kissed him on the cheek and looked out the window at the snow that had been piled up off the road onto the bank. Norman let a long slow breath out of his nose and unclenched his jaw. That was another barrel of porter for Jimmy. He really knew his shit when it came to women.

THEY GOT to the cottage in the late afternoon. Mikey Pat had already been there and had rung to say that it was empty. It had been since at least yesterday, because there was no footprints or tyre tracks in the snow. Aesop had been there, though. The kitchen was a mess and the bed in his room looked like he'd been playing football in it. Mikey was going to drop home and then head down to the sergeant's house, to fill him in on everything.

Norman got out of the car and looked around. There was nothing much to see. Everything looked normal. They went into the house and Norman checked all the rooms thoroughly. Nothing. It was all exactly as it should be. Well, exactly as it would be if that messy bastard had spent a couple of nights there. There was a bag in the bedroom. The one Aesop used to carry his music gear around. There were no drumsticks or anything in it now though, just a pair of jeans and some underwear. He went back out to Trish.

'Nothing.'

'Does it look like anything's the matter?'

'No. Not really. Except that he's not here. And he's not on his way back to Dublin or he'd have brought his bag with him. And if he *was* going back to Dublin, he'd have cleaned up because he knows what I'd do to him if he left the place in this state. Christ. Where is he?'

'No idea. He didn't have a car, did he?'

'Not unless he rented one.'

'Could he have walked anywhere?'

'No. Sure there's nowhere to walk to. Not in this weather. And not Aesop. He'd get a taxi from the couch to the kettle if he could.'

'I don't know, Norman.'

'You need to go, don't you?'

'Ah no. No, I could stay for a bit.'

'There's no need, Trish. Mikey Pat said he'd be here in half an hour. I'll have his car then if I need it.'

'Well, if you're sure.' She checked her watch. 'I could get home before it starts icing up too much again.'

'Off you go. I'll be grand. Really.'

'Are you sure?'

'Absolutely. Look, come on and I'll walk you to the car.'

'Thanks. You're sure now?'

'I'm sure. C'mon.'

'Okay. You'll call me as soon as you know anything?'

'I will of course.'

They went out and Norman looked around the landscape again, sighing. Then his eye caught something and he frowned.

'What it is?'

'The well.'

'What?'

'The well. Look. You can't really see it with snow all over it, but there's a holy well over there. See it? In that field?'

'I think so, yeah. What about it?'

'I'm just going to check something. Hang on a minute, will you?'

'Yeah. No problem. Can I do anything?'

'No. Actually … just … see the shed there?'

'Yeah.'

'There's a length of rope in it. Will you get it for me? The shed's not locked. The rope is hanging on a nail on the wall.'

'What are you going to do?'

'I just want to check something.'

'Norman, you're not going to do something stupid, are you?'

'Of course not. Won't take a minute. I'll see you over at the well, okay?'

He crunched through the snow in the garden and over the small fence that led into the next field. The well was about a hundred metres further on, and the snow was pretty deep. At least twelve inches. When he got there, he looked down the opening. It was less than a metre wide, but a good fifteen metres deep by all accounts. Or so Mikey Pat had once told him anyway. Obviously, Norman had never been down there. His Granny would have kicked his arse if he or any of them had ever tried that when they were kids. He started kicking snow away from around the base of the well to see if anything looked awry. But it was impossible to tell. The ground was hard with packed ice and muck. He looked up to see Trish coming over the field towards him.

'You all right?' he called.

'Yeah. I'm fine. Jesus, like going out with feckin' Indiana Jones this is.'

She reached him and handed him the rope.

'You're not going down there,' she said, when she saw him look over the side again.

'I want to just take a quick look.'

'Norman, no! What are you talking about? That's just crazy! It's dangerous and it's stupid and you're not to do it.'

'Sure haven't I done this kind of thing a million times. It's grand. I just want to take a quick look and I'll be back up to you then. Won't take a minute.'

'Norman, you're not in the army now. Will you give over? What happens if the rope breaks, or slips? Or if you slip off it and fall? Come on, stop being silly.'

'Trish, I just want to check the place out properly before Mikey Pat gets here okay? Make sure the eejit didn't fall in or something stupid.'

'Jesus. Can you not use a torch, for Christ sake?'

'Do you have one?'

'Of course not. But there must be one in the shed or something ...'

Norman grunted.

'I could be half an hour looking for a torch, sure. This'll take me a couple of minutes. Get it over and done with. I'll just tie the rope to the tree there and ...'

'You're mad! Will you stop messing.'

'I've done this hundreds of times, Trish. It's grand.'

'You're not bloody Rambo, Norman! The rope is damp and ... God, why are we even having this conversation?'

But Norman already had the rope around the thick sycamore that stood about six feet from the well.

'Won't be a minute.'

'Jesus, please Norman ...'

He had the rope wrapped around one hand now, slack in the other. He stepped up to the lip of the well and sat on it, swinging his legs around.

'I'll just ...'

'What the hell is that?' she said, pointing.

'What?'

'That. Around your ankle.'

'Oh. That's ... eh.'

'Fuck sake, Norman, why have you a bloody big knife strapped to you? Listen, this is getting ...'

'Here. Take it.'

'What? What am I going to do with it?'

'Just hold it. I don't want to lose it.'

'Jesus ... and ... and how are you meant to see down there?'

'I've a lighter.'

'And what about the bloody water in the bottom of the well? How deep is it?'

'Only about three feet usually. There's a grate across it then. In case anyone fell in.'

She sighed.

'You're going to go down there no matter what I say, aren't you?'

'I'll be back up in five minutes. You can keep talking to me if you like.'

'God. What'll we talk about? The bloody weather? Football? You abseiling into a well in the middle of winter on a damp, oily tow-rope with nothing to stop you falling to your death?'

'Whatever you like.'

He gave her a quick kiss on the cheek and then he was gone. All she could hear was the occasional mumble echoing up. She looked over the edge, but he was already just a murky shadow in the blackness. She waited for a minute or so.

'Anything?' she called.

'Hang on,' came the booming voice back up to her.

'Okay.'

Another minute or so. She could see the faint glow of his lighter, but she couldn't make anything out down there. Norman's voice came up again, but it was all muffled.

'What?' She leaned further in. 'I can't hear you.'

'I said I think I … I think I found … something.'

'Jesus. What?'

'Fucking hell! Fuck!'

'What? Norman, what is it?'

The light went out.

There was more mumbling, but she didn't know what he was saying. She felt sick, her heart hammering. She jumped back from the well and over to the sycamore tree to check the knot. It looked fine. You couldn't undo it even if you were trying to, not with Norman's weight pulling it tight.

'Trish? Trish, I'm coming up.'

'Okay Norman. Come on.'

The rope started to twitch and jerk even more. She looked back around at the tree, but there was no way it would slip and unravel on its own. No way. It was solid. She was sweating now, despite the cold. She looked at the knife in her hand and shuddered.

'Come on up.'

Chapter Thirty

THE DOOR of the cottage opened and Aesop stood there.

He stared.

'What the … ?' he said.

Trish went to stand up from the couch.

'Stay the fuck where you are, you mad cow,' said Aesop, pointing at her and taking a step back. 'I'm bleedin' freezing and I've had enough of your psycho shit.'

'What? Jesus, Aesop, where have you been? Everyone's been worried sick!'

'What are you doing here? Where's Norman?'

'He's dropping Mikey Pat home and then coming back with his car.'

'Me bollocks he is.' Then he saw the knife next to her on the couch and took another half-step backwards. 'Wha … why have you got his knife?'

'What? Oh, he gave it to me to mind. He said …'

'That's his Da's knife. No one's allowed touch it, you lying fucker.'

'Aesop, I swear, he's just …'

'Stay fucking sitting down!'

'What? Aesop, I'm just …'

'Where is he?'

'Who?'

'Norman!'

'I told you. He's getting Mikey Pat's car. My car won't start and he's going to drop me to the train. The spark plugs are gone again. It keeps happening.'

Aesop took a quick glance behind him.

'That car?'

'Yeah. It's my Dad's.'

'The spark plugs are gone, are they?'

'Yes! Look Aesop, will you come in and shut the door, for God sake!'

'You think I'm a fuckin' eejit? That's a diesel car.'

'What? I don't …'

Then he saw something else on the couch.

'Where did you get that?'

'What?'

'That's my phone.'

'Norman found it.'

'Norman found it? How did he manage that?'

'It was down the well.'

'I know where it was. It bleedin' fell down there the …'

Aesop's eyes jumped from the phone to the knife and then to Trish's face.

'Holy fuck,' he said, backing even further out the door and grabbing the handle. 'What are you after … you sick fucking …'

'Aesop? Aesop come back. Where are you …'

'Get the fuck away from me!'

She stood up and started to move towards him. He ran outside, slamming the door shut behind him. He heard the door open again but he just kept going, down the short gravel driveway and out the gate. He was twenty yards down the road, his name from her mouth echoing in his ears, when the car came bouncing over the hill.

And straight into him. He just had time to jump a couple of inches into the air and then he was collected up by the bonnet, his legs flung in an arc over his head, which smashed against the windscreen. The car kept going, sliding over the black, packed ice on the road and colliding with the gatepost of the cottage. Aesop had a brief sense of cold and noise in his head … and then he was gone.

JIMMY WAS fuck-ways in the head with worry. There was no word from anyone. Norman hadn't called and wasn't answering his phone. Aesop's was still dead. He called Dónal to tell him the latest and spent five minutes being told to sit down and try and relax. He couldn't though. As soon as Dónal hung up he was back to pacing his living room, cursing at his phone and rubbing his face. At least the coppers knew. That's what Norman had said the last time he called. Mikey Pat was with the sergeant and telling him what was going on. That was something.

Jimmy was about to call Shiggy, just for something to do, when the phone rang and vibrated in his hand, making him jerk.

'Jesus …'

The screen said nothing only that a call was incoming.

'Hello?'

'Jimmy?'

It was Susan in London. Fuck, what now?

'Susan?'

'Yeah. Hi.'

'Eh … hiya.'

'What's wrong?'

'What?'

'You sound awful.'

'Nothing … eh, nothing. I'm grand.'

Norman had asked him to say fuck all to her.

'Are you sure?'

'Yeah. I'm sure. What's up?'

She spoke quietly then.

'Jimmy, I can understand if you're annoyed. I'm sorry I never got back to you when you called me in London.'

'It's all right.'

'No. Listen, I knew you'd be around and I just didn't want to deal with it.'

'It's okay, Susan.'

'I went to my Mam's for the weekend. In Surrey. I just couldn't face the idea of seeing you and … y'know … getting into everything. So … eh …'

Will you get to the fucking point, woman?

'Susan, it's fine, okay. I mean … whatever.'

'Oh. So you're pissed off. I see. Well I won't keep you then.'

'Look Susan, I'm sorry. There's … stuff going on at the moment and I'm a bit on edge. Can I call you later?'

'Is everything okay?'

'Yeah. Well, no. Look, Aesop's gone missing and we're a bit worried about him.'

'Aesop?'

'Yeah. He's been gone for a couple of days now. And someone's been threatening him recently. We're all ... y'know? We're worried that something might have happened to him.'

'But Jimmy, that's why I called. I wanted to tell you that Amanda is okay.'

'Wh ... Amanda?'

'Yeah. It turns out that she was in Ireland. She went over to see Aesop. She hadn't planned it, but ... oh, I don't know. She remembered the great time we all had in Thailand, and she just wanted to see him again. I don't think she expected much, but she figured that Aesop was pretty easy-going and was hoping they could hang out for a bit. She was going to surprise him.'

'Right. Eh ... and have you spoken to her? I mean, today or ... recently?'

Christ, what was going on?

'Yeah! I talked to her this morning.'

What?! Jimmy swallowed. He might be able to find out something at long fucking last.

'And what did she say?'

'She said that she spent the last couple of days with Aesop.'

'She said that?'

'Yeah. They went to see some dolphin or something? Aesop insisted. She had a car and they drove to the coast and went out in a boat. Had a great time.'

'But ...'

'Actually, she was a bit embarrassed. Apparently, it took ages to track him down. She ended up talking to one of your friends' mothers to find him. She lied about who she was, she says. But she just thought that with him being famous and all, that's why he was so hard to find, because he was laying low. She didn't want to just arrive when he was too busy to talk to her or anything. She wanted to find the right moment, she said. But then ...'

Susan started laughing on the other end of the phone. Jimmy frowned at his phone. This was getting mental.

' … and then when she did find him, she went and walked straight in on him with another girl!'

'What girl?'

'Oh I don't know. Some fan I think. Jessica? I don't know if you know her. Anyway, this other girl was all embarrassed too. She left in quite a hurry and then Aesop and Amanda got chatting. Ended up spending the weekend together. They went off looking at this dolphin.'

Jimmy was scratching his head furiously now.

'Susan, did she say where they are?'

'Well, Amanda's back here. She flew in this morning. I met her for lunch.'

'She's … she's back in London?'

'Yeah. And she's a new girl. It's fantastic, Jimmy. You should see her! She had such a good time with Aesop. I mean, I don't even think anything happened. Y'know … anything like that. They were just like old mates. She loved it. Aesop really gave her a lift. I haven't seen her like this in so long. It's great. She said that first thing tomorrow morning, she's going to …'

'Susan, where the fuck is Aesop?'

'What?'

'Where is he? Is he in London?'

'What? No. He's in Ireland. They said goodbye in the airport in Cork and she flew back. I think he was going back to his friend's house or something.'

'So … are you sure about all this?'

'Yeah. I just left Amanda an hour ago. She's gone home to …'

Jimmy stopped listening. It was all okay. The dopey fucking idiot had spent the weekend in Dingle. He was grand. He must be on his way back to Dublin now. Christ.

'We were … we were just worried about him,' he said. 'We haven't heard from him in days and … we didn't know what to think.'

'Oh. Well … look, do you want Amanda's number? We were just

chatting, so I wasn't really paying attention to every little detail.'

'Yeah. Can I have it?'

He took the number down on the edge of a newspaper.

'I'll talk to you later Susan, okay?'

'Okay. Jimmy, are you sure everything's okay?'

'I think so. Now I do, anyway.'

Five minutes later he was talking to a very confused Amanda.

'And you never, y'know, wrote him notes or put flowers through his letterbox?'

'What? Why would I do that Jimmy?'

'Just … so you didn't then? You're sure you weren't breaking into his house and pissing on his bed there last month?'

'Piss … Jimmy, what's gotten into you? I didn't even know where he was until last week. What's the matter?'

'Nothing, Amanda. I just … look, can I call you later?'

IT WAS cold. Freezing. Numb. No pain.

Aesop tried to open his eyes. They both seemed to open all right, but he could only see out of one of them, and everything was blurred. He went to wipe at his face, but nothing happened. He couldn't move. He heard someone screaming and then everything was black. A bit later – seconds or hours, he couldn't tell – his good eye opened again. He could just make out two figures, one lying down and the other one kneeling. He recognised Norman's coat. His legs were still in the car but the rest of him was out, lying on the ground. The other figure was Trish. Aesop tried to call to Norman, to reach out to him, but nothing happened. Nothing came out of this mouth and his arm still wouldn't move.

He saw Trish look up. There was blood on her clothes.

'I'll be over to you in a minute, Aesop.'

He heard that, but it sounded like it was coming from the end of a tunnel. He tried to call again to Norman, but Norman didn't look around. He seemed to be struggling with her. Fighting. Then Aesop saw the knife. She held it, pointing it down at Norman as she pinned him with her knees. Tears filled Aesop's eyes. He couldn't do anything. And then he could barely see anything, his one eye becoming blurred again with the tears. His mouth made the shape again. 'Norman.' But if it made any sound, Aesop couldn't hear it. The figures just a few metres away were more like shadows now than real people. He blinked and for a split second the fog was gone. The last thing he saw before he blacked out again was Trish plunging the knife into Norman. That was it. He faded in and out a couple more times, but both his eyes were gone now. All he had left was the cold that seemed to be spreading from inside him instead of seeping into him from the ground.

And then his heartbeat. It thumped in his head and he could start to feel the pain now with every new beat. But it didn't sound right. There was something wrong. It suddenly didn't even sound like his heart any more. More like the thud of footsteps.

Getting louder.

Chapter Thirty-one

THERE WAS an exodus from Dublin to Cork.

Jimmy and Dónal, Aesop's family and Marco, Norman's Mam. Even Shiggy. Everyone flew straight down as soon as the news reached Dublin. It was fucking horrible down there. Crying, confusion, everyone running about trying to find out what the fuck had happened. Garda Ní Mhurchú had also gone down. This wasn't just another traffic accident. She stayed with Jimmy all through it. Sergeant Harmon was there for most of it too. He'd been ten minutes behind Norman coming over that hill, Mikey Pat in the front seat next to him, and when he'd seen that girl crouched over Aesop on the ground, both of them covered in blood and muck, he knew it was the one thing in all his years as a policeman that would visit him in the night afterwards. He locked Trish in his car as soon as he'd called the ambulance, and she'd gone quietly. They usually did once they knew it was over. Then he did what he could for Norman and Aesop. Christ, it looked awful. Smeared in scarlet around the frozen white of snow, he didn't think he'd ever seen so much life seep out of one person.

As Jimmy and everyone else were making their way to Cork, Norman and Aesop lying in hospital, Sergeant Harmon stood over Trish back at the station and tried to talk to her. But she wouldn't say anything. She just sat on a chair and rocked back and forward, pale and trembling. At one stage, she asked to go to the hospital to see Norman. When he told her that that was out of the question, she just looked down at the tiled floor and wouldn't speak again. He offered her tea and coffee, a cigarette, food, but she wasn't interested. A female colleague managed to get her cleaned up as best she could, but Trish didn't even help her. She just sat and stared as the woman wiped her face with a wet towel. Eventually, they called a doctor in. He took one look at her and told Sergeant Harmon that she couldn't stay there. She had to go to the hospital too. Shock. The sergeant cursed under his breath and ordered the female Guard who'd cleaned her up and another one to go with them. She wasn't to be let out of their sight.

THAT FIRST evening in the hospital, Jimmy paced in front of another doctor, biting at the skin in the bend of his thumb. He looked up.

'Look doctor, I didn't understand most of that,' he said. 'Do you want to tell me what's happening?'

'Mr. Kelly is going to be fine,' said the doctor. 'The quick attention he received at the scene undoubtedly saved his life. His physical condition is quite remarkable actually. I don't think we'd be having this conversation at all only for that.'

'Right. Is he awake?'

'I'm afraid not. He's just had pretty major surgery. You can see him tomorrow.'

'And Aesop?'

The doctor sighed and looked away for a minute. Jimmy felt his stomach lurch. He thought he was going to be sick.

'Doctor? What about Aesop?'

'Mr Collins, Mr Murray suffered serious internal injuries, the most significant of which is a ruptured spleen.'

'Jesus.'

'We've dealt with that problem and I'm hopeful that there won't be complications.'

'Okay. What else?'

'It's really the head injury that I'm concerned about. He suffered coup-contrecoup impact damage ...'

'Fuck sake doctor, what does that mean? Come on, will you? Jesus ...'

'He's undergoing some scans now. We'll know more when we get the results. I'm afraid I can't tell you much more than that.'

'Will he be ... ?'

'I'm sorry. It's far too early to tell. We've stopped the bleeding now, but all we can do is wait.'

'And ... and you don't know ...'

'No, we don't Mr Collins. But as soon as we do, I'll talk to you again.'

'Okay. Fuck … okay. Thanks.'

'There's one thing you should probably know, though. About what happened.'

'Jesus … what is it?'

The doctor told him.

Then Jimmy found himself wandering out in the grounds of the hospital, smoking and feeling nauseous and weak.

IT WAS the next night, small flurries of snow appearing out of the darkness of the sky and whipping tightly in the eddies around the hospital, caught in the glow of the lights.

Aesop was alone in his room. Not awake, exactly, but things were starting to happen in his head. He'd hear things, or he'd be able to make out light and dark shades around the room. He'd had a vague sense of people around him, but he couldn't concentrate. He kept drifting in and out. He didn't know where he was or why he couldn't move. There was music, playing softly. It hurt his head, but he couldn't see to turn it off, or talk to ask someone to turn it off for him. There was something in his mouth. Once he was aware of the pain, it got worse. Like a conversation across a room, where you hear your name. Once you hear it, you tune everything else out until that's all you can hear. And that music. Jesus … why couldn't they turn it off. It hurt.

A couple of fingers on his hand twitched and he became aware that he was holding something. Something … something … it came back to him then. It was a button, but right now it was an anchor that allowed him to set an order to things that had happened. He was in a hospital. He'd been run over. A female voice had told him at some stage earlier that pressing his thumb would help with the pain. It wasn't much, but being able to put some cause and consequence together in his mind gave him some comfort; almost as much as pressing down with his thumb, although that was a completely different kind of comfort. It was on a timer though. There never seemed to be enough in one shot to do him until the timer clicked over and he was allowed have another dose. The first couple of minutes after he pushed the button were absolutely fucking magic and he'd be buzzing like a mad thing in the bed. But the last while before it would reset was usually pretty bad.

And he was in pain now. He started to press his thumb down every couple of seconds, but he mustn't have been due yet. Fuck, this was the king of headaches he had. It was like having the worst hangover in the world and then someone smacking you hard with a stiff pillow on every count of your pulse. He could feel the sweat rolling down his face. His gown thing was damp and hot. Press … press … press. Nothing yet. He was going to release the button so that he could try and find that other one, the one that he'd been told called the nurse, but he didn't want to let go. This button was the only thing between the pressure in his head and release from it. Press … press … press. It wouldn't be long now, surely. He'd already put up with it for long enough. Could they not just knock a few minutes off the bloody timer? Fuck sake, he was in bits. His mouth was open, the one eye he could barely see out of squeezed shut. His face was soaked. Press … press … pr …

It hit him. A blissful rush that seemed to literally squeeze the pain out of his body like water from a sponge. Light danced behind his eyelids and then he felt himself settle back onto the mattress as though the pain had been lifting him off it on pointed barbs. He could breathe properly now. Slowly and deep. His hands and feet tingled for a second and then he felt nothing much. Just a kind of dopey oblivion. Then a sudden coldness wrapped around his chin and exposed cheek. It wiped down his chest, cooling him and making him sigh. It felt beautiful. Like slipping into a pool as the sun beat down on you. He opened his eye to try and thank the nurse through the slowly-moving shapes that weaved in front of him. One of the shapes stopped moving.

It was Trish.

'Aesop?'

No. Aw Jesus … no.

370

JIMMY HADN'T slept in two days. If he'd needed something to focus on, to try and take his mind off everything that had happened, he got it when the press arrived. The news was all over the country now. The drummer of the biggest band in Ireland had been in some kind of accident. They wanted stories, they wanted pictures. Jimmy wanted to kick the living fuck out of them, but after the first encounter between Jimmy and a photographer, which had ended with a camera being fired out the door of the hospital and into the street, he'd been led away from the public areas of the hospital and into a special waiting room where he wouldn't have to deal with them. Dónal talked to the throng outside. It was while he was sitting there on his own, staring at a cold cup of tea in front of him, that the words of the doctor the previous night came to him again. They'd figured out what had happened on the road outside the cottage. Jimmy had listened and then just shook his head, barely able to take it in.

It had been Trish.

She'd saved their lives.

The emergency tracheotomy that she'd performed on Norman, opening his throat after it had been closed by the smack of the steering wheel, had kept him alive until the ambulance had arrived. And she'd kept Aesop warm and conscious, his neck held rigid by her own coat, until the sergeant's car had crested the hill and she'd been locked in it. Once the staff at the hospital realised who this shaken girl was that had been brought in that evening, they told the two Guards what she'd done and then led her away to be looked after.

Jimmy had sat with her for an hour in the hospital when he got down there that first night, talking to her softly, his arm around her.

'Thank you,' he said.

She just shook her head, crying.

'It's my fault.'

'It's not. Shush. It was an accident.'

'He was running away from me.'

'He didn't know what was going on. It's okay. You saved them.'

But she didn't want to hear it.

'My fault,' was all she'd say.

'AESOP?'

No. Aw Jesus ... no.

Why couldn't he hear that? There was no sound, as though he was only imagining that he'd spoken. That thing in his mouth ...

'Aesop, listen to me. Can you hear me?'

Don't ...

'Please, Aesop, I'm not going to hurt you. Do you understand me?'

Aesop tried to press the button to call the nurse, but he was holding the wrong one.

Don't ... didn't ... do ... anything ...

'Please. Just listen to me. I need to tell you something.'

Her hand came up to his face. There was something white in it.

No ... no ...

He tried to turn away, but he couldn't.

'Shhh ...' she said. 'It's okay, Aesop.'

She wiped the new sweat from him.

'Shhh ...'

He drifted off for a minute or two. When he came back she was still there, still wiping him down and telling him that everything was okay in a soft voice. The effects of the drug weren't as strong now. He could make her out clearly but her voice was still distant, like a television turned down. She reached down and pulled the button out of his hand, leaving his thumb still pressing steadily on air. She sat forward then – closer to him, leaning over him – and held his hand.

'Aesop? Are you okay?'

No!

'Are you in pain?'

No ... no.

'I promise, I won't hurt you. I know what you think happened. It wasn't like that.'

The dizziness was starting to go. The pain was already gone, along with the feeling of drunken helplessness. He was halfway back to knowing what was going on. It was Trish. He remembered seeing her on the couch. Some couch. Somewhere. She'd had a knife. She was coming for him. That was all he had. And now she was here.

'I just want to tell you something.'

I don't love you. Please ...

'I just need you to listen to me for a minute. Okay?'

Jesus ...

'Okay?'

What did she want?

'If you can understand me, just squeeze my hand.'

She wiped his face again. It felt good, brought him closer to wherever they were. The world outside his head. He couldn't do anything anyway. What difference did it make now? Maybe if he could drag this out, someone would come along.

He pressed his thumb against her fingers.

She started to tell him then. Her hushed voice was like a breeze outside, but he heard it all. And then, as he lay between the two ends of pain and confusion, neither quite able to reach him now, he understood.

'HI,' SHE said, red with excitement and embarrassment.

'Hello yourself,' said Aesop, the big grin shining. 'Enjoy the gig?'

'I did. You were brilliant.'

'Thanks very much. I'm Aesop.'

She laughed.

'Yeah, I know. I'm Trish.'

'Hiya Trish. Can I get you a drink?'

'Ah no. I'm fine with this, thanks.'

'You sure? Band gets them for free.'

'No, really. We're all heading off after this one.'

'Where yis off to?'

'Oh I don't know. Leeson Street I s'pose.'

'Why don't you have a proper drink first then? You'll only get shite down there.'

'Yeah, I know. God. Okay then. Pint of Budweiser?'

'Bud? Grand. Hang on there Trish.'

He ordered and turned back to her.

'Is that a Cork accent?'

'Kerry.'

'Ah right. I'm shite with accents. And what are you doing up here in the big smoke then, Trish?'

'I'm a nurse.'

'Yeah? Tough job.'

'I like it though.'

'Are they all nurses?'

He nodded over to where another half-dozen girls were talking to Jimmy and the new bass player, Beano. Jimmy's mot, Sandra, was hovering there too, looking pissed off. No change there.

'Most of them, yeah. It's her birthday. In the black? That's Bronagh.'

'Ah right. Out on the razz then.'

'A bit, yeah.'

'So c'mere, where do you do your nursing?'

'Well …'

She looked down at the drink he was handing to her. He caught a hint of something in her eyes as she did.

'Well, actually, I'm not working at the moment.'

'Oh right.'

'I'm just back from Romania. I did some work over there for a bit.'

Aesop looked closely at her for a second.

'I saw some stuff on the telly about that.'

She nodded.

'Were you working with the kids over there?'

'Yeah.'

'Fuck. Those poor babies in the …'

'Aesop, sorry. But I'd rather not …'

'Okay. Okay, no problem. Anyway, you're back now. Out with your mates.'

She was still looking down at her drink.

'You okay?'

She sniffed and looked up at him.

'Yeah. It was just a bit …'

'Do you want to sit down?'

'They'll be kicking everyone out now, sure'

'They can't kick me out. I haven't cleared the stage yet. We're grand. C'mon and sit down for a sec with me. Over there, look.'

He caught Jimmy's eye and gave him a small nod. Jimmy just raised his eyes to heaven and got back to talking to Bronagh and her mates.

Once they were sitting down, next to the stage and away from everyone finishing up their drinks, Aesop took out a smoke for himself and held out the pack to her.

'No thanks.'

'Mind if I have one?'

She smiled.

'No. I've heard things about you, Aesop. But you're not really like I was expecting.'

'Jaysis. What were you expecting?'

'Just … y'know …'

'A mad sexy rockstar who thinks he's brilliant and only has one thing on his mind when he gets a girl into a dark corner like the very one we seem to find ourselves in right now?'

She laughed.

'A bit, yeah.'

'All lies and fabrication. I'm a dote.'

'Are you?'

'Ah yeah. You should hear me talking to mammies, sure.'

'I can imagine.'

'Altar boy and everything, so I was.'

'Right, yeah.'

'You okay?'

'I'm fine.'

'Cos over there, you looked a little bit …'

'No. I'm fine. It was just … it was hard being in Romania. I only got back the other day. This party is kind of for me too. Welcome back, y'know?'

'How long were you over there?'

She twisted her pint around on the table.

'Not long.'

'Right. I'd say it was tough all right.'

She nodded.

'It was.'

Her eyes started to glisten.

'It was awful.'

'You want to tell me?'

'God no. I haven't even told them yet. I can't.'

'Well tell me. Come on.'

'You don't want to hear it.'

'I do. Trish, it's been on the telly. Christ, it's heartbreaking. Tell me.'

'I'm sure you have better things to do than listen to …'

'I don't. Believe me, I don't.'

She looked up at him properly.

'You don't want me to ruin your night, do you?'

'You'll ruin it if you don't tell me now. C'mon. Please.'

His eyes were huge. Blue and deep and looking at her in a way she'd never imagined they could from what she'd seen of him earlier up on the stage. Either this was for real or he was the best chatter-upper she'd ever met in her life.

'I … I thought I'd get used to it,' she said, sighing. 'I went there full of good intentions. I was going to help. Make a difference, y'know?'

He nodded back at her, drawing on his smoke.

'The first day I walked into the orphanage, I had to run out again. I had nightmares that night. The children were piled into old cots, with bars like prisons. There were hardly any bedclothes, and what there was was filthy and torn. They were naked, most of them, and covered in their own and each others' mess. Half starving, sick and cold. Crying. Jesus, Aesop, you should have heard them crying.'

'They'd look up at me with their big beautiful eyes and hold out their arms, like they were begging me to take them away. And I wanted to. I wanted to take every one of them and make it better. It was so hard to go in there every day and see their little pleading faces. The kids I'd worked with here, before, that was different. They were loved and cared for as best we could. But these ones ... they had nothing. They weren't loved and nobody cared. Aesop, they hadn't done anything wrong. They were just children. Why, y'know? It wasn't fair. When they saw me pass they'd call my name and every time it broke my heart. I was supposed to stay for three months, but I could only do it for two weeks. I couldn't help them any more. I just couldn't. I hated to leave, but it was killing me to stay there. I had to go, Aesop, and I've been hating myself ever since I got on that plane back here.'

She was sniffling into a hanky now. He put a hand across the table onto her arm.

'God,' she said, a small laugh through the tears. 'Well, there you go. Got more than you bargained for there, rockstar, didn't you? Here in your dark corner, like.'

He gave her a little squeeze.

'Actually I did a bit, love, to be honest.'

They both laughed.

'But listen, you can't go around smacking yourself in the head over it. You did what you could, didn't you? That's all anyone can do.'

'But I'm *s'posed* to be the person that does that stuff. Properly, y'know? Goes the distance.'

'Says who?'

'Bloody hell. Says everyone. Ever since I was a kid, I was one that ...'

'Ah, don't mind all that shite. You're not living for anyone else. You do what you have to do and what you can do. Not what you're expected to do. That's only a one-way ticket to a wrecked head. And,

Christ, in a job like that there's enough pressure on you without worrying about who you're letting down. Fuck sake, Trish, you did what you could! You helped those kids. Who else is helping them?'

'But I'm not helping them now, am I?'

'Trish, you did your bit. And now you're back here with your mates and when you start working again you're going to be helping more people. I could never do the job you do.'

'But I should be ... over there and ...'

'Only if that's what you want. But if you're thinking of going back, for fuck sake just worry about the kids and yourself, right? Not people back here. Fuck them. Look, I only just met you and I don't know what your story is, but I definitely know that you can't always be what everyone expects. Who can?'

Her eyes were nearly dry now.

'I s'pose you'd know.'

'Hmm?'

'You're not exactly what everyone expects, are you?'

'Oh. Ah Jaysis, I am a bit, Trish. There's not much hidden in here.'

'I think there is. I heard you were all lies and come-ons and one-night stands.'

Aesop gave her a small sheepish smile.

'In my weaker moments, maybe ...'

'But you weren't with me. Tonight. Just now.'

'No, I s'pose I wasn't. Well ... except the bit about being an altar boy. That was bollocks.'

'Yeah, I gathered that. But that's okay.'

'Your mates look like they're getting ready to head.'

'Yeah. I'd better go.'

'Okay so.'

'Do you and the guys want to come out with us? It'd be a laugh.'

'Would love to Trish, but we'll be another hour at least here getting all this stuff together.'

'After that?'

'After that it'll be one in the morning and we've to get it all back

378

home. That'll be two in the morning and we've a blues gig in Slattery's tomorrow afternoon, so …'

'Okay then. Well … thanks Aesop. Really. It was nice talking to you.'

'And you.'

'Yeah, right.'

'No, I mean it. And listen to me … look after yourself, right? You've got a gorgeous smile, Trish. Make sure and show it off.'

'Oh God. Is this the come-on part or the lies part?'

'Neither.' He smiled at her. 'This is the part where I tell you you're the most beautiful and generous person in here tonight and you should go out with your mates knowing that about yourself. It's important. More important than anything else. And that's no word of a lie.'

She stared for a minute and then shook her head at him.

'I didn't … really didn't expect anything like this when I said hello. God, here of all places. You.'

'Yeah, I'm an enigma. That's what Jimmy over there calls me.'

'Does he?'

'Well … no. But he does call me names.'

'Aesop?'

'Yeah?'

'Would you mind if … if I kissed you before I go?'

'Eh … sure. Why, but?'

'I just want to. Help me remember what you said. Is that all right?'

'Yeah.'

'Really?'

'Yeah. No tongues.'

'I WENT back to Romania a week later,' whispered Trish, her head close to Aesop's ear. She could see his chest rising and falling slowly, hear his breath. He was relaxed now.

'You still with me, Aesop?'

She felt his thumb pressing her hand.

'Are you okay?'

Press.

'There's so many things I could tell you, but I know you're tired. I stayed for the rest of the year. It was the most amazing thing I've ever done. Of course there were days just like the first time, when I wanted to run to the airport and get out of there, but after a while I could see what I was doing and why I was doing it. Those beautiful innocent children were so strong and so brave. They gave me the strength to stay.'

'But there was one little girl I wanted to tell you about. And then I'll finish. She was nearly blind and very sick, but she told me through the Sister that she always knew when I was coming to her because she could just make out my uniform against the dark of the rest of the room. I always kept it clean and bright after that. No matter what. My uniform shone even if I had to stay up half the night washing it again and again. Her name was Hilda. She was with us for a couple of months. She used to say that when she saw my uniform, she thought that I was like an angel, coming to take her to God. Little Hilda. So beautiful. When I got there, she was covered in filth and cried every second she was awake. I'd try and talk to her as I cleaned her up. She'd see me coming in my white uniform and her little face would light up and she'd stand in the cot with her arms out until I picked her up and sang to her. She died then.'

Trish paused to take something out of her pocket. A tissue to wipe her face, and something else.

'Nobody could do anything about that. She was so sick. You don't want to know what she looked like the first time I saw her. But this is what she looked like a couple of days before the real angel took her away.'

She held a picture up in front of Aesop's face and turned on the small reading lamp over his head.

'Do you see her?'

Aesop's thumb pressed her again.

In front of him, a tiny girl grinned out at the camera from a cot, her huge green eyes clouded but defiant.

Trish put the picture onto Aesop's bedside stand.

'You gave me a lift, Aesop. Just when I needed it. I want you to have that picture. I never would've met Hilda if I hadn't gone back. It's because of you that she was able to go to God with soft words and music in her ears instead of the sound of her own crying. And all the others ... I never would have had the chance to help. And all I ever wanted to say was thank you. I love Norman. I think he loves me, but ... he's got something inside him and I don't know if it'll ever go away. I'd love to help him make it go away, but he won't let me. That's why it was so important for me to talk to you. I was nearly sure that Norman and me wouldn't work and then I'd probably never see you again to tell you about Hilda. He can be so jealous, the eejit, and all I wanted was a private moment just to tell you what you did for me ... for so many people. I'm sorry about everything, Aesop. Making everything so complicated instead of just talking to you. But it was so important to me. I'm sorry.'

She picked up his hand and kissed it.

'Get well,' she said, switching off the light over him.

And then she got up and left him in the dark, a single tear rolling onto the pillow under his neck. He couldn't wipe away the trail it left so he just lay there, waiting for it to dry.

Chapter Thirty-two

JIMMY HAD to go home that same night. Nothing was happening in the hospital anyway. They had to just wait. He needed to see his Mam, who his Da said was up the walls with worry. He walked into the house first thing the next morning and suffered the third degree for the best part of an hour, Peggy boiling the kettle and making pot after pot of tea as she demanded to know everything about what was going on down in Cork. The doctors were happy enough, that was the latest. Aesop was stable, but it was too early to know anything for sure about what would happen later on. But she wanted to know more than that. How did he look? Was he in any pain? What did the doctor say *exactly*? No, but Jimmy, what did he *say*? Jimmy just sat next to Seán at the kitchen table and went over it all about four times, stuff she already knew anyway from his calling her. When she moved on to asking about Jennifer, Aesop's Dad and Norman's Mam, he knew the worst of it was over. She'd wrung him dry.

She was putting out sandwiches for the two of them when his phone rang. Jennifer. He spoke into it for a couple of minutes and then looked up at his folks.

'He's awake.'

HE GOT a taxi straight to the airport and was running through the corridors of the hospital in Cork not three hours later. Before he even got to Aesop's room, though, he almost bowled over the doctor who was looking after him as he rounded a corner. Jimmy stood, panting, and asked him how everything was. The doctor took his time, going over everything in detail and outlining the various ways things could go from here.

Jimmy looked at him, his mind reeling from all the information. Bloody doctors.

'I'm afraid Mr Murray's injuries were serious, as you know. But he is stable for the moment. And he's awake, which is excellent news.'

'Will he be okay?'

'As I said, he's very ill. It's too early to say exactly how his recovery will progress. He seems to be doing well and that's all I can tell you. I'm optimistic, but there's a long road ahead of him.'

'Can I see him?'

'Of course. But, please, not for too long.'

'Okay. But is he … is he … when you talked to him, y'know … is he … okay? In his head, like.'

'He can't talk yet, due at least in part to the severe bruising to his face. We've given him a pencil and pad, although he hasn't used it yet. He's lost at least some function down one side, Mr Collins. He'll have more scans today so we can try and find out why.'

'Fuck … okay. Thanks doctor.'

JENNIFER AND Marco were coming out of the room when Jimmy got there. He hugged them both. They looked wrecked.

'What's up?' said Jimmy. 'Is he okay?'

'He looks awful,' said Jennifer. 'But I think he's okay. Comfortable anyway.'

'Yeah?'

'Yeah. Well, it's hard to tell with all the … but …'

'Come on Jen,' said Marco, an arm around her shoulder. 'Coffee time. We'll be back in a while Jimmy.'

They left Jimmy standing outside the door and moved off down the corridor. Jimmy took a deep breath and went in.

Aesop was lying there on the bed, covered in wires, his head wrapped up in a huge bandage. Machines everywhere, beeping and flickering. Jimmy stood just inside the door, rooted to the spot and his legs shaking.

'Jesus.'

He walked closer to the bed, both hands over his mouth.

'Aw Aesop, you … you stupid fucker. Jesus Christ … look at you …'

The bandage covered all of one eye, right down past his cheek and back up again so that his other eye was half visible, although that one was almost completely closed from the swelling. Almost. Jimmy could see that the eye was following him. He shook his head slowly and moved a bit closer.

'Can you hear me?'

It was really weird, talking to a big bandage like this. The guy in the bed looked nothing like Aesop. Nothing at all.

The corners of the lips tugged a little. Was that a smile? Recognition?

'Listen Aesop …' said Jimmy.

He grabbed a chair and pulled it closer to the bed.

'Listen, everything's going to be okay, man. The doctor says you're grand. You're awake now and he's delighted about that. Means you're going to be grand. Everyone's here to look after you. Fuck sake, every single nurse in Ireland has been trying to get transferred to Cork since they heard you were here. Queuing up to give you sponge baths, they'll be, watch.'

Aesop lifted his left hand onto his chest and Jimmy put one of his on top of it.

'I know you're in a bit of pain. He says that'll go away. And your other arm is a bit fucked, and your leg, but he says you'll just need to get to work with a physio when you feel a bit better. You'll be back playing the drums in no time at all. Right? As soon as you're ready, we're going to be back. The Grove, man. Look, I know all about Helen and all. That must have been fucking terrible for you. I'm sorry it didn't work out. We heard from Alison that you wanted to pack it all in and join Leet. I understand that completely. I do. Fuck knows, I'm the one who always gets the shite kicked out of me over women, right? I know how it feels. Just getting the fuck away from everything and trying to forget about it always seems like the best idea. But c'mere, it doesn't have to be like that. We don't need to do any of that. They can all get fucked, right? Me and you. Soon as you're better, we're going to start playing again. Anything you want. Megadeth, Anthrax, Pantera … all that horrible shite you like, whatever you want is fine with me.'

He thought he saw the smile get a tiny bit bigger.

'I'm telling you, man, I'll play any fucking thing at all just as long as you get yourself better. Fuck sake, I've been listening to nothing but the new Maiden album since you've been in here. Don't mind all that Celtic stuff I was on about before. Trad and all. I know you hate that stuff. And we don't have to do it, right? But I was talking to Dónal. He's on for your girl trad band idea. We can work on that together. Whatever you want to call them. That's grand with me. We'll have a laugh, right? It'll be deadly. Just … just you get better and then we'll put The Grove back together. Properly. Get a bass player. Do the tour, do another album. They way it should have been. Fuck Senturion and all that. Fuck Leet. They can all go off and do what they want. That's not us. It's not you. We'll go ahead and do things our way, okay? The way we always have. Fuck them. They can all … they can all …'

Jimmy's eyes were moist and stinging now.

'They can all go and … and …'

The hand came up and Jimmy leaned in. Aesop stretched out a finger and put it on Jimmy's lips.

'Sshhh …'

It was barely audible, but Jimmy caught it and stopped talking.

Then the hand fell back onto the bed and Aesop started to grab at something. Jimmy leaned over to see a pad and a pencil at Aesop's other leg. He picked up the pencil and put it into Aesop's hand, positioning the pad under it. He wiped at his eyes and nose while Aesop wrote. And then he leaned over and picked up the pad to read it.

You had me at 'stupid fucker'.

Jimmy's eyes filled up again, properly this time, as he tried to laugh. This was the first time that he knew something the doctors wouldn't or couldn't tell him.

His best mate was going to be okay.

Chapter Thirty-three

JIMMY FELT a weight lifted off him when Aesop was finally fit to be moved to Dublin to finish getting better. He'd been up and back to Cork so many times in the last two months that he reckoned he could probably fly the bloody plane himself. Being in Dublin meant that it was easier for everyone. Things were getting back to normal now. They all still thought of Aesop constantly, called him and dropped in, but now that he was out of danger and the extent of his recovery was down to the work he was doing with the physio, they were able to drift back to their jobs and lives. Jimmy realised that it was happening after he got a call from Shiggy to meet him in town. He found the little guy sipping on a pint in McDaids on his own.

'What's the story, Shiggy?'

'Hiya Jimmy. Pint?'

'Yeah, lovely.'

When two fresh ones were calming on the bar in front of them, Shiggy turned to Jimmy.

'Jimmy, I go home tomorrow.'

'Oh. Right. I see. Aw man, that's a shame.'

'Sorry Jimmy. Have to go.'

'Not at all, Shiggy. Christ, you've been here for weeks longer than you were meant to be. You're very good to hang about. They must be going mad in work.'

'Ah, fuck work, Jimmy. I don't care.'

'Don't be silly man. You've been there … how long now?'

'Twenty years. Too many.'

Shiggy sighed, rubbing his head, and looked at his pint.

'Twenty years, Jimmy. Is enough. More sings in rife than Kyotosei, *ne*? When Aesop get hurt, I sink I need … need to change sings.'

'I think we all did. Shit like that … puts things in perspective.'

'Yeah. I want to pray music. Ainu music, maybe. I buy *tonkori*. Go home and study. Quit job. Job is just … you know, Jimmy. You quit already.'

'Yeah. I know what you mean. And you'll be brilliant on the *tonkori*, man. You're brilliant on fucking everything, aren't you, ye bastard? When you get the hang of it, come back and we'll do that album. Irish rock and Ainu trad. Together at last!'

Shiggy giggled.

'Yeah. Deadry. You know, Jimmy, when I decide to quit job, first I sink I stay and pray with you guys.'

'But Shiggy …'

'Yeah, I know. Aesop can't pray, so no Grove.'

'Not for a long time yet, man. Might be a year. More, even.'

'You find new bass prayer some day?'

'He'll be shite compared to you, no matter who he is.'

'Yeah. Plobabry.'

They both laughed and took a pull of their beer.

'I miss you guys.'

'We'll miss you. It wasn't the same when you left the last time.'

Shiggy nodded.

'Hey, when Aesop is better, if still no good bass prayer …'

'I'll be sending a plane ticket to Tokyo. I promise. But you're sure?'

'Sure?'

'About quitting your job? That's a big step.'

'Oh. Yeah. Sure. I have money, Jimmy. No plobrem. But, *ne*, I work hard for twenty years for other people. Now I work hard for Shiggy. Aesop is okay now, but first when he was … you know … everybody afraid … so, now I understand. Rife berry short, *desho*?'

'Fucking tell me about it, Shiggy. What time is your flight tomorrow?'

'Two o'clock.'

'You going in to say goodbye to Aesop?'

'Sure. I go in morning. Take morning off work. Work say "rah-rah-rah … where is Shiggy … oh, big plobrem … rah-rah-rah". Ha Ha. Shiggy say "Fuck off, work! I quit!".'

Jimmy laughed and put down his empty glass.

'Maybe you shouldn't tell them to fuck off.'

'No? So … do what you do rast year is better?'

'Eh … well, maybe not,' said Jimmy, blushing at the mere memory of it. 'Fair point.'

'Is okay, Jimmy. Wait when I go back to Tokyo and then I quit.'

'Yeah.'

They said nothing for a minute, each one remembering all that had happened between them. Then Jimmy looked up. He didn't want to get all fucking depressed and bummed out again. There'd been enough of that shit going on around here recently. Too much. And anyway, Shiggy deserved a better send-off than that. There was only one fitting way for an Irishman to send one of his best mates away onto a plane.

'Pint?' he said.

WHEN THEY'D finished making love and were lying there in the candlelight, Trish began to trace one of Norman's scars with her finger. He didn't move; just lay there looking at the ceiling.

'Norman?'

'Hmm?'

'Do you think we'll ever be able to …'

'To what?'

'Be together.'

'What? We are together.'

'No we're not. Not since the accident. And not really before that either.'

'What do you mean, Trish?'

'I love you Norman.'

He paused.

'I know.'

'And you say you love me.'

'I do.'

'But you won't let me inside you.'

'Jesus, Trish, you are inside me. I never stop thinking about you.'

'Yeah. Maybe I'm in here.' She touched his head. 'But I need to be in here.' Her finger went to the scar on his chest.'

'You are.'

'I'm not. There's too much other stuff in there already.'

'Ah Trish, I don't know what you're talking about.'

'You do, Norman. Sure, isn't that the problem?'

'There's no problem.'

'Of course there is. You can barely sleep at night. And over the past while, you've been getting more and more distant from me. I don't know what to do.'

'I … I just have bad dreams sometimes. It's nothing. It'll go away.'

'It's getting worse!'

'Look Trish, it's nothing. Please, I just … it's nothing.'

She sat up and looked down at him.

'Norman.'

'What? Jesus, what is it Trish?'

'Look at me.'

'I am looking at you.'

'Do I look like a feckin' eejit to you?'

'No. Of course not.'

'Tell me what those dreams are. Tell me what happened to you. And tell me what you're planning to do about it, because I can't help you if you don't.'

'Nothing happened. I don't …'

'What's this?'

She jabbed one of his scars.

'And this?'

She poked at another one.

'And this one? This one goes all the way around your back for God sake.'

'I told you about them …'

'Collapsed lung my arse, Norman. Tell me.'

'I … you don't need … to know …'

'I do! Because otherwise I don't know you and I'm not spending the rest of my life with someone I don't know.'

'What? Who said …'

'I'm saying, Norman. You think I'm only here for giggles? What's your plan for us then, if it's not that? Might as well tell me now.'

'Jesus, Trish, I haven't thought that far ahead. But of course … I mean, you're everything I have.'

'Am I? Come on then. You know my story. Everything. You know everything about me, good and bad. What's your story?'

He lay back again against the pillow and closed his eyes, his fists over them.

'Jesus, Trish, I … I can't.'

She took a deep breath and got out of the bed. As she put on her dressing gown, she turned around to him.

'You better find a way, Norman. Soon.'

She went out and closed the door. She stood for a minute, waiting for him to call her back, and when he didn't, she went into the bathroom and locked the door. Would he ever tell her? Whatever it was, it was locked up so deep inside him, filled so much of him, that he probably wouldn't even be the same person if it was ever let out. She was afraid of that. She needed to know that the best of him would still be there. She needed to know now more than ever, because she'd lied to him earlier.

There was one last thing about her that he didn't know.

IN BED, Norman was staring at the ceiling. A hand crept to his neck, to the bruised flesh that now covered the hole she'd dug in him to save his life. Another scar would cover the whole thing over one day. Now it was still tender and vulnerable. One day it would be hard and tough, like the rest of them. He might be able to forget about it then, as it just became part of him. Or maybe he wouldn't. Forgetting things wasn't his strong point.

The images bubbled up from where he kept them, a place as familiar to him as the pocket of a favourite coat.

They'd kept him for over a month in that cell. He got used to the pain after a while. He didn't think he would, or could, but he did. What never went away was the fury. They'd come for another session with him and his head and chest would almost boil with a rage so deep that he'd wonder that his heart didn't explode. He'd try and think of something else; scenes from the farm in Cork with Mikey Pat, hurling games he'd played, gigs with the lads, anything at all. But sooner or later all of these would be edged out of the way by that ferocious loathing that seethed inside him. They saw it and laughed and stoked it up even more.

Later on he realised that he'd never be able to make anyone understand what it had felt like to be there each time they came for him. He didn't even bother trying.

So maybe now it was time to tell someone. Because he did love her. Now it was time, because … because he knew he had to go back and get the bastards. Because it would never fucking stop until he did. Ever.

He turned his head and looked at the door Trish had just walked through.

TRISH FINISHED wiping her mouth with some toilet roll and flushed it down the toilet. Then she rinsed with the blue mouthwash from the windowsill. She checked the mirror and held her breath against the next wave of nausea that swept upwards from her stomach. She saw her reflection grimace, still not used to it.

It had only started a few weeks ago.

Chapter Thirty-four

JIMMY GOT a call from Dónal the next day. He was needed in the studio.

'Sure,' said Jimmy, checking his watch. 'What's up?'

'Ah, it's a bit of a ... well, not a problem exactly ... but will you come in?'

'What? Man, what's going on?'

'Just come in and we can have a chat about it. That all right?'

'I'll be there in half an hour.'

Jimmy caught a taxi into town and pulled up outside Sin Bin. He trotted up the stairs and opened the door to the studio. Sparky was there as always, headphones on and pushing sliders around on his mixing desk. Dónal was there too, drinking coffee and taking notes on something.

'Lads,' said Jimmy, taking off his coat.

'Howya Jimmy,' said Dónal. 'Thanks for coming in.'

'No problem. How's Sparky?'

'Grand Jimmy. Just getting a bit done on the Leet album.'

'Right. So what's the story Dónal?'

'Yeah, eh listen Jimmy, let's sit down out there.'

'Grand.'

Once they were sitting opposite each other on the couch, Dónal put his hands together in front of his chest.

'Right. The thing is, Jimmy, the album is going great guns.'

'I know. It's great.'

'Yeah. Except there's a lot of people out there who are wondering if it's going to be the first and last one from The Grove.'

Jimmy shrugged.

'Everyone knows what happened to Aesop.'

'Yeah, I know. But things move on, y'know?'

'What things?'

'Everything. Senturion and their US partner have been at me all week. Seems they misread your potential. That's what they said.

Fuckin' eejits. Anyway, the fans are screaming for you and Senturion are screaming now as well.'

'For what?'

'A tour.'

'A tour? How are we meant to tour? There's no band, Dónal.'

'I know that. And that's kind of the point. Look, in one way, The Grove is Jimmy Collins, right?'

'No. It's not, Dónal. It's Aesop as well.'

'But I'm just saying that you're the songwriter, the front man … all that.'

'Yeah. So what?'

'So, if … and I'm just saying *if* here … you had another drummer and another bass player, then it wouldn't be too bad, would it?'

'It also wouldn't be The Grove, Dónal, would it? It'd be me and some pair of cunts.'

'Well … right. But that's not how some people see it.'

'Fuck some people. How do you see it?'

'I'm just telling you what's going on, Jimmy. That's my job. I'm with you no matter what. Whatever you want to do, that's what we do.'

'Well that's good. Because I'm doing fuck all without Aesop and Aesop can do fuck all at the moment.'

'Okay, okay. That's fine Jimmy. But this thing will get cold on us, right? That's what will happen. We'll have to start again.'

'Then we start again.'

'Right. So … and you're going to do nothing until Aesop's better?'

'I'm not doing gigs. We'll just write new material and wait for him.'

'Okay. But …'

'Dónal, do you know what Aesop's doing right now? While we're sitting here shooting the breeze, I mean. He's doing what he's been doing for weeks. Staring at his bad hand and wondering if it'll ever hold a drumstick properly and smack a drum ever again. He's doing exercises eight hours a day or more, and he's getting there, but the physio reckons he could be a year away from a gig. At least. And that's assuming he keeps getting better, something no one's giving any fucking guarantees about, by the way.'

'I know that Jimmy. I know …'

'And you want me to tell him I can't wait? That we're firing him and carrying on? The only thing in his fucking life, the thing that gives him a reason to wake up in the morning and not throw in the fucking towel as he's sweating buckets lifting weights and squeezing rubber fucking balls, and you want me to take it away from him? Me bollix, Dónal.'

Dónal held up his hands.

'Jesus, Jimmy, I'm your manager and I'm just telling you what's going on around you, okay? But we're going to play this your way no matter what happens.'

'Glad to hear it Dónal.'

'Okay. So … would you consider a solo tour?'

'What?'

'Just you. Acoustic. A few small venues. Just to keep your face in the news while he's getting better?'

Jimmy sighed and thought about it for a bit.

'Acoustic?'

'Yeah. Just you on the stage. What do you think?'

'Ah … Jaysis. Look … I'll have to think about it, Dónal.'

'That's all I'm saying, Jimmy. It's just business. But The Grove can wait. Forget I even said that.'

'I'll talk to you about it again, right? The fucking last thing I want right now is to get up there without Aesop and start doing all those songs. He nearly fucking died man. He nearly …'

'I know, Jimmy.'

'And getting back into it is the only thing that's keeping him fired up now. If he hears that I'm off gigging without him …'

'Okay Jimmy. No problem. Really. Look, don't worry about hiring anyone for The Grove, okay? But maybe you can talk to Aesop about the other thing. Just to see what he thinks. Yeah?'

'I don't know man.'

'Just mention it to him. A couple of sets for the punters and the press. Let them know we're making progress. He can be in the audience if he likes. Mug it up for the girls and all, y'know? He'd love that.'

'I'll talk to him.'

TRISH'S FACE was a mixture of disbelief and horror.

'You can't go back there, Norman. Jesus. You can't …'

'I can't not go back, Trish. Listen to me, I'm after realising that I'll never be able to love you properly until I get rid of this thing that eats at me. The only way I can do that is go back and … finish it.'

'Finish it? Murder people. Become like them?'

'Stop, Trish. I never said that would happen, did I?'

'Why are you going then? And what about your Mam? This will kill her!'

'Mam has always known this would happen. I think we both tried to convince ourselves it wouldn't, but fuck it Trish this is who I am.'

'Norman, will you listen to me for Christ sake? Look what happened to you the last time you were there. Look what they did to you. They nearly killed you! And you were a bloody soldier then. You haven't been … training, or … or … and now you want to go back?'

'But they didn't kill me, Trish. They just fucked me up, didn't they? Christ, you know they did more than anyone after what I just told you.'

'And … and you have to go now? Today? Jesus, why didn't we talk about this yesterday or … or … how long have you been planning all this?'

'I only just decided yesterday that I need to go as soon as possible.'

'But …'

'Trish, I'm not going to be gone long. A couple of months probably. I'll come back then and this thing will be over.'

'Norman, *this* thing will be over if you get on that plane. Jesus, this is fucking madness!'

'Listen to me, Trish. I do love you. You know that, all right?'

'How is this love?'

'I'm doing it now, so that it doesn't fuck everything up later. I'm doing it for us as much as anything.'

'You're not doing any bloody thing for me. Afghanistan, Norman? And what's going on in Afghanistan at the moment. A hippie festival? They're fighting over there, for God sake.'

'And I'm a soldier.'

'You're not a bloody soldier any more, Norman!'

'No Trish. I never stopped being one.'

'Jesus …'

Trish looked at him through her tears and didn't know him.

'Why?' she whispered, shaking her head.

'I have to. I'm so fucking sorry. But … I have to.'

'Get yourself … killed?'

'That's not going to happen. When I come back, we can … it'll be finished. I promise.'

She could barely speak now, or see him through her seeping eyes.

'Norman …'

He shook his head, and moved towards her, to hold her.

'There's no other way to make it stop. You've no idea what it feels like. This anger. It's like a fucking ball of rage in my stomach and it's there all the time. I can't do it any more.'

She opened her mouth but then she closed it again. Her hands didn't go around him as he hugged her. They stayed pressed on her belly as the rest of her reeled in hurt and confusion. What if she told him and he went anyway? What would that tell her about him? Something she didn't want to know.

So she just sat, surrounded by his huge arms, and cried.

'I need to pack and get to the airport,' he said then.

JIMMY WENT to visit Aesop later in the afternoon. He opened the door to find him tapping out a Led Zeppelin drum solo on one hand.

'Howya Aesop.'

'Oh, hiya Jimmy. What's the story?'

Jimmy looked again and frowned.

'What are you doing?'

'Just doing a bit of Moby Dick.'

'No, I mean, what's that on your face?'

'Oh. Sparky was in yesterday. He took a look at me chart and went mad when he saw the drugs I was taking. Sparky's your only man for drugs, I'm telling you.'

'But …'

'He said I didn't need all the painkillers. I should just put two teabags over me eyes for the headaches. That's what he uses, he says, when the voices start annoying him. So I'm giving it a go.'

'Right. Is it working?'

'I don't know. I only just started.'

'Aesop …'

'Jimmy, I need to get out of here. I'm going mad.'

'But you can't walk properly yet,' said Jimmy.

'I'm grand,' said Aesop. 'It's just a bit of a limp.'

'A limp? You're like bleedin' Quasimodo trying to get around.'

'Piss off. Anyway, don't I have me wheelchair?'

'And how are you going to … Aesop, will you ever take the fucking teabags off. This is stupid.'

'But Jimmy, Sparky says they work wonders.'

'For fuck sake Aesop, you're s'posed to make tea with them first.'

'What?'

'He didn't mean … nothing. Look, just take them off, will you? You're a fuckin' eejit.'

Aesop took the teabags off his eyes and blinked at Jimmy.

'Would they not burn you if you're after making the tea with them?'

'You wait for them to get cold, don't you?'

'Ah, I don't know, Jimmy. Are you taking the piss?'

'Jesus … are you? Listen, Aesop, how are you meant to get around your house in a wheelchair?'

'I can get around grand. I only need the chair for long distances.'

'The doctor says you've to stay another couple of weeks.'

'The doctor can pull the plum off himself for all I give a shite.'

'Ungrateful bastard. Aesop, they've done a great job looking after you. Dr Phelan said you got a terrible bang on the head.'

'Did he? Jaysis, he's a great doctor isn't he? What gave it away? The fucking big car-shaped dent in me skull, was it?'

'It's just another couple of weeks. You need the rest anyway.'

'All I've bleedin' done is rest! And I'm getting very fucking tired of it.'

'And who's going to drag you in and out of here every day for your physio?'

'You.'

'Me bollocks.'

'Why not? Some mate you are. I'm sick!'

'Look, just stay put for another little while.'

'But Jimmy …'

'Christ, I think it was better when you were in a coma, you know that?'

'C'mere, how's Norman?' said Aesop.

'He's grand.'

'How's the bodyguarding business going for him this weather? Does he need any references?'

'I think he's back at the gardening.'

'Poor flowers. I hope they have insurance.'

Jimmy noticed Aesop flexing his left wrist. He had to use it for everything now and it got sore.

'How is it?'

'Ah, it's all right. Nearly getting used to writing and everything with this hand now. I'm going to end up as … what do you call it?'

'Ambidextrous?'

'No. No, I mean … when you can write with both hands.'

'Ambidextrous.'

'No, Jimmy. You know the word I want …'

'Fucking ambidextrous is the word you want, Aesop.'

'I don't think so, Jimmy.'

'Jesus. Do you want a glass of water?'

'Nah, I'm grand. Unless you've a pint in your pocket, do you?'

'No.'

'Any chance you could run over to Beaumont House and get me one?'

'Not unless the doctor says you can have one.'

'He's not the boss of me.'

'Afraid he is, man.'

'I'd kill for a nice creamy pint.'

'Won't be long now. Actually, I had a few nice ones with Shiggy yesterday.'

'Yeah. He was in this morning. It's shite to see him go.'

'Yeah. Well, he stayed as long as he could.'

Jimmy looked at the iPod that Aesop had next to him in the bed.

'Need any more music?'

'Nah. I've loads of stuff on there. Y'know something, when I was in a coma I kept imagining I heard fucking Bronski Beat in me head. It was driving me mad.'

'Yeah. That was me.'

'What?'

'I told them to play that.'

'What?! You torturing cunt! And me not able to move …'

'We were trying to wake you up! I knew that …'

'Bastard! I thought I was after dying and going to hell and this was me punishment for all the gee. Fuck you anyway, Jimmy. I've been nearly afraid to go asleep ever since, in case it starts up again. You're a gee-bag of the highest order, Collins. I'll bleedin' get you for that. You know that gay one they do?'

'Were they not all gay?'

'Yeah. Well thanks to you I'm waking up in the mornings tapping away to the fucking bass line on me leg. I have a reputation, so I do.'

'I won't tell anyone. Shut up whinging a minute, will you, and tell me how you are anyway.'

'How I am?'

'Well … just for instance, like … you've barely mentioned Helen's name since the accident.'

'Ah, right. Only a matter of time, wasn't it Jimmy? I was wondering what was keeping you.'

'None of my business, man. I was just wondering how you're getting on.'

'None of your business my arse, Jimmy! You've only been fizzing at the bunghole waiting for me to spill me guts about that, look at you.'

'I haven't!'

'Yeah, right. Well anyway, what do you want to know?'

'Are you all right? I mean, I know you really liked her …'

'Yeah. I did.'

'And?'

'And I got the red card, didn't I? So I got shitfaced and rode Jessie out of badness.'

'That wasn't very nice.'

'Jimmy, I was hurt, sad and very fucking drunk. When you're like that, it's just like Shakespeare said, y'know? *Everybody needs a bosom for a pillow* …'

'Shakespeare, yeah …'

'And anyway, I can't tell you how nice it was Jimmy, I was that drunk. But if you mean that it was a prick of a thing to do, then yeah. It was. Riding Helen's mate … stupid.'

'Well, she didn't have to …'

'Ah, what was she s'posed to do, Jimmy? Once I started going for it, like. She's only human.'

'So is Helen.'

'She's not man. That was the problem. She was … something else. Really.'

'But you're okay now?'

'Yeah. Well, no. I mean, I haven't had a bounce since Jessie. Can you believe that?'

'Really? No nurses or anything?'

'No. And it's not for the want of a fucking horn either, I can tell you that for nothing.'

'Lovely. So, why then?'

'Ah … just … there's a difference between the sex I've been getting since we got famous and whatever I felt with Helen. I haven't been able to … get it right in me head yet. Not that me head was a hundred percent anyway, with Bronski Beat milling through it, ye bastard. But anyway, yeah, I just felt something with her. And it was nothing to do with riding I don't think. But it was really good. Until it wasn't.'

'Love?'

'If that's love, man, keep it the fuck away from me. Love gave me brain damage, didn't it?'

'Aesop, running forehead-first into a fucking Volvo gave you brain damage.'

'Whatever. One thing led to the other.'

'So this is a whole new sensitive Aesop in our midst?'

'I don't know about that, Jimmy. Let's just say that once I start … eh … dating again, I'll have an idea what I might be looking for.'

'I s'pose that's something.'

'Yeah. But I haven't been able to … y'know … just forget about her.'

'That's normal. Fuck sake, look who you're talking to.'

'Yeah, but you're a homo, Jimmy. I'm not used to it.'

'You'll get used to it.'

'I don't want to, man. I want Helen and all the shit that goes with her out of my head so I can just …'

'Move on?'

'Yeah! Move on, play on, ride on … get me fuckin' life back, y'know? I need to get out of here and up on a stage so I can play my bollocks off and score some chick and pretend that none of this ever happened.'

Jesus, thought Jimmy. Maybe this wasn't the best time to talk to Aesop about what he'd come to talk to him about.

'What's wrong?' said Aesop.

'What?'

'What's with the head on you?'

'Oh. Nothing. Just …'

'Just what?'

'Look man, I was talking to Dónal and he … well first of all he just mentioned that Senturion are mad for us to tour.'

'Jesus. Aren't we all?'

'Yeah. Well, apparently, they want me to get a couple of session musicians and tour the album.'

Aesop just nodded, but he seemed to shrink a little in the bed.

'Of course I told him to tell them to fuck off.'

Nothing.

'And then he said I might just do a couple of acoustic gigs. Small ones, y'know? Just around town or whatever. Say hello to the punters.'

'Right,' said Aesop. His face was blank. 'What did you say?'

'Well, I told him I'd talk to you about that.'

'Why do you need to talk to me?'

'Because … well, I don't want you thinking of me up there doing it without you.'

'But I can't do it.'

'I know. But even an acoustic gig … I'd feel shite knowing that I was only doing it because your arm and leg are fucked.'

Aesop nodded again and looked over at the other side of the room for a minute.

'Fuck it,' he said then. 'Just do it, Jimmy.'

'What? Ah no …'

'Jimmy, listen to me. I want nothing more than to do a gig. Nothing. It's the only thing I see myself doing when I get out of here. The only thing I give a fuck about because I know that once I do it, then all this shit is over. Okay?'

'Okay.'

'So … the next best thing would be to see you do one.'

'Aesop …'

Aesop's bad hand came up and held Jimmy's arm.

'Not bad,' said Jimmy, looking at it.

'Yeah, well if I could give you a decent slap on the head, I would. Do the fucking gig, Jimmy.'

Jimmy nodded, still looking at Aesop's hand. It was great to see some strength in it, but he was a long way off his Comeback Special. What would The Grove be by then? Something they just trotted out of The Vault during nostalgia week on MTV?

'Are you sure?' he said.

'Jimmy do the gig. Just one, even. See what it feels like.'

Jimmy nodded and looked down at Aesop's hand on his arm again, the pencil and pad where he'd been writing his name over and over, the little rubber ball for squeezing on his lap, the half-kilo weight on the bedside table. Aesop was right.

Just then Bronski Beat came on the iPod. The bass intro to 'Small-town Boy'. They both looked at each other and laughed. Jimmy spotted Aesop's hand tapping away on his arm.

'Look at that!' he said, pointing.

'Oh God. See what you've done to me, Collins? See what's after happening to me?'

'I'm putting this on the website, man.'

'You said you wouldn't tell!'

'Me bollix, Aesop. The world needs to know that the brain damage is permanent.'

'Bastard!'

Aesop picked up the remote and flicked forward to a Buzzcocks song.

'Ah, that's better,' he said, putting his head back onto the pillow.

'You're really cool with me doing a gig, Aesop?' said Jimmy.

Aesop sighed.

'Yeah. Fuck it. I'll be back up there with you one day, Jimmy. Keep the stage warmed up for me.'

'It won't freak you out to see me up there in front of the punters?'

'I'll get up and give them a wave. Show them how I'm getting on. I'll be grand.'

NORMAN SLUNG his bag onto his shoulder. Trish had two fist-

403

fuls of his coat, but she wasn't pulling him back. She just wanted to feel him there with her. He walked out the door with her and they stood in the small garden of her house.

'I've to go,' he said. 'The plane …'

'Norman … there's … I …'

'Yeah?'

She paused, biting her lip. Then she just shook her head, hair sticking to her soaked face, and let go of his coat.

He walked down the driveway to the waiting taxi.

JIMMY WALKED out of Beaumont Hospital slowly, not even noticing the bustle in the lobby, the crying of a child, the pale sun in the sky. He stood just outside and sat down on a bench to light up a smoke. The pox of it all was that Aesop might never be the drummer he was before the accident. And Shiggy was gone. That Grove was over. He had to think of it like that. Maybe it *was* time for him to move on, do this gig. He thought of Aesop back in his room, the only thing in his head being the day he played again and always the crushing feeling somewhere else in him that it might never come. That would be the worst thing that could happen to someone like Aesop. He needed that crowd like other people needed air.

Jimmy closed his eyes and imagined a solo gig. He could see the hollering crowd, hear the thundering echoes of his guitar, feel the heat of the lights. It would be brilliant of course. Being back in the middle of all that. But then he imagined himself turning around and seeing nothing but a black curtain behind him and suddenly he didn't want it any more. He wanted his fucking band back. His mates. He stared at the butt in his fingers, twisting and squeezing it until it was dead and hard.

But it was time to start thinking about the future. He sat and thought about that. His future.

Finally, he took out his phone and called Dónal, telling him to book a gig in McGuigans for six weeks time. Dónal knew not to ask too many questions, and just said he'd sort it out. Jimmy hung up, an almost-forgotten buzz settling into his belly. Okay. He was committed now, but that was okay. This gig would be the best thing he'd ever done. He'd make sure of that. For all of them. Whatever it took to put it together, he had six weeks and Jimmy had always worked better when he had a goal. They wanted a gig? He'd give them a gig they'd never fucking forget.

He dialled another number then. One he should have dialled a long time ago, and would have only for the fucked-up priorities he used to carry around with him. But not any more. Shiggy was right. Life was short.

He heard her voice.

'Susan?'

Then he had to wait, one finger in his free ear, as a sudden roar shook the air around him and made him look up to the sky. But that was okay. A few more seconds? He'd already waited a lot longer than that to tell her that he needed her more than anything else in his life. That he loved her.

He could wait now for the climbing plane overhead to disappear into the clouds, bringing whoever was in it to wherever they had to go.

Epilogue

JIMMY STOOD in front of the crowd, his guitar hanging down in front of him. It had been a couple of minutes since he'd walked onto the stage and they were still screaming and clapping. Talk in the music press had been about nothing but this gig ever since it had been announced. Jimmy Collins was going to perform for the first time since the accident nearly four months ago that had claimed the drumming, and very nearly the life, of Aesop. Leet had finished playing about half an hour ago. They were good lads. Interrupted their tour of the UK to fly back and open this gig for Jimmy. Now he just stood there, his ears rattling against the noise of the punters and smiled out at everyone as best he could. He couldn't see much against the lights in his face, but he caught a few eyes and gave a few little waves. Jennifer and Marco, his folks, Dónal and Sparky, his ex-bird Sandra and Beano, her fiancé. He knew his old mate Johnnie Fingers was out there somewhere. He was home from Tokyo to do a bit of business and said he'd get up for a couple of songs. The punters would lose their minds when they saw him. A few of the lads from Kíla were there too. They'd be getting up later to help out with 'Caillte'. Jimmy couldn't wait till the Irish public got an earful of that. Dónal was already talking about re-releasing it.

Eventually Jimmy held up a hand so that he could say something, but that only made the noise louder. He shook his head and grinned, leaning in to the mike.

'Will yis shut bleedin' up a minute?'

They laughed then and soon there was only the sound of coughs and whispers.

'Thanks.'

He adjusted the strap of his guitar, looking for the right words.

'Eh … well, I s'pose … I don't want to say too much. But there's a couple of things I have to say before I start. Eh …'

He looked down at the floor.

'Eh … first of all, just … thanks. We've had a bit of a hairy time of it since … the accident. We've, as you know, we've had our share of mishaps. I won't go into the whole thing now, cos the papers just about have it all covered anyway. Aesop … all of us … were just blown away by the generosity of everyone over the last few months. It's been amazing to know that you're all behind us. So … thanks very much.'

He stepped back from the mike and gave a little bow as he waited for the cheering to die down.

'So, obviously, Aesop can't play the drums at the moment. But I guarantee you that he's working on it!'

More shouts and cheering.

'And of course Shiggy went back to Japan, so … eh … well, I s'pose you might say that The Grove has been on a bit of a hiatus. But before you went and forgot all about us, I just wanted to play here tonight and to tell you that we appreciate everything that all of you – and a lot of other people – have done for us over the last few months.'

There was no cheering this time. Just clapping. Lots of it, with a few whistles.

'So … well, the last thing I wanted to say for the moment is that Aesop is very sorry that he's not out there with you. But if you know Aesop, you'll understand that he'd go mad being down in the crowd instead of up here. He told me to pass on his apologies and he'll see you all very soon.'

Jimmy didn't want to drag this out. It was hard enough. Aesop had barely been able to speak when he'd seen him earlier. He tried not to think about it. He waited for the noise to ease off and then he strummed down on his guitar to check the tuning. The lights on the stage collapsed, leaving him standing there on his own in a single shaft of white.

He opened with 'Wish You Were Here'. He'd played it the last time himself and Aesop had been on a stage together down at the Open Mike night in Cork. The punters swayed and hummed along, lost in it. He hadn't planned on trying to turn on any waterworks. Certainly not this early. But it was happening now, a few girls right in front of him gazing up with shining, wet eyes. Well fuck it. This gig would have a vibe of its own and he wasn't here to put clamps around it. Everyone joined in on the chorus, the sound of it thudding against the walls and the ceiling and making Jimmy's mike resonate against his lips. Everyone in McGuigans tonight was on the same page. Good. He needed them that way.

He went through the set for another hour without stopping or talking. It wasn't all deep and emotional stuff. He played acoustic versions of 'Landlady Lover' and 'Alibi', two old Grove favourites. Then he took out a slide and did a Rory Gallagher number, fast and thumping. Jimmy wanted to show off some new stuff, so he played a couple of songs that no one knew. They were tasters from the new album, but he didn't introduce them. He wanted them to speak for themselves. They were based on two Carolan airs. He just closed his eyes and played and did his best to let the songs fill the room without any help from his hips or his grin or that part of him that needed punters to like them more than anything he'd ever written. Then he finished out with 'Caillte' and 'More Than Me'. The song that broke the Grove and the song that made them the biggest-selling artists in Europe.

Once he'd taken his bow and looked back out at them, he felt the nerves building in him again. He'd told Dónal he might take a break at this stage of the gig, but he knew he couldn't do that now. He had to keep going. His belly was writhing, sweat on his hands, as he took the mike in his hand again.

'Thanks very much.'

He waited.

'Eh, I spoke to Aesop … oh, a good few weeks ago now … and I told him I'd be doing this gig. Y'know what I mean … I didn't know if he'd be all pissed-off that he couldn't play and I wanted to make sure he'd be okay with it. Of course, he was grand. He actually threatened to slap me if I didn't do it!'

Laughter.

'Anyway, our manager Dónal had already suggested that maybe getting a couple of new people in to take over on the drums and the bass might be an idea. Just temporary, like. It'd be good for the band to be out there, doing concerts for everyone … all that.'

'So, once I agreed to do this gig, I started thinking about that again. I mean … thinking about getting a new drummer and a new bass player and touring with The Grove again. So anyway, I talked to Aesop about it, and he said I should do it too. He wanted to see The Grove out there.'

Now there wasn't even any coughing or whispering. Even the staff were staring up at him, not really sure about where this was going.

'So then I called Shiggy in Japan. Just to see. But he said the same thing. He told me that The Grove shouldn't stop just because of what had happened. So, anyway, to be honest with you … I guess tonight was never really a Jimmy Collins gig. Jimmy Collins is part of a band. And now I think it's time for you to meet the rest of that band …'

Jimmy stood back from the mike and looked stage left with one hand out.

Shiggy walked out first, but the crowd didn't even get a chance to roar.

Aesop appeared, grinning, and limped over to the middle of the stage. The three of them hugged and waved out at the erupting scene in front of them.

Jimmy stepped up to the mike again and grinned.

'Weren't expecting that, were you? Yeah. Well you wouldn't believe how nervous we all are, I'm telling you.'

He pointed to Shiggy next to him.

'He never fuckin' told us he played the drums!'

Shiggy pumped the air with two sticks and leaned into the mike.

'Never fuckin' ask, Jimmy.'

Jimmy turned around and helped Aesop strap on the bass as Shiggy got in behind the drum kit. Back at the mike he put on a pair of dark shades and pointed over to his left.

'Hit it Aesop.'

Aesop started the bass line to 'Strut' and then Shiggy came in on the high-hat.

Jimmy leapt up into the air and the roar of his guitar as he came down was the only thing that could have drowned out the noise of the crowd as nearly three hundred people screamed and rushed the stage.

He looked around at the lads and grinned. He was home, at long fucking last. Then he shuffled over to the edge of the stage and got down on his knees, his guitar still wailing and screeching. He leaned down without missing a note and planted a big one on the beautiful girl that was dancing there. She kissed him back and said something, but he couldn't hear what it was. Didn't matter.

He'd ask her later when they got home.

DOWN IN the audience, they were feeling nothing but love. A mother wiped away her tears as she looked up at the stage. She only had one son, but they were all her boys up there. She'd never felt so proud, even as she grimaced against the noise. A policewoman held her girlfriend's hand and tried not to allow herself get too caught up in the gig. She'd promised Dónal that she'd keep an eye out, just in case. An old sound engineer frowned down at his desk and made sure that every nuance that Jimmy had planned would come out of the speakers for him. Occasionally, he'd yell abuse at the young guy doing the lights next to him, but on the whole he was pretty happy. He pulled out a banana and peeled it. An English girl gazed up at her man. She'd never seen this before, never imagined it would be like this, and would have pinched herself if her hands weren't punching the air.

Further back, a big guy from Cork stood against the wall with his girl, grinning and tapping his foot. He'd seen it loads of times, but hadn't expected ever to see it again. The young nurse stood in front of him so that he could fold his hands across her belly. He leaned down and kissed her neck and remembered when she'd called him back that day as his hand was swinging his bag into the back of a taxi. How she'd told him and then how every bad thing that had ever happened to him, in that instant, didn't matter any more and never would again.

Right at the back wall, a father held his son on his shoulders. They were coming out of a rough time too, although they'd never be completely free of it. They'd lost a daughter, a sister. Little Philomena was gone, but things were slowly getting better again. Liam roared laughing and sang as he held on around his Dad's chin. His skinny frame was lost in the folds of the huge black Cradle of Filth t-shirt that he'd suddenly produced and started to wear a few months ago, when things had been really bad. But he'd been seeing someone since then, getting some proper help. Now he didn't keep spending all his money on flowers for her grave. He didn't sit reading her diary any more for hours on end, drawing little lovehearts in it to match the hundreds she'd drawn on it for herself and her favourite rockstar. He'd stopped running away at night too.

And he hadn't wet the bed in a long time now ...

CRÍOCH

First in the trilogy

Superchick
Stephen J. Martin

ISBN: 978 1 85635 464 6

'All women are bastards ...'

JIMMY COLLINS – competent middle manager by day, suburban rockstar by night – has just been dumped and he's not taking it very well. Even a visit to his stylist can't cheer him up.

He decides to take control of the situation, convincing his friends to help him find the perfect girl – beautiful (but loyal), smart (but not too smart), confident (without being feminist), an expert bun-maker, who's indifferent about shopping, enthusiastic about *Star Trek* and scornful of self-help books.

As lead singer and guitarist with one of Dublin's best-known pub bands, The Grove, Jimmy decides to kick things off by writing a song for her; the mythical babe who's got it all – Superchick.

Rock and a Hard Place

Stephen J. Martin

ISBN: 978 1 85635 549

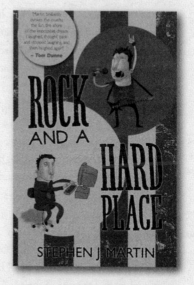

Play drums, drink beer and ride as many women as possible ...

... HIS mate Aesop isn't a complicated person. For Jimmy though, life just isn't that simple.

Being a rockstar was all he ever wanted but it was supposed to happen when he was seventeen, not in his thirties. Now he has this big important job and his boss thinks he's ready. He's being groomed for stardom all right, but in the boardroom, not a beer-soaked, panty-strewn concert hall.

When The Grove suddenly becomes the band everyone's talking about, Jimmy starts to feel the pressure. Something's got to give. Even his doctor says he needs to relax and Jimmy's not inclined to argue with a woman wearing a latex glove.

Ta very much ...

DESPITE WHAT you may have heard, writing a novel isn't all about sitting around in your underpants and shutting out the world as you dig repeatedly down into yourself to nose out fragrant truffles of literary brilliance. That was the drink talking. And I'm sorry for what I said about your bird too – it was probably just the way she was standing.

Anyway, I owe the following people a big bowl of jelly and ice cream for helping me out with *Ride On* ... Jonie Hell, Mick O'Gorman, Shane Harmon (legend), Rebecca Prince, Andy Plester, Miles Essex, Villads Spangsberg, Alan Baxter, Kevin English, Rob Wrixon, Joe Burke, Damien Murphy, Neil Clarke and Declan Burke. Also, Johnny O'Reilly, John Tierney and Will Murray for reminding me what it's like to be young and mad – cheers lads ... always a pleasure.

It's about time that Dave 'Kitty' Barry got a special mention all for himself. He knows why ... I'll say no more.

Colm Ó'Snodaigh from the band Kíla was an enormous help and I'd like to thank him and the rest of the band for allowing me to have a laugh with their fictional doppelgängers in the book. *Míle buíochas!*

Every book needs a shower, a shave and the rub of a cotton bud or two before being let out into polite society. Joe Burke, Brian Dolan, Ruth Kelly, Fiona Lodge and Stewart Ward were on hand – again – to help me perform the necessary ablutions. And it wasn't like they didn't have enough to be doing!

It takes a unique blend of talents to edit a book so that everyone wins, and my editor, Isobel Creed, has them all in abundance. Many thanks to Isobel and Mercier Press for helping *Ride On* out of my head and into your hands.

And, always, thanks and love to Ruth, without whom there'd be no Jimmy, no Aesop, no Grove, no Sparky, no Shiggy, no Norman, no Peggy, no gigs, no Caillte, no laughs ... no nuthin' ...

SJM
Hong Kong, 2007.
[www.pointedshoe.com]